Still Life, More Drama

By Regina N. Smith

Disclaimer
Copyright 2025 © by Regina Smith
All Rights Reserved

Cover design by Elena Dudina.

For Ken, Lillie, and Kisses

Prologue
1966

Flipping through the pages of a women's clothing catalogue, twelve-year-old Cindy Spearman admired the photos of the store's latest spring designs: laced trim dresses, A-line jumpers, hip-stitched skirts, and jacket dresses. Each model had a flawless smile and a calm, elusive pose. To young Cindy, each model held her own story. Using her imagination, she pictured them living the lives everyone dreamed of: vacationing in far-off places, meeting friends for weekend lunches, or having admirers stop them to say just how beautiful they looked. That was the life Cindy dreamed of for herself: to be like them, to be part of that beautiful world, and to soak in every joyful experience it had to offer. Often, she caught herself mimicking their poses, attempting to step into their world, even if only for a moment. She hoped she'd be happier than her mother, and with luck, she'd never marry a bitter man like her father, who seemed angry at the world for trapping him in a job that forced him to go door to door selling encyclopedias on commission to support a family. Cindy prayed her future husband wouldn't gripe about eating pot roast too often or about not making enough sales to earn a promotion.

Next door lived a boy named Duke Collins, a boy Cindy's age. The two became fast friends since Duke and his family moved into the neighborhood a month ago.

They found each other fascinating, especially because they had so much in common: board games, comedy shows, riding bikes, and peculiarly enough, an interest in girls.

Untethered by Cindy's interest in girls, one day, Duke shared an object he stole from his father's closet. It was a tiny, red and white, trapezoid-shape device that the boy said was a photo viewer souvenir. Duke instructed Cindy to peek into the viewer, which she did with one eye. Inside, the girl viewed the tiny pinup image of a woman posing in nothing but her undergarments. Fascinated, Cindy later sketched the image into her notebook.

Chapter 1
1973

If anyone was looking for a good time, Dan Jones's gatherings were the place to be. His legendary events were known for their laughter, music, camaraderie, and best of all, an endless supply of booze and drugs, all secretly circulated on the Camellia University campus in Camellia, Alabama. Quietly known as the Crowned King of Trips by his ever-growing cult of followers, Dan was a tall, bearded, smooth-talking twenty-four-year-old hippie from California, known for his nonchalant zest for life and access to drugs. He wore his shoulder-length blond hair loose, and his blue eyes were usually hidden behind dark-tinted shades. His signature look included a white bohemian shirt, worn blue jeans that dragged along the ground, and, when he was not barefoot, a pair of brown sandals.

Though he tried to keep a low profile, Dan's rare appearances in class were always accompanied by the unmistakable scent of marijuana, which spurred university officials to try to have him arrested and expelled. Yet time and again, the King of Trips slipped through their fingers, untouched by consequence.

That night at the Bolton Apartments, Dan's unofficial headquarters, his followers and the curious alike were welcome to unwind, get fried, and get laid. The apartment was thick with smoke as Dan, in his usual mellow fashion, encouraged everyone to relax, "do their thing," and listen to stories from his travels. He spoke of drifting from California through various states, preaching a rejection of materialism, the pursuit of spiritual connections, the liberation of sexual freedom, and the beauty of living simply. No one knew exactly how Dan managed to keep his apartment, but rumor had it he'd struck a private arrangement with the building's elderly owner, though the nature of that deal was anyone's guess.

When taking a break from one of Dan's bizarre tales, visitors were treated to impromptu guitar or autoharp performances by anyone with a bit of musical talent. The melodies stirred the room into clapping, sing-alongs, and even dancing, while a few guests slipped away to indulge in more sexual pleasures.

Leaning back into the soft brown couch, Dan slowly exhaled a thick cloud of dope smoke, his expression loose and content. He passed the joint to one of his brunette lovers, who took it casually, unbothered by the couple nearby, tangled in a heavy make-out session.

Among Dan's most loyal followers was Cindy Spearman, a nineteen-year-old art major who quickly joined his circle after arriving at the university. Almost immediately, she became entangled in the cult's drug-fueled lifestyle. The teen was an attractive blonde with a short pixie haircut, deep brown eyes, and a magnetic presence. She often went braless beneath a multicolored, V-shaped minishirt, paired with a blue miniskirt and, when not barefoot, a pair of worn brown sandals. She was a sophomore with notable artistic talent and had earned a full scholarship from the university's art department the previous year by putting her skills in painting and drawing to good use.

In her pursuit of an unrestrained life, Cindy had fully immersed herself in Dan's world, rejecting everything her hopeful mother had once tried so hard to protect her from. Letting herself be swept up in the night's wild energy, she danced freely, smoked dope, and drank whatever passed her way, the mix leaving her pleasantly giddy.

Amid dancing with a stranger, someone caught her eye. Mid-move, she froze, her gaze locked on a figure across the room. Without a word, she slipped away from her partner and crossed the hazy apartment to get a better look.

What she saw made her breath hitch. The man looked like he'd stepped out of a glossy magazine: jet-black hair, storm-gray eyes, and an athletic build that stirred something primal in her. He wore a red, white, and blue plaid shirt tucked into well-fitted jeans and brown leather shoes. Desire flickered through her body and mind, pulling her toward him with the same intense, reckless curiosity that had drawn her into Dan's world.

Who is that, Cindy wondered, her gaze sweeping over the hunk from head to toe. *I've never seen anyone like him around here before. I wonder if he'd go for someone like me.*

Without hesitation, she strutted over, flashing a sly grin as her finger traced a teasing line toward her breasts.

"You're cute," Cindy giggled, giving him a playful look. "Wanna dance?"

"What?" the hunk mumbled, rubbing his eyes and coughing.

"Wanna dance?" Cindy asked again, louder this time, her grin unwavering.

"No."

No? Cindy's mouth dropped open. *What's wrong with me? What kind of person is he looking for? Is he going steady with someone? Whatever. Who cares? He'll be leaving with me, whether he realizes it or not.*

"Okay then," Cindy responded coolly, dismissing the rejection like it was nothing. "I'll get to the point. Wanna fuck?"

The guy raised an eyebrow, did a double take, then started snickering. The laughter started slowly, then picked up like he couldn't help himself.

What the hell's so funny? One hand planted firmly on her hip, Cindy froze. *Does he think this is some kind of joke? What a jackass. What's the point of being here if he's not down to have a little fun?*

"No, really," Cindy insisted, leaning in. "I want to." *Last chance!*

"Could I at least know your name first?" the hunk laughed, finally reining in his amusement.

"Cindy Spearman. What's yours?" she asked, her tone softening.

"Paul Boudreaux."

"Ok, *Paul Boudreaux*," Cindy said, raising an eyebrow. "Wanna fuck?"

Waiting, Cindy crossed her arms, one foot tapping against the beat of the music as someone dropped a vinyl on the record player, beginning a new song.

Paul cocked his head and grinned.

"Sure, we can do that," he answered with a smirk, "but first, let's go ahead and dance. One of my favorite songs just came on, and it's been a while since I danced with someone beautiful."

That's more like it! Her cheeks flushed, Cindy stepped in, meeting Paul on the dance floor. To her surprise, he had impressive moves: smooth, confident, and effortlessly cool. A jittery thrill bubbled up within her as she imagined what the rest of the night might bring.

As the song faded out, Paul leaned in and gave Cindy a brief but surprisingly tender kiss, like a quiet thank you. Without a word, they slipped out of the apartment.

Outside, Paul led her to a gleaming blue convertible that looked like it had just rolled off a showroom floor. It had a white leather split bench seat, an immaculate dash panel, an 8-track AM/FM stereo, and armrests that were nothing short of pristine.

Cool, Cindy thought. *Is he trying to show off, or does he really drive this thing every day?*

Paul drove to a nearby corner store and left Cindy alone in the car. She looked around, then ran her hand gently over the smooth leather upholstery, marveling at the luxurious interior. Never in her life had she imagined riding in a car like this; it felt like something out of a movie.

If he'd left the keys, she thought with a mischievous grin, *who knows what I might've done?* The idea of stealing the car was ludicrous... but wickedly amusing.

Paul returned a few minutes later and started the engine again. He turned down a side street, then into a dimly lit alley. There, things escalated quickly. Paul slipped on a condom, and the two had sex.

Afterward, Paul offered to drive her home, but Cindy shook her head.

"Take me to Gardere Apartments," she said, satisfaction in her tone as she smoothed her skirt. "A friend of mine lives there. So... are you a Camellia University student too?"

"Yeah," Paul replied, his tone relaxed and content as he guided the car toward the address Cindy had given him. "It's my first semester. I just got home from Vietnam and wrapped up orientation not too long ago... I might've bitten off more than I can chew, telling my advisor I wanted to major in both Business and Physical Education. But the freshman courses should give me some time to figure things out."

"How old are you?" Cindy asked.

"Twenty," Paul said, "but I'll be twenty-one in a few months. You?"

"I turned nineteen last week."

"Cool, happy belated birthday. Did you do anything special to celebrate? And what's your major?"

"My momma came to visit, and we had a birthday dinner," Cindy said with a smile. "My friends made me cookies and pound cake... I'm an art major. My building's right next to the business building, so we might run into each other again. Who knows?"

"Most of my freshman classes are on the other side of campus," Paul said. "But I've got a break around one on Tuesdays and Thursdays. I usually grab lunch then."

"I'm at the art building every day," Cindy replied. "On Tuesdays and Thursdays, I've got Beginner's Spanish from 8:30 to 9:30, but the rest are all art classes, like studio stuff and art history. I practically live there because of my scholarship and work-study job."

"Neat. You must be really good to have earned that scholarship," Paul told her. "What kind of art is your specialty?"

"I'm best at painting and drawing...mostly portraits of people," Cindy replied.

"I'd love to see them sometime," Paul smiled, glancing over at her. "Maybe I'll swing by during my break."

They pulled into the parking lot of the Gardere Apartments, a single-story complex painted a soft shade of blue. The grounds were well-kept: freshly trimmed grass, tidy flower beds, and an outdoor pool. Tall fixtures along the walkway cast a gentle glow, lighting the path ahead.

"Here we are," Paul said, easing the car into a parking spot. "I can walk you to the door, if you want."

"Nah, I'll be fine," Cindy assured him. "Don't sweat it."

Before stepping out, Cindy rummaged through her purse, pulled out an old receipt, and scribbled her name and number with a pen that was nearly out of ink. Letting out a quiet groan, she went back over the faded parts to make the writing legible. She handed the slip to Paul, who folded it and tucked it into his shirt pocket.

He's a nice guy after all, she thought. *I hope we really do run into each other again. Hmm... I wouldn't mind having sex with him again either...*

"Peace out, Paul," Cindy stated.

With that, she stepped out of the car and made her way down the walkway. A cool breeze brushed against her skin, raising goosebumps along her arms.

She approached apartment 134 and knocked on the door. From the corner of her eye, she caught the glow of Paul's taillights as he pulled away from the complex.

She knocked again. The door creaked open to reveal a tired-looking man she recognized as Joel Duncan. He was twenty-one, with curly blond hair and hazel eyes. He wore green and white striped pajamas and stood barefoot on the threshold.

"Hey, Cindy," Joel greeted her, opening the door wider. "Hanging out at Dan's again?"

"Yeah," Cindy answered, stepping inside. "It got late, so I had a guy give me a lift. Is Margo already in bed?"

"Well, it *is* midnight... on a *Monday*," came a sleepy voice from the hallway.

Margo Burnett appeared, leaning against the doorway. She was twenty years old, with soft brown eyes and short brown hair that fell loosely over her shoulders. Dressed in a pale pink nightgown and barefoot, she gave Cindy a weary but familiar smile.

The two had been close ever since taking a couple of classes together during Cindy's first year at Camellia. Nearly a year into their friendship, this kind of late-night visit wasn't uncommon.

"I'm heading back to bed," Joel yawned. "Night, Cindy."

He brushed past Margo and disappeared down the hall, leaving the two women alone in the living room to talk on the couch.

Margo rubbed her eyes. "I'm surprised. I thought you went to Dan's with Clair, and she'd be the one taking you home."

"Let me give you the skinny," Cindy confessed, her voice buzzing with excitement. "I met the dreamiest guy, like the kind you'd see in magazines, only better. And get this, he was actually sweet! I think we really hit it off, so I gave him my number."

"Ooh, spill it!" Margo squealed. "Describe this dreamy guy. I want to picture him!"

"Black hair, light eyes, and the body of a god," Cindy gushed. "Margo, he said his name was Paul and he goes to our school, so I hope I might run into him again."

"I think I met him earlier today," Margo said, her eyes lighting up. "Joel was showing a guy named Paul around campus who fits that exact description. He's super handsome and definitely not hurting for cash. His grandfather's portrait is hanging in the business building. The name's Beau Dupont. And honestly, he's not bad looking himself. Check it out next time you're on campus. That family's big in banking and loaded."

"Wow, I will!" Cindy gasped, her eyes wide with curiosity.

Margo placed a hand gently over her friend's and gave it a soft squeeze.

"Cindy," she said, her tone serious, "I think you should reconsider spending so much time at Dan's. I know he seems cool and all, but he's bad news. I'd hate to see you get wrapped up in the middle of something."

"Oh, come on, Margo." Cindy let out a light chuckle and waved off the concern. "I'm not doing anything different from anybody else on campus. Everyone's been to Dan's at least once or twice. I just go a little more often, that's all. There's nothing wrong with having a little fun. Isn't that what college is for?"

"Not if it risks losing your scholarship," Margo said firmly.

"That won't happen." Cindy shook her head. "As long as I keep my GPA where it needs to be, show up for class, and handle my work-study, I'm golden. If Dan were as awful as you and a few administrators say, other people wouldn't keep showing up at his place, so he can't be all bad. Why hate a guy who only wants peace, freedom, and for people to be their true selves? Don't be so uptight. Relax and open your mind a little."

"Dan's out for himself! He's slick and uses vulnerable people. He talks a good game about peace and freedom, but convinces people to give him money, trade their bodies—especially the girls, and gets drugs from who knows where. He should have been booted from campus ages ago."

"I'm not being used, and I'm not vulnerable. We're doing each other a solid. I help him stay afloat in our classes, and he helps me mellow out with whatever I need. It sounds like a sweet deal to me. So, if anything, we're using each other."

"That sounds crazy. What well-meaning person cheats in all his classes and gives drugs and alcohol to a nineteen-year-old like candy?"

"It's my life," Cindy groaned. "I'm nineteen and not some kid anymore. I can make my own choices."

She glanced at the wall clock. It was 12:15 a.m.

"Mind if I crash here tonight and catch a ride home later?" she asked. "I'd appreciate it."

"You know the drill," Margo sighed, already heading toward the hall closet. "I'll get a pillow and blanket. The couch is yours, your majesty."

Margo handed over the bundle, and Cindy offered a grateful smirk.

"You're the best," she said in a mocking yet playful tone, taking the items from her friend.

The sleepy teen crashed on the couch for the rest of the night. By early morning, Margo drove her across town to her apartment at Hollow Oaks, a name that sounded a lot nicer than it looked.

The place was a total drag. The low-rent complex consisted of cramped one and two-bedroom units, a rundown communal laundry room, and a corroded row of mailboxes. Years of slumlord ownership had left the property in shambles. What was once a green lawn had become a scraggly expanse of dirt patches and weeds, boxed in by cracked concrete and pothole-ridden parking lots.

The current landlord, Mr. Tanner, was notorious for being a real cheapskate, always cutting corners and dragging his feet on repairs.

Her ears reddening with embarrassment, Cindy muttered a quick thank you and goodbye to Margo, then unlocked the door to apartment 157. The second she stepped inside, the stench of stale air and neglect hit her like a smack.

The inside was a total wreck, far worse than the building's sorry excuse for a courtyard. Piles of junk covered every surface: old newspapers, cracked sketchbooks, dirty laundry, tubes of paint, crumpled fast food bags, and the unmistakable stink of something that should have been thrown out days ago. The place was part artist's studio, part packrat's dream, crammed into one claustrophobic mess.

The couch was buried beneath a mountain of clutter: fashion magazines, crushed potato chip bags, and layers of paint-stained clothing. Just to the left, an obvious dip in the pile marked Cindy's personal crash zone. That was where she ate, studied, and slept most nights.

She didn't bother picking up a thing. With a heavy sigh, she collapsed into the familiar dent to unwind. Her mind drifted as she stared up at the ceiling. Yesterday hadn't been so bad. Her new classes seemed promising, the scene at Dan's had been fun as always, and she'd ended the night with a guy who looked like a dreamboat.

Sniffing, Cindy opened her eyes and turned her head toward an odd, moldy smell wafting from the equally littered kitchen. The scent of spoiled food and stagnant water hung thick in the air, a grim reminder of the dishes she had left soaking and the glass jars filled with paintbrushes steeping in murky brown water.

She didn't move, convinced the mess could wait, just like everything else. Slowly, she closed her eyes again, letting the silence settle around her.

Chapter 2

Later that Tuesday morning, Cindy changed into a fresh outfit and stepped out of her cluttered apartment, catching the city bus along the route closest to Camellia University. In one hand, she nibbled her breakfast on the go: a half-eaten banana.

The bus made its routine stops, pausing to pick up or drop off passengers who paid seventy cents for the day or thirty-five cents for a one-way fare. It was cheap, even for students living on scraps.

Cindy recognized a few of the regulars. They were the people who kept the university running behind the scenes without ever getting much recognition: custodians, cafeteria workers, and groundskeepers. A couple of fellow students doing work-study rode too, slumped in their seats, either staring out the windows or half-asleep with textbooks in their laps.

It didn't take long for Cindy to notice the common thread among them: everyone was hustling just to stay afloat, trying not to drown in bills, jobs, or expectations.

Sometimes, she missed the ease of having her mom's old coupe. *Ole Reliable*, they used to call it. The car had seen better days and had plenty of mileage, but it ran smoothly and didn't ask for much fuel in return. Now, she had to settle for a seat near the back of the bus, eating her banana in silence.

Cindy's mind drifted as she stared out the window. Intrigued, she began to wonder what else was out there beyond the usual routes and classroom walls.

One day, soon, she would have enough money saved to buy herself a new bike, something to ride through hidden backstreets, explore the town's quiet corners, and chase moments that couldn't be found in textbooks.

When the bus eased to a stop near campus, Cindy stepped off with a small crowd. They split off in different directions, each headed somewhere with a purpose. She made her way toward the foreign language building for her first class of the day: Beginner's Spanish.

Initially, she considered taking German. It had a bold, unfamiliar ring to it, all sharp consonants, fierce vowels, but she decided against the risk. Spanish felt safer. She had studied it in high school, and with a scholarship on the line, this wasn't the time to gamble with her GPA. *Better to stick with something familiar.*

Cindy finished the last bite of her banana and paused, eyeing the peel in her hand. For a second, she thought of keeping it—maybe for compost, maybe just out of habit—but the idea of carrying it around campus all day didn't appeal to her. She tossed it into the nearest trash can and wiped her fingers on her skirt.

Mmm, she thought. *That was a good breakfast.*

She made her way up the steps of the foreign language building and pushed through the door into the cool hallway. A few students lingered near the entrance, slowly scanning posters for study abroad programs in Spain, Mexico, and France. Cindy barely glanced at them. Her focus was on finding Room 14.

She turned into the first corridor, scanning the numbers until she found it as the second-to-last door on the right. Inside, a few early arrivals had already claimed their desks. Among them was a familiar face:

her friend, Laura Sanders, hunched over her notebook while doodling a silly drawing on the first page.

Laura was the same age as Cindy. She had brown hair and eyes that complimented her yellow and green striped blouse, blue bell-bottoms, and white wedged shoes. Like Cindy, she came from humble beginnings, until her mom married a pilot who made things much easier for the family.

The two young women had known each other for about a year now, long enough for Cindy to appreciate Laura's easygoing energy and kind-hearted nature.

Cindy slid into the desk beside her friend and flashed a warm smile.

"Morning, stranger," she said, setting her belongings down with a soft thud. "I'm glad we managed to get this Spanish class together. This semester will go by in no time, but I still wish I had you in one of my art classes! That would have been so cool."

"Morning; this is still good," Laura responded, glancing up from her notebook where she'd been doodling the image of a sleeping cat. "We'll get a chance to brush up on our Español and sneak in a few laughs along the way! Do you have any classes with Margo or Clair?"

"Margo's in my World Art class," Cindy replied, "but I've got nothing with Clair...Oh! After class, I need to give you the full rundown on this dreamy guy I met last night at Dan's. Trust me, you're gonna want to stick around and hear every detail."

They both giggled as an older woman stepped into the classroom and introduced herself as Mrs. Garcia, the Spanish professor. She had warm brown eyes, salt-and-pepper hair, and wore a crisp white blouse tucked into a brown skirt with sensible black shoes. As she greeted the class, the last student slipped into the room just as she began calling the roll.

The usual chorus of "here," "present," and awkward silences filled the space. Predictably, when she called Dan's name, there was no answer. Moving on, Mrs. Garcia continued down the list and soon had the class flipping open their textbooks to page one, at least for the students who had them.

The lecture began with a straightforward review of basic pronunciations, greetings, introductions, nouns, and verbs. For Cindy, it was smooth sailing. She'd seen it all before in high school and quickly found herself predicting the kinds of questions that might show up on a quiz or test. Still, she dutifully took notes, keeping her pen moving until the class finally let out.

After class, the friends strolled down the corridor, their chatter low and quick as they swapped gossip about Cindy's midnight fling. Every few steps, they'd burst into muffled giggles, drawing a curious look or two from nearby students. Laura clutched her books to her chest, wide-eyed at the juicy details, while Cindy recounted everything with a dreamy smile and the occasional dramatic sigh. By the time they reached the main hall, it was time to head to their separate classes, and Cindy promised to spill more later.

Drawing II was next on Cindy's schedule at the art building across campus. She had to hustle, which she absolutely despised, but this wasn't just any class. It was *Ryan Mills's* class. One of the rare things that the professor was lenient on was being called by his first name, just Ryan, like most of the other art professors who favored comfort over formality in both address and clothing. Ryan was in his late thirties, wore glasses, and had brown hair and eyes. His outfit consisted of a light blue shirt, dark blue jeans, and black shoes. Though easygoing in style and form of address, his studio expectations were anything but. He didn't play.

Cindy learned early that Ryan didn't care for excuses. His class was sacred ground, and you showed up on time or not at all. The man had a reputation in the art department for being tough, and Cindy had seen the casualties herself over the past year: students getting the door slammed in their faces without hesitation, followed by a pointed, "Class starts when it starts, not when you feel like showing up."

Previously, a student explained that she had car troubles, but Ryan told her that it was not his concern. He simply said she should have left earlier or taken the car to a mechanic. Another time, a classmate brought a toddler to class, and Ryan asked her to leave, stating, "This is a drawing studio, not a daycare. Come back when you've found a babysitter."

Not wanting to give the professor any leverage to call her out, Cindy, as always, made it a priority to arrive at class on time. Punctuality was non-negotiable in Ryan's world, and she had no intention of becoming one of his cautionary tales.

The art building was Cindy's oasis; yet, Ryan was a constant shadow. Like it or not, she was tethered to him. He wasn't just her Drawing II instructor; he was also her painting professor, her academic advisor, and the one overseeing both her work-study and her scholarship.

Trying to catch her breath, Cindy slipped into the studio and made a beeline for the table where the sketchbooks were stacked. She rummaged through the pile, found hers, grabbed a handful of drawing pencils, and headed straight to her usual working area. Around her, other students mirrored her actions with familiar precision.

Within seconds, Ryan entered the room, shutting the door behind him. The atmosphere shifted. Without a single word, the students instantaneously turned their attention to the still life arrangement in the center of the room and went to work drawing it.

Ryan had trained them well. Once he walked in, it was time to work, and those unfamiliar with his unspoken rules always stood out: they loitered, waited for instructions, and were unsure of where to begin. But the rest of the class? They worked and didn't dare say a word of warning. Instead, they watched as Ryan stood silently at the front of the room, arms crossed, expression unreadable, letting the clueless few figure out, for themselves, that they were already behind.

Ryan didn't bother with roll call. He knew nearly everyone by name, having taught most of them the previous semester, except two newcomers. Cindy recognized one of the newcomers as Ronald Foster, a student she's seen before in a different drawing class. He had red hair, sharp green eyes, and wore a solid green shirt tucked into brown slacks, paired with white tennis shoes. Luckily for him, Ronald was already working on his drawing in his sketchbook, unfazed. However, the other student sat awkwardly still, clearly waiting for instructions.

"Alright, line them up," Ryan said coolly, stepping to the front of the room like it was a stage.

Chairs scraped against the floor as students carried their sketchbooks to the chalkboard ledge. The students lined their work in a long row, each page a reflection of the still life arrangement drawn from different perspectives.

Without saying a word, Ryan's eyes scanned each drawing with the scrutiny of a seasoned critic.

The confused student who hadn't drawn anything remained at his seat, eyes darting between his peers and the row of displayed sketches, clearly unsure whether to join or stay put.

Meanwhile, the others returned to their seats quietly, some exchanging glances, others focused on Ryan as he began the silent ritual of reshuffling the work. He moved with purpose, shifting drawings up or down the row, adjusting the lineup from strongest to weakest in his opinion.

Ryan picked up the second-to-last drawing, wedging it somewhere in the middle of the lineup with a nonchalant flick of the wrist. Then he reached for Cindy's. Without hesitation, he placed it second from the top, a familiar position. Cindy stared at it, numb. She didn't flinch, didn't scowl, but the sting settled in all the same.

Second. Again. It was always second, never first. Like some twisted joke, someone else had managed to surpass her, and once more, she was left trying to understand how. To her eye, their piece had less drawing, less detail, and certainly less talent. But of course, that was just her opinion, and Ryan never cared about any but his own.

Now came the part most students dreaded: the critique. It came with one crucial rule that everyone had drilled into their heads: never start with *"I like..."* Anyone who did would feel the full force of Ryan's infamous tongue-lashing. He demanded specifics. What technique stood out? What did the artist do well or poorly? Could you compare it to another artist's style or approach? Vague praise was useless in his class.

Before addressing the first drawing, Ryan turned his attention to the unfamiliar newcomer.

"Where is your drawing?" he asked, his voice flat but sharp.

"I didn't know I had to draw anything," the student replied, his voice uncertain.

The room went still.

"Let me get this straight," Ryan said. "You walk into class, sit for ten minutes watching everyone else draw, and decide to do nothing?"

"This is my first day in this class," the student countered. "I didn't know. Nobody told me anything."

"It's also *his* first day," Ryan said, motioning to Ronald. "Yet he showed observation and initiative by doing what he saw his peers doing. You lack both. My next question is, can you draw?"

The other students stayed silent. They knew better than to interfere.

"N-no," the student confessed.

"Then why are you here?" Ryan asked. "Who put you in this class?"

"Chill, man. I needed an elective to graduate. My advisor put me in here because she said art would be an easy class."

Cindy grimaced, knowing that, unbeknownst to the clueless student, he had just committed a crucial sin in the art community.

He's toast.

Calling art "easy" to professional artists was like swinging a bat at a hornet's nest. It dismissed all the hard work, vulnerability, and creativity they poured themselves into.

"Excuse me?" Ryan said, removing his glasses and tilting his head slightly. "What did you say?"

"I'm just taking this class as an elective," the student repeated, his voice trailing off as he realized he was suddenly very alone in a now ice-cold room. "I mean, I didn't mean anything by it. It's not my fault. That's what they told me!"

Ryan stared at him for a long moment, then raised his hand to silence him.

"You think art is *easy*?" he scoffed, sliding his glasses back on. "And they stuck you in *my* class? Absolutely not! Get out. Take your schedule and beat it. This is an advanced drawing class, not interpretive jogging or some nursery where you take naps and glue macaroni to construction paper."

"But what else should I take?" the stunned student asked.

Ryan had already moved on.

He squinted at Ronald's unfinished sketch like it had personally insulted him. "The paper looked better when it was blank. What made you think this was acceptable? Weren't you in Brenda's class last semester? No wonder you aren't very skilled."

Ryan's critique of Cindy's drawing wasn't nearly as harsh as it had been for others. After all, he'd been one of the deciding voices on the scholarship committee that made her being there possible, and by now, Cindy had learned how to tune him out when necessary. Whatever a nerdy bigot with glasses had to say about *other* people wasn't *her* problem.

While Ryan moved on to critique the other students, Cindy's mind wandered. She hummed the lyrics of her favorite tunes under her breath, contemplated what the cafeteria might be serving for lunch, and wondered about the films playing at the local theater. Anything to pass the time until the critique ended. When it finally wrapped up, she snapped back into focus as students shuffled forward to collect their sketchbooks.

Ryan began assembling a new still life arrangement for the next assignment, this one meant to stretch across several sessions. Students reached for their oversized drawing pads that were nearly three times the size of their regular sketchbooks, signaling the shift to a more ambitious project. As always, everyone was expected to begin working right away. But for Cindy, expectations were a little different.

She worked quickly and with impressive speed, guided by a trained eye for proportion, line quality, and subtle value shifts that made her compositions stand out. Cindy didn't just understand the elements of art and principles of design; she mastered them. Because of that, she had to do more.

Alongside the regular assignments, she had an extra one: assemble her own objects and develop an independent drawing to submit to Ryan. It was more pressure, but Cindy didn't mind. In some ways, she thrived in it.

During Cindy's first year at the school, whispers floated through the art department about a heated showdown between Ryan and Brenda, an argument over who would get to advise her and whose classes she'd ultimately join. In the end, Ryan came out on top. While he and Cindy didn't always see eye to eye, she had to admit he pushed her harder as an artist. Brenda, by contrast, had a laid-back approach.

One thing Cindy loved about her art classes was the freedom to listen to music while they worked. The studio radio, parked on a dusty windowsill, was always tuned to a local station that spun a cool blend of jazz and swing music, just enough rhythm to keep imaginations going and pencils moving. Swaying her head from side to side, Cindy's hand glided effortlessly across the paper, quickly sketching Ryan's still life set with ease. She was already building up value and texture in her sketch while many of her classmates were still holding pencils up like measuring sticks, squinting one eye to gauge proportions.

Ryan's latest still life arrangement, however, earned a few groans from several students, especially over the cluster of plastic grapes. The overlapping spheres demanded precision, patience, and a sharp eye for layering and depth. But this was Drawing II under Ryan Mills, and anyone expecting shortcuts was in the wrong class.

As the Drawing II class wrapped up, students tucked away their drawing pads and supplies, leaving the carefully arranged still life untouched for the next round.

Remembering her promise to Margo, Cindy headed next door to the T. Tilberson School of Business in search of the portrait of Beau Dupont. It didn't take long to spot the image of the distinguished older gentleman; his likeness framed neatly among the original Board of Directors lining the entrance hallway.

That family must still be doing pretty well for themselves, Cindy thought. *Margo said they were in banking, but how'd they manage to hold on through the Depression?*

Her thoughts drifted.

Maybe Paul will clue me in the next time I see him, if I run into him at all. I could certainly do with some financial advice...He mentioned he'd be out of class right now... Would he be hanging around the union? Or somewhere else?

Deciding to head toward the cafeteria, Cindy stepped into the warm afternoon light and hadn't gone far before encountering a group of students handing out flyers informing the public about an equality march for women that would take place in a few days, sparking her immediate interest.

Cindy took a flyer with a quick "thanks" and tucked it into her purse, a spark of enthusiasm flickering in her chest. It felt like something worth sharing. She made a mental note to show it to Laura and Margo later, certain they'd be just as fired up.

She picked up her pace as the gnawing hunger in her stomach made itself known. Fishing around in her purse, she pulled out a crumpled pack of gum, unwrapped a stick, and popped it into her mouth. The sharp mint flavor danced over her tongue, and for a moment, the pangs dulled. Still chewing, she swallowed the burst of cool saliva and kept walking, determined to get some real food before her next class.

Minutes later, Cindy stepped into the student union, where the cafeteria line snaked halfway down the corridor with students waiting impatiently for a hot meal.

Eyeing an uncleared table like a hawk spotting prey, Cindy weaved through the crowd and dropped into a vacant seat, barely missing a guy with a tray that had a sloppy joe and French fries. A fork sat beside a half-eaten scoop of coleslaw and a few limp fries. Without hesitation, Cindy stabbed at the coleslaw and ate it. It wasn't her favorite, but free always tasted better. She didn't have to wait in line, and the food didn't go to waste. She dipped the fries into the leftover slaw juice, savoring the weird, tangy taste. She tossed the fork down and left the table without glancing back.

On the other side of the union, couches sagged beneath groups of lounging students, some watching the TV that played sitcom reruns while others were talking about music, politics, or the upcoming march.

By a big sunlit window, lounged nineteen-year-old Clair Adams, who had red hair and green eyes that complemented her soft green minidress and yellow clogs. She giggled at something her boyfriend, Micky Watts, whispered in her ear.

Clair had promised to be Cindy's ride home the night before, but, as usual, had vanished without a trace, leaving Cindy stranded. That had become a pattern, and while Cindy should've been furious, she'd let it go. Maybe it was guilt. After all, one sweltering afternoon when Clair wasn't around, she allowed Micky to kiss her, sneak his hands under her skirt, and taste her like candy. The sneakiness of the deed itself turned Cindy on, until Micky pulled back before things went all the way. Since then, they barely acknowledged each other in public, pretending, for Clair's sake, that nothing had ever happened. But today, Cindy wasn't feeling so polite.

Catching Micky's eye, she smirked and slowly dragged her tongue across her lips, teasing, daring him to react. His face flushed instantly, and like a guilty schoolboy, he jerked his head away, pretending to be engrossed in a nearby television. Cindy laughed to herself and strolled past.

Yum, yum, yummy. Cindy chuckled to herself, toying with the idea of tormenting Micky a bit more. But her fun was cut short; she needed to get back to the art building before time ran out. With a sigh of mild disappointment, she slipped out of the union, determined to satisfy her thrill another day.

Cindy's last class of the day was *World Art* with Dr. Ritter, a petite woman with curly salt-and-pepper hair who often wore a white blouse, a multicolored scarf, and a blue skirt with black shoes. Unlike the more laid-back art professors who didn't fuss over titles, Dr. Ritter insisted on being called "Doctor" because, as she put it, she *earned it* after years of hard work toward her PhD.

She had a student pass around copies of the lecture outline. Roll was called. Dan's name was mentioned, but he was absent. Without wasting time, Dr. Ritter dimmed the lights and launched straight into a lecture on Prehistoric Art, clicking through slides as she spoke.

There was a required textbook for the course, but Dr. Ritter lectured without it, relying instead on her memory and years of personal research. Cindy had heard plenty about the professor, mainly that she'd just returned from sabbatical and that her classes were anything but easy. Former students often grumbled that despite getting meager grades on their weekly written summaries, the real challenge came with the midterm and final: each consisted of a single, open-ended question. If a student didn't know the answer in full detail, failure was almost guaranteed. Dr. Ritter's art history courses were mandatory for all art majors, and even Cindy knew she'd have to buckle down to pass on the first try. As the professor spoke, Cindy took notes in her own version of shorthand, capturing key terms to review later when she had time to study more thoroughly.

Dr. Ritter's lecture was extensive but surprisingly engaging. To her surprise, Cindy found herself genuinely interested, jotting down ideas as the professor clicked through slides of cave paintings and ancient figurines. When the class ended, Dr. Ritter dismissed everyone but asked Cindy to stay behind.

"Cindy," Dr. Ritter stated, "my colleagues and I had the pleasure of viewing more of your exceptional drawings from Professor Mills' class, and they've been nothing short of remarkable. Since last year, several have noted that your skills in both painting and drawing rival those of our graduate students. We're genuinely impressed, and I'm pleased the department made the right decision in selecting you as our first woman recipient of the full scholarship in our department."

"Thanks," Cindy replied flatly, thinking how ridiculous the woman sounded. For all the praise Dr. Ritter was dishing out, none of it matched her reality. If she was as exceptional as they claimed, then why did

Ryan always rank her second during critiques? Why was her scholarship stipend barely enough to cover rent, art supplies, meals, and the basic cost of living? And if her work truly rivaled that of graduate students, then why not just hand her the bachelor's degree and let her move on to a master's degree?

"I was talking to a good friend not too long ago, and I'd like for you to meet her," Dr. Ritter said. "Her name is Mrs. Lucy Everett. She's the new Assistant News Editor for the school paper, and she's interested in doing a feature on you, especially with the upcoming student art show. She plans to attend, and there's talk of possibly including photos from the show in the upcoming yearbook. It could inspire both current and future students."

"Neat. I'd love to help with the article and yearbook," Cindy replied.

Dr. Ritter handed her a business card. "Mrs. Everett will be reaching out to you soon."

Cindy thanked her, tucked the card into her purse, and stepped out. A few doors down, she slipped into an empty classroom and quietly shut the door behind her. Inside, she began copying notes from her notebook onto clean sheets of paper, notes from the classes she shared with Dan. A deal was a deal. In exchange for a small bag of acid, she handled his notes, signed him in when professors didn't bother taking roll, and if the coast was clear, might even take the occasional quiz or exam in his place.

Sure, it was a dishonest little setup, but for Cindy, it beat shelling out cash for drugs, and so far, the professors never noticed a thing.

Finishing the last of the notes, Cindy carefully tore the pages from her notebook, folded them with care, and tucked them inside to hand off to Dan later. Stepping outside, she felt a soft breeze brush against her skin. Beaming, she admired how the tall trees cast dappled shade along the walkways between the university's grand old buildings, stirring a mellow curiosity about its storied past.

"Go away and leave me alone!"

"I didn't do anything," Cindy said, her voice cracking with confusion. "Why are you mad at me? What did I do?"

"You're weird and gross," Jane Norris snapped, rushing down the hallway without a backward glance.

In the hallway, a few classmates looked their way, smirking, snickering, and whispering.

Everything that could have gone wrong went wrong. A few weeks ago, Jane was the new girl, and she and Cindy had hit it off instantly. They were inseparable: sitting next to each other during class, eating lunch together, whispering in class, and crashing at each other's houses outside of school.

Then, that one evening in Jane's bedroom, both girls were lounging on the floor flipping through teen magazines when Cindy made a move she couldn't take back. She kissed Jane softly on the cheek.

Startled, Jane touched the spot like it burned. When Cindy, acting on instinct and emotion, leaned in to kiss her on the lips, Jane shoved her hard and increased the distance between them.

"What are you doing?" Jane shouted that day. "Get away from me!"

The panic in Jane's voice still echoed in Cindy's ears. That night, she ran home, devastated, too ashamed to cry, too numb to sleep. She hated herself for misreading the moment, for being too bold, too wrong.

Now, Jane avoided her at every turn, asked to be moved to another desk in class, pretending Cindy didn't exist. The teachers, unknowing or indifferent, granted the request without question.

Left behind, Cindy could only watch the pieces of their friendship scatter, powerless to pick them up.

It had been a long day, and Cindy rode the bus back to her apartment. When she stepped off at her stop and rounded the corner to her building, she spotted Mrs. Grigsby sitting outside on an old wooden chair. She wore a faded gray dress and a pair of brown shoes. Her thick black hair was tied back with a gray scarf, and her blue eyes were sharp.

Her four kids, ranging between the ages of four and nine, chased each other back and forth between the buildings and the partially filled parking lot.

Mr. Grigsby was nowhere in sight, as usual. Cindy rarely caught glimpses of him with his family. Word around the complex was that he held down two jobs. One was with the city involving maintenance. The other? Cindy didn't have the slightest clue.

Cindy gave a lazy wave as she passed her neighbor, trying to appear unfazed, but her heart sank when she spotted the eviction notice taped across her front door. She peeled it off and slipped inside.

Why worry about my little bit of money when there are other tenants to worry about, Cindy thought, scrunching the notice into a ball and tossing it to the floor.

She walked over to the kitchen table, where two half-finished acrylic paintings were sprawled across the surface. With the tip of her finger, she checked the surface, determining that both paintings were dry enough to be stacked on the growing pile by the kitchen counter. Clearing the table down to an old newspaper, she reached into her purse and pulled out a tiny bag of white powder. With practiced care, she poured out a small amount and shaped it into a neat line. The bag disappeared back into the purse, and out came a rolled-up dollar bill. Cindy leaned forward, placed one end to her nostril, and snorted the line in one smooth motion. Eyes closed, she sank back into the chair.

Knock! Knock!

Crap! Cindy wiped her nose with the back of her hand, stuffed the dollar bill back into her purse, and quickly set one of the paintings on top of the newspaper covering the kitchen table. She made her way to the front door and cracked it just enough to see who it was.

"Yeah?" Cindy uttered, swiping under her nose again.

"Ms. Spearman," Cindy's landlord, Mr. Tanner, spoke. "I need to talk to you about the notice left on your door."

The middle-aged landlord stood with authority, dressed sharply in a dark blue two-piece suit, a black and white striped tie, and polished black shoes that caught the late sunlight. His short brown hair thinned at the crown, and his green eyes held the tired firmness of someone who'd had this conversation too many times.

"I can't right now," Cindy said, barely opening the door. "I'm not decent."

"I can wait."

"This isn't a good time," she added quickly. "I'm sorry."

Mr. Tanner paused. "How about tomorrow before the office closes?"

"I already read the notice," Cindy admitted, her voice thin but firm. "I know I'm three months late. I'm gonna pay the money as soon as I can. I just need more time... I can't give what I don't have until I get paid."

"Actually, now it's *four* months," Mr. Tanner corrected her. "*This* month's rent was due a week ago. I'm going to need that money in my office by Thursday. I'll be out of town Friday and won't be back until next Tuesday. If I don't have it in hand, the lease won't be renewed. As for the rest that's late, I need it in a lump sum in two weeks."

"Yes, sir. Thank you," Cindy murmured, closing the door.

The teen walked back to the kitchen and opened the refrigerator. A carton of milk and a few sad-looking bottles of condiments greeted her. The sour stench hit her the moment the door cracked open, and she slammed it shut with a wince.

The counter wasn't much better. There were empty noodle wrappers, crumpled pudding cups, and beneath a crinkled flyer of grocery deals, a half-flattened loaf of bread. She pulled out the bag and took out two slices, tearing away the moldy corners before popping the good bits into her mouth.

"Dinner!" came Mrs. Grigsby's voice through the thin apartment wall, followed by the stampede of little feet and a door slamming next door.

Mr. Grigsby must be home, Cindy thought. *I bet they're having something good...* Her stomach turned, not from the bread but from longing.

Momma, I sure do miss your home cooking. I hope you and Jacob are okay... One day, I'm going to make it big, and we'll never have to worry about money again. You'll both see.

Chapter 3

"She's insane, and this proves it," Mr. Spearman snapped, smacking the notebook with the back of his hand. "Look at it! What more proof do you need to see that your daughter's a freak?" He shoved the notebook inches from his wife's face, then turned to glare at Cindy with absolute disgust.

Earlier that afternoon, Jane's mother had come by to speak with Cindy's parents, explaining what had happened and asking that Cindy stay away from her daughter.

"Jack," Mrs. Spearman pleaded in her soft, mousy voice, "please don't raise your voice or say such things. She's still our child."

"Don't argue with me, Louise." His voice cut sharply through the room. "If that's what she is, then that's what I'll call her."

"All this fuss over a simple kiss on the cheek?" Her voice rose with desperation. "Hasn't everyone done that at least once in their life?"

"Then explain these drawings!" He held up the notebook like evidence in a trial. "Nothing but filthy garbage!"

"I didn't do anything wrong," Cindy protested. "I wasn't thinking, that's all! I don't even know why I kissed Jane on the cheek—I just... I thought I wanted to. I'm sorry! I won't do it again! And the drawings—what's wrong with them? Don't artists draw naked people too? What about the naked people in the science book?"

"Cindy, you're still a child," her mother said gently, wringing her hands. "It's inappropriate."

"She got it from you," Mr. Spearman accused his wife, rolling the notebook into a cylinder and jabbing it toward her. "All that coddling and those damned catalogs—no wonder the girl's mixed up. If it weren't for you, she'd be normal instead of a lunatic!"

Early the next morning, the campus bookstore was still closed when Cindy knocked at the back door. After a pause, it creaked open, and Betsy Jordan, a young woman in her early twenties, peeked out. She wore a yellow and white maxi-dress with white shoes, her brown hair parted down the middle, blue eyes cool and guarded. Stepping outside, she pulled the door shut behind her with a firm click.

"What do you want, Cindy?" Her arms folded tight. "We don't open for another thirty minutes."

"I'm sorry for what I did," Cindy's voice was barely above a whisper. "I don't know why I do the things I do, but I am sorry..."

"Saying you're sorry doesn't change what you did to my grandmother's wedding ring," Betsy replied. "That ring was everything to my mother. To me. And you sold it like it meant nothing."

"I—I was messed up..."

"Don't," Her tone sharpened. "Don't stand there and act like you didn't know better. I trusted you. I let you into my life, into my home. And you went behind my back and sold something precious—for drugs."

"I got it back, didn't I?"

"Yeah. After you had sex with a *man* to do it. What kind of sick, twisted thing is that, Cindy?" Her voice cracked, her expression pained. "You really think that makes it right? I can't even look at you without feeling sick to my stomach. Just... go away."

"At least I'm someone who *tried* to make things right!" Cindy snapped, her voice sharp with frustration. "Stop acting like you've never done anything wrong!"

Betsy didn't flinch, but her eyes narrowed.

"You spend all your free time with Fran," Cindy went on. "You ignore me when you're supposed to be free. Don't think I don't know what you two have been up to."

Betsy's jaw tightened, but she stayed silent.

"And you're making a big deal over some *stupid* ring that you got back anyway?" Cindy's voice rose. "I bet you don't care about it as much as you say you do!"

Cindy's eyes welled, but her anger held steady. "If you and Fran are together, just admit it!"

For a moment, neither said anything. The early morning air hung still, tense and heavy.

Cindy threw her hands up. "I'm so sick and tired of everyone acting like I don't have feelings—like I'm nothing! All over *one* incident!"

Her voice cracked as her frustration spilled out. "Why is it always me? Why do I have to be perfect all the time, like I'm not allowed to screw up? One stupid thing, and it's *always* over for me!"

Her chest rose and fell, her eyes glossy with unshed tears. For a second, she looked less like a young woman and more like a lost child, pleading to be heard.

"The mistake is *you*, Cindy," Betsy said coldly. "Go ruin someone else's life and stay out of mine."

"You are such a hypocrite," Cindy shot back. "As if you've never slept with a man before!"

"I *have*," Betsy admitted, her voice flat, "but the difference is I stopped a long time ago. Bye, Cindy."

Betsy turned around and reentered the building. The door slammed shut. A second later, the lock clicked.

Cindy stood frozen for a moment before slumping to the ground, leaning her back against the cool brick wall. Reality settled like dust in her lungs...heavy and choking. It was over. Betsy was gone, just like the rest. Every relationship she'd ever had was ruined. Somehow, it always ended like this. In a disaster.

I guess I'm a walking lunatic, Cindy thought bitterly, slowly pushing herself up. *I hate being who I am. And what's worse? I don't think I can change it.*

Her gaze drifted toward the alley where trash bins buzzed faintly with flies. *I didn't even sell that dumb ring for drugs. I only kept it to remind me of her, that someone could love me for who I am...Oh well, so much for that... I wasn't even attracted to the guy she caught me with. I just needed one part of him to quiet a craving. She never wanted to understand anything about me. What did she expect if we both stopped having sex long before I did anything? I bet she was doing something with Fran...Maybe we really are better off apart. Oh well. I gave her that stupid ring back. She acted like it meant the world, but I know now she never truly cared about me. Not one bit. I don't need anything left to remind me of her. Not a ring. Not a memory. Not a damn thing.*

Cindy took the long trail to campus, her thoughts as heavy as her steps. She entered the painting studio and went straight to the supply area, picking out an old canvas left behind for recycling. She set it on an easel, opened a tube of white acrylic, and painted over the old image, erasing someone else's past to make room for her own.

As her classmates slowly trickled in, Cindy grabbed another canvas of similar size, eyeing it thoughtfully. Maybe she'd turn it into a diptych. But of what? What two images could live side by side and speak to each other?

Reflection? she wondered. *Maybe both panels as mirrors? Something strange? Maybe something that doesn't play by the rules, like me.*

Unlike Drawing II, where Ryan micromanaged everything, Painting II was more relaxed. He gave the class freedom to explore their ideas, though the ranking system remained. So did the pressure. The upcoming student art show loomed, and every project still had to meet the standard. This time, Cindy wanted her piece to say something real.

Ronald frantically smeared thick globs of paint across his canvas, dragging colors into one another with his palette knife. He was chasing something immediately, something loud and wild: a masterpiece in minutes. Maybe if the chaos looked intentional, Ryan and the others would finally recognize his genius.

Ronald glanced at the petite woman beside him. "Lorin, tell me what you think," he whispered. "I'm going for a heavy abstract expressionism vibe. Think Ryan'll dig it?"

Lorin studied the mess, tilting her head before frowning slightly.

"Any feedback helps," Ronald said quickly. "We can paint whatever we want, right? It doesn't have to be perfect. Maybe this is my thing. I'll knock out a few of these and cruise through the rest of the semester."

Lorin scratched at her temple. "Ronald... It's got energy, I'll give you that. But, I dunno, man—it doesn't look *done*. How long did you even work on it? Ten, maybe five seconds? Have you forgotten that this is another one of *Ryan's* classes?"

"Okay, so it might need more work." Ronald shrugged. "But it still looks good, right? It's got spontaneity. Guts. There's a kind of primal motion to it."

"It... kinda looks like it was *rushed*," Lorin said cautiously. "Like there wasn't much thought behind it, just random smears wherever the paint landed. It doesn't say anything to me yet. Honestly, if Ryan walks over, I wouldn't count on him seeing past how unfinished it is. If you wanted to do this kind of work, maybe you should've taken Brenda's class instead."

"I *tried* to get into Brenda's class," Ronald muttered. "It filled up before I could register. This was my only option. I got an A with her last semester. Think there's hope for me?"

Lorin hesitated, then smirked. "Well, if you're Pandora's box, maybe there's still hope at the bottom."

At fifteen, Cindy kept her eyes shut, partly from the lingering effects of the medication and partly to avoid facing her parents. Her arms lay wrapped in clean white bandages, a fresh reminder of another failed attempt to escape. Her father's voice echoed with familiar cruelty as he called her names and grumbled that he was done trying and that she was no longer his problem. But that wasn't the worst part. The doctor's update cut deeper than anything her father said. Whatever hope she had been clinging to slipped further away, leaving her colder, emptier, and numb.

The rest of the painting class passed without incident, but Cindy couldn't shake the weight pressing down on her. She needed air to escape the constant barrage life kept throwing at her. She had talent, sure, but what good was it when everything else felt like a bad joke at her expense?

As she left the art building, she considered heading home. What was the point of going to another class? If Dan could coast through without showing up most of the time, why couldn't she? At least she'd made an effort. That had to count for something. Cindy dug through her purse for an acid tablet, not watching where she was going. She bumped into someone, lost her balance, and hit the walkway hard. She scowled and looked up, ready to snap, but her expression softened when she saw who it was.

"Sorry," Paul said, reaching down to help her up. "I wasn't paying attention to where I was going."

His hand was warm and steady. Cindy took it and let him pull her to her feet.

He smiled, just a little crooked, and it sent a flutter through her chest.

"Well, hello there, stranger," Paul said. "Looks like we ran into each other after all."

Cindy blinked, briefly forgetting the storm cloud she'd been under.

"Yeah... guess so." A faint smile touched her lips, surprisingly genuine. "I thought your classes were way across campus."

"They were," he replied, "but my schedule got changed again." One class was canceled because not enough people signed up. Then the replacement conflicted with something else. They had to change the entire schedule...It was a complete headache. But it's all fine now... Since we're both here, mind if I check out what you've been working on? I've got time if you do."

"S-sure," Cindy stammered, leading the hunk through the doors of the art building and into the drawing studio.

Cindy flipped open her sketchbook, holding it out for Paul, who studied the pages. Eager to show more, the teen grabbed her sketchbook from the previous semester to share, thrilled that her crush was carefully viewing them with a sincere interest. More enthused, she led Paul to the painting studio where her canvas sat on the easel in the stage of a mid-transformation.

"I started this one earlier today," Cindy informed him. "But, there's one from last semester."

The teen walked to the back of the studio and carefully brought over a painted canvas that had been propped against the wall. Gazing over the painted image of a woman, Paul cracked an excited smile.

"*You* did this?" Paul exclaimed, eyes wide with surprise. "Wow! This is stellar! It's got to be one of the best paintings I've seen in a long time!"

"Thanks." Cindy blushed.

"Hey, my class is about to start soon," Paul said, carefully returning the painting. "We should hang out. Want to grab lunch today, if you've got time?"

"Um, sure. How about 1:30?" Cindy offered.

"That works," Paul replied with a grin. "I'll see you then."

A pleasant tingling spread across her skin as Cindy watched Paul head for the door. *He came back... and wants to have lunch? Am I dreaming?* She pinched her arm and smiled when it stung. Nope, this was real. Still giddy, she floated to printmaking with a heart lighter than it had been in weeks.

At exactly 1:30, just like he said, Paul stood outside the art building. Together, they walked toward the student union.

"The art really impressed me," Paul told her. "Portraits aren't easy, and you've got real talent. What else do you like to paint?"

Pretty much anything," Cindy said. "People, landscapes, flowers, still life... but I prefer painting women, especially since I am one. I'm still figuring out printmaking. Next semester, I'll be diving into ceramics and sculpture."

"Cool, I should look into taking an art class as an elective. Got any suggestions?"

"Well, it depends. Do you like drawing or are you better with building things with your hands?"

"Anything you're willing to teach me," Paul smirked. "I can handle it!"

They both laughed, the tension quickly melting away.

"Thanks again for the ride that night," Cindy said. "I really appreciated it. I've never been in such a nice car before. I usually take the bus unless I can catch a ride from a friend."

"No worries. My car's my pride and joy. I call her Wilma. I know it's kinda dorky, but she gets me where I need to be, so I take good care of her."

Paul walked a step ahead and held the door open for her.

Wow, he's a gentleman, Cindy thought as her heart gave a soft flutter.

They joined the short lunch line at the cafeteria, but as they inched forward, a knot of worry twisted in Cindy's stomach.

Wait, we never talked about who's paying!

Sure, Paul seemed like he could cover both meals without blinking, but what if he expected them to go Dutch? Cindy's fingers touched the lone dollar bill tucked in her purse. That was all she had. Just the thought of standing there empty-handed in front of everyone made her chest tighten. Her cheeks flushed at the thought.

God, that would be humiliating.

Reluctantly, Cindy grabbed a tray and followed Paul down the cafeteria line. Around them, trays clattered, students chatted, and servers dished out steaming food.

Paul loaded his tray with beef stroganoff, roasted vegetables, and a thick slice of garlic bread.

Cindy, her nerves bubbling beneath the surface, picked up a small bowl of pasta salad and placed it quietly on her tray.

When they reached the end of the line, Paul glanced at her tray, then at her.

"That's it?" he asked, brow raised.

"I'm not very hungry," Cindy lied, forcing a faint smile.

Paul eyed her, clearly unconvinced.

"Come on," he said. "I'm hungry, and I bet you are too. Go grab something else. I'll wait."

What? Cindy stared at him, heat flooding her cheeks. *I can't afford anything else! Wasn't that obvious from the pathetic little pasta salad sitting on my tray? Just because most people here were born with silver spoons in their mouths doesn't mean we all were. I'm broke! Thanks for making me feel like trash, you clueless jerk.*

Leaving her tray behind, Cindy stepped out of the line. She turned and walked quickly toward the student union doors before the tears could spill. A few escaped anyway, even as she blinked hard to keep her vision clear.

"Cindy?" Paul's voice called out.

Ignoring him, Cindy didn't look back. All she could think about was getting out of there as fast as possible. Near hyperventilation, she could feel the imagined stares closing in from every direction. *They're all laughing. Watching. Judging.* Her steps slowed, and her vision began to spin.

"She's insane, and this proves it," Mr. Spearman's voice echoed.

"You're weird and gross," Jane's voice chimed in. *"Get away from me!"*

"I can't even look at you without feeling sick to my stomach," Betsy's voice added. *"Just... go away.... The mistake is you, Cindy..."*

A hand closed around Cindy's arm, snapping her out of the spiral of voices.

She spun around and yanked her arm free, eyes blazing.

"Don't touch me!" she snapped.

Paul stood there, brows furrowed in concern, his hand still halfway raised.

"Cindy, what's wrong?" he asked. "Is everything okay? Why'd you take off like that?"

"I-I'm not hungry," Cindy lied again, her eyes flicking to the ground. "I need to get back to the art building. I forgot I've got a lot of work to finish."

Paul tilted his head, unconvinced. "Since it's lunchtime and we're already here, doesn't it make sense to grab something before going back?"

"I can't afford it, Paul. I can't afford *anything*!"

Cindy's face broke before she could stop it.

Heads turned. Eyes settled on her. Cindy could feel every one of them.

It's happening again! They're all going to turn on me and say everything's my fault! It's always my fault! My fault! My fault! My fault!

Cindy's breathing quickened again, but Paul spoke before panic could take over.

"I was the one who invited you to lunch," Paul said, his voice gentle and steady, like a hand reaching through fog. "I planned to cover both meals, so there's no need to worry about money...Why don't we head back to the cafeteria, grab something to eat, and hang out for a bit? I'd like to get to know you better."

He waited, giving Cindy space to breathe and think. She braced for the worst: him walking away in frustration, calling her names, or rolling his eyes.

But none of it came.

Paul stayed relaxed, his expression patient. No trace of judgment. Just calm.

Cindy's heart pounded as she shifted restlessly. Finally, she turned and walked slowly back toward the cafeteria, Paul beside her.

They returned to where their trays still sat, untouched. Cindy didn't add anything, despite Paul's quiet glance. He said nothing, just paid for both and carried the trays to a nearby table.

The silence felt heavier than it should have.

Cindy frowned, staring down at her food. *He's definitely done with me now. I didn't just embarrass myself. I embarrassed him. And now he knows I'm broke. Great. Just great.*

She slumped slightly, pushing her pasta salad around with her fork. Her appetite was already gone.

"It seems we both have a thing for pasta, huh?" Paul stated, breaking the silence between them.

"I didn't mean to overreact," Cindy apologized. "I'm sorry..."

"Don't be," Paul reassured her. "I should've told you I was covering lunch before we got in line. That's on me. So, what's your favorite food?"

"Shrimp," Cindy replied, her voice a bit more relaxed. "What about you?"

"Meatloaf," Paul answered with a grin. "I'm a meat and potatoes kind of guy, but this looked too good to pass up. Want to try some? It's actually pretty good."

He lifted his fork, offering her a small bite from his plate.

Cindy nodded, and Paul carefully scooped a bit of food into her bowl. Cindy took a bite, and slowly, a smile spread across her lips.

Paul quietly added another generous scoop. Then another.

"Okay, okay," Cindy laughed, raising a hand and pulling her bowl closer. "If you keep giving me all your food, you won't have any left."

"There's enough for two," Paul pointed out. "I don't mind sharing. Ever been to Ackerman's Buffet? I heard they got plenty of seafood. Some of my classmates swear by it."

"Yeah, I've been," Cindy replied. "It's popular with families on weekends. Big portions for cheap."

"Cool. Let's go sometime. My treat."

"That's generous, but you've already done enough. I'll cover the next one."

"Too late," Paul grinned. "I already offered, and you didn't say no. So, I'm paying. No takebacks!"

Cindy gave him a sidelong glance and smiled despite herself.

"So, where are you from originally, Cindy?" he asked, continuing the conversation.

"Buggy, Nebraska," she told him. "I lived there until my parents divorced. Then my mom and I moved to Tennessee to be near her folks."

"Buggy?" Paul beamed. "That's an actual place?"

"Yup, and it's exactly what it sounds like, small and dusty," she said with a laugh. "Not much to do but farm, go to school, and hit church on Sundays. There was one thrift store, two gas stations, a little hotel, and a beef-packing plant that made the whole town smell weird on hot days. The nearest town was forty minutes away, and the closest big city was four hours away."

"Interesting," Paul said. "I'm from Wood Oak, Louisiana. It's a small suburban place with plenty to do. My friends and I were big at football and baseball games. We went to drive-ins, parks, skating rinks, bowling alleys, and malls. Sometimes we packed lunch and flew kites or had picnics. Other days, we'd drive to other nearby parishes to explore old buildings, do a little hunting, or visit the swamps."

He smiled at the memory. "I miss it, but this place is starting to feel like home too. I like it more each day."

Cindy took another bite and looked thoughtful. "Do you think you'll go back to Louisiana after school?"

"Hard to say," Paul murmured, his gaze drifting. "I want to, but I can't. It's a long story."

He took a breath, then added, "I did two years in the Marine Corps. I'm in the reserves now, just trying to figure out what I want to do with the rest of my life. For a long time, I thought I'd either become a P.E. teacher and coach or take over my father's business. But if neither of those works out, I might end up going back into the military full-time."

"Thank you for your service," Cindy said, her voice sincere.

Paul nodded with a quiet smile.

"I've thought about moving back to Tennessee," Cindy sighed. "To be closer to my family. But I'm keeping my options open. What kind of business did your family run in Wood Oak?"

"We had a business called *Sal's Country Store*," Paul explained. "It started small, but when my father took over, he expanded it. We sold everything: food, clothes, simple auto parts, toys, and electronics. You name it. If folks needed it, we tried to carry it."

He paused, and his voice tightened.

"He was planning to open a second location," Paul continued. "He had notes on everything, but he passed away before he could make it happen."

Paul fell silent. His eyes shimmered with held-back tears as he drew in a slow, shaky breath. Cindy saw the shift in his voice and the softness in his expression. This wasn't small talk anymore.

He had been close to his father. That much was clear.

"Sorry," Paul said with a soft chuckle, wiping his eyes. "Just good memories. They hit me all at once."

He cleared his throat and sat up straighter.

Cindy nodded and asked, "Did you play any sports in high school?"

"Sure did," he replied, his face lighting up. "I was quarterback of the football team and captain of the baseball team."

Cindy blinked. *Quarterback? Captain? Of course. One of those golden boys.* The kind who ruled the hallways and landed on prom court without even trying. Good-looking. Charming. Confident. No wonder.

If we went to the same high school, she thought, *he'd probably have walked right past me. Or worse, joined in when the others called me a weirdo or a freak.*

A small pang pressed in her chest.

Too bad. He's nice, but he's out of my league. Lightyears away.

"Neat," Cindy said, feigning interest as she scooped the last bite from her bowl. "Thanks for the food. It was good, and I liked talking with you."

"Anytime," Paul replied, casually digging into his roasted vegetables.

Yeah, Cindy thought bitterly. *He's as good as gone.*

She glanced at him while pretending to focus on her empty bowl.

This is the worst part. He has so many qualities I like. He's patient, easy to talk to, thoughtful, good-looking, and confident, but not cocky. He knows what he's doing, and not just in conversation.

She exhaled softly, keeping her face neutral.

He's got so much going for him. He's probably loaded and could have his pick of any girl on campus... the kind who doesn't need a bus pass or worry about whether she can afford lunch.

Cindy nudged her bowl forward, the clinking of silverware grounding her thoughts.

What would someone like him want with someone like me? I'm nobody here. I'm just a student who doesn't belong anywhere except in the art department.

Her gaze dropped.

He's the kind of guy girls line up for. The kind you don't get to keep.

She smiled faintly to herself.

Oh well. It was nice while it lasted.

"Hey," Paul said as he speared the last of his vegetables, "if you're free Friday evening, we could head out to Ackerman's."

Cindy perked up a little. "Sure, I'd like that. What time?"

"Let's say 7 p.m.? Meet me at the Gardere Apartments. I'll pick you up."

"Okay," she nodded, a small, genuine smile playing on her lips.

Paul began gathering their empty dishes and utensils onto his tray. "I'll be right back."

He made his way to the dish return, then strolled casually to the cashier. Cindy watched as he leaned in to speak with the woman behind the counter. He smiled and handed her something. *A receipt? Cash? A note?*

The cashier glanced over at Cindy and then unexpectedly left her station.

Cindy's stomach tightened. Her thoughts, once beginning to settle, started to race again.

Were they talking about me? Did I do something wrong? Did she recognize me from somewhere? Her eyes followed the cashier until she disappeared through a door.

Something fishy is going on...

She shifted in her seat, nerves bubbling back up. *Maybe I misread him after all.*

The cashier returned to her station, now holding a small to-go box. She handed it to Paul. He took it, thanked her, and walked back to the table.

"This isn't much," Paul said as he set the box in front of Cindy, "but... happy belated birthday." He gave her a wink before turning to head out.

Cindy blinked, surprised. *Why did he...?* She watched him go, caught somewhere between speechless and floating.

She slowly opened the box. Inside sat a generous slice of rich chocolate cake.

Her breath caught. *He cared.*

The cafeteria around her buzzed as usual, but it all faded into the background as warmth spread through her chest. Her heart swelled, and she could almost feel her insides glowing from the unexpected sweetness.

When's his birthday? she wondered, already wishing she had thought to ask.

Chapter 4

"Duke, mind your manners," Mrs. Collins said sharply, her voice cutting through the rising tension. Her son's face had turned a deep shade of red as she turned back to the Spearman family, her posture rigid with indignation. "My son wouldn't lie to me, and I believe him."

Mr. Spearman responded with a quiet firmness. "Listen, son," he said, looking Duke straight in the eye. "I understand this must be frightening, being caught up in something bigger than you at your age, but Cindy's going to need your help now more than ever."

"I am telling the truth!" Duke argued, voice cracking under pressure. "Cindy knows that I am!"

Then, with fire flashing in his eyes, he turned to face her directly.

"For once in your life, stop lying to everyone!"

Cindy returned home after classes, her body heavy with exhaustion, but her spirit was a touch lighter. She had eaten the slice of chocolate cake Paul had given her, the small act of kindness still lingering on her mind. For the first time in a while, she could admit the day hadn't been a total disaster. Yet beneath that small flicker of peace, the old weight still pressed down. She was tired. She was tired of feeling broken, of chasing closure that would never come, of mourning a love that had long since abandoned her. Betsy. Always Betsy. No call. No message. Not even a "happy birthday." Just silence.

A while ago, Cindy had tried one last time, dialing a familiar number through a haze of tears, but Betsy didn't answer. She didn't want to. And so, Cindy had done what she once threatened in a desperate cry for help: swallowed a handful of pills and curled up on her bed, quietly hoping her body would just give out.

But it didn't.

Her heart kept beating. Her lungs kept breathing. And morning came.

She had thought about trying again. She really had. But the idea, once so urgent, felt distant now, as if even her despair had grown tired. Would Betsy have cared if she had succeeded? If the news had come through a phone call or an obituary? If the girl who once loved her with everything simply ceased to exist? Probably not. She hadn't even picked up the phone.

Scoffing to herself, Cindy cleared the kitchen table, making space for the ritual she had fallen into after school: snorting a line. The powder sat ready, like a quiet promise. As she rolled the bill, she couldn't help but think of how ironic it would be to one day show up in the school's yearbook or newspaper. *Cindy Spearman: Artist of the Fucking Year.* Like some prize-winning hen on display for the whole campus to gawk at.

If luck ever tilted her way, maybe future students would sit in dark lecture halls, watch slides of her paintings, and write research papers on her life. Maybe her work would be dissected in classrooms, her name spoken alongside the greats. After all, weren't most artists tortured? Didn't some claw their way through the dark and come out famous?

The better question was: if any of that ever came true, would she even be alive to see it?

She bent over the table and inhaled sharply.

The burn surged through her nose. Numbness followed. Then the rush: pure, electric, unfiltered joy tearing through her bloodstream. Her eyes fluttered closed.

Oh, yeah...

"I'd like to take a look," said Mrs. Lincoln, one of the teachers, extending her hand.

Cindy didn't say a word. She slammed the notebook shut and pulled it closer to her chest.

After much pleading, her now-divorced mother had convinced her father to let her enroll in an evening school program for underage girls who were expecting. Though Cindy went through the motions, completing assignments and attending class, she refused to speak to the other students or the staff. She floated through the days like a ghost, present but unreachable.

Only her notebook, full of drawings and scribbled thoughts, held any evidence of the girl she used to be, or might still become.

Mrs. Lincoln sat quietly in the empty seat beside Cindy, offering no pressure, just presence. The classroom clock ticked softly in the background, marking time until Mrs. Spearman would arrive at the school. Cindy was always the last to leave.

After a long silence, Mrs. Lincoln finally spoke.

"Cindy," she said gently, "I've noticed how passionate you are about drawing. We don't have an art program here, unfortunately, but my father was a gifted artist. He taught my sister and me how to paint when we

were young. With the talent you have, I think it's worth passing that knowledge along."

She paused, measuring Cindy's reaction before continuing. "I have paints and canvases at home. If you're willing, I could bring them here. Of course, I'd need to get permission from the administration first, but only if you're interested."

Hours later, Cindy sat at the kitchen table, debating whether to hand over any rent money to her landlord. It amused her to imagine how absurd it would be if food were included in the rent. *Cheap old Mr. Tanner would probably hand out a half slice of stale bread and a swig of tap water, then raise the rent for the* "amenity." Classic lose-lose.

She wondered where the man actually lived. *Probably across town with the uppity crowd,* she guessed. He likely spent tenants' money pampering a spoiled wife with expensive tastes who had a shopping addiction. *Lucky bitch...*

Rising from the chair, Cindy rummaged through cluttered piles until she found the old drawing pad she'd been searching for. She flipped through the pages, past doodles and half-finished sketches, until she reached the blank sheets in the back. Setting the pad on the table, she laid a metal ruler across the paper and, using a technique she'd learned in printmaking class, tore the sheet down in a clean, precise divide. With the two pieces she had, she stacked one on top of the other and halved them, repeating the technique until she had four sheets. She set them aside and started on a new sheet from the drawing pad. She repeated the process—line, press, and tear—until she had a tidy stack of twenty neatly cut pieces. Satisfied, she dug out a jar of drawing pencils and stuffed as many as she could into her pencil case, along with a small handheld sharpener.

Okay, she thought, *that should do it.*

Deciding it was time for a short break, Cindy picked up the phone to call her mother. She picked up the handset and held it to her ear. She dialed her mother's number and waited until a soft voice came through the line.

"Hello?" came Mrs. Spearman's soft voice.

"It's me, Momma," Cindy said. "How are you and Jacob doing?"

"Aww, we're doing just fine, sweet angel," Mrs. Spearman replied warmly. "How are you?"

"I'm fine."

"Sunshine and I miss you. He's asleep right now, but he's been learning his ABCs and is getting bigger by the day! I told him we'd be visiting again soon."

"I can't wait," Cindy said, a small smile tugging at her lips. "But how are your wrists? Are they still bothering you a lot?"

"Yes, and the doctor said the surgery for the carpal tunnel should help a great deal, so I'm looking forward to it," her mother said. "Darling, since that day's almost here, would it be okay for Sunshine to stay with you until I've recovered enough to take him back home with me? That would help me a great deal."

"Sure, Momma. I'd do anything to help."

"Thank you, sweetheart. I still worry about you being all alone in Alabama, though."

"Everything's fine, Momma. Actually, I have some good news! One of my professors is setting up an interview for me. It's with someone from the school's paper about being featured in an article! And don't forget, the student art show is happening this semester too."

"I'm so proud to hear that! I've always said my sweet little girl was talented. Now, even more people will get to see just how special you are."

"I'm not a little girl anymore..."

"You'll always be *my* little girl."

"Yes, Momma... Well, I have to go. I love you both."

"We love you too, sweet angel. Take care."

Cindy ended the call and allowed herself to sink into the worn couch in the living room. The comfort was brief. Something tickled her skin. She flinched and brushed at her arm, but the sensation returned, this time on the other side. Glancing down, she froze. A trail of ants wove their way through the clutter: over piles of clothes, across scattered stacks of paper, and now crawling along her arms.

"Shoot," Cindy exclaimed, swatting at the ants with her hands, but they kept coming.

She lifted part of the clothing pile, uncovering a hardened, half-eaten chocolate muffin swarming with ants. Disgusted, she pinched it between two fingers and hurried to the front door. Flinging it outside, she shut the door with a sigh, trying to remember when she had even eaten the muffin.

Unable to remember the last time she'd seen the laundry hamper, Cindy grabbed an armful of clothes and dropped them on the floor. She picked through a few shirts and gave them a sniff. There was no question; they needed washing. She laid out an old blanket and began piling as many clothes onto it as it would hold. In the kitchen, she reached into a cabinet and pulled out a jar containing a small amount of leftover change and coins she'd found around the parking lot and campus. Sorting out the quarters, she slipped a handful into her purse. Then she grabbed the nearly empty bottle of laundry detergent, tucking it under her arm, and gathered the blanket by its corners, using it as a sack.

The community laundry room was already occupied when she arrived. One machine was in use by the elderly woman who often monopolized them, and another by a woman in her early forties, someone Cindy vaguely recognized as a caretaker for a handicapped relative, usually after her shift at a local fast-food place.

"I'll still be able to finish school and graduate on time?" Cindy asked, her voice thin with worry.

"Yes, sweet angel," Mrs. Spearman replied gently, placing her hand over her daughter's on the table. "The evening school has a special program for families like ours. They'll help make sure girls like you can continue their education. Everything's going to be just fine, you'll see."

"What about Duke and his family?" Cindy asked quietly. "Are they still mad at me?"

Mrs. Spearman's expression darkened as she gave a slight nod.

"I'm sorry," Cindy whispered, trying to choke back a sob. "It's all my fault."

"Don't worry about them," her mother said firmly. "You have me. I'll do anything for my little girl. Anything."

Cindy hesitated. "Where's Dad? He hasn't come to visit..."

"He... he's gone," Mrs. Spearman said, her voice softening. "Things had been rocky for a while, and he chose to leave. So, money's going to be tight, but we're moving to Tennessee to be closer to Gran-gran and Grampy. I accepted a secretary job at the elementary school on Meadow Brook Avenue since Alice is retiring."

"But what about your hands?" Cindy asked. "Aren't they still hurting?"

"I'm fine," her mother replied. "Let's worry about you for now and the new move. Who knows? It might turn out to be a blessing in disguise."

By the time Cindy finished her laundry, the other two women had already left. She didn't bother folding the clothes or towels, just heaped them onto the same blanket and hauled them back to her apartment. Once inside, she dropped the bundle onto her makeshift sleeping area and let it be.

Threading her way through the narrow pathway carved between clutter, she reached the bathroom. Several items were precariously left in the bathtub: a nearly empty shampoo bottle, a small decorative basket with half-used bath items, a bar of soap, and two towels. She removed them one by one, setting them on the floor.

Turning the faucet, she let the water run until the tub was half full. Then, shedding her clothes, Cindy stepped in and sank beneath the surface, the warm water enveloping her like a temporary escape.

For now, the mess could wait, and so could everything else.

Cindy wondered how different her life might have been if she had chosen to attend a community college or public university instead of a private university. She had been accepted to all three, but Camellia University had offered her a full scholarship with a small stipend, along with the promise of meaningful connections, a fresh start, and the chance to figure out where she truly belonged. It seemed like the right decision at the time, a path toward independence and adulthood. But never in her wildest dreams had she imagined it would be this hard.

Now, as she looked around her cluttered apartment, she couldn't quite explain how things had gotten this way. She hadn't meant to collect so much. At first, it was just one item: a small ceramic cup found near the dumpster. Aside from a chip on the handle, it was perfectly usable. It had felt wrong to leave something so salvageable behind. So, she brought it home, and then it became a habit: discarded objects from the apartment complex, leftovers from campus move-outs, and forgotten things abandoned on the city bus. She kept them all: things no one else wanted but things she couldn't ignore. Each piece felt like a quiet testimony to being overlooked yet still having value.

Everything, Cindy believed, had a purpose: some potential to be useful one day. But lately, she found herself wondering when that "later" would finally come.

She had given away a few things before, hoping someone else would see the beauty in them, but the flicker of disappointment in their eyes at a scratch, crack, or stain always left her disheartened. It made her question whether they had been better off with her in the first place. At least here, she could guarantee they were appreciated. So, the rest stayed. They had a home now, one that understood them.

After her bath, Cindy returned to the couch, the place she now called a bed, and slept for the remainder of the night.

By morning, she dressed quickly, skipped breakfast, and caught the bus back to campus, carrying her stack of carefully torn drawing paper and a pouch of pencils. She was ready to give the day a chance.

During the lunch rush in the student union, Cindy slid a few coins from her purse and fed them into a vending machine, selecting a candy bar. The sugar gave her just enough of a jolt to push past her nerves.

She wandered into the common area, where clusters of students were chatting, watching television, or lounging between classes. The room buzzed with laughter, gossip, and the clatter of trays from the nearby cafeteria. Though humbling, Cindy knew she had to take a chance.

Her eyes landed on a seating area occupied by four young women, all dressed in coordinated pink and white sorority colors, unmistakable. They were laughing over something in one of their textbooks.

Still, the teen took a breath and approached them.

"Excuse me," Cindy said, her voice steadier than she felt. "Would any of you like to be sketched for a few dollars?"

If there was one thing that flattered people, it was being asked to be sketched.

Two of the young women exchanged nervous giggles. A third gave Cindy a once-over, her expression sharp with judgment. *Who is she, and why is she speaking to us?*

The fourth woman tilted her head, curiosity softening her features. "Will it be good?"

"Yes," Cindy replied with quiet confidence. "It will."

"How much are we talking?" the second woman asked, still unsure if this was a joke or a real offer.

"Wait," the third woman cut in, her voice edged with suspicion. "We need to make sure she can actually draw first. I'm not paying for some stick figure."

"I'm an art major," Cindy replied, trying to stay composed. "She won't have to pay anything if she doesn't like it. But if she does, she can pay whatever she thinks it's worth. The sketch will be simple and quick, but if she wants something more detailed, we can talk about a commissioned price."

She held her breath, praying the woman wasn't the type to take advantage, the kind who wanted something for nothing just because they could.

After a brief pause, the fourth woman gave a small nod. "Okay. I'll do it."

Cindy pulled out her materials and got to work, her hands moving with practiced rhythm as she blocked in the shape of the woman's head, then carefully sketched her eyes, nose, lips, and hair. As she worked, the other three grew quiet, their earlier giggles replaced by focused curiosity.

"Wow, it really *does* look like Bonnie," the second woman gasped, leaning in for a better view.

Bonnie's smile widened, a soft blush blooming across her face. The sketch seemed to melt away the earlier tension at the table. She turned the paper in her hands like it was something precious.

"This is so cool," Bonnie said, reaching into her purse. She handed Cindy a few bills, then added more. "Can you do me a solid and do another one for my old man?"

"Got it," Cindy said, her voice steadier now.

The others, now clearly impressed, asked for their own sketches. Cindy drew quickly and skillfully. By the time she finished, each of them had paid her, some offering more than she expected.

As they stood to leave, Bonnie glanced back. "You should come tomorrow, same time. Some of our other sisters would love to have their own sketches done."

"Definitely," the first woman added. "You've got real talent."

Ecstatic, Cindy nodded, her heart racing with excitement. "I'll be here."

Later that day, after her classes, Cindy roamed the campus, doing quick sketches of students and even a few staff members until her hand began to ache. Grimacing, she rubbed the cramping muscles with her other hand, trying to coax the sting away. She'd earned enough to cover the overdue rent, but the rental office was likely closed by now. Still, she held out hope for a small miracle.

After stuffing the hard-earned cash into a makeshift envelope, just a folded scrap of drawing paper, she boarded the evening bus back to her complex with her head leaning against the window.

Sure enough, the *CLOSED* sign was posted at the office door when she arrived. Her heart sank until she spotted Mr. Hines, the maintenance man, flipping off the lobby lights inside.

Cindy rushed forward and knocked urgently. Mr. Hines, startled but kind as always, opened the door with an inquisitive look.

"I know it's after hours," Cindy said, breathless, "but could you please give this to Mr. Tanner?"

She held out the envelope.

The man looked at it, then nodded. "Alright, I'll make sure he gets it."

"Could you... maybe write a note or something? Just in case? He needs to know that I turned it in today."

Mr. Hines didn't hesitate. He pulled a notepad from the front desk and scribbled a quick receipt listing the amount, Cindy's name, the date, and time, then signed it with his initials. He also left a note for Mr. Tanner and slipped it underneath his office door.

"Here you go," Mr. Hines said, handing the first note to Cindy.

"Thank you," she said, the tension in her shoulders finally loosening.

Cindy returned to her apartment, carefully placing the signed note into her purse.

Inside the dwelling, Cindy let out a dry, bitter laugh. After all the sketching and hustling, she was *still* behind on rent, broke, and hungry. Her stomach grumbled, a reminder that vending machine candy wasn't dinner and that payday from her stipend was still a week away. Even then, the amount wouldn't be enough to cover what she owed in full.

Cindy wished she had found the willpower to let go of Betsy sooner. Regret sat heavy in her chest. So much of her money, which could have gone toward rent or groceries, had been wasted on foolish hope.

In the depths of heartbreak, she'd turned to seers and storefront mystics who lit candles and flipped tarot cards, offering vague assurances: *Her lover would return in two weeks. She'd been cursed by a jealous woman. Bad karma from a past life was blocking her happiness. A new romance would appear soon, once she learned to let go.*

Each prediction fed her desperation. Now, burning with quiet rage, Cindy resented them all. Maybe some had truly believed what they said. Maybe not. Either way, the money was gone, and there was no magical fix. From now on, she would have to let life play out on its own without any spiritual cheat sheet.

I can't believe I wasted so much money and time stressing over someone who clearly didn't give a damn about me, Cindy thought, exhaling as she let her head fall back, eyes fixed on the ceiling. *Never again. I won't make the same mistake twice.*

If I had known someone like Paul was on the horizon, I would've moved on a lot sooner. Damn, I should've asked more about him instead! A faint smile tugged at her lips despite the frustration. *Technically, someone did say a new person would come into my life once I let go, but I saw so many psychics and tarot readers, I can't even remember which one said it...*

She sighed again, softer this time. *I wish I knew more about Paul. Is he really as kind as he seems? Would he accept me, truly accept me, for who I am once he learned everything about me? Could we grow together, not just coast on attraction or sweet words?*

A pause, then a quieter thought: *It's still early and too soon to make a big deal out of everything, and I guess I'll find out. All I know is, I really, really like him.*

Excitedly, Cindy picked up the phone, twirling the coiled cord around her finger as she dialed Margo's number.

"Hello?" Margo's voice answered after a few rings.

"Guess who's got a date with Paul Boudreaux?" Cindy teased, her voice bursting with energy. "This girl! We're going to Ackerman's Friday!"

"No way!" Margo squealed. "Oh, I'm so happy for you. Paul is such a great guy!"

"He is! I just hope he's not putting on some kind of front, you know?"

"I don't think so. A guy like that doesn't waste his time if he's not feeling it. And Ackerman's? That place has the best spice cake in town and the cornbread is so good. If things go well, maybe we can double date! Wouldn't that be fun?"

"It would! Only... there's one small thing. Paul thinks I live at the Gardere Apartments. Would it be okay if I came to your place before he arrives? He's supposed to pick me up at seven."

"Yeah, but Paul already knows you don't live here... Joel let it slip," Margo informed her.

Cindy's eyes grew wide as she sucked in a sharp breath.

"What? Why would Joel do that?" she burst out, her hands opening and closing like she was squeezing the air. "Paul could get upset or bail on me! Oh no, did Joel say anything else? What did Paul do? What did he say?"

"He was surprised, for sure," Margo replied, "but honestly? He didn't seem mad or anything. I don't think he cared much. He just nodded, said, 'okay,' and they both started rambling on and on about sports..."

Cindy blinked, slower now, trying to process. "Still... that doesn't tell me much...I don't get it. I'll be crushed if he backs out. I really like him."

"He hasn't called it off yet, so there's still a chance he'll show," Margo assured her. "My only worry is... does he know about Jacob yet?"

"Oh, so Joel didn't spill *that* part?"

"Not that I've heard."

"Margo, you've got to talk to Joel. Tell him not to say *anything* else about me to Paul. We're still figuring each other out, you know? He doesn't need to know *everything* about me all at once. I want him to know *me*, not what someone else decides to share. I don't want to scare him away..."

"I'll talk to Joel. I'll see what I can do."

"Thanks... I've got to find something halfway decent to wear. Everything I have at home is awful."

"*How?* It's *Ackerman's! E*veryone dresses casually there."

"Yeah, but I'm going with *Paul*," Cindy stressed to her friend. "I've got to wear something that'll knock his socks off."

"What about that yellow dress you wore to the student art show last year? It was super cute."

"Cute isn't gonna cut it this time. I need something that'll make him lose his mind."

"Try nothing," Margo joked, and both of them cracked up. "Or," she added, "we hit the mall real quick and find something new."

"I wish I could, but I can't afford a new dress right now," Cindy said with a sigh. "Any chance I could borrow that red minidress you wore to Joel's birthday last year?"

"Sure. I'll drop it off at the art building in the morning. Just get it back to me soon, okay?"

"Thank you, Margo, you're a total lifesaver! I'm so excited, I could burst! I never thought I'd get a date with someone I liked *this* much. He's just... amazing."

"I'm happy to help, but I'll be even happier when I hear all about it."

"So, basically, you *want* me to kiss and tell?"

"Absolutely. If you want the dress, I want *details*."

Chapter 5

"He's perfect, Cindy," Mrs. Spearman beamed, cradling the newborn in her arms.

Cindy turned away, her face pale and hollow with exhaustion, and something deeper. A boy? Perfect? No way. Boys grow up to be men, and men only learn how to harm. She didn't want him. She didn't even want to look at him.

A nurse stepped quietly into the room, clipboard in hand. "Are you ready to name the baby for the birth certificate?"

"I don't care," Cindy snapped, not bothering to look at her. Her voice cut through the sterile air, sharp and cold. "Just let her name it."

Mrs. Spearman flinched. Her color drained. "We... we'll call him Jacob," she said softly, glancing toward her daughter, hoping for approval.

"Just call the stupid thing Jacob," Cindy muttered, dragging the blanket over her head and shutting the world out.

Cindy sat alone on a bench near the parking lot of the Gardere Apartments, bouncing her leg and checking the time on her watch for the eleventh time in five minutes. It was Friday evening, and though the clock ticked forward, it felt like the closer it got to seven, the slower time moved.

She wore the borrowed red minidress and paired it with her best yellow wedges. A touch of makeup, a soft mist of alluring perfume on her neck and wrists, and hair styled just right to frame her face, all of it carefully chosen to make an impression.

Chill, Cindy kept telling herself. *He's not going to be mad. He's not going to call me a liar. It's going to be fine. It has to be fine. It will be. It will.*

She repeated the words like a chant, trying to drown out the rising nerves in her chest. *Just breathe. Just wait. Everything will be okay...*

Right on time, Paul's blue convertible rolled into view, gliding toward the lot. *He's here!*

Cindy jumped to her feet, her pulse quickening. She instinctively reached up to smooth her hair, wishing she had a mirror for one last check to make sure everything was still perfect.

She watched as Paul parked, stepped out, and flashed that easy smile of his. Her heart thudded wildly.

Then, he opened his arms, and she walked straight into them.

Relief, joy, and something close to disbelief surged through her as he held her close. Cindy tilted her face up, kissed him, and felt her whole body light up when he kissed her back.

He showed up for me. Dreams really do come true.

"Hey, you," Paul grinned, sneaking in another soft kiss that made Cindy's heart flutter. "You look beautiful."

"Thanks." Cindy offered a shy smile. "I almost thought you weren't gonna show..."

"Why would you think that?"

"Well... I figured you might hold it against me, finding out I don't really live here," Cindy admitted, then quickly added, "Anyway, I heard Joel's been helping you around campus. I'm good friends with him and Margo. She and I got close after taking a few classes together last year. Small world, huh?"

Paul shook his head gently. "Nah, I don't mind. That was the day we met. You weren't ready to show me where you lived. People do that. I get it. What mattered was that you got somewhere safe. Yeah, Joel's been helping me a lot. He and his old lady are real solid."

Cindy's eyes shimmered. *He's not mad. Thank God.* A wave of relief washed over her.

"Before we head out," Paul said, slipping his fingers gently through hers, "I want to swing by and say hi to our friends."

He led her back toward Joel and Margo's apartment. Inside, he kept things brief, offering warm greetings and tossing out excitement about an upcoming baseball game. Afterwards, the couple made their way back to the convertible and took off toward the restaurant.

As they cruised down the road, Cindy stared out at the passing lights, her thoughts spinning. *Maybe I'm overthinking... but why is someone like him single? Does he like blondes? What's he doing with someone like me?*

Trying to quiet her nerves, she turned to him and asked, "So... what made you come over to Dan's that night?"

"To see what it would be like. Try a few things." Paul's voice was casual but slightly guarded. "It helped with the transition, getting back to civilian life."

"I did that my first year too," Cindy replied, nodding. "It's kind of cool, right? People say stuff about Dan, but I think he's misunderstood. There aren't a lot of places where folks can just *be*. No judgment, no pressure. I mean, sure, it's not for everyone, but for some of us... it's a lifeline."

She glanced at him, curious. "I'm sure someone like you probably doesn't deal with that kind of thing. But maybe I'm wrong."

"It was okay," Paul replied, "but there was too much smoke for my taste. Honestly, I'm no freer than anyone else, believe it or not. If I were, I wouldn't have ended up at Dan's in the first place."

"Do you think you'll go back?"

"Maybe," he said thoughtfully. "Now and then, sure. But nothing regular. Being in the reserves means I can't afford to mess up. Getting caught would be a disaster."

Cindy nodded. "I've been going for a year, and no one's been arrested. If anyone called the pigs, it sure wouldn't be one of us. And Dan's landlord? He's cool. He'd deny everything in a heartbeat."

A small silence followed, then Cindy added, trying to sound casual, "So... are you single, or...?"

"I'm single," Paul said easily. "You?"

"Single," Cindy replied, then tilted her head slightly. "When was your last serious relationship, and how long did it last?"

Paul thought for a second. "Senior year of high school, back in '69. It went a couple of months into '70."

Cindy blinked. *His senior year? Only a couple of months?* His ex must've been crazy to let him go. *Well, I'm not stupid. I'm not letting this one slip away.*

"She didn't want to wait, huh?" she asked, fishing gently.

"I wouldn't say that," Paul replied, his tone even. "Life happened. We just ended up going separate ways."

Cindy watched him closely. "Are things... over for good?"

"Yeah," Paul said, nodding. "We haven't talked in years. It's over; time to move on. How about you?"

"I liked someone," Cindy admitted. "We dated for a few months, but... I did something stupid. Something the person couldn't forgive." She glanced out the window briefly before continuing, "I apologized and learned my lesson. So, that's that."

She studied Paul's face, bracing for a shift in his tone or posture. But he stayed relaxed, nonchalant, even. There was no judgment in his eyes.

Emboldened, Cindy asked, "So... what are you looking for now, in a relationship?"

Paul pulled the convertible into the restaurant's parking lot and eased it into a space. He shifted into park, then looked at her.

"Honestly?" he said. "Nothing, really. I'm just going with the flow. I'm not chasing anything serious right now. There's still a lot I've got to figure out before I can be in something like that."

"Oh," Cindy said softly, her voice dipping with disappointment. *Nothing serious?* Her heart sank. *Maybe he's just as broken as I am.*

Why does it have to be this way, now that he's here, now that I finally feel something real? She stared out the windshield, trying to push back the ache. *We'd be perfect together... I know it. But if he's just going with the flow, maybe, just maybe, he'll be ready later. Maybe with me.*

She forced a casual tone, masking the hope behind a practiced smile. "Same here. Just seeing where things go, you know? Whatever happens, happens."

Then, as if the words came out too easily, she added carefully, "When you *are* ready to be serious... would you ever want kids? Or date someone who already has one?"

"No," Paul said, not realizing the quiet crack that opened in Cindy's chest. "I like kids, always have. I even want to work with them someday. But I wouldn't date someone who already had one."

Cindy blinked, trying not to react. *Just breathe. Just chill.*

"I thought I could," Paul continued, eyes on the dashboard, "and I tried. But after a breakup... it's not just the relationship you lose, it's the kid too, especially if you get close. That kind of goodbye...it wrecks you."

He exhaled slowly. "Truth is... I already have a kid. With my ex. Somewhere out there."

Cindy swallowed hard, silent.

"As much as I hate to admit it... I've been a terrible father. I never thought I would be. I always figured I'd be like my dad: present, steady, the kind of man a kid could look up to. But it didn't turn out that way."

His voice dropped lower, almost a whisper. "So how can I be a good father to someone else's child when I've failed with my own? I can't. I won't put myself, or anyone else, through that again."

Paul has a kid?

Cindy's heart pounded. *What did he do that was so bad that he thinks he's a terrible father? Maybe he's just being hard on himself... or maybe, it was something really awful. God, I hope it's not the latter.*

It must've been serious, she thought, *if his ex took the kid and they've been out of his life for this long. Was the child born around the same time as Jacob?* Her stomach turned. *He must've become a dad right out of high school...*

A cold shiver slid down her back. *What if he's hiding something big? Like he hit his ex. Or something even worse, God forbid, something creepy, twisted, or disgusting. He's so calm, so put-together. Too put-together?*

Daddy had a mean streak too, she remembered bitterly. *He looked just as normal to everyone else, but behind closed doors...*

She bit the inside of her cheek. *I can't go through that again, not with someone like Paul. I don't care how good-looking or sweet he seems now. What if he's just like Daddy? What if he hasn't changed?*

Then, quieter: *Or maybe... maybe he has.*

Cindy followed Paul along the walkway toward the restaurant entrance, her senses sharper now, every movement under quiet scrutiny.

Is he hiding something? Could there be warning signs I'm just not seeing?

But there was nothing out of place.

Paul walked with an easy stride, casually confident. He opened the door for her without hesitation, offered a small smile, and pulled out her chair once they reached the table. Every gesture was thoughtful, almost old-fashioned in the best way.

If there was darkness in him, it was buried deep. Too deep for her to see tonight.

. Cindy sat quietly, watching her date as he settled into his seat across from her.

He seems so normal. So nice. But that's exactly how people like Daddy fooled everyone too.

The restaurant buzzed with the chatter of large families, the clatter of dishes, and the constant shuffle of waitstaff darting between tables refilling drinks, clearing plates, and scribbling down new orders in a rush.

Paul and Cindy both decided on sodas, then made their way through the crowd to join the line at the buffet.

Cindy filled her plate with shrimp creole supreme, a scoop of macaroni salad, and a helping of potato salad. Paul's tray was more down-home: braised beef tips, white rice, field peas, and a generous serving of cabbage.

By the time they returned to their table, their drinks had been delivered. They sat and began to dig in.

Cindy took a bite of shrimp and almost sighed out loud. *Mmm.* Her taste buds lit up. *Way better than last time.* Across the table, Paul nodded with approval as he chewed, clearly impressed with his own choices.

"Wanna try some shrimp?" Cindy offered, holding out her fork.

Paul leaned in and took the bite. "Mmm, that's good," he said, eyebrows lifting in pleasant surprise. "It tastes like home, real Louisiana flavor. No wonder this place is so busy."

He wiped his mouth with a napkin and grinned. "If it's always this good, we've gotta come back. How about this, each time we come, we try something different until we've tasted everything on the buffet?"

Cindy smiled. "Deal. Margo said the cornbread and spice cake were amazing, so we've gotta try those before we go."

"Deal! I'll save room!"

Cindy's heart fluttered. *Paul is so my type, more than anyone I've ever met. He's fun, easy to talk to, and open to new things...Please let him see what I see: how right we could be together. Keep things chill, girl. Keep the ball rolling.*

"There's going to be an undergraduate student art show coming up in a few weeks at the Crimson Gallery," she said, trying to sound casual. "The opening reception is on a Friday at 7 p.m., but after that, it stays open weekdays from 8 to 6."

"Where's the Crimson Gallery?" Paul asked, interested.

"It's in the art building, just downstairs. There's this black railing that leads to a staircase. It's kind of tucked away, but the space itself is cozy. Not huge, but we usually get a decent crowd. People from other departments usually drop by to support us."

"I'll be there," Paul said. "After all, an artist I know has made a pretty strong impression on me."

Blushing, Cindy gave herself a quick pinch beneath the table. *Did he just say that?*

"Here, try this," Paul offered, holding out a bite of beef from his plate.

Cindy leaned in and took it. Her eyes widened as the flavor hit. "Wow," she murmured. "At this rate, we might as well just switch plates."

"Why not?" Paul chuckled. "Food is food. I'm not picky. Do you cook much at home?"

"Not really," she replied before flashing a teasing smile. "But I would... for the right person."

"I know how to make the basics: spaghetti, sandwiches, mashed potatoes, meatloaf, stuff like that," Paul said. "I didn't really have to cook much while I was enlisted. Most of our meals were either prepped for us or came in MREs."

"MREs?" Cindy tilted her head, curious.

"Meals Ready to Eat," he explained. "Prepackaged food that's designed to last a long time. Not exactly gourmet, but food is food."

Cindy made a face. "Yikes. I guess anything fresh probably tastes like heaven after that."

"Exactly. That's why I appreciate food like this even more."

He wiped his mouth and leaned forward slightly. "Okay, your turn. Besides art, what do you like to do for fun? I know you're creative, so I'm sure it'll be something interesting."

Cindy smirked. "Well... I'm kind of an oddball, so you might want to be careful asking that."

"Try me," Paul said. "Nothing really surprises me anymore."

"Well..." Cindy paused, watching his face for any flicker of judgment. "I like riding bikes. I had this old one that got rusty, and the chain came off. I kept telling myself I'd fix it, but life got in the way. Last time I checked, the tires had gotten bad. Now I'm trying to save up for a new one."

Paul nodded. "Sounds normal to me."

"I like traveling, catching movies, and hanging out with people I like..."

Her date raised an eyebrow playfully. "I'm still not hearing anything odd."

Cindy inhaled sharply, then let it out. "I like guys a lot... but I also like women. A lot. Like... the way a guy would."

Cindy closed her eyes for a moment, then rolled her shoulders back like she was letting go of a weight.

"Far out," Paul said with a small, nervous chuckle.

"Would that be a problem?" Cindy asked, her voice edged with uncertainty.

"No," he said, shaking his head. "I mean, I like women too. You're just... the first person I've met who's ever told me something like that. So yeah, it's different, but not bad."

"I like men too," Cindy added quickly. "I guess I'm wired a little differently. Most people wouldn't get it, so I usually keep it to myself."

"Your secret's safe with me," Paul said gently. "It's not something I'd judge you for."

Cindy smiled, heart skipping a beat. To test the waters, she leaned in and kissed him, slow and deliberate.

Paul didn't hesitate to kiss her back, passing the test.

When they parted, Cindy smirked and teased, "Your turn. What are you into?"

"Sports and anything military," Paul answered. "I like everything you like, but I'm also big on music, dancing, and trying new things. All the typical things an everyday person would enjoy."

"I like that... and I like you," Cindy said, her voice soft.

"I like you too."

After dinner, Paul surprised her by taking them downtown to hear a local rock band perform. Cindy beamed when Paul boldly grabbed her hand, leading them to be the first couple to dance. Others soon followed, but it felt like the world had melted away, leaving just the two of them swaying under the lights. When they paused to rest, they stayed close, singing along to the lyrics like old friends reliving a favorite memory.

As the night wound down, Cindy found herself wishing time would stretch, just a little longer. She wanted to bottle every moment: the laughter, the music, the closeness, and live inside it forever.

Paul chatted briefly with a few band members and some fellow concertgoers before walking back with Cindy to the car. As they approached his blue convertible, she caught a glimpse of weariness in his eyes. When she realized they were headed down the familiar route back to Gardere Apartments, her heart dipped slightly.

She didn't want the night to end. Not yet.

"We could head back to your place," Cindy suggested, her fingers gently resting on Paul's thigh.

"You sure?" Paul asked, his gaze flicking toward her with a hint of surprise.

"Yeah."

Without another word, Paul made a smooth U-turn, heading away from Gardere and back towards downtown. The scenery changed quickly from familiar sidewalks and neon lights to a more refined part of the city. Eventually, they arrived at a gated community on the outskirts known as Lakeland Square.

Cindy stared in awe at the pristine setting: a modern complex of penthouses with sleek architectural lines, a shimmering pool, a gym, a courtyard fountain that bubbled peacefully, and perfectly manicured lawns.

Inside Paul's home, her amazement grew. The space was open and bathed in soft lamplight. Tall windows stretched toward the ceiling, showing off the city's distant skyline. Modern furniture in muted tones gave the place a calm, grounded feel. There was a staircase leading to an upper floor, houseplants thriving in the corners, and books and records neatly shelved along one wall.

"Home sweet home," Paul said, setting his keys in a tray by the door. "Let me show you around."

Paul led Cindy through each room of his home, casually pointing out small details such as momentos from his military service, where he liked to study, a framed photo of his family, and much more. The tour left Cindy more than impressed. It opened her eyes to something she hadn't let herself fully imagine before: the possibility of a life filled with peace, beauty, and care, something far from the chaos she had known.

Boldly, Cindy turned up her seductive charm, resulting in the pair having sex in Paul's bedroom. When it was over, Paul lay beside her, one arm still loosely draped across her hip, his steady breathing soft and deep in sleep.

Cindy remained beside him for a few minutes, listening to the quiet. She traced the outline of his shoulder with her eyes, yet curiosity stirred in her.

Carefully, she slipped from the bed and quietly stepped across the room. Paul's pants lay near the foot of the bed. She picked them up, her fingers moving quickly but quietly through the pockets.

In one pocket, she found his wallet. Inside were the expected contents: his driver's license, military ID, social security card, and a modest wad of folded bills. She flipped through it slowly.

No pictures of a woman. No images of a child.

A quiet sigh of relief left her lips. *So, he was telling the truth... Good. But I wish he had at least one picture of his kid inside. Maybe there's one somewhere else...Did he ever say if his kid was a boy or a girl? I don't remember.*

Maybe she really could let herself believe in him. Maybe, for once, it was safe to hope.

Cindy closed the wallet and tucked it back into the pocket. Her hand brushed against something in the opposite one. It was soft and delicate. *What's this? Underwear?* Her stomach fluttered uneasily as she pulled it out.

Relief washed over her when she realized it was just a handkerchief. She quickly folded it back and placed everything where she found it, laying Paul's pants neatly on the floor.

Padding silently across the room, Cindy entered the bathroom. After relieving herself, she turned on the faucet and began washing her hands. That's when it happened: a loud crash followed by a dull thud.

Her breath caught.

She shut off the faucet in a snap and froze, eyes locked on the bathroom door. Heart hammering, she scanned her surroundings, then yanked open the cabinet near the sink and grabbed a towel to wrap around her body.

Cindy pressed her ear against the door. Silence.

Then, gripping the toilet plunger like a weapon, she carefully cracked open the door and crept back into the bedroom.

Her eyes widened.

Paul was on the floor beside the bed, grimacing, his face twisted in pain. One arm clutched the other near the elbow. Beside him, a shattered lamp lay in a mess of broken ceramic and tangled wires.

"Oh my God—Paul!" Cindy dropped the plunger and rushed to him, kneeling at his side. "What happened?"

"I fell," Paul muttered, wincing.

"I'll get some ice—" she started, but he shook his head.

"I'll be fine. Don't worry about it." He grimaced again, pushing himself upright. Carefully, he gathered the broken pieces of the shattered lamp and tossed them into the nearby trash bin. Then, he flipped on the ceiling light and sat back on the edge of the bed, breathing heavily.

Cindy hovered for a moment, unsure whether to sit beside him or give him space. He answered that uncertainty for her, opening the drawer of the nightstand and pulling out a joint. He lit it with a flick from a silver lighter and took a slow drag before offering another to Cindy.

She accepted without hesitation and eased onto the bed beside him.

"Wanna know a little secret?" Paul asked, his voice quieter now, eyes fixed on the glowing tip of the joint. "Sometimes...I wish I never made it back home."

Cindy turned to look at him, but he didn't meet her eyes.

"Sure, I may *look* fine," he continued, "and act like things are normal, but on the inside...whether I'm awake or asleep, I'm haunted by things I can't take back. Things I'll never be able to forgive myself for."

He paused to take another slow drag.

"If I had to describe it without saying too much," he added, "it'd be like...guilt, bitterness, fear, and anger, all twisted together. I get tired of feeling like this. But it keeps coming back."

A faint chuckle escaped him, dry and humorless.

"I guess that's another reason I went to Dan's. I wanted to be around people who were just...living, even if things were messy. Maybe I thought being there would help me not view myself as losing my mind or thinking of myself as a lost cause."

"Try taking some acid," Cindy suggested, her voice casual. "It can really take the edge off. Just make sure you think about stuff that makes you happy while you're on it, or else it can get ugly. Bad trips are no joke. If you want, add some booze for extra measure."

"I don't drink," Paul replied, shaking his head. "It doesn't sit well with me."

"Drinking's not that bad," Cindy shrugged. "Think about it. What's the difference between that and medicine? My folks used to give me a shot of brandy whenever I had a cold or fever as a kid. Same concept. Only this time, it's not for a sore throat. It's to put you in a cool place where you can view life from a different perspective. Who knows? Maybe you'll come out the other side feeling better about yourself. About life."

She nudged him lightly. "Plus, everyone's doing it anyway."

"Someone has all the answers, huh?" Paul asked, arching a brow.

"Ha, ha, very funny," Cindy replied. "Yet I'm not the one having trouble sleeping, am I?"

"No," Paul said, rubbing his temple, "but I'm not trying to end up an addict either. Maybe I should just ask my doctor for a stronger prescription..."

"Those doctors? Please," Cindy scoffed. "If those watered-down sleeping pills actually worked, you wouldn't still be up at night. They keep the good stuff for themselves and hand out sugar pills to everyone else while preaching their holier-than-thou nonsense."

Paul didn't say anything, just looked down.

"Why deal with all that crap," she continued, "when you can just go straight to Dan? He'll hook you up with whatever you need. The key is moderation. If you don't overdo it, you've got nothing to worry about. Some stuff even gives you a wild burst of energy, and when you crash, it's the best sleep you'll ever have. Just do it at home, kick back, and that's that. Nobody needs to know, except you and Dan. He won't rat anybody out."

"What a way to market his products," Paul laughed.

"Give it a try," Cindy coaxed with a playful nudge. "We've got the whole weekend to see what works. Some know-it-all doctor would have you doing the same thing anyway, only slower, and way more boring. You've got nothing to lose. I can stick around and help you ride it out."

Paul hesitated, then shrugged. "Well... okay. Just to see how things go."

"Right on," Cindy grinned, her eyes sparkling. "This is already shaping up to be the best weekend ever!"

The next day, they paid a homeless man outside a liquor store to buy a large bottle of booze, then headed over to Dan's apartment to pick up a mix of pills, powders, and tabs, whatever promised relaxation, revelation, or escape. Once back at Paul's place, they started drinking and sampling their haul.

The first wave brought waves of euphoria, laughter, heightened senses, and a charged sexual energy. But as they began mixing old favorites with the new drugs, the experience shifted. Some combinations lit them up with manic bursts of energy and chatter. Others hit like bricks: inducing panic attacks, vomiting, dizziness, and fits of irritability.

Neither of them could tell where the thrill ended and the edge began.

Though the plan was to experiment through the weekend, the binge blurred into midweek before the high finally began to wane. Time lost all shape. It wasn't until the distorted haze of a Wednesday afternoon that Cindy, mid-trip, suddenly remembered: school.

Wide-eyed, she jolted up. "We have class!"

Disoriented and unable to find Paul's car, they wandered the streets until they finally caught a city bus toward campus. Once they arrived, Cindy and Paul parted ways.

After mistakenly wandering around several of the wrong buildings, Cindy somehow ended up in the building she had been searching for. Dragging her feet inside, the teen squinted her eyes and pushed open an art studio door. Inside, students worked quietly, focused on their projects. Cindy stumbled in and clipped the edge of an easel, knocking someone's painting to the floor.

"Oh, sorry," she muttered with a giggle, plopping down heavily onto a barstool.

Heads turned. Eyes narrowed.

Cindy blinked. Their faces were familiar, but she couldn't recall having class with them before. Maybe they'd switched sections or added late.

Cool... very, very... cool...

"Watch where you're going next time," the angry student protested, scooping up the fallen canvas.

"Ugh, someone stinks," another student muttered, burying his nose in his shirt.

"Gross," a third gagged. "It smells like body odor, weed, puke... and something else."

"Did someone *pee* on themselves?" a fourth whispered, eyes darting around.

Across the room, the door opened again as Ryan entered, helping a student maneuver a large canvas through the doorway. As he turned to assist further, he froze mid-step. His eyes locked on Cindy.

She sat slumped on a barstool, clutching a paintbrush with a loose grip, her eyes wide and glazed. She moved the brush slowly up and down in the air, as if painting something on an invisible canvas.

Ryan blinked, stunned.

Without thinking, he handed off the canvas to the other student and crossed the room, but halfway there, he stopped cold. His nose wrinkled. The stench hit him like a wall.

A mix of sweat, weed, vomit, and stale alcohol clung to the air around her.

Ryan coughed, pinching his lips into a tight line.

"What on Earth—" the professor choked, covering his nose with one hand as a short heave escaped him. "Cindy, in my off—no, *outside. Right now.*"

As they exited, students exchanged pinched expressions and murmurs, the stench still lingering.

Outside, Ryan kept his distance, still shielding his face. His voice was calm, but taut.

"How are you, Cindy?"

"Fine..." she said, her words loose, voice trailing like a forgotten thought. "Have you seen Paul? We're trying to find the art building...Wow, look at all those colors, man...They're sighing...I just want to touch...and feel them."

She reached out toward the sky, as if trying to wipe away something invisible.

"Listen," Ryan continued, his tone firmer, "I don't know what convinced you to show up to one of my classes like this, but you need to leave campus. Go home. Right now."

"I'll be missing my classes, and Ryan'll get mad..."

"They're excused for today," he said. "Just go. And... take a bath, for heaven's sake."

"...Yes, sir."

Cindy shuffled to the nearest bus stop and caught the next ride home. When she arrived back at the Hollow Oaks apartment complex, frustration set in as she realized several doors were locked, preventing her from getting inside. She ran into Mrs. Grigsby, who seemed shocked by the request to help guide her to her apartment. Reluctantly, the woman agreed and walked Cindy next door to her unit. Cindy didn't bother to shower. She collapsed on the couch, where exhaustion overtook her, and slept for the rest of the day.

Chapter 6

Thursday morning, Cindy was anxious and moody. Her purse was empty: no beloved acid tablets, no mesc, no nothing to take her on another craved trip. Frustrated, she turned the tiny bag inside out and licked it, hoping to taste even the faintest trace of the substance it once held.

Groaning in disappointment, she skipped breakfast and trudged into the bathroom. A bath, fresh clothes, and the thought of doing laundry gave her just enough purpose to move. After taking a quick bath, she headed to the laundry room.

The laundry room was empty and quiet. She flicked the lights off and sat in the darkness, nodding off while the washer and dryer did their magic. It was the only kind of magic she had left.

Of all the clothes she washed and dried, only Margo's dress was neatly folded and carried under her arm. The rest were dumped onto the couch inside her apartment. She stared at them blankly, then sat and waited until it was time to catch the bus and return to school.

During Spanish class, Cindy discreetly handed Margo's dress to Laura, knowing she'd probably run into Margo later that day. When Laura pointed out that Cindy didn't look well, Cindy ignored her. She didn't need sympathy, and she definitely didn't want to talk. The only thing that mattered was whether Mrs. Garcia noticed anything.

Just in case, Cindy had her answer ready: she was recovering from the flu. That explanation would be enough to shut down any further questions and keep the professor at a safe distance.

The class had already moved on to new topics: days of the week, months, and numbers. It was material Cindy had learned before, but now she found herself needing small reminders. Her brain felt foggy.

Later, when Cindy entered the art building, her mood soured further as Ryan requested that she follow him into his office. Behind the closed door, he kept his voice low but firm.

"Yesterday, you disrupted a class you weren't enrolled in," he said. "And let's be clear about this. If you show up on campus under the influence again, I'll be forced to report it to the Dean of Students."

As if that weren't enough, he added a jab about the importance of maintaining personal hygiene.

"I don't know what you mean," Cindy replied flatly, lying without hesitation. "I didn't do anything wrong. I've been sick with the flu and haven't been feeling like myself lately."

"We're going to stop right there," Ryan said, cutting her off like he'd heard it all before. He raised a hand, his expression unmoved. "Go to class and think about what I said. If it happens again, even under the *slightest* suspicion, your time in this program is over."

"But—" Cindy started to protest, but stopped cold at the sight of Ryan removing his glasses. That gesture said it all. She'd seen it before. One more word, and it would be the final nail in the coffin.

"Yes, sir," she mumbled, swallowing her anger.

Ugh! Ryan gets on my nerves! Why can't he just go on sabbatical like all the other professors nobody likes? Who is he to tell me what to do? I'm an adult!

Stomping into the drawing studio, Cindy snatched up her materials and threw herself onto the barstool where she usually worked. One by one, other students trickled in and began setting up their projects.

Oddly, Ryan didn't appear until eighteen minutes into class, and he wasn't alone.

With him walked a woman Cindy had never seen before. She looked to be in her late forties, with greying brown hair pulled into a tight twist, sharp green eyes behind glasses, and a stiff, professional outfit: white blouse, blue blazer, matching skirt, and sensible black shoes. Everything about her screamed "uptight authority figure," reminding Cindy of her junior high school principal.

They walked together toward Cindy's station.

Oh, crap! He ratted me out after all! What about my second chance? Ugh! Of course! He's had it out for me since day one! That's it, isn't it? Goodbye scholarship. Goodbye future. I should've known better than to trust a word that came out of his mouth! My life is officially over.

"This is Cindy," Ryan told the woman. "She's the student we've been talking about. Cindy, this is Mrs. Everett."

Where have I heard that name before?

"Hi, Cindy," the woman said, extending her hand. "I'm Lucy Everett, from *The Rumble*. Dr. Ritter and I spoke recently about interviewing you as the university's first female recipient of this scholarship. Mr. Mills has been telling me so many wonderful things about your work. He says you're his best student, both in drawing and painting!"

Excuse me?

Cindy blinked, drawing her head back slightly, tilting it like she hadn't heard right.

"His *best* student?" Cindy echoed. *Since when was second place considered the best?*

"Yes," Mrs. Everett confirmed warmly. "And I'm really liking what I see in this drawing. I'd love to view more, especially the paintings I've heard so much about! Could you show me the ones planned for the Crimson Gallery?"

"S-sure," Cindy stammered. *I'm not finished with the paintings or the drawings... but if that's what she wants to see, I'll show her what I've got.*

She led Mrs. Everett through the hallway and into the painting studio, where she pointed out the monochromatic diptych she'd been working on: two mirrored figures of a woman, still clearly in progress, but already hinting at emotional depth and technical skill.

"Such fine detail," Mrs. Everett murmured, studying the canvases. "When it's finished, I wouldn't be surprised to see it in a museum. Truly impressive work. Tell me, young lady, when did your journey as an artist begin?"

"I've been drawing for as long as I can remember," Cindy replied. "But I didn't start painting until I was fifteen."

"And who taught you?" Mrs. Everett asked, clearly intrigued.

"One of my old teachers—Mrs. Lincoln. She told me her father was a landscape painter, but she leaned more toward realism. She took me under her wing during a rough time in my life. Honestly, she's one of the few people who pushed me to finish high school and apply for the art scholarship."

"Fascinating. What was her father's name?"

"Gustave Auclair... if I'm remembering correctly."

"The world-renowned French artist?" Mrs. Everett gasped. "Oh, my! That should be included in the article, but I'll need to confirm that detail."

Be my guest, Cindy thought. *I just learned about Auclair in art history. Thanks, Dr. Ritter. Mrs. Lincoln never said what her father's name was, but I'm sure they're related somehow. Aren't we all connected to Adam and Eve anyway?*

"I'm certainly looking forward to seeing the finished diptych at the student art show," Mrs. Everett said, her eyes still tracing the painting. "We'll have one of our photographers drop by later this week to get a shot of you with the piece. When we conduct the interview, it'll be great to capture you in your element."

She turned back to Cindy with a smile. "Let's plan to meet again next Thursday at this same time. I can't wait to see what else you're working on!"

Mrs. Everett bombarded Cindy with questions and praise as they returned to the drawing studio, and although the attention was flattering, it started to grate on Cindy's nerves. She forced a polite smile and nodded along, secretly relieved when the woman finally turned her attention to other students.

Once Mrs. Everett left, the remainder of the class went by uneventfully. Cindy attended her World Art class afterward, then joined her friends in the campus equality march. To make ends meet, she resumed sketching portraits of people around campus for extra cash. She told herself she'd keep it up until she could cover her back rent and finally afford the bike that she'd been eyeing.

Ugh. Never again. I swear, I'll never blow through money like that again. I hate doing extra work. Lesson learned!

Fatigued, Cindy dragged herself to Dan's apartment, where the louse was slouched on the couch, puffing smoke and sipping booze, surrounded by the usual crowd of slack-jawed ramblers spewing nonsense.

Christ. Do any of these morons ever go to class?

Without a word, she handed Dan the class notes she managed to scrape together, praying he wouldn't notice the gaps, casualties of her recent downward spiral. He glanced at them briefly, gave a lazy nod, then handed her a tiny plastic bag.

Cindy stared at it. It was barely a third of their usual deal.

"The heck is this?" she asked, trying to keep her voice even and staring at the tiny bag in her palm. "This isn't what I'm supposed to get. Where's the rest?"

Dan yawned. "Supply and demand, baby. Stuff's getting scarce, and people are lining up, ready to pay whatever it takes. We're gonna have to renegotiate our agreement. I don't need your notes, and I definitely don't need you taking tests for me anymore."

Cindy blinked. "What?"

"I've got better deals now," Dan added. "Other cats can get me the real tests for any class I want on campus, no sweat. I don't have to play the long game anymore."

Cindy's voice rose, tight with panic. "Dan, come on. I'm already behind on rent. I don't have a lot of money right now."

Dan gave a mocking shrug. "Can't that rich cat of yours do you a solid? Wasn't it just last week you two came in here throwing money around, buying up everything like it was Christmas?"

"Can't you give me a break?" Cindy pleaded. "I've been loyal since day one! If it weren't for me, Paul wouldn't have come back. He wouldn't have spent half as much as he did! I'm the one who kept people from bailing when they started doubting you. Doesn't that count for something?"

"True..." Dan said, rising from his seat. He slung a casual arm around Cindy's shoulders and began guiding her outside to the porch and then the sidewalk. "Everything you said is true, and I trust you more than anyone here, Cindy. Not many people stick around the way you have. That loyalty means something."

Cindy side-eyed him warily.

"So," he continued, "how about we help each other out? I'll give you your usual amount, no questions asked. But I need a favor in return."

"What kind of favor?" she asked, her stomach already tightening.

Dan stopped walking and gestured toward the neighboring house. "Go next door and make good 'ole Sam happy for me, and we'll call it even."

Cindy recoiled.

"What?" Her voice cracked. "Are you out of your damn mind? I'm not sleeping with your landlord! I won't even do that for mine!"

Dan didn't flinch. "Why not? If you ain't got the cash, how else you plan on payin'? Sam won't mind. He likes young college girls, and it'll be quick and easy. It's a fair trade, and everybody wins. Just do it... unless, you'd rather do it with me instead."

Cindy froze, her breath caught in her throat. Her body trembled with rage and disgust. Without thinking, she slapped Dan hard across the face.

He froze, stunned for a moment, then touched his cheek slowly. His expression twisted in fury. In one violent motion, he backhanded her.

Cindy cried out as she hit the ground, clutching the side of her face in shock.

"Hey! Chill out!" one of the guys from the porch shouted, jumping down to pull Dan back. Dan yanked his arm away.

"What's going on?" one woman gasped, grabbing her friend's arm as they both stood to get a better look.

Dan loomed over Cindy, his voice sharp and cold. "Don't come back around here again. Next time, it'll be worse."

Cindy glared up at him through her tears, defiant. "I'd like to see you try."

Dan raised his leg, ready to stomp her, but the other man lunged in, yanking him back.

"Come on, man, let her go," he said firmly.

Dan jerked his arm away, hurling every foul name he could muster at Cindy. He shoved past the group, stormed into the apartment, and slammed the door hard behind him.

"Cindy!" one of the women called out, rushing toward her. "What happened? Are you alright?"

The guy beside her reached down to help, but Cindy slapped his hand away, forcing herself to her feet, trembling but proud.

"Fuck you too, Dan!" she screamed, her voice cracking as she walked away, stiff with rage and pain.

After everything... he treated me like garbage. Like I was nothing. Like I was his worst enemy. Dan, I hate you. I fucking hate you, man!

"Cindy, the door," Mrs. Spearman called out, her voice weary from a long shift and a detour to the grocery store. Arms full, she fumbled with the knob until it finally gave way.

She stepped inside and froze.

Her newborn grandson lay on the living room floor, crying weakly. The air was sour with the smell of an unchanged diaper.

"Oh, no..."

Gently but urgently, Mrs. Spearman set the grocery bags on the coffee table and rushed to scoop the baby into her arms. His cries were hoarse, nearly ragged. She cradled him close, whispering soothing words as she made her way to the kitchen, where she grabbed a bottle of formula from the fridge. With practiced hands, she changed his diaper, trying to calm both the child and her rising panic.

Tears welled in her eyes, and one escaped down her cheek as she carried the baby toward her daughter's room. She knocked, holding her composure together with fraying threads.

"Cindy," Mrs. Spearman said, gently but firmly. "Cindy, if you could hold the baby... I need help."

Silence.

She tried the doorknob. Locked.

"Cindy," her voice broke this time. "Why was Sunshine on the floor? Didn't you hear him crying? Please, answer... I need help. I can't do everything alone."

Chapter 7

Friday arrived, but Cindy was still reeling from what had happened.

He hit me.

The thought echoed in her head like a broken record.

Dan hit me. That bastard actually raised his hand to me, a woman. Her stomach turned at the memory. *Men aren't supposed to do that. Ever.*

Then came the rest: the twisted "deal," the smug way he tried to coax her into using her body like it was currency.

He had the nerve to ask me to sleep with his landlord—his damn landlord! She clutched her head, fingers digging into her scalp. *What the hell was I thinking, trusting him? I thought we were friends...*

Tears welled, but she blinked them back.

I can't believe it... All this time, I thought I was in control. That I was using him, too. But he never saw me as anything more than someone to use. I feel so stupid.

Her chest ached with the weight of betrayal and self-blame. *This isn't who I want to be anymore. How'd things go so far to end up like this?*

Cindy studied her reflection in the mirror. The bruise on her cheek had darkened overnight, a harsh reminder of what Dan had done. She dabbed on makeup to cover it, but no matter how much she blended, she couldn't erase what happened. Disgusted, she turned away from her reflection and left the union bathroom.

Her purse still held a few dollars, enough for a breakfast bar from the vending machine. In the cafeteria area, a few students chatted over plates of steaming eggs, bacon, oatmeal, and toast. She didn't join them. Instead, she kept circling the lounge area with her sketchpad, offering to do more sketches.

Two more sketches were completed, quicker, looser, but still good. There was something calming about the rhythm of her pencil moving across the paper. *Maybe if I keep at this, I'll make enough to catch up on rent.* She approached a student gazing at the bulletin board and offered to draw him, but he politely declined.

Fair enough. Cindy lingered in front of the board, reading through the fliers for concerts, plays, sporting events, and beauty pageants. *Maybe I could draw outside one of these events and get more people that way.*

The teen circled the student union aimlessly, her feet dragging slightly from exhaustion. She came across a seat that had an abandoned newspaper that caught her eye. She picked it up and folded it open to the *Help Wanted* section.

There's got to be something in here that I can do to earn extra money, she thought, scanning the ads.

Ryan would kill me if he knew I was looking for a job. Cindy glanced around as if he might appear from behind the vending machine. *Yeah, yeah, I know the scholarship rules: no outside work, focus on school, blah, blah, blah. But I need more money; so, what he doesn't know won't hurt him. If it's under the table, it's not like it counts... right?*

She skimmed through the classifieds. Most of the listings might as well have been written in another language. *Wig stylist? Nope. Stenographer? Not a chance. Licensed nurse? Seriously? Correctional officer? Yeah right! As if anyone would want to see me doing that.*

Only two ads seemed remotely possible: one for a modeling gig, and another for kitchen help at a diner a few blocks from campus.

Modeling could be quick money, but what kind of modeling? And the kitchen job... She sighed. Long hours on my feet, grease popping in my face like acne, and rude customers that I'd probably argue with. But it's something.

The modeling job seemed like the better of the two, at least on the surface. But the ad was vague. No mention of pay, no details about the kind of modeling they were after. Just a number to call after 5 p.m. on weekdays and the promise of "training included." *Sketchy,* Cindy thought, *but still... intriguing.*

The kitchen job ad, on the other hand, was straightforward. $350 a month, not bad as a supplement to her scholarship. But the hours might clash with her class schedule. *Still,* she considered, *I've juggled worse.*

She tore both ads from the newspaper and tucked them neatly into her purse. *Maybe I can swing all three,* she thought—*the stipend, the drawings, and one of these jobs. Who says I can't?*

Her mind flickered with hope. *If I play this smart, I might finally be able to get ahead. Pay rent, get that bike... maybe even breathe a little. Heck, the possibilities are endless.*

"Cindy, we need to talk about your essay," Ms. Snow said gently, placing the paper back on the desk in front of her student. Only Cindy's name was written on it. "I don't want to give you a zero, but this is the second time you've turned in a blank assignment. You've passed your other work, but this essay is a big part of your final grade."

Cindy ignored the teacher. She picked up her pen and started doodling in her notebook, eyes fixed downward.

Ms. Snow sighed and eased into the desk directly in front of her. "I know talking isn't your favorite thing, but I need to understand. Why didn't you write anything? Don't you want to pass this class?"

Still, no answer.

"Mrs. Lincoln showed me your paintings," Ms. Snow continued, her voice softer now. "They're stunning. She and I have been talking, and she's asked me and another teacher to write recommendation letters for your scholarship application. I want to write one, Cindy. I really do. But if you don't pass this class, your GPA won't be high enough to qualify for the university you're aiming for."

"I won't get in," Cindy muttered. "So, why waste time? Essay or no essay, I'll still finish high school."

"But why risk your grade?" Ms. Snow asked, softly. "Why not leave with an A instead of a D?"

"That's how the class was set up."

"Cindy," she said, leaning in, "you can write this essay. You've been one of the top students. We've gone over this topic for weeks. Your mini-essays? Some of the best in class."

"Didn't I say I won't get in?" Cindy snapped, her voice breaking with frustration. "Nobody's going to give me a chance. Not once they see where I go to school and find out I've got a kid."

Ms. Snow started to speak, but Cindy pressed on.

"That's why my daddy left my momma in the first place. He said I wouldn't amount to anything. He said it over and over—and he's right. So, what's the point of writing some dumb essay? They're gonna look at my application, laugh, toss it in the trash, and pick someone better. Someone with a clean record and a perfect life. And even if I got in, what good is an art degree? People will laugh at it and call it basketweaving. The only time your art's worth anything is when you're already dead. So maybe I'd have to be dead to be worth something at all."

"There are good fields out there for artists," Ms. Snow said. "You could become a college professor, an art historian, a museum director, a registrar—so many things. But they all start with higher education."

"Yeah," Cindy muttered, "and we're right back to my original point. I won't get in."

Ms. Snow didn't argue. Instead, she lowered her voice. "At least try. Finish this class with a grade that reflects everything you've learned and are capable of, not one that reflects someone who's chosen to give up on herself. At this point, it's not the school that is determining if you'll be accepted or not. It's you, starting right now, with this last chance."

She placed the blank essay on Cindy's desk.

"I'll be grading papers for the next thirty minutes. If you choose to write, I'll read it. If not, then that's your choice too. But I hope you make the right decision."

Cindy made it to all her classes and returned to the student union, where she quickly found herself surrounded by more sorority groups eager for sketches. The women loved being the center of attention, laughing and posing while their friends watched the drawings take shape. Two of them even asked for group sketches, three girls to a page, which took longer, but Cindy didn't mind. As long as the cash kept flowing, she'd draw until her fingers gave out.

Which, unfortunately, they nearly did.

Her hand began to ache halfway through the second group drawing, but she pushed through it.

Keep going, she told herself, *just a little more.* But by the last sketch, it felt like someone was swinging a sledgehammer into her hand. Her grip trembled. She couldn't bend her fingers without pain shooting through her arm.

Reluctantly, Cindy told the remaining students she'd return Monday to continue. She slipped away, in discomfort, ducking into a quiet corner to count her earnings. The wad of bills in her palm nearly made her forget the pain, almost. It was enough to cover at least two months' worth of back rent.

Worth it, she told herself.

Cindy stopped at one of the payphones and pulled the crumpled newspaper clipping from her purse. Slipping the required change into the slot, she dialed the number listed under the modeling ad. No pay. Just "exposure" and "training." *Great.*

She sighed and called the second number: the kitchen job.

"Sorry," the voice on the other end said. "Only morning shifts are left."

Cindy's stomach sank. *All during class time... Figures.* She hung up the phone, the dull clank of the receiver matching her mood.

"Cindy..."

The voice made her turn.

Two familiar faces stood a few feet away: Eileen Livey and Ann Hensen. Eileen, nineteen, had long red hair and brown eyes. She wore a soft brown blouse, a dark orange skirt, and white sandals. Ann, twenty-one, had brown hair and hazel eyes. She wore a yellow shirt, a green skirt, and yellow shoes.

"Hey," Cindy mumbled.

"We've been looking for you," Ann said. "What happened back there with Dan? We heard yelling, and then someone said you got into a fight."

"Nothing," Cindy muttered.

"*Nothing?*" Eileen's voice rose. "Dan *hit* you, Cindy. How is that nothing?"

"It was just... a misunderstanding," she insisted, eyes dropping to the floor.

"No, it wasn't," Ann said firmly. "Stop covering for him. He didn't bother protecting you when he didn't hesitate to hit you in front of other people. That's not a misunderstanding. It's who he is."

"In all fairness... I hit him first," Cindy said quietly.

"So what?" Eileen countered. "He's stronger than you. He could've walked away. He *should've* walked away. I'm mad, but what gets me the most is that *you're not*. You're still trying to defend him after what he did? After all that talk he feeds everyone about peace, spirituality, and some 'higher consciousness' crap?"

Cindy said nothing.

"Did you at least report him?" Eileen pressed. "The dean? The campus police? Someone?"

"No," Cindy answered. "Why should I? If I talk, Dan'll get in trouble, and then he'll send people after me. Just like he did when Gail spoke up about him dealing on campus. She's gone now, and he's still here. So, what do you think will happen to *me*?"

"We'll back you," Eileen assured her. "He hit you in front of a crowd. Anyone could've reported him, not just you."

"He'll still blame me," Cindy replied, her voice brittle. "He'll twist it and make it sound like I started it. He always does. And I'm not going to the dean, or the police, or *anyone*. Don't bring me up. I'll deny it. So, just don't."

"But Cindy," Ann pleaded, "you don't have to face this alone. You've got *us*. Let us stand with you. If enough people speak up, maybe they'll kick him off campus for good."

"They'll get rid of me too," Cindy replied. "Dan's got stuff on me, and if it gets out, I could lose my scholarship. I'll be *ruined*. If you really want to help, just keep my name out of it."

"It's still not right," Ann muttered.

"Either of you got any acid tablets?" Cindy asked, her voice low but urgent. "That would really be doing me a solid. I ran out and need some, bad. I've got money."

Ann hesitated, glancing briefly at Eileen before rummaging through her purse. Silently, she slipped one small bag into Cindy's hand once the cash was exchanged.

Cindy didn't stick around any further. She turned and walked away, wishing they'd just mind their own business. Still, buried under all the frustration and fear, a small part of her was touched. Someone *did* care. That mattered, even if she didn't want to admit it.

She caught the bus home, collapsed onto the couch, and took one of the acid tablets. The bag didn't have much, but for now, it would have to do.

Mmm... Her body melted into the only clear spot on the cluttered couch as kaleidoscopic shapes swirled in slow motion across the room. *Such a beautiful world... I want to stay here forever...*

Hours later, now in the haze of the following day, Cindy walked to the front office. She handed over what she could to Mr. Tanner to chip away at her back rent.

"Cindy," Mr. Tanner stated, "I need to step inside your unit for a moment. There've been several complaints about a strong, unpleasant odor coming from around your apartment."

"Today's not a good day," Cindy replied quickly, her heart pounding. "Can you come back in a few days?"

"I've already heard that a few times," Mr. Tanner countered. "I just want to make sure there's nothing rotting or damaging the property, nothing that's a health risk."

"Seriously, I can't today," Cindy insisted, her voice sharpening with frustration.

"Alright then," Mr. Tanner said coolly, pulling a folded document from his folder. "This will be noted as a failure to comply under your lease agreement. You've refused multiple inspections. That's grounds for termination."

Cindy's eyes widened. "What?"

"You've got thirty days to vacate unless I'm allowed to inspect. Your choice."

"But I can't! I need more time!" Cindy pleaded, her voice cracking.

"Today," Mr. Tanner said firmly, "or I'll proceed with litigation to have you removed from the property."

Cindy's face tightened. Whether she let him in or not, she was screwed.

"If I let you in, that means I've complied, right? This paper doesn't apply anymore?" she asked, gesturing to the document.

"That depends on what I find," Mr. Tanner replied. "Shall we go now?"

Shit.

Cindy hesitated, then gave a reluctant nod.

"Fine."

Together, they left the office and headed toward Cindy's apartment. Each step felt heavier than the last. Cindy dragged her feet, mind racing for a way out of the mess. Drugs were strictly forbidden. Thank God she hadn't smoked weed on the property in the past few days. Still, that didn't mean she was in the clear. When they reached the unit, she hesitated, then reluctantly unlocked the door and pushed it open for the landlord.

Immediately, Mr. Tanner's face twisted in disgust. He coughed, raising his hand to cover his nose and mouth as the stench hit him. Navigating the narrow walkway between piles of papers, clothes, and broken junk, he stumbled on a toy truck that was partially buried beneath the clutter. Forced to let go of his face, he reached out for balance, only to grab a precarious mound of clothes that collapsed under his weight, pulling him down with it and nearly blocking the path behind him.

Cindy winced, her stomach tightening as she watched him struggle to his feet. When he gave her a sharp, disapproving look after spotting the covered couch, she let out a slow, defeated sigh and sat down, staring at the floor.

In the kitchen, the sounds of coughing, objects clattering, and her privacy unraveling filled the silence like needles under her skin. Cindy kept her gaze low, wishing herself to be invisible or that she could vanish into any other life, any other place. All she wanted was to be left alone. She didn't bother the neighbors. She didn't make any noise. Why should it matter what went on inside her own four walls?

Mr. Tanner headed for the bathroom but couldn't wedge himself through the cluttered hallway. He stood there a moment, staring at what used to be a door to the bedroom, now barricaded by a mountain of forgotten things.

"Let's talk outside," he said flatly.

Cindy followed, her steps heavy, each one dragging like the guilt sitting in her gut.

Out on the breezeway, Mr. Tanner turned to face her, his brow furrowed and jaw tight. "Look, Cindy, I get it. You're juggling school, life, and whatever else you've got going on. I've tried to be patient. But what I saw in there? It's unacceptable! That isn't just a mess, that's a danger zone."

Cindy kept her eyes on the ground and arms folded across her chest like armor.

Mr. Tanner exhaled, rubbing the bridge of his nose. "What's going on? That apartment's a wreck. Where'd all those things come from? Does your mother know you're living like that?"

Silence.

"The place smells awful, like something crawled in and died. You can't even get to the bedroom. That's not just a code violation, but a health hazard. If a fire broke out, you would have trouble getting out safely."

"I let you in," Cindy said defensively, her voice tight. "I did what you asked. I said I needed time, but you wanted to come in anyway..."

"It's not about letting me in," Mr. Tanner sighed. "The place is a disaster, and every tenant has an obligation to keep their unit clean and up to code. That's part of the terms in everyone's lease. Your unit is not only filled with clutter, but it has a moldy stench. At this point, it may not even be safe for you to stay there."

The landlord paused to collect himself.

"I don't want to evict you, kid," he continued. "But you gotta meet me halfway and get the place cleaned and up to code. I'll give you two weeks, and I mean it. Two weeks to turn it around, or I'll have no choice but to move forward with the eviction. Don't test me on this."

Cindy's blood boiled. Her fists clenched at her sides as she snapped, "Then give me my money back! I'm gonna need it for another place!"

Mr. Tanner didn't flinch. "Not a chance. That money is what was owed, and you're still behind a month."

Tossing her head back, Cindy released a muffled groan as she clenched her fists.

"Fine," she argued, "Once it's paid off, I'll just move somewhere else. I don't like living here anyway. This isn't the only apartment in town."

Mr. Tanner shook his head, frustration rolling off him in waves. "You think another landlord's gonna take you with this kind of mess on your record? Good luck. Most won't even let you fill out the application."

Cindy opened her mouth, but he cut her off.

"Two weeks," he repeated, voice like steel. "No more. And I *still* expect the rest of that overdue rent. You want a roof over your head? Earn it."

Fuming, Cindy stood frozen as Mr. Tanner walked off. She spun on her heel and kicked a loose rock with such force that it clattered across the pavement. Storming back into the apartment, she slammed the door behind her and collapsed into sobs, not knowing where to begin.

The place was a wreck, and it was all on her to fix it. Just one person, drowning in clutter, rot, and the weight of her own life. How was she supposed to clean all this without the neighbors catching on? One wrong move and they'd all be whispering. Pointing. Staring.

Who ratted me out? Probably some nosy neighbor who couldn't mind their own damn business. Acting like a hero, like they saved the day.

If the smell was so bad, how come she couldn't smell it herself? What did Mr. Tanner know, anyway? Those piles weren't trash. They were *her* things. Things that mattered. Things that might mean something someday. Maybe even be worth something. These people didn't get it. *Idiots, all of them.* One day they'd see. They'd regret every smug suggestion.

Who did Mr. Tanner think he was, anyway? How dare he talk like she couldn't find another place? Heck, apartments needed renters too, didn't they?

Then the thought hit like a slap: *Momma.* Cindy would have to ask her to co-sign again, and Mrs. Spearman would ask *why.*

"Shit," Cindy muttered. "What am I gonna do now?"

Cindy sank into the couch, her hands covering her face like a veil of shame and exhaustion. Her tears came silently at first, until her breath hitched and she wiped at her cheeks with the heels of her palms. When she finally opened her eyes, the piles around her loomed like towers, threatening to cave in at the slightest movement.

I can't... I... can't... but if I don't, I'll get kicked out...

A sharp inhale stung her lungs as panic gripped her chest. She bent forward, clutching her stomach, trying to breathe through the pressure. Back and forth, she began rocking herself.

Help me... Oh, God, help me. I can't take anymore... Please, God...

Her chest rose and fell like a ticking bomb. The room swayed, bending in angles that didn't make sense. Dizzy, she shut her eyes and curled up into herself, folding her legs beneath her, and arms wrapped tight.

I can't do it... I can't, I can't...

Cindy stayed like that: still, small, swallowed by the wreckage around her, for nearly an hour. Not crying anymore, just breathing in the quiet that followed panic. Then, almost mechanically, she got up and wandered to the kitchen phone.

With trembling fingers, she dialed the number. Her thumb hovered over the receiver, ready to slam it back down. But before she could, the line clicked.

"Hello?" came the voice. Familiar. Warm. Tentative.

Cindy's throat locked.

"Hello?" the voice answered again, firmer this time, but still curious.

Cindy hesitated, her breath hitching as she tried to speak through the lump in her throat. She slowly brought the handset back to her ear, her knuckles white around the cord.

"...Laura, it's Cindy," she choked out, her voice breaking, barely above a whisper. "I really... I really could use a friend right now."

"What happened?" Laura asked. "Did Paul break things off?"

"No," Cindy sniffed, brushing her tears on the shoulder of her blouse. "It's got nothing to do with him. I just— I can't tell anyone else about this. I need... I need so much help..."

"Help with what? Cindy, what's going on?"

"I'm gonna get kicked out of my apartment," she confessed, the words tumbling out like a flood. "If I don't clean it up. It's— it's a disaster, and I can't... I can't do it alone. I'm overwhelmed, scared, and— I can't breathe—"

"Oh no," Laura gasped. "Okay, calm down! Just breathe, all right? I'm on my way, okay? I'm coming!"

The line clicked as Laura hung up in a hurry. Cindy stood there, still holding the receiver against her ear long after the dial tone returned. Her hand shook as she placed it back on the hook. For a moment, just a moment, she let herself believe that maybe she wouldn't have to face this alone.

Fifteen minutes later, there came a knock at the door. Cindy cracked it open just wide enough to see Laura standing there. She greeted her friend with a lingering embrace that slowly calmed her nerves.

"I came as fast as I could," Laura said softly.

Ashamed, Cindy let go, stepped aside, and let her friend into the apartment. Laura stepped in carefully.

"Whoa," she said under her breath, not unkindly. "What happened, Cin? Where'd all this stuff come from?"

"I don't know; everywhere," Cindy mumbled. "It just...built up...I didn't mean for it to happen."

"Oh, Cindy..." Laura frowned, glancing around again before asking, "Alright, where do we start?"

"I don't know," Cindy sniffled back a sob. "It's too much for me to think about."

"How about the living room, since we're here?" Laura suggested. "Got any trash bags?"

Cindy handed her friend a crinkled shopping bag that she had recycled. Laura began stuffing items into the bag, but after a few items, Cindy stopped her.

"Wait," Cindy stated, a nervous edge in her voice. "What's in the bag?"

Laura froze mid-reach and said, "Just junk. It looked like trash, so I put it in."

"Let me see," Cindy murmured, reaching for the bag. "I wanna check first. I don't want anything important thrown away by mistake."

Laura handed it over, and Cindy sifted through the contents. Her fingers brushed over an old, folded newspaper. Next came a hardened, shriveled orange peel. Then, there was an empty bottle of floral perfume, and a slip of paper stuck to the waxy remains of a melted white candle.

"I can still use these," Cindy insisted, clutching the wrinkled orange peel and empty perfume bottle like they were rare artifacts. "The orange peel helps freshen the air. And I can reuse the perfume bottle. The papers could be used for wrapping things."

Laura crouched beside her, eyeing the brittle peel with a skeptical look. "Cindy, that peel's old and dried up. It's not deodorizing anything anymore."

"It still has a little scent."

"Barely....and you don't need that perfume bottle. There's more like it over there on the side of the couch. As for the paper... look around. You've got more than enough."

Cindy's brows drew together, defensive but tired. "But what if I need it later? I don't want anything wasted."

Laura sighed. "You haven't needed it yet... Look, what if I load up the old papers and take 'em to the recycling center myself? They'll make new paper out of it, and none will be wasted. Would that be okay?"

Cindy hesitated.

"Yeah," she finally agreed after a minute of thinking. "Okay."

They carried several old newspapers outside, stacking them in a small pile in the trunk of Laura's car. They went back and forth until the trunk was filled with papers.

Then, Cindy reentered the apartment and caught sight of another pile Laura had quietly made, this one full of clothes. Her stomach dropped. She waited for Laura to start rummaging through another pile of clutter before she darted forward, scooping up as many garments as she could. Blouses, scarves, and a stained poncho were all clutched tightly against her chest as she stormed into the kitchen. She yanked open the cabinets and stuffed the clothes inside, slamming the doors shut before Laura could follow.

"What are you doing?" Laura called from the other room.

"Nothing," Cindy lied.

Laura stepped into the kitchen. The silence between them was heavy, filled with the weight of everything unsaid.

"Cindy, there's no reason to cram clothes into the kitchen cabinets," Laura said. "Sure, it works as a temporary fix, but we'll have to move them eventually. They don't belong there. Just think how nice it would be to have the place looking like it did that time we all came over for fondue. And with Valentine's Day coming up, I'm sure you'd want it to look nice in case Paul stops by, right?"

Cindy considered Laura's words, silently admitting it would be nice to have people over again. It had been a long time since anyone had spent time with her inside the apartment, especially since the breakup with Betsy.

So, I have to let more go... again. I don't want to, but I need to... if I'm going to move forward, I guess.

The place hadn't felt like home in a while, not with just a couch serving as her anchor in an otherwise empty space.

It would be nice to have room to breathe... to not feel so confined... and alone...

For several hours, Cindy and Laura sorted through the items, discarding what was no longer needed. By the end of the day, they had cleared nearly half the living room. Back and forth, they walked, loading Laura's vehicle with recyclables and tossing the rest into the dumpster.

When it was finally time to stop, Laura promised to return after school on Monday to continue helping with the cleanup. Cindy thanked her, then pushed through another hour of organizing on her own.

Exhausted, she finally collapsed onto the couch, this time without piles of clothes, papers, or clutter surrounding her. For the first time in a long while, she had room to stretch out her body and legs.

I haven't been able to do this in forever... I almost forgot how good it feels to really stretch out here...

Rrriiiinnnggg! Rrrriiiinnnnggg! The phone chimed.

Cindy walked into the kitchen and picked up the phone.

"Hello?" she answered.

"Hey, Cindy," the familiar masculine voice spoke. "It's Paul. Wanna hang out?"

"I would, but I'm so tired," Cindy exhaled. "I've been cleaning most of the day, and I'm just now winding down."

"Need any help?" Paul offered.

"No, but thanks. That's awfully sweet of you."

"Okay, just wanted to let you know I won't be around next weekend. I'll be at the armory for my reserve duties most of the day, so I'll be tired too once I get home."

"In that case, maybe we could meet up tomorrow to make up for the time we'll miss?"

"Sure! Where and when?"

"How about the outlet mall on Bolton Street? Say, 10 o'clock?"

"I'll be there. Later, Cin!"

Grinning, Cindy hung up the phone, her exhaustion fading as excitement for tomorrow took over.

Chapter 8

Rrriiinnnggg! Rrrriiinnnggg!

"Hello?" Cindy yawned as she answered the phone that Sunday.

"Hi, may I speak to Ms. Cindy Spearman?" came a polite, feminine voice.

"This is she. Who's calling?"

"Hi, my name is Debbie Kirkland. I'm the manager at the Camellia Art Studio. A few days ago, you sketched my niece at the university. Beautiful work, by the way. I wanted to reach out because we're launching a summer arts program for kids between the ages of eleven to fifteen, starting the second week of June. We're inviting local artists to give art demonstrations, and I immediately thought of you."

"Oh wow, thank you!"

"The pay isn't much, I'll be honest," Mrs. Kirkland added, "but it's a great way to give back to the community and there's potential for it to lead to other opportunities."

The pay isn't much? Of course not. Here we go again! Everyone wants artists to give back, to make a difference, to inspire the community... but no one wants to actually pay us. How about giving us a decent check? These supplies aren't cheap, and neither is my time.

Cindy clenched her jaw, tempted to hang up right then and there, but the reality of her empty wallet weighed heavily. She couldn't afford to be proud right now. Any money—any—was more than what she had. She swallowed her frustration and forced herself to stay on the line.

"Sure, sign me up," Cindy said, forcing a cheerful tone she didn't feel. "I'd love to! Anything to give back!"

They still better pay me...

"Excellent!" Mrs. Kirkland replied, clearly pleased. "I'll get everything set up and send over the details as soon as I can."

Great. Now hang up before I change my mind, Cindy thought. *Not even a thank you for all this so-called charity work... Figures.*

Mrs. Kirkland ended the call with a brisk goodbye. Cindy set the phone down, then reached into her purse and pulled out another acid tab. She stared at it for a second before putting it in her mouth.

She muttered Dan's name under her breath, cursing him for the fight that had blown everything apart. Sure, she'd thrown the first slap, but what woman wouldn't after what he had the nerve to suggest that day? Still, she was the one paying for it now.

There was another guy off campus who sold some of the same stuff Dan had, but his supply was weak, barely worth the cash.

Maybe I could ask Paul... she thought. *He's decent. He could probably get what I need...*

But that thought twisted into something uneasy.

Of course, then I'd owe him. And what could I possibly offer someone like him? He already has everything. I don't want to screw things up between us... but I need what I need. Maybe Ann or Eileen could do me a solid, but I barely run into them as is, and they probably will stop going over to Dan's place too...

She rubbed her temples, trying to push the tension away.

*I'll figure something out. I always do…
eventually.*

Later that day, the outlet mall buzzed with shoppers drifting in and out of stores, hunting for the latest deals. Paul and Cindy weaved through the crowd and made their way into the radio store.

Paul purchased a cassette recorder along with a few blank tapes to record his class lectures. As Cindy continued to browse, she spotted a familiar music system on display, the same model she'd seen in his apartment.

Lining the shelves were sleek new gadgets: a bold display of headphones, shiny AM/FM stereo receivers, automatic stereo changers, and stereo phonos.

Their second stop was a sporting goods store, where playful flirting took over. Paul showed Cindy how to hold a baseball bat properly and demonstrated a quarterback stance, laughing as he coached her through a few poses. She played along, occasionally tossing a teasing jab his way as they turned the aisles into their own impromptu playing field.

Next came the furniture store, where they wandered through staged living rooms and bedrooms, pretending to be serious buyers planning to furnish a dream home.

In the hobby shop, surrounded by toys, roller skates, robots, and colorful board games, they got nostalgic. Between laughs, they swapped stories about their favorite childhood memories, the embarrassing holiday gifts they'd ever received, and the long-wished-for items they'd finally collected as adults.

From there, they dove into the packed record store. Flipping through the selections, they picked out and purchased new records from their favorite singers and bands to listen to for later.

There, the evening unraveled in familiar rhythms: smoking weed, having sex, and lounging together in a haze of comfort and connection. Cindy stayed the night, relieved that she had thought ahead to bring over a change of clothes. Everything was calm, quiet, until the now-familiar thud broke the silence.

Once again, Paul had fallen to the floor in his sleep, caught in the grip of whatever troubled his dreams.

"I... I'm sorry," Paul muttered, his voice heavy with exhaustion and frustration.

"Are you okay?" Cindy asked softly.

Paul drew his knees to his chest, eyes closing as he took a long, slow breath. "Yeah..."

"Things'll get better, Paul. Just... chill, okay?"

Cindy lit another joint, then slid out of bed and sat beside him on the floor. She handed it over, and Paul accepted it with a quiet nod, taking a drag like it was the only thing keeping him grounded.

After a pause, he spoke again. "I think you should leave."

Cindy blinked. "Why?"

He didn't look at her. "Aren't you scared? I...I don't want to do anything to hurt anybody, especially you. It's not safe to be around someone like me. When I'm awake, I'm fine...but when I fall asleep, I can't control myself."

Cindy leaned in closer, her voice calm but firm. "You wouldn't hurt a fly; you're just jumpy at night, is all...Sometimes, people get that way after trauma and want to push people away."

Paul took a slow drag from the joint, holding the smoke for a second before exhaling. He passed it back to Cindy, who placed it between her lips as they leaned into each other's arms.

"People come and go," Paul murmured. "They don't stick around, no matter what."

I will, Paul. I promise... if you let me.

"Sounds like you were really hurt," Cindy said gently.

"I was," he admitted, his voice low. "But, oh well... Nothing matters anymore."

Cindy looked at him, soft but steady. "I'll stick around. I think you're neat."

He glanced over, the corner of his mouth twitching. "Why?"

"You're good looking and know how to fuck," she said with a teasing grin.

They both burst out laughing, and the tension briefly lifted.

"That's a straightforward way of requesting for someone to stick around," Paul chuckled.

"Also, you seem to be a nice guy and easy to talk to" Cindy added, nudging his shoulder. "I know you're not looking for anything serious, but until then, we can be there for each other."

Paul didn't answer right away, but the way he pulled her closer said enough.

"Deal," he said. "I think you're cool too. You're down-to-earth and creative. I like the paintings you showed at the studio. I wish I could paint as well."

"I got this job at a studio downtown," Cindy said. "We can check it out later today, if you're up for it."

"Sure," Paul replied. "I'd like that."

They shared an affectionate kiss, then curled back into bed together, the morning light slipping quietly through the blinds. This time, there were no interruptions, just peace between them.

Monday morning arrived, and Cindy and Paul drove by the art studio to take a quick look before heading to campus. Afterward, Cindy slipped into her usual routine: attending classes, working on new sketches, and meeting Paul for lunch.

In a rare quiet moment, she paused to offer a silent prayer of thanks. Things felt like they were falling into place. She could finally see herself as genuinely happy.

Later that afternoon, Cindy met up with Laura, and the two picked up where they left off: sorting, cleaning, and packing items to be recycled. They worked well into the evening, making steady progress.

After Laura left, Cindy continued on her own for another hour before finally calling it a day. Between them, they had cleaned nearly three-fourths of the living room, with plans to tackle more on Tuesday.

Rrriiinnnggg! Rrriiinnnggg! The phone chimed.

"Hello?" Cindy answered.

"Hey," the voice said. "It's Eileen. Just calling to see how you've been."

"I'm fine, thanks. How'd you get my number?"

"Stellar." Eileen paused, then added, "Oh, I got it from a friend who had it. I wanted to apologize. Ann and I didn't mean to upset you that day. We were just trying to stand up for what we thought was right. Anyway, the offer's still on the table, if you ever change your mind."

"Thanks..."

Eileen continued, her tone shifting. "So... everyone's saying you're hanging around with a new guy. Does that mean Betsy's out of the picture for good?"

Cindy didn't answer right away. *So, what if she is?*

"Well," Eileen said, her voice softening, "what I'm getting at is... if you'd ever like to go to a movie with me sometime, I'd really like that."

"I... uh..." Cindy hesitated, unsure of how to respond. "It's true. I am seeing someone new. So... sorry."

"Great," Eileen said flatly, then forced a lighter tone. "If you ever change your mind, the door'll always be open."

There was a pause on Cindy's end before she finally asked, "I don't get it. Why now?"

"Well... you were with Betsy, and I figured you needed time to move on after the breakup. Then I heard you were possibly seeing someone else, but... I don't know, I still wanted to take a chance and ask."

Cindy hesitated, weighing her thoughts. Things were going well with Paul, better than she'd expected, and she was undeniably drawn to him in every way. But deep down, she knew he wouldn't be willing to accept her son, and a committed relationship wasn't on his radar anytime soon.

Was he seeing other people on the side? Was she supposed to wait around until he decided what he wanted? The more she thought about it, the less fair it seemed.

Then there was Eileen. She was attractive enough, sure, but Cindy wasn't certain if she was truly her type. They'd shared the occasional chat at Dan's place, but never anything deep or meaningful. Nothing that stuck.

"Yeah," Cindy said. "I'll keep that in mind... I gotta run, but I'll see you around."

Cindy hung up the phone, deciding that she'd rather stick with Paul. Still, there was something thrilling about being wanted by someone else. The idea of a fling teased her imagination, and for a brief moment, she let it play out in her mind like a scene from a movie. Giggling to herself, she shook her head and pushed the thought aside.

She stepped back into the now-roomier living room, which still felt small but no longer stifling. Spreading her arms, Cindy gave herself a slow spin, smiling widely. She could move freely, see the warm wooden walls, adjust the blinds without knocking something over, and look out the window at the world beyond.

Only a few more rooms to go, and this place will feel like home again... I'm so close.

Her heart swelled with gratitude. *I wonder how I'm going to thank Laura. She's been such a huge help with all the cleaning... and Paul makes me feel special, every single time.*

Forget the bike for now, she thought. *I'll do something meaningful for them. Maybe drawings: pieces that reflect what brings them joy, something personal, something lasting. Yeah... that's it.*

Cindy grabbed her drawing pad and a few sharpened pencils. She began settling into the quiet of her space as she prepared to work on something more meaningful than anything she'd drawn in weeks. This time, she worked large, giving herself room to breathe, to stretch the lines across the page like her thoughts taking form.

For Laura, she sketched a black and white tuxedo cat, curled neatly in a loaf position, paws tucked beneath its body. There was something serene in the cat's stillness, and Cindy smiled as she drew in the dark patches of fur, imagining Laura's face when she saw it.

Next, she turned to Paul's drawing: a baseball player caught mid-motion in a powerful batting stance. She wanted to capture not just a player, but *Paul*—his energy, his quiet strength.

Time passed unnoticed. Cindy leaned in, her hand steady but tiring. She pushed through, layering detail after detail until her fingers cramped and her wrist throbbed. Still, she kept going, only stopping when the ache was too much to ignore.

She flexed her fingers and looked down at the images, her heart full. These weren't just drawings. They were gifts and pieces of herself, shaped in graphite and gratitude.

Reluctantly, Cindy called it a day. Carefully, she slid the drawing pad and pencils beneath the couch, making sure they were safe. Letting out a long yawn, Cindy stretched across the cushions, her body sinking into the softness.

She glanced between the kitchen and the hallway that led to the bedroom and bathroom. The apartment still needed work, but she was close.

Almost there...

With that thought, Cindy closed her eyes and sleep gently overtook her.

On Tuesday evening, after their classes, Laura and Cindy returned to Cindy's apartment to finish clearing out the last section of the living room and part of the kitchen.

As they peeled back layers of old dishes, unopened envelopes, and takeout containers, Cindy couldn't believe the number of roaches. Some were dead, but many were still very much alive, scurrying out from the mess.

Then it happened: one particularly bold roach took flight, soaring across the room like it owned the place.

Laura let out a sharp scream, followed by a string of cuss words, surprising Cindy, who had never heard such language come out of her friend's mouth before.

"Shit! Kill it! Oh my god, kill it! Damn it!" Laura cried, trembling as she swatted at the air with a folded newspaper.

"Wait, wait!" Cindy shouted, ducking. "I don't want it dead! Just trap it! We can take it outside!"

"You want to *save* it?!" Laura gawked at her. "It's *flying*, Cindy. That's not a houseguest! Kill the damn thing, shit!"

The two launched into a frantic, half-serious argument over the roach's fate, dodging and ducking as the insect zipped around the room.

"I'll take care of it!" Cindy finally said, grabbing an empty bowl and a piece of cardboard. "I'll take it out myself."

But as she approached, the roach darted down into a cluttered corner and disappeared into the cracks beneath a pile of clutter.

Cindy rose onto the tips of her toes, peering into the cluttered corner, hoping she could somehow coax the roach out from its hiding place.

Wham!

"What happened?" Cindy asked, spinning around.

"There was a huge spider, and I got scared," Laura admitted, her voice shaky as she flung the folded newspaper, now with a squashed spider inside, into the recycling bag. Grimacing, she shook her hands wildly, as if trying to fling off some invisible, revolting substance that clung to her skin.

Cindy opened her mouth to protest, but quickly shut it. When it came to spiders, she knew Laura had a hard line: no mercy, no debate. There was no changing her mind.

Cindy turned back to the task at hand and resumed cleaning. The rhythm of back-and-forth trips to the dumpster continued, and with each haul, the apartment felt a little lighter. However, as she stepped outside with another bag, she noticed Mrs. Grigsby watching from her doorway while her children played nearby.

Great, Cindy thought, cheeks warming. *I'm so embarrassed...*

She gave a quick, awkward nod and carried on, hoping her neighbor wasn't judging the chaos too harshly.

"Hello, Cindy," Mrs. Grigsby called out. "Moving out?"

"No," Cindy replied, forcing a polite smile. "Just making a little room."

Not wanting the conversation to go any further, she quickly turned and hurried back into the apartment, shutting the door behind her.

That was close, she thought, exhaling as the lock clicked into place.

The women finished cleaning the living room and managed to tackle about a third of the kitchen. With a packed schedule for the rest of the week, Laura promised to return over the weekend to help finish up.

Cindy hugged her friend tightly. "Thanks for everything," she said, truly grateful.

I'm going to try to finish the rest of the kitchen on my own, she thought. *That'll be a nice surprise for Laura when she comes back.*

She considered working on the drawings again but decided to give her hands and her mind a break. Instead of staying cooped up in the apartment, Cindy stepped outside for a change of scenery. She wandered through the complex, then down the street, breathing in the early evening air, letting it clear her head.

Along the way, Cindy passed neighbors returning home from work, some sitting outside in chairs, catching up with each other, while others called their kids in for dinner. She took her time outside, soaking in the everyday life around her, quietly wishing she had a television of her own to return to.

But that was okay. Back inside, she still had stacks of old newspapers and magazines to flip through.

When she returned home, the teen picked up a worn magazine and sat with it, thumbing through the pages. Her eyes lingered on the bright, cheerful faces.

What a bunch of lies, she thought bitterly. *Nobody's ever that happy. Not for long, anyway. Most of these people are smiling because they're next to some expensive thing. Sure, maybe you're happy for a moment, before you get it, when it's still a dream. But after? It fades. I was so stupid to believe in that over and over again...*

She turned the page slowly, her expression hardening with thought.

If all of that was a lie, then what actually brings happiness, the kind that lasts? Margo was right. I was vulnerable...I still am, maybe. But I'm going to fix things. I already am.

On Thursday, Mrs. Everett arrived at the art department with a staff member in tow to conduct the interview with Cindy. They spoke at length about her current work and upcoming creative goals, while the photographer snapped photos of Cindy standing beside her artwork, which she had carefully arranged on a display board for the occasion.

The article was slated for the front page of an upcoming edition, set to release a week before the art show. The thought of it made Cindy's heart race with excitement.

After school, still riding the high of the moment, she called her mother to share the good news.

"I'm so proud to hear this," Mrs. Spearman said, her voice bubbling with excitement after Cindy shared the news. "Send me several copies, please! Gertrude and Agnes are going to be just as thrilled. I have the best daughter in the entire world! Oh, I could just burst!"

"I will, Momma," Cindy promised. "I'll mail them as soon as I can. When the yearbook comes out, I'll get one for us to share too."

"I'm so happy, I'm crying, just so you know that..." Her tone softened. "Sunshine and I can't wait to be there for the art show and see you again. Don't forget to keep an eye out for the envelope I'm sending. I'll include a few things he'll need when he stays with you before the surgery."

Cindy hesitated. "Of course, Momma. I'll do what I can. I just worry about handling everything while I'm still in class. I won't have much time with him, and daycare's just not something I can afford right now."

"I've got that covered, remember," Mrs. Spearman assured her. "I've been putting money aside for a rainy day, and it should be more than enough to help with daycare and anything else that comes up. Just make sure to give them a copy of the documents once they arrive. I'll also bring the originals when we come, in case something goes wrong with the delivery. It's best to have everything in order before Sunshine arrives."

Cindy paused, guilt tugging at her. "I feel awfully bad about missing your surgery... Maybe I should talk to Ryan and ask for time off so I can be there to help."

"I'll be fine," her mother reassured her. "Besides, I'd never let you put your education or your promising career on hold just to take care of me."

"Okay... well, if anything changes between now and then, I'll do whatever's necessary."

"Thanks, sweetheart. I'll call you later, alright? I love you."

"I love you too, Momma. Take care."

Cindy hung up the phone and immediately began rummaging through her purse, searching for the last of her acid tablets. Her fingers brushed the small bag. It was light, nearly empty. Only two tablets left.

Uneasy, she slung the purse over her shoulder and headed out, crossing campus with the hope of spotting Gordon Burns, the guy who usually sold acid nearby. But no matter how many familiar corners she passed, he was nowhere to be found. *Shoot!*

Her footsteps carried her further, down a path she hadn't taken in a while, one that led just beyond campus, to a place once filled with celebration and reckless freedom.

The teen stopped in front of the door and hesitated, the memories pressing heavy on her chest. Taking a deep breath, she swallowed hard, then knocked.

This is ridiculous, Cindy thought. *Why am I even worrying? Maybe if I just apologize, things can go back to normal. It's been a few days, and we've been friends before. I didn't do anything so awful that it can't be forgiven. He'll forgive me... I hope.*

A moment passed. Then another.

Cindy knocked again and waited.

Finally, the door creaked open.

"Didn't I tell you not to come back here?" Dan said coldly, standing in the doorway.

"I have money," Cindy replied quickly, handing over a small wad of bills. It was money she had scraped together, originally meant to cover her back rent. "I'm sorry about before. I didn't mean to hit you. Can we just... let bygones be bygones?"

Dan took the cash but didn't move aside.

"You still did it," he muttered, his voice low and cold. "You think throwing money at me makes it all go away?"

"I'll pay double," Cindy snapped, her voice rising. "Just give me the tablets, the usual amount this time. Come on, I need my acid, and you'll get your money."

The weight of the past hung heavily between them as their eyes locked. Cindy stood her ground, determined to get what she came for.

Finally, Dan sighed. His body softened, and his eyes became less sharp.

"*Double*, huh?" Dan said, a smile slowly building with a little laugh. "Now, you're talking."

He opened the door and stepped aside.

"Alright, come in," he spoke. "I'll see what I got in the back."

Cindy stepped inside, and Dan closed the door behind them. She stood by the couch while Dan disappeared down the hallway like he always did dozens of times before.

Waiting, Cindy glanced around. It felt good to be back. The place was just as she remembered: the lingering smell of weed and incense and the soft psychedelic music playing from a record player nearby. There was the infamous comfortable couch everyone loved, partially covered with a brown, yellow, and orange crocheted throw and the "rug of love" surrounded by floor pillows guests used to sit or hug while sharing stories and music.

I knew he wasn't such a bad guy after all, Cindy thought, taking in a deep breath and focusing on the comfort of being somewhere that once felt like home. *What was I thinking? I guess I overreacted when I hit him…I shouldn't have done that. No wonder he was mad. I should make it up to him, especially since he's willing to bury the hatchet.*

Dan returned with a small bag of acid tablets and handed them to her after she paid the extra cash.

"That's all I got right now," he said, removing his wallet from his back pants pocket to stuff the money inside. "It should be enough to last you a few days until I get more in."

"Thanks," Cindy said, gawking at the bag. "I knew I could count on you. I even threw in a few extra bucks for —"

Dan's hand shot forward, closing around Cindy's throat. Her eyes widened. Gasping, she clawed at his hand. The bag slipped from her fingers and fell to the floor.

"You want pills from me?" Dan said slowly, a smile creeping in. "Good, because I've been thinking about what I want too."

An hour later, Cindy finally made it back to her apartment. Her makeup was a mess, streaked down her cheeks from tears that hadn't stopped for most of the way back.

She grabbed the hem of her blouse and brought it up to her face, wiping roughly at the smudges. Her body ached with every step, but she pushed through the pain, forcing herself toward the bathroom.

Flicking on the light, she grimaced as she painfully leaned over the sink and turned on the faucet. The cold water pooled in her cupped hands. She splashed it over her face, then rinsed her mouth, spitting the saliva down the drain.

She reached for the mouthwash, unscrewed the cap, and took a swig straight from the bottle. The sting of it filled her mouth as she swished and spat again, trying to erase the aftertaste of her shame.

What have I done? Cindy choked, her body trembling and muscles aching. *Why did I go back? I'm so stupid.*

Her tears welled up again, hot and blinding.

Oh God, everything hurts...

She gripped the edge of the sink for support, breath ragged.

Dan... you fucking bastard. Her jaw tightened, rage mixing with pain. *I swear, you'll pay for this. You will, you fucking jerk...*

Groaning, she made her way back to the couch. Flinching and gasping as increased pain surged in places that touched the couch cushions.

Cindy lay awake all night, her body aching and her thoughts unraveling into knots. Sleep was impossible. Each time she closed her eyes, the memories clawed their way back. Her body still ached, and the thought of checking for bruises unsettled her. She wasn't ready to see the evidence of what had been done.

She kept going back and forth in her mind: *Should I go to a clinic? Should I go to the police?*

But then came a few additional thoughts. *What would I say? That I went over to Dan's to get more acid? That he tried beating me to a pulp? That I had to fight back? That I had to bite, kick, scratch, and do whatever it took to get out of there? I hope I hurt him. I hope I hurt him good. I hope those bite marks stay on him forever and that he's in just as much pain, if not more. That'll teach him.*

Cindy contemplated Dan being bold enough to report her and say that she was the one who attacked him. After all, after everything that occurred, she wouldn't be surprised that if he went to jail or got expelled for anything she would say about him, he'd find a way of dragging her down with him. Her addiction, their fight, and everything they knew about the other would all be dragged into the light.

But he did this. He chose this. He beat me and shouldn't get away with it! Why does that bastard always get away with everything he does?

Still, that didn't silence the voice that whispered: *You chose to go back. You asked for it. But I didn't! I didn't ask for any of this! I tried to bury the hatchet, had the money, and wanted to make a deal! Ugh! I wish I could murder that son of a bitch!*

Then another thing hit: she didn't leave with the acid tablets she had paid for.

Shit!

The teen's mind raced again. Who was Dan really, and why hadn't she seen that side of him a long time ago? Not once had anyone ever said the man had physically beaten a woman. Why her? Why choose her to physically beat? Was there more to Gail's story than she knew about when she reported Dan to the dean a while ago? If Cindy were to go back to Ann and Eileen, would they still agree to come forward with her to the dean to help her report Dan? What about the other witnesses to Dan's behavior from that same day of the first fight? Would they back her or turn away?

Damn it... I should've sided with Gail instead of Dan. I should've spoken up when I knew the dean was digging for proof about him selling drugs.

Now it was too late to help Gail. Where would Cindy even begin? Both she and Dan had physical wounds. It would come down to her word against his. Her stomach flipped at the thought of Dan's victory over Gail. Everyone knew she had taken back her statement and decided not to return to the university the following semester. In the end, she and the dean had both failed.

It wasn't fair, and everyone in Dan's inner circle had celebrated the victory. It was ridiculous. Everyone on campus knew he was supplying drugs. And still, there hadn't been a single arrest. No one else had the nerve to fight back.

Yet, Cindy did have something. She managed to steal Dan's wallet before taking off. Quickly, she had shoved it deep into her underwear. It wasn't justice, but it was something, for now.

Cindy pulled out the wallet and flipped through it. Inside was Dan's driver's license, a folded wad of cash, far more than enough to cover her rent for the next few months, his Social Security card, his driver's license, a credit card, a library card, and a few old photos of people she didn't recognize.

Cindy took the cash without guilt and tucked it into her purse. *I bet I could make better use of the money than he ever would.*

Next, she removed all of Dan's cards, one by one. She had no intention of using them. She wasn't stupid. But just because she wouldn't use them didn't mean someone else out there wouldn't take the opportunity. Not in a town like this.

A slow, burning fury stirred in her chest. *Let someone else recycle Dan's precious identity and money, if they dared.*

She made up her mind. Over the weekend, whether riding the bus around town or walking across campus, she'd discreetly toss them, one by one. His credit card. His driver's license. His Social Security card. His library card. *That'll teach that son of a bitch a lesson...*

Over the weekend, after paying the last of her overdue rent with Dan's money, Cindy quietly set her plan in motion. She boarded the city bus, where she, one by one, dropped Dan's belongings in random places around town: a phone booth, near the pump of a gas station, a bench at the mall, and the table in a busy fast-food restaurant.

When Cindy returned home, she spent the rest of the afternoon cleaning with Laura, and together they managed to tackle most of the kitchen. Before Laura left, Cindy surprised her with the drawing of the cat and a generous offer: dinner at any restaurant she wanted, her treat. Paid for, of course, with the cash she had taken from Dan's wallet.

By Sunday afternoon, Cindy had finally bought the bike she'd always dreamed of from a local shop. Without a second thought, she tossed Dan's empty wallet into a gas station dumpster and left without looking back.

Cindy returned home and quietly shut the door behind her.

Finally, she thought, surveying the space. *The kitchen looked almost as good as it had the day she moved in.*

She stretched her arms above her head, let out a long sigh, and took a deep, cleansing breath.

Her eyes landed on the calendar hanging on the kitchen wall. A few more days, and she'd receive her university stipend, but that was no longer a concern.

Since Paul will be free next weekend, I think I'll surprise him. I'll take him out for a change and give him that drawing I've been working on. He's going to love it.

. On Monday, Cindy was genuinely happy to see Paul again for lunch. Her eyes lit up the moment he greeted her with a smile and an affectionate kiss. When he offered his arm, she slipped hers through his, her heart skipping a beat as they walked together toward the cafeteria. This time, the lunch was her treat, paid for by Dan, of course. They picked out their favorite items and headed to their usual table, the one they had started to think of as their spot over the last few lunches.

When they were seated with their food, Cindy leaned in.

"So," she said, "tell me how things went over the weekend."

"Not much happened," Paul replied, taking a small bite of macaroni casserole. "We did morning formation to see who was there, the gunnery sergeant read the plan of the day, and we practiced maneuvering and infantry squad tactics."

"What's that?" Cindy asked.

"Shooting and moving," Paul said with a smirk. "But mainly sitting around when not doing that. Some went to the motor pool to perform maintenance on the unit's vehicles."

"What do you mean? Sorry..."

"Checking the oil, checking the exterior, and making sure it's clean. Things like that. Your turn: how did you keep busy over the weekend?"

"Cleaning. Cleaning. And more cleaning," Cindy said with a mock sigh.

"More cleaning?" Paul laughed. "Are you moving or something?"

"No, just catching up on everything at home. School's kept me pretty busy, and I let things pile up. But I should have it all done by the end of the week."

"Need any help?" Paul offered.

"No, thanks," Cindy replied. "There's not much left to do, but I appreciate the offer."

"Okay, cool... So, I've been telling everyone I know about the art show, and most said they'd stop by to check it out. I mentioned you do portraits, and one of my buddies is interested in getting one done, if you've got the time."

"Sure, who is he?"

"His name's Greyson Joslyn. He lives across the hall from me and goes to school here too. Real nice guy. Joel and I were planning to hang out at his place this weekend, if you want to come. Joel said he was gonna ask Margo to join us too, probably later today."

"Sure," Cindy said, smiling softly. "I like spending time with you."

They shared a gentle kiss, the kind that lingered just a moment longer than usual.

"Let's meet up a few minutes after your last class today, okay?" Paul said, brushing her hand with his thumb. "We've got a lot to make up for after the weekend."

"I can't wait," Cindy giggled, leaning in for another quick smooch.

Once they finished their meals, Cindy and Paul parted ways. Cindy headed to her printmaking class, where she and her classmates continued working on their relief prints using linoleum, lino cutters, ink, brayers, and paper. One of the perks of the class was the ability to produce multiple copies of a single design, something Cindy found both practical and rewarding.

That day, the professor introduced an upcoming print exchange: by the end of the semester, each student would trade prints with their classmates, creating a shared collection of everyone's work. Cindy loved the idea. Not only did she plan to participate in the exchange, but she also made a mental note to create extra prints for her friends and family.

After class, Cindy carefully cleaned her tools and tidied her workspace. A quiet sense of relief settled over her. She didn't have to worry so much about squeezing in extra sketch work before and after school anymore. There was a lot to be happy about. Her rent was up to date, her apartment was almost cleaned, Paul was back, and she'd finally gotten the bike she'd dreamed of. The article was set to bring her the recognition she'd longed for, and everything felt like it was going right.

Cindy glanced up at the clock on the printmaking studio wall. *Fifteen minutes past the hour.*

Hmm... Paul must be running late. She shrugged to herself. *Oh well, it's only a few minutes. No big deal.*

To kill time, Cindy wandered into the drawing studio, where Ronald was still working and clearly having a hard time.

Still, he showed persistence, often staying after hours to work on his piece. From what Cindy could see, his drawing was riddled with inaccuracies: subtle proportion issues, awkward angles, and other mistakes he probably hadn't even noticed yet.

"Draw what you see," Cindy hinted. "Not what you *think* you're seeing."

"What do you mean?" Ronald asked, glancing up. "I *am* drawing what's there."

Cindy shook her head slightly. "Not exactly. Look at the grapes. You're drawing them like a bunch of separate circles. But real grapes overlap. You need to show how they connect, not just float in space."

Ronald frowned and started erasing the clumsy cluster.

"And go easy on the paper," Cindy added. "You don't want to tear through it."

As she watched him hunch back over his drawing, she couldn't help but sigh inwardly. *Geeze... doesn't he know anything? Maybe he should go back and retake the first drawing class under Ryan...*

Cindy's gaze flicked upward as she stepped out of the art building.

Where was Paul?

He'd said he wanted to meet, so why hadn't he shown up? If he'd changed his mind, he could've at least told her. She'd already missed her usual bus, didn't have access to her new bike, and still had cleaning to do back at the apartment.

With a sigh, Cindy sank onto one of the benches in the courtyard. *Maybe if I sit here, I'll spot him when he shows up...*

She folded her arms and scanned the paths crisscrossing the quad. *This isn't like him. I hope he's okay... Where is he?*

Twenty minutes later, Ronald exited the art building, tossing Cindy a small wave as he passed. She barely noticed. Still seated on the bench, she was moments away from giving up and heading home when she spotted a familiar figure coming down the sidewalk.

It was Paul, but something was wrong.

His face was flushed and drawn tight, jaw clenched. One hand was balled into a fist, the other wrapped protectively around his midsection. He moved with a slight hunch, each step looking more like a struggle than a stride.

Cindy stood quickly, alarmed.

"What happened, Paul?" Cindy gasped, rushing up to him.

"I got in a fight with Dan," he said, his voice tight. "But what do you care?"

"What?" she blinked, confused.

"Don't play dumb," Paul pointed out. "I went to Dan's, hoping to grab the tablets you like and surprise you. Instead, that loser starts trash-talking you, going on and on about some fight and accusing you of stealing his wallet. What's going on, Cindy?"

Cindy froze. *He found out. Shit! I can't deal with this right now! I don't want to talk about it. I can't!*

His stiff stance and impatient eyes made her panic rise.

"Don't be mad," she blurted. "Dan's the one who started the fight. He started everything!"

"Oh, so you *were* at his place over the weekend," Paul stated, his voice flat and eyes narrowing.

"Ok, so I was," Cindy confessed, crossing her arms over her chest. "All I did was drop by to get more tablets, but he's the one who went crazy and attacked me first. So, yeah, we got into a fight! What, are you trying to blame me?"

"That's not what I'm trying to say, but I had to beat the crap out of him for putting his hands on you and threatening to do it again. I don't get it. You've never said a bad word about the guy. It's always Dan this and Dan that, like he's this great guy. Now, I'm finding out, from him, that he's beating you up. Why didn't you tell me? I thought we were closer than that."

Paul paused, his eyes narrowing.

"Has he hit you other times before?" He asked.

Cindy pinched her lips thin. She took a shaky deep breath.

"Just keep out of it," she told him. "You'll only make things worse... Okay, I didn't mention it before. So what? You know now, so just drop it. I...I don't want to deal with this right now."

Paul squinted his eyes.

"What?" he gasped. "After everything I've done, this is what I get? Where's the trust, Cindy?"

Cindy tossed her head back to gaze at the heavens. Her eyes began to brim with tears. She choked back a sob and lowered her gaze to the ground.

"And what do you mean by that?" she snapped. "What were you hoping for? A medal? Or for me to let my guard down so you could end up hurting me too?"

Paul took a step back, his eyes becoming dull.

"Oh, I don't know, maybe more honesty and trust," he scoffed, rolling his eyes. "So, stop trying to flip things around on me. I'm not falling for any of that. The main point is, he knew things about you that I didn't. Earlier, why did you tell me that you spent all weekend cleaning, but not tell me something that important?"

"So, I'm supposed to tell you everything I do?" Cindy yelled, "What if I didn't want to talk about it? Who would? What are you? Some possessive psycho?"

Paul stepped back, his gaze momentarily ping-ponging between Cindy and the surrounding area.

"What?" he countered, his voice now harsh. "Dan treats you like trash, yet it's always Dan this, Dan that. Like he's some sort of god or something. But *I'm* the psycho? That says a lot about the men you choose to respect."

"Will you stop blaming me! Just drop it already!"

"Then stop calling me something that I'm not. I'm only trying to help!"

"I don't need your help! I didn't ask you to get my tablets or fight for me. Next time, stay out of it. I don't need your charity, and I sure as hell don't need you fighting my battles. I can handle everything myself. I always have! So, why don't you mind your own damn business and keep out of mine!"

Paul swallowed hard. There was an awkward moment of silence between them.

"Fine, understood!" He finally uttered, his tone flat and taking a moment to look past her into the distance. "I'll remember that from now on."

Silently, they both stood there until Paul proceeded to walk away.

Cindy's eyes began to brim with tears. She sniffled back a few tears and wiped away those that escaped. Taking a moment to breathe, she dragged her fingers through her hair before rushing behind him.

"Listen," she said, her voice faltering. "I'm sorry. I just don't want to talk about it, is all. Can we just move on and forget all of this happened?"

Paul stopped, lowering his head and shaking it.

"Why?" he asked. "What's the point in doing so? We now know where we both stand, and there's nothing here to salvage...I really cared about you, Cindy. I thought what we had was the real deal, but I was the one fooling myself. Maybe I am a psycho, like you said."

"What?" Cindy cried out, her heart racing. "Are you breaking up with me? Over this? Why are you giving up on me already? Paul, we've never even fought before any of this! Give me another chance!"

Paul shook his head again, cold and unwavering. "For what? We clearly don't know each other, so why pretend things are fine? Don't follow me. I can't think straight... Just leave me alone."

Cindy reached for Paul's shoulder, but he jerked away from her touch and walked off.

Cindy's whole body began to tremble.

Choking back a sob, she slapped a hand over her mouth to muffle the sound, but it was no use. The dam had broken. Stumbling back toward the art building, she ducked into a quiet corner and collapsed to the ground.

How did I get here?

Tears poured down her face as she drew her legs in tight, curling her arms around them. She buried her face in one hand, trying to block everything out. But the ache in her chest only grew heavier.

I just lost the best relationship I ever had... I ruin everything. I can't do anything right. Never, never, never...

The sobs came harder, shaking her shoulders. There was no stopping them now.

"I'm sorry, Paul," she whispered through her tears, hoping that somehow, he would hear her plea. "I'm so, so sorry..."

Chapter 9

Over the next few days, Cindy tried again and again to reach Paul, calling and even approaching him on campus to apologize. Each time, he turned her away with an excuse that he was too busy or needed to be somewhere else. He no longer met with her for their usual walk to the cafeteria, and the silence between them deepened the ache in her chest, leaving her feeling more desperate and alone with each passing day.

In the meantime, she and Laura managed to finish cleaning the kitchen, bathroom, and most of the bedroom in time for Mr. Tanner's inspection. With the apartment in much better shape, the eviction was called off, and Cindy was told she would be allowed to renew her lease, on the condition that her mother also signed the paperwork once she arrived in Alabama for her visit.

Despite the small victories, Cindy's mind remained consumed with Paul. She was tempted to confide in her friends, to ask what she should do, but the shame kept her silent. She already knew what they'd say: what she'd say if the roles were reversed. It was her fault, all of it. And yet, she couldn't stop thinking about him. The laughter, the closeness, the genuine affection, the comfort of just being near him. It all felt so far away now, like a dream she couldn't return to.

Deciding to take a chance, Cindy remembered Paul mentioning that he'd be spending the weekend at his neighbor's place and that Margo might be there, too. The idea of seeing him again made her stomach twist with nerves, but she couldn't let things end without trying. Still, she prayed he wouldn't lash out or humiliate her in front of their friends if she showed up.

By Friday evening, Cindy called Margo and asked if she'd be willing to take her to the gathering the next day. To her relief, Margo agreed, but noticeably said nothing about Paul. That silence settled uneasily in Cindy's chest, sparking new questions. *Why didn't she mention him? Did she know what happened? Was she keeping something from me?*

On Saturday afternoon, Margo and Joel arrived to pick Cindy up from her apartment. Determined to make a good impression, Cindy had chosen her outfit carefully: a solid yellow dress paired with white wedge shoes, and she clutched the drawing she had worked so hard on, hoping it would help mend things with Paul. Her heart pounded as the three of them made their way to the door across from Paul's unit in Lakeland Square.

Joel knocked, and a moment later, the door swung open to reveal a stocky young man, about twenty-one, with brown hair and matching brown eyes. He wore a thin brown jacket over a green, red, and white checkered shirt, crisp white pants, and polished black shoes. Cindy tried to steady her breath, unsure if Paul would be inside, and if he was, how he'd react to seeing her.

"Hey, Greyson," Joel greeted the guy. "You remember my old lady, Margo? And this is our friend, Cindy."

"Nice to finally meet you, Cindy," Greyson said, extending a hand with a friendly smile. "I've heard a lot about you."

Wonderful... Before or after the fight with Paul? Just perfect...

"Nice to meet you," Cindy replied, masking her nerves with a forced smile as she shook his hand, doing her best to sound cheerful.

Greyson's penthouse had all the makings of a classic bachelor pad: part patriotic shrine, part sports haven. The American flag and souvenirs from sporting events lined the walls, and a large television set, locked onto Channel 5. The sportscasters were already deep in debate over which of the two baseball teams had the edge, their voices rising above the hum of conversation.

A long, sturdy coffee table held an impressive spread clearly intended to impress: finger sandwiches, chips and dip, platters of chicken wings and hot dogs, frosty soda bottles, a few open beers, loaded potato skins, and burgers stacked high.

Cindy glanced around the crowded space, counting at least twenty people milling about, laughing, eating, and shouting at the screen. But Paul wasn't among them.

She frowned.

Why wasn't he there? Wasn't this supposed to be his friend's gathering? No one seemed to be asking about him. No nervous glances toward the door. No calls or updates.

Did something happen? Cindy wondered. *Did they have a falling out too, and no one's talking about it? Or is it just me he's avoiding?*

Cindy lingered close to Margo and Joel as the three of them sunk into the couch cushions as the baseball game played on. Cindy picked at the seam of her dress, her rolled drawing placed carefully in her lap.

"So... is Paul coming?" she finally asked, her voice low and uncertain. "I wanted to give him this drawing I made."

Margo took a sip from her soda. "I'm not sure. Maybe he's running late. He does live across the hall, though. You could always check."

Cindy hesitated, then nodded, muttering a quick "Be right back" before rising to her feet. She made her way out into the hallway, nerves pricking her skin like static. Standing before Paul's door, she drew in a breath and knocked softly.

No answer.

But from within, she could hear faint music, something mellow and slow, and then a woman's laugh, carefree and familiar.

Her stomach twisted.

She knocked again, louder this time.

A moment later, the door creaked open, and Cindy's heart dropped.

Ann stood in the doorway, her body swaddled in nothing but a white towel. Her eyes were bloodshot from whatever she'd been smoking. She blinked in surprise, then gave a lazy grin.

"Well, hey, Cindy," she slurred. "Didn't know you were delivering pizza now."

Cindy stared, frozen. Her throat clenched, and for a moment, she couldn't summon a word.

Her world tilted, and her stomach turned. Shoving Ann out of the way, Cindy rushed inside, her heart pounding in her ears. The place reeked of weed and had music blasting from the downstairs radio.

"Cindy, where's the pizza?" Ann called behind her, but she was already moving, already climbing the stairs.

Each step felt heavier than the last, her body dragging itself toward the sound she didn't want to believe. Then Cindy heard it: moaning, grunting, breathless cussing, and her worst fear solidified into truth.

At the top of the stairs, she stopped in the doorway of the bedroom.

Paul.

Eileen.

Having sex.

Cindy's world shattered in an instant, like a broken mirror. Everything she thought she had with Paul was gone: the tenderness, the promise to be there for each other, and the once steady growth of a budding relationship. Gone. All of it.

Swiftly, the sounds of both Eileen's and Paul's moans burned into her ears, fueling Cindy's fury and jealousy like a bomb being tossed into an already raging fire. Fueled by heartbreak and humiliation, Cindy couldn't think. She couldn't breathe. But, what she could do was drop the drawing on the floor, storm toward the bed, releasing a scream she barely recognized as her own, and punched Paul with every ounce of pain bottled in her chest. Stunned by the unexpected blow, Paul's body lurched, but Cindy couldn't stop. Next, she lunged at Eileen, yanking her by the hair and dragging her off the bed.

"You sneaky, lying bitch," Cindy bellowed, her voice cracked with tears.

With every ounce of hurt and fury surging through her, she unleashed a relentless storm of punches.

Eileen kicked and shrieked, scrambling away as Paul grabbed Cindy's arm from behind. But she twisted and struck again, blindly, needing to make them feel even a fraction of what she felt in that moment: betrayed, thrown away, and angry.

"What are you doing here?" Paul demanded, struggling to separate the women. "Get out, right now!"

Eileen scrambled to her feet and lunged at them, wildly throwing punches between Paul and Cindy.

"Hey!" Ann shouted, rushing into the room.

"Stop it!" Paul yelled, forcing himself between them and using all his strength to wedge them apart. "Cindy, get out of here!"

"So, this is what's been going on?" Cindy shouted, her voice shaking with rage. "You've all been two-timing me behind my back! You're nothing but liars!"

She turned on Paul, fists flying. He grabbed her by the waist, trying to pull her from the room, but before he could, Eileen snatched a shoe from the floor and hurled it at them, barely missing Paul's head.

"Leave, bitch!" Ann shouted at Cindy.

"Fuck you!" Cindy snapped, shoving Paul away. She stormed down the stairs, her fury trailing behind her like fire. Paul followed close behind.

At the bottom of the stairs, the shouting continued: Cindy and the women hurling slurs and insults at each other, their voices echoing through the unit.

"This is all your fault!" Cindy screamed at Paul.

She grabbed a small vase from a side table and hurled it at him. Paul flinched as it missed, shattering against the wall behind him.

Next, the teen grabbed an armful of records stacked on top of the music system and began hurling them, some at Paul and others toward the women upstairs. The records flew like sharp, flying saucers. While the women dodged them, Paul wasn't as lucky; a few struck him squarely.

Upstairs, the women began hurling pillows, shoes, and even framed pictures ripped from the walls at Cindy as they tried to descend the stairs. Paul struggled to block their path, shielding them while also ducking to avoid more of the vinyl records Cindy was still launching in their direction.

Hurt and furious, tears streaming down her face, Cindy hurled the last record. It struck Paul directly. From behind him, Ann and Eileen lunged at her, desperate to land a few blows. Paul remained in place, using his body as a shield, grimacing as he absorbed each hit, determined not to let them reach each other.

Finally, Cindy bolted out of Paul's place and stormed straight into Greyson's apartment, heading straight for Margo.

"Take me home," Cindy demanded, her voice sharp and shaky.

"We just got here," Margo replied, confused. "Why are you so upset? Was Paul home?"

"Don't ever mention that name to me again! I want to go home! Right now!"

Joel and a few other guests glanced in their direction, puzzled by Cindy's distress. Around them, the mood remained upbeat with people laughing, chatting about the game, watching TV, and enjoying food in high spirits.

"Okay, chill," Margo responded, turning to her boyfriend before uttering, "Let me grab the keys from Joel."

Margo retrieved the keys, and the two women hurried out of the building and into Joel's car. The moment Cindy closed the door, she burst into tears.

"What's going on?" Margo asked. "Cindy, what happened? I can't help if I don't know what's going on."

"I ruined everything," Cindy sobbed. "And now Paul and I hate each other."

"Wait, what? Since when? I thought you two were solid. Joel never said anything about a breakup. What happened between you and Paul?"

"I'm ashamed to say it, but I did something I'm not proud of... and Paul ended things. He's already moved on, fast. It hurts so much. I tried to apologize, but..." Cindy's voice cracked. "He won't forgive me."

"Sounds like he's trying to get revenge," Margo said. "I mean, why else would he jump into something new this quickly, unless he was seeing someone else the whole time?"

"Don't say that; I can't handle it! I'm so hurt, Margo... I feel like I could kill myself," Cindy whispered.

"No! Don't say that, Cindy," Margo replied firmly, grabbing her hand. "Killing yourself over some guy isn't worth it. That's never brought anyone back; it just ends everything for you. He'd move on, and you'd be gone. You're hurting, but this isn't the answer. Please don't let him have that kind of power over you."

"Why won't he forgive me?" Cindy cried. "I tried apologizing so many times... Why wouldn't he let me explain before he decided to fuck Ann and Eileen?"

"What? Ann *and* Eileen? Both of them? You've got to be kidding me!" Margo gasped.

"Why them?" Cindy's voice cracked with disbelief. "Paul's such a hypocrite! He said we'd be there for each other, and the first chance he gets, instead of talking things out, he fucks them! Just to hurt me! How could he do that?"

She shook her head, fists clenched. "No wonder he kept saying he wanted to 'keep his options open.' He meant it! How can he be sweet one minute and a total jerk the next, just because of *one* fight?"

"I wish I had an answer for everything," Margo replied, "but I don't. Maybe it's best to just leave all of them alone, especially if being around them makes you feel like hurting yourself. What about talking to a campus counselor?"

"Ha! Yeah, right," Cindy scoffed. "So, they can tell me *I'm* the problem? I don't think so."

"That's not what I'm saying," Margo countered, her voice trembling slightly. It's just that we've been through this before with you mentioning that you want to harm yourself, and I'm getting scared."

"Whatever," Cindy muttered, turning toward the window. "Am I getting a ride home or not? I'll walk if you're just going to sit here and act like I'm the one who's crazy."

Releasing a heavy sigh, Margo started the car to drive Cindy home.

Counseling? Her? Margo must've lost her mind, just like everyone else around her. If anyone needed counseling, it was *them*. Weren't they the ones turning her life upside down? Weren't *they* the ones acting crazy? Still, maybe Margo was right. Maybe she *should* leave them all alone, starting with Margo herself, for suggesting she was the one who needed help.

That's it, Cindy thought bitterly. *Once I get home, we're no longer friends. Who needs anybody? I don't need anyone!* All people ever did was get on her nerves and stab her in the back.

Her thoughts shifted to Eileen and Ann, the traitors. *What was that even about?* What had she ever done to deserve it? Eileen had *just* asked her out a few days ago, and now she was having sex with Paul... and ready to fight her? The betrayal stung deeper the more she replayed it.

Can't I trust anybody? Cindy thought bitterly. Of all the people who'd hurt her, she hated and felt betrayed by Paul the most. Never in her wildest dreams did she imagine that his warmth and sweetness were nothing more than an act.

She scoffed, remembering how he accused *her* of keeping secrets. *Really, Paul? What about you?* How long had he been seeing Ann or Eileen—maybe both? Maybe those weekend "reserve duties" he mentioned were just an excuse. He was probably having sex with them instead.

What a jerk! But I'm the one who needs counseling, Cindy sneered to herself.

Minutes later, Margo pulled into the parking lot of the Hollow Oaks complex. Flashing red and blue lights lit up the area. Several police cars were parked along the side of Cindy's building. Officers were scattered around, speaking with residents and taking notes.

What's going on here? Cindy wondered as Margo eased the vehicle to a stop nearby.

Mrs. Grigsby stood with one of the officers, who scribbled notes on a clipboard as she spoke. Several neighbors gathered in small groups, murmuring among themselves or speaking with other officers. A few had dragged out chairs and bar stools, content to sit and watch the scene unfold like television.

"What happened?" Cindy asked the nearest neighbor.

"There was a break-in," the woman replied, tilting her head as she looked more closely at an officer interviewing another neighbor. "Someone tore through one of the apartments pretty bad."

Poor Mrs. Grigsby, Cindy thought, her stomach sinking. *She's always so kind to everyone. She didn't deserve this. What has she ever done to anybody? Her husband works hard, and their kids keep to themselves. Why would anyone target them?*

As Cindy and Margo edged closer to her apartment, a gnawing sense of dread crept in. Something wasn't right. Her eyes locked onto the shattered front window. Glass sparkled like broken ice across the pavement. But then she noticed Mr. Grigsby sitting in the chair where his wife usually sat and their youngest child clinging to him while the others hovered near their doorway.

Cindy's gaze drifted past them and suddenly froze.

Her breath caught. She raised both hands to her mouth, gasping in horror.

It wasn't the Grigsby's unit that had been broken into.

It was *hers*.

The apartment door stood wide open, exposing her, as if she were standing there completely naked for everyone to view.

The apartment door stood wide open. Officers moved in and out with their radios crackling. The sight made Cindy feel like the floor had dropped beneath her, like she'd rather be dead than face one more thing.

"Oh no," Margo breathed, her mouth falling open before she covered it with her hand.

One thing after another, Cindy thought, her vision blurring. *I—I can't take it. I can't take it anymore. I just... can't.*

Defeated and overwhelmed, she froze in place before her legs gave out. Margo caught her just in time.

"Oh, no, Cindy!" Margo cried, lowering her friend carefully to the ground, fanning her with her hand in panic.

A nearby neighbor rushed over, but before anyone could say another word, Cindy's eyes rolled back, and she fainted.

Chapter 10

When Cindy regained consciousness, she found herself cradled in Margo's arms and an officer kneeling beside her, fanning her mildly while the two spoke in hushed tones.

"Oh, thank God," Margo breathed, relief flooding her voice.

"Wha—" Cindy tried to speak, her head spinning. "What... my apartment? What happened?"

"Someone broke in," Margo reminded her. "Just sit tight, okay?" She turned quickly to the officer. "We need an ambulance."

"No," Cindy insisted, her voice shaky but firm. "I'm not going anywhere."

The officer looked at her closely. "You live in this unit?"

"Yes, sir," she replied, leaning on Margo as she slowly got to her feet.

"I noticed some bruising on your stomach," the officer said, eyeing her carefully. "Would you mind explaining how that happened?"

"It's nothing," Cindy lied, trying to wave it off. "How long was I out? And... how long has all this been going on? Did you catch who broke in?"

"You were out for just a few minutes," the officer told her calmly. "We're wrapping up statements from the landlord and a few witnesses. No suspects have been caught yet. It's still under investigation. For your safety, I'd recommend staying with a friend for the next few days. Unless, of course, you'd prefer an officer nearby."

Cindy pressed her lips into a thin line, uncertain. After everything, who could she even ask? Guilt twisted in her chest as she remembered the harsh thoughts she'd had about Margo just moments earlier.

"She can stay with me," Margo offered, giving Cindy's hand a reassuring squeeze.

"Thanks," Cindy uttered, her voice stripped of pride.

She turned to the officer. "When can I grab a few things?"

"Right now," he replied with a nod, before stepping aside to speak briefly with a departing colleague as the other officers began to clear the scene.

With her heart heavy and her mind reeling, Cindy walked beside Margo toward the apartment where chaos greeted them.

The apartment had been ransacked. The rooms she and Laura had worked so hard to clean were now a disaster. Spray-painted scribbles and ugly lines covered the wooden walls. Her couch was flipped over, its cushions slashed open like wounds. Books and magazines were torn to pieces and scattered across the floor.

In the kitchen, shattered dishes lay in heaps, crunching underfoot, and the cabinets were tagged with more spray paint, obscene and meaningless.

Frowning, Cindy stepped into the bathroom, her stomach churning. Shampoo and conditioner had been poured everywhere: across the sink, counter, floor, and inside the tub. Her toothbrush and hair accessories floated in the toilet bowl, and her bath towels were crumpled on the floor, reeking of urine.

Cindy turned away, her face tightening, and walked into the bedroom. The destruction continued. Her pillow had been slashed open. The mattress was half-dragged off the bedframe. The sheets were twisted and hanging, covered in torn, spray-painted clothes. It was like someone had taken a knife to her life that was deliberate, personal, and cruel.

After all the effort Laura and I put into getting this place back in order... this happens. Just great. Story of my life—one mess after another. This has got to be one of the worst weekends I've ever had.

It took some time, but eventually she and Margo managed to gather a few articles of clothing Cindy could wear for the week. Margo folded them and carried the small pile out to her car.

Cindy stayed behind a little longer, moving slowly through the wreckage, trying to think clearly. She realized she'd have to replace her toothbrush, hairbrush, undergarments, clothes, and much more.

Perfect, she thought bitterly. *Just perfect.*

She groaned loudly as a new, sinking realization hit her—her precious new bike was gone.

Shit! I just got the damn thing!

Grumbling under her breath, Cindy stomped out of the apartment, pausing to debate whether it was even worth locking the door. *What's the point? It's already trashed.* Still, out of habit or stubbornness, she locked it anyway, then headed to Margo's car, where her friend waited patiently.

They drove to a nearby store where Cindy grabbed the essentials she'd need to get through the week. As she tossed items into the basket, including new toiletries, undergarments, a hairbrush, and a few other basics, she couldn't shake the creeping thought that maybe all of this was karma.

It was some twisted payback for fooling around with Micky behind Clair's back and stealing from Dan. Maybe there was some spiritual lesson that she had to learn and show repentance to be forgiven.

She thought about Clair.

Well, I'm sorry for sneaking around with Micky. We didn't go all the way, but that's no excuse. I shouldn't have done it. I knew better and still chose to go through with it. I regret betraying a friend like that, and I'll never do something like that again. Maybe a part of me was jealous because Clair had something I thought I wanted...I was so upset that things weren't working out with Betsy, but now I understand. I can see how Clair must have felt, or would have felt, if she caught me with Micky. It hurts, and I'm sure she would have hurt just the same. What was I thinking? It felt fun and exciting at first, but now I feel ashamed and awful for ever believing it was okay.

Then, came the thought of Dan, immediately causing her to roll her eyes.

Cindy scoffed. If anyone expected her to feel sorry for Dan, that wasn't going to happen, not after the way he tricked and tried to beat her to a pulp. He deserved it, and she'd do it again, if she had to.

The teen glanced up at the heavens. *I don't give a damn about him. He had it coming.*

Margo and Cindy returned to Lakeland Square after leaving the store. Cindy remained in the vehicle while Margo entered the building.

Still sorting through the mess of her feelings, Cindy prayed not to run into Paul, Eileen, or Ann. She was in no mood to deal with them. Her patience hung by a thread, and she dared anyone to test it. She didn't care who it was. The next person who so much as looked at her the wrong way might be the one she ended up going to jail over, and honestly, right now, it felt worth it. Every ounce of rage boiling in her blood needed somewhere to go, and she was ready to unleash it.

It didn't take long for Cindy to spot Margo and Joel making their way back to the car. They were deep in conversation. Well, Margo was. She spoke with animated gestures, her expression tense, while Joel walked beside her, hands buried in his pants pockets and brow furrowed, clearly annoyed but quietly listening. In Margo's hands was a small stack of neatly wrapped to-go containers, which shifted precariously as she tried to balance them in one arm, gesturing animatedly with the other as she spoke.

When they reached the car, Joel did exactly what Cindy expected. He apologized for what had happened to her and her apartment. As upset as she still was, his words took the edge off her anger, if only slightly. But they also stirred something else: embarrassment, humiliation, and a heavy sense of shame. The way he looked at her, sympathetic, maybe even pitying, made her feel like a charity case.

For a moment, she considered asking them to drop her off at a nearby hotel instead. It would be easier and less awkward. But then the thought of being alone crept in, bringing with it a quiet fear she couldn't ignore. As much as she hated the situation, being by herself tonight might feel worse.

Swallowing her pride, Cindy returned with her friends to the Gardere Apartments. The familiarity of it all hit like a punch to the gut. It was déjà vu in the worst way. She was back on someone else's couch with her heart shattered, her apartment in ruins, and her life unraveling yet again.

Why does this keep happening to me? she wondered, staring blankly out the window as the complex came into view. *Why is this a pattern I can't seem to break?*

The questions haunted her, heavy and unrelenting. She had sworn off going to seers. Not again. Not this time. She couldn't afford the expense, especially when every dollar would need to go toward replacing what little she had left: clothes, toiletries, bedding, and maybe even furniture. The list felt endless.

Cindy let out a dry chuckle, more bitter than amused.

Full circle, she thought. *Same story, different couch.*

At least their home was solid, warm, intact, and untouched by chaos. It made her think of the roach she'd once considered saving in her own wrecked apartment. Now, *she* was the roach: small, displaced, and clinging to someone else's stability.

But maybe, just maybe, she could mend, even if it was slow.

The moment they entered the unit, Joel headed straight for the hallway closet and pulled out a pillow and blanket for Cindy. Meanwhile, Margo tucked the leftovers into the refrigerator.

"Thanks," Cindy said to Joel as he handed her the items.

He gave a quick nod, then plopped onto the couch and turned on the television to watch the remainder of the baseball game. Cindy couldn't help but roll her eyes slightly. *Of course.* No matter what turmoil surrounded them, Joel's priorities remained blissfully consistent.

Margo beckoned Cindy into the kitchen. Complying, Cindy entered, stopping beside her friend, who leaned casually against the refrigerator.

"I was thinking on the ride back," Margo said, her voice low but thoughtful. "I know a place where we could get some good used furniture for cheap. They're closed on Sundays, but we could check it out Monday, if you're up for it."

"Sure. Thanks," Cindy replied, trying to sound more upbeat than she felt.

"I know this is a horrible time," Margo added, reaching out to give her a quick, comforting hug, "but we'll help you get through it. You're not alone. I feel awful about what I said earlier... about the counseling. I didn't mean to imply anything bad about you. I guess I wasn't thinking. The timing couldn't have been worse...I can't wrap my head around the break-in... or what could've led to it. No wonder you've been so stressed. I didn't realize things had gotten *this* bad...I'm sorry."

"It's okay," Cindy said. "It's no big deal; you were just trying to help."

Margo gave a small nod, visibly relieved. "Well, there's food in the fridge. Help yourself to whatever you need. I grabbed everyone a plate of leftovers from Greyson's. Make yourself at home, alright?"

Monday rolled around. Cindy attended her usual classes, then stuck to Margo's plan and visited a used furniture store. She was grateful to have the money she did. Without it, the purchases would've been nearly impossible. Still, she had to admit, Margo's idea of *cheap* didn't quite align with hers. The prices made her wince, but the quality was undeniable for secondhand pieces.

She ended up buying a used couch and a few chairs to replace the ones that had been destroyed. Most exciting of all was the bed. It was far more comfortable than the one she'd had before. They arranged to have everything delivered within a few days, once the damaged furniture was cleared out.

Cindy appreciated how Margo had stepped up, taking charge of the cleanup and helping her replace what had been lost. It made her think of Margo as an angel, just like Laura, who had also offered to return on Wednesday to help with the cleaning. That was the next plan: a fresh start, a second cleanup, this time with more hands, more support, and maybe, just maybe, a little more hope.

The day of the cleanup, after school, Margo, Laura, and Cindy were the first to arrive at Cindy's apartment. Without wasting time, they got to work. Back and forth they went between the apartment and the dumpster, arms full of what was now useless debris: shattered dishes, slashed pillows, broken chairs, and everything else that couldn't be salvaged. The shattered window had been covered with a rough sheet of plywood, nailed tight.

With each trip, the space inside the apartment felt a little less heavy, a little less like a crime scene, and a little more like the beginning of something new.

An hour later, Joel arrived with extra help. He brought along Greyson, the guy Cindy had briefly met at the weekend gathering, and unfortunately, Paul.

The moment she saw him, her stomach clenched, and her blood began to simmer. *What is he doing here?* Didn't Joel know better? Of all people, Paul was the *last* person she wanted to see, especially now, in such a vulnerable moment.

His presence stirred a storm inside her: embarrassment, anger, jealousy, all tangled up and rising fast. Just seeing him again was like ripping the bandage off a wound that hadn't even started to heal.

Cindy wanted to scream, to cancel the entire cleanup, kick everyone out, and slam the door behind them. Her chest burned with anger as her eyes locked onto Margo's, shooting her a glare filled with betrayal.

"What's *he* doing here?" she demanded, her voice sharp and low.

"I don't know," Margo whispered quickly. "I didn't ask him to come."

Cindy turned a harsher glare on Paul and Joel as they casually greeted her, like everything was normal, like she had no reason to be upset with either of them. Her expression said otherwise, ice cold and unapologetic.

The only person she acknowledged was Greyson, offering him a brief nod when he greeted her. Everyone else, as far as she was concerned, could disappear.

"You need to leave," Cindy said through clenched teeth, pulling Paul off to the side. Her voice was low but sharp. "I don't want you here."

"Joel asked me to help," Paul replied, his tone flat. "That's why I'm here."

"So what? Get out." Her voice rose before she could stop it, louder than she intended and sharp enough to silence the room.

Everyone turned to look. A hush fell over the apartment as all eyes locked onto them.

Paul's lips pressed into a thin line, his glare cutting. Hurt, anger, and offense flashed in his eyes before he turned away. Without another word, he walked out the door, got into his car, and drove off.

"What was *that* all about?" Greyson asked, raising a brow.

Cindy shot him a glare so sharp it could slice glass. *Seriously?* Of all people, he should've known better. At that moment, she wanted him gone, too.

Before Cindy could open her mouth to yell at Greyson for asking such a stupid question, Joel cleared his throat loudly, cutting in.

"Greyson, help me get this couch to the dumpster," he said firmly, already moving toward the damaged furniture.

Joel wasn't off the hook either, not by a long shot. Cindy narrowed her eyes at his back.

I'll cuss him out later, she thought. *After that damn couch is gone...*

The two men lifted the battered piece and began carrying it out in awkward silence.

Idiots, she fumed, crossing her arms. *I'm so sick of stupid people!*

Cindy made her way to the bathroom, where Laura was already hard at work scrubbing. Quietly, she pulled on a pair of rubber gloves, steeling herself for the task ahead. She crouched beside the toilet and, with a grimace, began fishing out her ruined belongings: hair accessories, her toothbrush, and other soggy remnants. She stuffed them into a trash bag without ceremony.

Together, she and Laura cleaned up the mess of shampoo and conditioner that had spilled across the floor, dripped down the sides of the tub, and clung to parts of the toilet and bathroom walls.

From the corner of her eye, Cindy spotted Joel and Greyson maneuvering the damaged mattress and its foundation out of her bedroom. Something stirred in her. A sudden, irrational urge to rush over and inspect it, to see if maybe, somehow, it could still be salvaged.

With a quiet exhale, she forced the thought out of her mind and turned her focus back to the task at hand, cleaning the bathroom walls and reclaiming what little control she could from the turmoil.

"The kitchen's done," Margo said, appearing in the doorway between the hallway and bathroom. "I'm gonna tackle the rest of the bedroom now that the guys cleared the bed out."

"Thanks," Cindy replied with a tired but grateful nod.

"Ms. Spearman?" Mr. Tanner's voice called out.

"In the bathroom," Cindy called back, catching a glimpse of him near the door.

"I'm going to have maintenance install a new lock, and I'm bringing you the key," he said, stepping inside. "They're working on it now. We'll also have someone remove the spray paint from the walls first thing tomorrow."

He handed her a small key and left without waiting for much of a response.

Cindy stared at the key in her hand.

That's awfully nice of him, she thought. *But he better not hike my rent after all this.*

By Friday, the spray paint had been cleaned, the replacement furniture delivered and arranged, and Cindy had officially moved back in. It felt good, really good, to be in her own space again, with a real bed that was far more comfortable than her last. But comfort didn't erase fear.

The thought of the intruders still haunted her, leaving her restless. Sleep came in shallow, broken stretches. Each distant sound outside made her jolt upright, hand instinctively gripping the knife she now kept under her pillow.

She hated thinking about it, but the question still loomed: *What would've happened if I had been here that time?*

And no matter how many times she told herself it was over, that single thought refused to leave her alone.

Cindy wanted to feel safe. She considered calling Margo or Laura, maybe asking if she could crash at their place for a few more nights. But it was late. They were probably already asleep, tucked into the warmth and security of their homes. She didn't want to disturb that.

Her apartment, though cleaned and refurnished, still felt violated.

Swallowed by unease, Cindy grabbed a pillow and blanket and quietly slipped into her closet. It was cramped, but it gave her a strange sense of security. If someone came back, she would at least have a few seconds to either hide or strike.

I'll be fine, she told herself, trying to steady her thoughts. *I will be. I always manage to find a way.*

Chapter 11

Saturday morning, Cindy retrieved the mail from her overstuffed mailbox. Among the usual clutter, one envelope stood out. It was from her mother. Inside were the documents she needed to enroll her son in a nearby daycare.

Good thing this wasn't inside the apartment when it got ransacked, she thought, slipping the envelope safely into her purse.

The rest of the mail was mostly junk: donation requests, insurance offers, and flashy advertisements. She flipped through them briefly, tempted by a few of the deals, but she knew better. After overspending on replacement furniture, there was no room left in her budget for impulse buys.

With a sigh, she dumped the junk mail into the nearest trash can and made her way to the bus stop near the complex. As she waited, she glanced down the road and couldn't help thinking of her stolen bike, her dream ride.

Now, she was back to waiting. Again.

The bus finally arrived, and Cindy took it to a familiar stop, not far from a local daycare she often passed on her way to school. *Happy Time Daycare,* the sign read in cheerful block letters.

It was a modest building, nothing fancy, but every time she saw it, the children outside were laughing, running, or playing games behind the sturdy metal fence. There was something comforting about it, something in the normalcy, the joy, and the playfulness that made her feel almost steady again. The small play area out back wasn't much, but it was well-kept, and she imagined her son fitting right in, smiling like the others.

Cindy stepped inside the daycare and approached the front counter, where a woman sat behind a small desk.

"Hi," Cindy began, trying to sound more confident than she felt. "I'm here to ask about enrolling my son."

The woman gathered some papers to add to a clipboard and handed them to Cindy with a pen.

"Yes, ma'am," the woman said. "We just need a few things to get started."

She listed the requirements: a copy of her son's birth certificate and immunization records, a copy of Cindy's driver's license, the names of authorized individuals who could pick him up by 6 p.m., and emergency contact information.

Cindy nodded along, mentally checking the list. *I've got most of that already... just need to make a few copies.*

Handing over her driver's license felt bittersweet. The last time Cindy had driven anywhere was during her mother's visit, using her now-gone old coupe. Still, the license was valid, a small piece of independence she hadn't entirely lost.

She filled out the necessary forms, listing herself, her mother, and Laura as trusted adults authorized to pick up Jacob by the facility's 6 p.m. closing time. If needed, the woman explained, children could stay overnight for an additional fee, though Cindy hoped it wouldn't come to that.

After reviewing the contract, she signed it and handed over the required payment for her son's enrollment.

She also noted her mother's nickname for Jacob, "Sunshine," a name she'd used since he was a baby.

With the enrollment behind her, Cindy caught the bus to a nearby grocery store. She didn't need much; she rarely ate more than a few bites before feeling full anyway. She recalled how, early on, Margo used to joke that she ate like a bird, always pecking at her food while the others dug in.

Her grocery bag was light, just a few pieces of fruit and vegetables, two muffins, and a small chicken. It wasn't much, but it would stretch through the week.

Back at home, Cindy peeled one of the oranges and settled onto her new couch. The apartment was quiet, almost too quiet, with little to occupy her. To pass the time, she flipped through her Spanish notebook, but reviewing her notes took barely any effort and left her right back where she started: restless.

Needing something to lift her spirits, she made a decision. *Enough waiting around.*

She was going to return to the bike shop and buy a new bike to replace the one that had been stolen. It wouldn't erase everything that had happened, but it was something she could reclaim, something just for herself. The thought alone gave her a flicker of energy.

Cindy took the bus and bought the bike.

Her heart felt lighter. Finally, a piece of freedom returned. With her new ride beneath her, she cruised through the neighborhood at an easy pace, letting the day unfold around her. She stopped now and then to admire store window displays, take in the subtle changes to the block, or peer down quiet alleys she hadn't noticed before.

When nostalgia crept in, she lifted her hands from the handlebars for a moment, balancing herself with a carefree grin. The wind kissed her cheeks and threaded through her hair, tugging gently like an old friend.

I needed this, she thought, breathing deeply. *Badly.*

From that moment on, Cindy made herself a promise: wherever she went, her bike was going too.

It wasn't anything fancy, but it had wheels, it moved when she needed it to, and most importantly, it brought her peace. Riding it gave her the closest thing to flight, a small slice of freedom that made her feel light, untethered, like a bird finally escaping the cage.

She rode around town for a good while, eventually drifting toward the outskirts of campus. To her surprise, and a bit of luck, she ran into Gordon. Thrilled at the opportunity, she bought a new supply of acid tablets and some weed. It wasn't exactly what she wanted, but it was better than nothing.

Eager to try them out, Cindy rode back home and gave the drugs a go, but the effects fell short of her expectations.

Still, there was at least one positive: her window had finally been replaced. The ugly sheet of plywood was gone, and in its place was clean, solid glass.

On Tuesday, it was time to take the Spanish test. It wasn't as easy as Cindy had expected, but she knew the material well enough and was still one of the first students to finish. Per Mrs. Garcia's rule, everyone had to flip their test face down and wait silently until the rest of the class was done. That part wasn't difficult for Cindy, though she did wish she'd chosen a seat further in the back. Anything would've been better than staring at the chalkboard and watching Mrs. Garcia pace the aisles like a security guard on patrol.

Cheating wasn't as easy as it used to be, not with how alert Mrs. Garcia was, though Cindy wasn't entirely convinced the teacher even noticed how some students got away with it. Still, it didn't matter this time. Cindy was only focused on her test, not anyone else's.

And oddly enough, Dan didn't show.

Figures, Cindy thought. *Maybe he's even lazier than I gave him credit for.*

More and more tests were flipped over until the last student finally finished. Mrs. Garcia collected the stack and seamlessly transitioned into a new lecture, carrying the class to the end.

As soon as class was done, Cindy gathered her things, ready to rush to Ryan's class, but a voice called out to her from the hallway.

"What?" she asked, turning.

"Don't shoot the messenger," said Millie Fellows, a red-haired, blue-eyed student in a solid brown blouse, black skirt, and black shoes. Her tone was cautious, almost apologetic. "But Dan wanted me to ask if you knew where his wallet was. He's really, really upset and thinks you have it."

Cindy blinked, then folded her arms.

"No, I don't," she said, the lie rolling off her tongue half-smooth. Technically, she didn't have it anymore. "Why would *I* have it?"

"Beats me," Millie said. "I'm just telling you what he told me. He thinks you stole his wallet, and he said if it's not returned with *everything* in it, he's going to start sending more people after you."

Cindy's eyes widened. Her heart dropped, and it felt like her soul nearly leapt from her chest.

"I don't have it," she repeated, the lie tightening in her throat. "I never did."

Without waiting for a reply, she turned and bolted down the hallway, her breath growing rapid and shallow with every step. *Shit. I don't have his stupid wallet anymore!*

Her thoughts spun faster than her feet. *How the hell am I gonna get out of this? What if he's the one who sent people to break into my apartment? If that's true... I'm toast.*

Shit, she gasped. *This can't be happening now! Jacob and Momma plan on coming over soon! They can't get caught up in this! Shit! Fuck!*

Cindy's thoughts spiraled, her mind ping-ponging between cuss words and dread as she rushed toward her next class. Dan had connections. Too many. He knew people all over campus, and if half the rumors about him were true, he could probably get away with murder.

And I'd be his first, she thought grimly, *if I'm not just another unspoken name on a list from his California days.*

Oh my God, she wanted to cry out, picturing bullets flying past her and her only chance of escape being her damn bike, which, at this point, felt more like a child's toy than a getaway vehicle.

She imagined the whole campus turning on her, pitchforks in hand, torches blazing, ready to drag her out and burn her at the stake.

Cindy couldn't get to Ryan's drawing class fast enough. If there was any place on campus that felt remotely safe, it was there. Ryan didn't let just anyone walk through the door. Only enrolled students were allowed in, which, in her current state of panic, might as well have been Heaven.

For a fleeting, desperate moment, she even considered going back to the dumpster where she'd tossed Dan's wallet. *But that thing's long gone,* she thought bitterly. *Just like the rest of the stuff I left lying around town like a damn fool.*

The thought of returning to Dan's off-campus place to lie and claim she didn't have the wallet anymore crossed her mind, but it was pointless. He'd never believe her. She was probably target number one now, not just for the wallet, she realized, but for anything and everything that upset him.

Cindy's pencil moved more slowly than usual across the page during drawing class. Her hand sketched, but her mind was far from present, completely tangled in fear, anxiety, and frantic planning. She kept trying to piece together ideas, strategies, anything that might get Dan off her back. After their last interaction, she saw him for what he really was: a devil in disguise. And the worst part? She was in way over her head.

Was it really that bad? she asked herself. *Bad enough to even consider something desperate, like killing him?*

The thought chilled her. *Could I really do something like that? Would I even go through with it if I had the chance?*

Deep down, she already knew the answer.

I'd probably chicken out... or get caught... or worse.

And yet, the fear still clawed at her. Because if she didn't do *something*, who knew what Dan or the people he'd send would do next?

Class ended faster than Cindy expected, leaving her wishing for the critiques she used to find annoying. Rather than heading to the cafeteria for lunch, she lingered in the comforting quiet of the art building, opting instead for a vending machine snack. She inserted her money and punched a button for a candy bar, craving something warm and homemade, but settling for sugar and convenience.

"Nice bike," a voice said behind her.

Cindy turned to find a familiar face, Judy Bowman, one of the sorority sisters she had sketched once before. Judy, twenty-two, looked polished as ever in a crisp white blouse, pink skirt, and a matching thin jacket adorned with her sorority pin and emblem. Her glossy brown hair framed a composed face, her dark green eyes both curious and sharp.

"Thanks," Cindy replied, brushing a few crumbs from the candy wrapper off her fingers.

"I really loved the drawing you did," Judy said, her voice smooth and pleasant. "Do you have time to do another? I want to give it to someone special."

"Sure," Cindy agreed, leading her into the drawing studio where a few classmates still lingered, chatting or cleaning up their workspaces. She leaned her bike against the wall, pulled out her sketchbook, and got to work. Judy posed gracefully, the confidence in her posture making it easy to capture her essence on paper.

When she finished, Judy examined the drawing with a smile, handed Cindy some cash, and said, "Hey, baby."

Cindy froze.

To her shock, "baby" turned out to be none other than Ryan, her professor, who walked in and greeted Judy with a casual kiss.

What in the world? Cindy's eyes darted between the two.

Ryan? In a relationship? With a student? When did all this happen? Cindy couldn't tell if she was shocked, intrigued, or just plain grossed out. The sight of Judy and Ryan together scrambled her emotions like static.

"Look," Judy said, holding out the sketch. "Isn't it great? I loved the first one so much, I had to get another done."

"Of course it is," Ryan replied, smiling as he glanced at the drawing. "Cindy's good at what she does. That's why she's our scholarship recipient."

Cindy blinked. The world just kept flip-flopping. Bad to good, then back again, then maybe good? At least this felt like a *win*.

"She should do *you*," Judy suggested suddenly, giving Ryan's arm a playful squeeze.

"How about us *together*, then?" Ryan offered, already sitting down beside her with a casual grin.

Cindy blinked again, unsure if she was still in reality.

This is insane, she thought. *None of this can be real.* Maybe she hit her head. Maybe she finally cracked. Either way, whatever *this was*, it was a far cry from the hell Dan had dragged her through.

You know what? Yeah. I'd rather be here, Cindy decided. Even if it was all bizarre, even if her teacher was dating a sorority queen and asking for couple portraits, it beat feeling like she was being hunted.

She nodded silently and picked up her pencil, sketching them both: the professor and his polished, glowing girlfriend. It was weird. Unexpected. But peaceful, in its own twisted way.

The teen finished the sketch and handed it to Judy, who squealed with delight the moment she saw the image.

"Oh my gosh, this is perfect!"

Cindy smiled faintly, the praise cutting through the numb haze that had settled over her lately.

"I know you've been busy," Ryan said, his voice lower now, his eyes locking on hers in a way that made her feel like she'd just been caught with her hand in the cookie jar.

Before she could respond, he reached into his pocket, pulled out his wallet, and handed her a generous payment, more than she expected.

"Thank you," she muttered, startled by the gesture.

Turning to Judy, Ryan added, "I'll see you in about an hour, okay?"

"Yes, baby," Judy said, leaning in for a quick kiss before he headed out of the studio.

Judy turned back to Cindy, her eyes still glowing with excitement.

"Oh, I *wish* I could draw this well," she said. "Also, I saw that painting you've been working on. It looks *amazing.* I seriously can't wait to see it finished. Who knows, I might even buy it."

Sure, you can, Cindy thought bitterly. *Perfect time to collect art from a walking, near-dead artist. It'll be worth a ton.*

She began packing up her sketch materials, her fingers moving slower than usual. She wished she had a studio of her own, some quiet retreat like the graduate students or professors enjoyed. After tidying up, she headed to her art history class, then rode her bike home. On the way, she called Margo.

"Hello?" Margo answered, her voice warm.

"Hey, Margo. It's Cindy. Got a few minutes?"

"Yeah, I just finished putting the pot roast in the oven. What's going on?"

Cindy hesitated, her voice tight. "I think Dan's the one who wrecked my apartment. He had to be. One of my classmates said he sent her to tell me that if I don't give him back his wallet, he's going to send more people after me. *More*, Margo. That means it was him. He did it."

A pause. "You took his wallet?"

"No," Cindy said quickly, too quickly, trying to keep the guilt out of her voice. "Why would I have it? It could've been one of his dopey girlfriends who stole it."

"Yeah," Margo said slowly, "or someone from one of his stupid parties. It could've been anyone."

"I know! That's the problem!"

"Geez, Cin... but why blame you? You haven't even been back there in a while, have you?"

Define 'a while,' Cindy thought, chewing her lip.

"Not really," she admitted. "I stopped going after we had a falling out. I haven't been back since, but I guess I'm the easiest one to blame. He hates me after all."

Margo let out a slow breath. "I don't even know what to say... I mean, maybe you could call the police, see if there's anything they can do. Or ask your landlord if you could switch to another unit. Hell, even move somewhere completely different. That's all I can think of... unless..."

Cindy tensed. "Unless what?"

"Unless you try to talk to Dan. I mean, tell him straight up it wasn't you. Prove it somehow."

Cindy scoffed. "Talk to *Dan*? That's a death sentence. He's beyond mad, Margo. He'd never believe me even if I *was* telling the truth, which, for the record, I *am*."

"I know you are," Margo said gently. "I'm just scared for you, that's all."

You're scared? Cindy thought desperately, her throat tightening as tears welled in her eyes. *I'm the one who should be scared.*

"I don't mean to overstay my welcome," she said softly, forcing the words past the lump in her throat. "But... could I come stay at your place for a few days? Just until things calm down?"

There was a pause. Too long of one.

"I'd love to say yes," Margo finally said, her voice laced with hesitation. "But I can't, Cindy. I'm sorry. I'm... honestly terrified. I don't want to get caught up in something this serious. It's just too much for me, even as your friend."

Cindy's heart sank.

"Maybe try a hotel for a few nights," Margo continued. "Or ask Laura? You know how she is. She'd probably welcome anyone with open arms. I really hope you understand."

Cindy didn't respond right away. Her silence was answer enough.

This hurts. A lot. Cindy blinked away the burn in her eyes. *But I don't blame her. It's my problem, not hers... And if Margo's scared, then Laura probably will be too. I guess I really am on my own.*

"Yeah," she said quietly, doing her best to keep her voice even. "I'll figure something out. Thanks for listening, and for everything you've helped with so far."

There was an awkward pause before she added, trying to shift the conversation. "So, um... I found out Ryan's seeing someone. She's a student here. Isn't that against campus rules? Can professors date students?"

"They can," Margo replied. "As long as Ryan's not *her* professor, and she's not one of *his* students, it's technically allowed."

"Who would've thought," Cindy said with a dry chuckle. "I never imagined I'd see the day, but... here it is." She paused, swallowing the lump in her throat. "Well, I gotta go. I'll call you later."

"Okay," Margo replied softly, her voice heavy with guilt. "Bye, Cin. Stay safe."

Yeah... how?

Chapter 12

For the next several days, Cindy stayed in a cheap hotel wedged between campus and her apartment. Each time she handed over more money, her heart sank. She could feel herself slipping back toward the money-worrying lifestyle she'd fought so hard to escape.

Now and then, she'd take the bus to check on her apartment, just to make sure it hadn't been vandalized again. So far, it hadn't, and Millie hadn't said anything else about Dan either. But the silence only deepened Cindy's paranoia. Why hadn't she heard more? What was being planned?

She hated the unknown, being caught in the middle of it, and left to guess what might come next. It made her long for happier times, even the ones she used to think were bad. Compared to now, those days felt like heaven.

On Tuesday, Mrs. Garcia returned the Spanish tests. Cindy flipped her paper over and stared. Her mouth dropped open.

F.

How?

Adrenaline surged through Cindy's veins as she scanned the test. Her eyes darted from question to question, trying to make sense of the answers, but they didn't match anything she remembered writing. None of it looked familiar. Then her breath caught.

The handwriting.

It wasn't hers.

Not even close.

Yet there it was, her name scribbled across the top as if it were her test.

"This *isn't* my test," Cindy blurted out, her voice tight with panic. She shook her head and looked up at Mrs. Garcia. "It's not!"

Mrs. Garcia's face didn't flinch. "See me after class," she said, taking a moment to collect the tests after the class had seen their grades.

Wait, what? Cindy's mind reeled. *Why should I wait? This is an emergency! I didn't do this!*

She sat frozen, her heart hammering against her ribs. This wasn't just a mistake. It was a disaster. Her scholarship, her GPA, and her entire academic standing could crash from this.

An *F*.

And the worst part? It wasn't even hers.

Cindy wanted to scream out her frustration. She couldn't stay after class. Not when *Ryan's* class was next.

She lowered her head and pressed her hands against her forehead, trying to ground herself, but the pressure only reminded her of the rising panic inside.

Everything faded. Mrs. Garcia's voice became white noise, a dull buzz in the background of her spiraling thoughts.

Vocabulary words. Family. Friends.

Who cared?

The book could teach her that.

Not some half-hearted regurgitation from a professor who couldn't even tell a forged test from the real thing.

Her grade. Her scholarship. Her future was dangling by a thread over someone else's mistake. Or maybe it wasn't a mistake at all.

She shut her eyes, tuning out the lecture completely, counting the minutes until she could argue her point.

Damn, was all she could tell herself as the weight of it all sank in.

There was no point in going to Ryan's class today. She was still passing his, and missing one day probably wouldn't do much damage, not the kind of damage an F in Spanish would do if it wasn't fixed, and fast.

When class had ended, Cindy met with Mrs. Garcia in her office to discuss the test.

"It's not my test," she said firmly. "It's not even my handwriting."

She opened her Spanish notebook, flipping to a recent page. "This is how I write. See? It doesn't match at all."

Mrs. Garcia took the notebook, studied Cindy's neat script, then looked again at the test with Cindy's name written at the top. She frowned and pulled the stack of tests from her bag, thumbing through them one by one.

"Your name doesn't appear on any others," she said. "If this one isn't yours... then where is your test?"

"I don't know," Cindy said, frustration mounting. "But that one *isn't* it. I swear to you."

"Let's go through the rest again together," Mrs. Garcia said calmly, sliding the stack toward Cindy.

Together, they browsed through the other test papers. Laura had gotten an A, definitely her work.

Millie, too, had scored an A. But then came Dan's. Cindy froze. Dan, who hadn't even shown up to take the test, somehow had a paper... and it had an A as well. A low one, but still an A. The handwriting matched Millie's. Cindy waited, hoping Mrs. Garcia would notice, would say something, but she didn't.

How could she not see it? Cindy's mind spun. Maybe it was something only artists noticed, subtle differences in handwriting, the shape of letters, the pressure of the pen. They were trained to see.

That bastard got an A and I got an F, Cindy scoffed internally. *That's not fair.*

A wave of regret washed over her. Helping Dan cheat had backfired. Now he was coasting through, looking like a decent student, and she was the one failing!

What baffled Cindy most was that *none* of the papers were hers, as if her original test had vanished and been replaced with a forgery meant to sabotage her.

"It's none of these," Cindy said, frustration tightening her voice. "But I swear, I did the test!"

"I know," Mrs. Garcia replied calmly. "You were right there, sitting at the front of the classroom. I remember." She glanced again at the suspicious test. "I'm going to hold onto this one and investigate what's going on."

Relief started to bloom, but Cindy's nerves remained taut.

"In the meantime," Mrs. Garcia continued, "I'll give you another version of the test to take right here in my office."

"I have another class," Cindy said quickly. "I'm already late for it."

"I'll write a note for your professor," Mrs. Garcia offered, already pulling out a pen and notepad. "Take your time. I'll grade this one myself."

Cindy almost broke into tears, not from stress this time, but from sheer gratitude.

"Thank you," she whispered, voice cracking slightly.

Mrs. Garcia gave Cindy another blank test. It took but a few minutes for the teen to complete it, and she handed it over, watching the professor grade each answer, one by one. When the professor had finished, she adjusted Cindy's grade from an F to an A.

"When are we getting our tests back?" Cindy asked, relieved at the adjustment.

"I keep them," Mrs. Garcia replied. "The only time I hand them out is to show the grade before collecting them again."

"Yes, ma'am."

Mrs. Garcia adjusted Cindy's grade in the gradebook and scribbled a note for her to give to Ryan. Cindy accepted it gratefully, tucking it into her notebook before leaving the building.

Still, her mind spun. Somehow, Dan was behind all this. She could feel it in her bones. But if it wasn't Millie helping him, then who? The handwriting on the forged test didn't match Millie's or any other student's. It was off. It was strange. But one thing was clear. Someone wanted to see her fail. And Cindy was determined to find out who.

I bet it could be Eileen or Ann, Cindy thought. *They're always hanging around Dan, and they've already stabbed me in the back once. It's funny how they did what they did, and now I haven't seen either of them around. I wish I knew what their handwriting looked like. Then I could compare it to the fake test. But how could they have even gotten access to it? Are either of them even taking Spanish this semester?*

Her thoughts spiraled faster, darker.

If they managed to get my phone number and address, then why not my test? What if they snuck in somehow? Or worse... what if Mrs. Garcia helped them?

The idea chilled her. *Could she have sabotaged me on purpose? Maybe she changed her mind once she realized she could get in trouble...*

Cindy didn't want to believe it, but right now, she wasn't sure who she could trust.

The teen reached the art building and, as expected, the door to the drawing studio was shut. She paused, swallowing hard as her fingers trembled over the note tucked in her notebook.

Please, God, Cindy whispered in her head, *don't let me be humiliated again. Not today. Please. I've already been through enough. Aren't there other people in this damn world who could suffer instead of me for once?* She winced at her own words. *I'm sorry for cussing, but I'm tired... I'm so tired.*

She knocked.

The door opened, revealing Ryan on the other side. He frowned slightly as he looked at her, and her nerves spiked. With shaky hands, she held out the note. She half-expected him to roll his eyes or scold her, maybe even shut the door in her face.

Instead, he read the note silently, then opened the door wider.

Cindy blinked, stunned. No yelling. No judgment. Just... calm acceptance.

Without a word, she stepped inside. Her classmates were already hard at work, heads bent over their drawings. Cindy found her seat, pulled out her materials, and got to work, still a little lightheaded, but grateful.

I wonder if he's only being nicer because his girlfriend likes my work, Cindy thought, glancing at Ryan from the corner of her eye. *Well, who cares? It takes the pressure off. That's all that matters.*

She exhaled quietly, letting herself relax a little.

If everything else could just start falling into place... things might finally get back to normal. That would be great.

Her stomach growled faintly. *I wonder what the cafeteria has for lunch. I'm so tired of vending machine junk like chips, candy bars, and sugary snacks. I need something real.*

Then, just as quickly, her thoughts shifted again, unexpected and unwelcome.

It was nice when it used to be me and Paul... She blinked. *Wait. Why do I miss him?*

The memories flooded in before she could block them out. *He slept with those two sluts... and I threw a vase at him. And records. But... he still came to help clean the apartment, until I screamed at him to leave.*

Cindy stared down at her drawing, her pencil still. Her chest tightened.

Why would I miss him? Cindy scolded herself. *Here I go again, probably messing up. Just like always.*

He'd probably turn into someone like Dan…He'd sleep with me, then beat the crap out of me. I don't need that to happen again. I don't.

Nonetheless, she gathered the courage to head to the cafeteria after her drawing class. No Paul. Her stomach twisted, but she wasn't sure if it was relief or disappointment. Maybe both.

Frowning, she settled for a plain sandwich, eating slow, reluctant bites as she walked back toward the art building. Everything felt heavy. Numb.

She entered Dr. Ritter's art history class and took her usual seat. The room was half full, a few voices murmuring, but she barely noticed them.

Moments later, Ronald stepped through the door, his face lit with a cheerful grin. He spotted her immediately and made a beeline for her row, plopping down beside her.

What does this loser want? Cindy thought, rolling her eyes.

"Hey, Cindy!" Ronald grinned. "Thanks a million for the pointers! My drawing's looking way better. Ryan even said so! I stopped by his office before class and showed him. He told me my grapes, bowl, and vase were really improving, something about the proportions and overlapping looking more natural. I told him it was all thanks to you!"

"No sweat," Cindy muttered, hoping she didn't sound as annoyed as she felt. *Please don't think we're friends now. Go back to wherever you usually sit in the back, Ronald.*

More students trickled into the classroom, but Ronald didn't budge. He stayed planted beside her like he'd found a new permanent seat. *Great.*

Dr. Ritter entered and began setting up the projector for another lecture. Cindy leaned back in her chair, trying to settle in, until her body tensed with a jolt of panic, causing her to nearly urinate on herself.

There, standing at the door, was *Dan.*

Her breath caught.

Oh, shit!

Before she could sink lower in her seat or even look away, Dan spotted her. Cold dread wrapped around her spine. She barely had time to blink or run before he casually strolled across the room and slipped into the empty seat next to her.

And just then, as if the universe had conspired to mock her terror, the lights went out.

Pitch black.

No. No. No. This isn't happening!

The urge to flee nearly overwhelmed her. Her chest tightened, her breaths grew shallow, and her head began to spin. It felt like the walls were closing in. She was on the verge of hyperventilating.

Dr. Ritter, oblivious to the storm unraveling in Cindy's seat, asked a student to shut the door. The heavy click of it closing echoed like a prison gate. Without so much as a roll call, the lecture began.

"So," Dan whispered beside her, his voice low and chilling, "where's my fucking wallet?"

Chapter 13

Dan cracked his knuckles. Cindy swallowed hard.

"I don't know," she said, lying through her teeth. "Why would you think I have it?"

"Don't fuckin' lie to me," Dan hissed, his voice sharp and threatening, loud enough to earn a "Shh!" from Ronald.

"You were the last one around before it disappeared," Dan pressed, eyes drilling into her.

Cindy held her ground. "Well, I don't have it. I never stole anything from you before, so it couldn't have been me. I didn't even see your stupid wallet the last time I was there. Maybe someone else took it while you were high or too busy running your mouth."

"Shh," another student snapped from a nearby seat, holding a finger to her lips.

"If I don't get my fucking wallet back—" Dan began, his voice rising with each word.

"Maybe it was *Eileen* or *Ann*," Cindy cut in quickly, not hesitating to toss either of them under the bus.

Dan paused. "What?"

"It could've been one of them," she said, trying to sound more confident than she felt. "They've got a reputation, you know that. Always lying, always stabbing people in the back. One of them could've swiped it while you weren't paying attention."

Dan narrowed his eyes, silent for a moment, as if weighing the bait she just dangled in front of him.

"Dr. Ritter," a student near the feuding students raised her hand, interrupting the lecture. "Sorry, but I couldn't hear what you just said."

"Yeah," another student chimed in. "There's talking going on, and it's hard to listen."

Dr. Ritter paused, her expression calm but firm. "Class, please remember, no talking during the lecture. Be considerate of your classmates who are here to learn."

With that, she resumed the lecture.

"Something smells funny," Ronald spoke up, wrinkling his nose.

"I think it's weed," another nearby student added from the back.

That was Dan's cue. Without flinching, he stayed seated a moment longer, cool, composed, like nothing was wrong, then stood up just as Dr. Ritter resumed the lecture. He slipped out of the classroom silently.

Cindy exhaled slowly, her heart still racing. Relief washed over her, though she wasn't sure if it would last. She could only hope he'd taken the bait, for now.

Maybe, with some luck, even if Eileen and Ann denied stealing the wallet, Dan would start losing his mind, paranoia eating away at him until he trusted no one. His inner circle would see him unraveling, and maybe he'd end up locked away in a loony bin, far from everyone's lives for good.

A smirk tugged at Cindy's lips as she imagined Dan unleashing his wrath on her rivals instead of her. Whatever chaos he could cause them would be a welcome relief compared to what she'd been through. She wished she could watch their unsuspecting fates unfold firsthand, but even without that, just knowing

Dan might be turning his sights on them was enough to guarantee Cindy a good night's sleep, with the biggest, most satisfied smile on her face.

Oh, I'm not through with you, Dan, not by a long shot, Cindy thought, reflecting on the memory of how he'd humiliated her. *You'll regret everything you've put me through. Every damn thing.*

Cindy stepped out of the art building, ready to head back to the hotel. As she reached for her bike, she spotted a familiar silhouette seated on a courtyard bench. Her chest lifted with a flicker of hope, but when the figure turned around, it was a stranger. The weight returned instantly.

She dropped her gaze and climbed onto her bike, pedaling away from campus. Still, the ride soothed her, each turn of the pedals lightened her mood, like a rainbow slowly stretching across the sky after a storm. It took time, but eventually she arrived back at her temporary stay. Inside her room, she turned on the television, collapsed onto the bed, and let out a deep, weary sigh.

She rested for a while, drifting in and out of sleep until the clock read 7 p.m. With a firm press of her lips, she pushed herself off the bed, turned off the television, and grabbed her bike. She didn't care that the sun was already setting; the ache in her legs didn't matter either. What mattered was making her feelings known. Yes, things had fallen apart, but why did they have to stay that way? If there was even the faintest possibility of a second chance, she had to try. If it didn't work out, at least she could say she tried.

By the time Cindy reached Lakeland Square, night had completely taken over the sky. It was harder to slip through the gate at this hour, but luck was on her side. A car pulled in, and she followed close behind. Getting into the building wasn't too hard either. She slipped inside just as a resident opened the door. Head up, no hesitation. Blending in was half the battle, and she did it like a pro, all the way to Paul's door.

Taking a deep breath, Cindy knocked on the door and waited.

Paul, I'm sorry, she wanted to say. *I know "sorry" isn't enough, but if there's anything I can do to make it right, just tell me. We both messed up in our own ways, but I can forgive you...if you'll forgive me. I should've said this sooner. I just...appreciated everything we had before things fell apart. Maybe we can get through this. Together.*

She knocked again, her heart thudding harder with each passing second.

The door creaked open, and Cindy's heart skipped a beat. Paul stood in the entryway, leaning against the frame. But unlike before, his body blocked the doorway, guarded, distant. He wasn't inviting her in this time.

"Cin?" he asked, eyes squinting. "What are you doing here?"

"Paul, I'm sorry," Cindy began, her breath trembling.

"I can't talk right now," he cut in quickly. "I've got company."

"Oh." Her voice cracked. "But, it won't take a minute..."

He didn't close the door. He didn't invite her in either. Instead, he stayed planted in place, silent. At least he was listening. That was more than she expected.

"I'm sorry," she repeated. "I messed up. I took you for granted, and I shouldn't have. I didn't mean for things to go the way they did—"

The door edged open just a little wider.

And there she was.

Judy.

Her presence filled the gap behind Paul, and the shock of it stole the rest of her breath.

Judy's eyes met hers, and in that instant, everything dropped out from under Cindy.

What is she doing here?

"Cindy, hey," Judy greeted brightly. "I didn't know you knew Paul."

"Yeah," Cindy said, her tone flat. "We know each other."

"Well, come on in," Judy offered cheerfully, swinging the door open wider as if she lived there too.

What the hell?

Cindy hesitated, glancing at Paul. He didn't say anything, just turned and followed Judy back inside. With her heart sinking, Cindy stepped in behind them.

"I was just giving Paul the sketch you did of me," Judy beamed, picking up the drawing from the coffee table and holding it out like a prized possession. "He loves it. Don't you, sweetie?"

Sweetie?

Wasn't Ryan your 'honey'? Cindy thought, her eyes narrowing. *What was Judy doing here this late? Where was Ryan? And Paul—what the hell was going on?*

"Well, I better get going," Judy said with a satisfied sigh, as if she'd just scored a win. Cindy's shock deepened when Judy planted a quick kiss on Paul's lips, like *he* should have been Ryan.

Cindy stood frozen, caught between confusion and disbelief. She had no idea what she'd just walked into, but all she could do was silently process the strange scene unfolding before her.

"Bye, I'll see you tomorrow," Judy said to Paul, then shot Cindy a knowing smile. "Later, Cindy."

With that, she breezed out the door.

After a long, awkward silence, Cindy finally found her voice.

"W-what was that all about?" she demanded.

"Nothing," Paul said coldly. "I told you I had company. Just like you told me once before—'It's none of your business.'"

Tears welled up in Cindy's eyes, and her voice cracked as she broke down. "Why are you doing this to me?"

"Doing what?" Paul asked, his tone defensive. "I wasn't expecting for you to be here, so why would I be doing anything to you? I haven't done anything wrong, not that I see."

Cindy's sobs grew louder. "Then just stop! How many times do I have to apologize? I *get it*; I've learned my lesson! But you're only doing this to get back at me, aren't you?"

Paul's expression softened slightly, but his voice remained firm. "Actually, I'm not. You moved on... and so have I. It's that simple."

Cindy scoffed, stunned and struggling to hold on to the last thread of hope. "Judy has a boyfriend, just so you know."

"I already know that," Paul replied flatly.

"What? Then I don't get it. Why is that okay for her?"

Paul exhaled, his expression unreadable. "Listening isn't exactly your strong suit, is it? Haven't you figured it out by now? I don't trust you, Cindy. Not even close. And you know why. Every single reason. You know them, or are we going to pretend otherwise again?"

Cindy's voice wavered. "What about forgiveness? You don't believe in that?"

"I've forgiven," he said, his tone firm but tired. "But I haven't forgotten. And I'm not convinced I want someone like you in my life anymore."

His words hit like a slap.

"I fed you, supported you, treated you with respect, and defended you. And what did I get? You ran your mouth, told people things that should've stayed between us, humiliated me, hit me, destroyed my stuff, and called me outside of my name. I know damn well you'd do it again, if given the chance. I expected better from you, Cindy. A lot better."

"What about our promise?" Cindy pleaded, her voice cracking. "We said we'd be there for each other. Or does that mean nothing now? Is it that easy to forget, just toss me aside? Was all of it just pretend?"

Paul's eyes narrowed.

He stepped closer, his voice low but laced with frustration. "I *was* there. I fought Dan because of you. I stopped two girls from coming after you. I showed up and tried to help clean the apartment. And what did I get?" He pointed at himself. "Shoved further and further away. Every time I tried, you made it clear I wasn't wanted. I was the one unappreciated. I was the one thrown away."

Cindy headed to the door, her head bowed low as she reached the entrance. Another ending. Another loss. The same cycle, repeating again and again.

Behind her, Paul ran a hand through his hair, letting out a slow, heavy breath.

Resigned, Cindy grabbed her bike, stepped outside, and left the apartment. She made it as far as the building's edge before pausing to glance up at the night sky. It was cold and dark, but a few stars pierced through the blackness: quiet, distant, and defiant. A plane blinked across the sky, growing smaller with each passing second.

Reaching the sidewalk, she waited for a line of cars to pass. Just as she started to mount her bike, a familiar voice called out.

"It's not a good idea to ride home this late on a bike."

Cindy turned around. Paul had followed her. His face was softer now, the bitterness faded, though his eyes remained guarded.

"Let's go back," he said gently. "I'll give you a ride home."

Almost on instinct, Cindy considered refusing, saying she could make it home on her own. But the reality crept in fast: the long, dark ride to either her apartment or the hotel, the weight of isolation, the fear of Dan's people possibly lurking in the shadows...or worse, her own thoughts chasing her down.

"I'm at a hotel," she admitted quietly.

Paul looked at her, surprised. "A hotel?"

"Yeah… I was scared they might come back," she said, her voice low. "So, I've been staying there the last couple of days."

"Oh," he said, pulling out his keys. He motioned for her to follow. But instead of leading her to the parking lot, he opened the door back to his apartment. "You can crash on the couch tonight."

Cindy stepped inside, murmuring, "Thanks." She eased herself onto the couch as Paul nodded, saying nothing more. Her bike stood leaning against the wall, a silent witness to everything.

Paul turned and headed upstairs, leaving Cindy alone with the warmth of unexpected kindness and the heaviness of everything unspoken.

Cindy sank into the softness of the couch, her body curling into the cushions. He returned moments later with a pillow and a folded blanket, handing them to her without a word. She wanted, just for a second, to brush his hand, to feel some trace of connection, but it didn't happen. Without a glance back, he quietly retreated upstairs.

Left in the hush of the room, Cindy stared at the ceiling. Her fingers curled around the blanket's edge, her mind spinning with unspoken questions. *Was this just kindness? A habit? Or… something else?* Could there be a second chance waiting in the silence?

Grateful for the gesture, but haunted by uncertainty, she sat still for what felt like forever. Finally, unable to shake the pull in her chest, she slipped the blanket aside and stood up. Quietly, she climbed the stairs.

The door to Paul's bedroom was open.

He sat at the edge of his bed, his back hunched, head bowed in thought. The lamplight outlined the tension in his shoulders. When Cindy stepped softly into the doorway, he lifted his gaze. Their eyes met.

She wasn't sure what to say.

Neither was he.

He didn't say anything when Cindy sat beside him and gently rested her head against his shoulder. To her surprise, Paul wrapped an arm around her and gave her a small, comforting squeeze.

Could this be it? Cindy wondered, her heart fluttering with a fragile sense of hope. *Is this my second chance?*

She lifted her head slightly and leaned in, hoping for a kiss, something to seal the possibility of starting over. But Paul turned away just enough to miss it, avoiding her attempt.

"Good night, Cin," he said softly, climbing into bed and turning his back to her.

Cindy lingered at the edge of the bed, her heart aching in the silence that followed. Then, silently, she stood, descended the stairs, and returned to the couch. Wrapping herself in the blanket, she lay down and stared at the ceiling.

There was no anger in her, just an ache that settled in her chest like a weight. Hope had carried her up the stairs, but reality had brought her back down.

"Good night, Paul," she uttered, wishing he could hear.

Chapter 14

The next day, Paul drove Cindy back to the hotel so she could gather her things. Then, together, they went to her apartment. Relief washed over Cindy when she saw that nothing had been disturbed or vandalized on the outside.

Feeling a sudden surge of guilt for how Paul had been treated the first time he came by, Cindy hesitated before inviting him inside. But Paul quietly declined, shaking his head as he drove away.

Swallowing her pride, Cindy stepped inside the apartment. Everything was exactly as she had left it, unchanged, yet somehow heavy with the weight of her worries.

Cindy was still saddened that things hadn't worked out the way she'd hoped with Paul. Still, at least they were speaking again, with less tension, fewer tears. But something still gnawed at her: *Judy*. Why was she hanging around? She already had a boyfriend, so why *Paul* too? Then another question crept in: *was Paul ever really mine to begin with?* And worse: *would Judy be the one to take her place if Paul wanted something serious?*

There were too many questions and not nearly enough answers. Judy might have been all smiles and friendliness, but Cindy had made up her mind. *That tramp needed to go.*

Another question tugged at Cindy's mind: What about Eileen or Ann? Were they still lingering in Paul's life somehow? Maybe, if luck was finally on her side, Judy would vanish too, just like they had. Still, if she wanted Judy gone, she'd need intel, real details, not assumptions. And if anyone on campus knew how to get it, it was Margo.

Cindy made her way to the kitchen and picked up the phone, dialing Margo's number with purpose. The line buzzed once, then again.

"Hello?" Margo answered.

"Hey, it's Cindy," she said, trying to sound casual.

"Oh, hey! I can't talk long—Joel and I are about to head out. Did you and Paul patch things up? He's throwing a little hangout later and told us to swing by."

Cindy froze. *What?*

Paul hadn't said a word about hosting anyone. That meant she hadn't been invited. A sharp sting of betrayal crept into her chest, not just from Paul, but from Margo too, who hadn't mentioned anything until now.

"No, but that's okay," Cindy said, doing her best to keep the disappointment out of her voice. "I just had a couple of quick questions. You know Judy Bowman, right? Isn't she in the same sorority your sister Myra was in? I was wondering if I could get Myra's number, maybe ask her a few things about Judy?"

"I would, but Myra's not going to spill anything on Judy. It's against their sorority rules," Margo replied. "Why? What did you want to know?"

"I just wanted to see if she could tell me anything, anything at all that might be useful."

"Well, Judy's a senior," Margo said. "And she's the social chair of the sorority. She plans all their events, formals, charity stuff, mixers, you name it. Honestly, she's good at it. Plus, her family's in the hospitality industry. They own several hotels. Her sorority's Spring Fling is coming up in a few weeks, but you gotta be invited."

So, she comes from money too, Cindy thought, her expression turning sullen. Of course she did. Judy probably fit right into Paul's world, effortlessly and perfectly. But that didn't mean Cindy was ready to back down. No way. Just because Judy had wealth and all the right connections didn't make her better. It only meant she had a head start; doors opened for her that others had to break down just to peek through.

Strip all that away, the designer clothes, the family-owned hotels, the sorority power plays, and what would be left? Probably someone average and dull. *Probably some basic floozy hiding behind good lighting and charm.* Cindy clenched her jaw. No, she wouldn't let someone like that win, not without a fight.

"I have to go," Margo reminded Cindy. "I'll call you back later today, promise."

"Thanks," Cindy replied, hanging up the phone.

Well, I'm not just going to sit around and mope like before, she thought. *I'm tired of everyone else living their lives while I'm stuck feeling left out. Forget that. I can enjoy myself too; I will.*

With a sense of resolve, Cindy changed clothes and hid her bike in the bedroom closet, breaking an earlier promise to herself that she would never leave it behind. But there was no time to casually ride it on campus. Instead, the teen took the bus to campus, determined to make the day brighter than what it was starting to become.

Cindy returned to the art building. She pushed the door open and stepped inside, where a few graduate students were scattered throughout the open studios, immersed in their work. Some undergrads lingered in clusters, chatting, laughing, or hunched over their projects.

Through his open office door, Cindy glimpsed Ryan rifling through a drawer, clearly in search of something. She didn't linger. Instead, she headed for her workspace, determined to refocus her attention where it belonged, on her own art in the painting studio.

"Ah, Cindy," a voice called from behind.

Startled, Cindy turned quickly and blinked in surprise. Judy stood there, seemingly having appeared out of nowhere.

"You scared me," Cindy admitted, letting out a light, uneasy chuckle.

Judy let out a melodic giggle, delicately covering her mouth with her fingers. "I tend to do that sometimes," she said, her voice sweet but unreadable.

Grabbing a nearby stool, she dragged it near Cindy and sat down beside her.

"Such beautiful work," Judy said, her eyes tracing the diptych. "You know, there's this old saying that when artists paint people, they reveal pieces of themselves. I felt the sadness captured in her face. Such honesty in art always tends to pull people in and bring them together, like us. Don't you think?"

"Sure," Cindy replied, forcing a smile. "Like Ryan too, huh?"

Judy's smile didn't falter, but she didn't answer either. Instead, she moved on. "So, any idea on how much you'd like for the painting?"

"Not yet," Cindy said, unsure whether Judy was genuinely interested or simply playing games. "I'm still on the fence."

Yeah right! It's obvious that she's lying. Who does she think she's fooling? I wouldn't sell her any of my paintings, not in a million years.

"Well," Judy said, reaching into her purse. "I brought a little down payment. I figured it might speak your language."

She winked and added, "It's an investment we can both appreciate."

Cindy blinked, expecting a check or cash. Instead, Judy handed her a small bag filled with acid tablets.

Cindy stared at it, and Judy's smile didn't move.

What on Earth? Cindy's breath hitched. *She has acid tablets?* Her mind raced. *Where did she get them? How does she know? Does Ryan know?* A pit began forming in her stomach. *Is this a test?*

Her hands stiffened at her sides, eyes darting from the bag to Judy's flawless smile.

And then it hit her—Ryan's warning.

"We're going to stop right there," Ryan had said, *his voice clipped, his expression cold. "Go to class and think about what I said. If it happens again, even under the slightest suspicion, your time in this program is over."*

The memory slammed into her like a brick wall. Her throat tightened, and her heart pounded with familiar desperation. It had been a while since she touched real acid. If anyone on campus had the best stash, it would probably be Judy. Of course it would. With her wealth, charm, and connections, why wouldn't she have the best stuff? Didn't the best always have the best?

Cindy's fingers twitched.

She hated Judy, loathed everything the girl represented. But this? This wasn't cruelty. This was... an offer. A business transaction. Just an exchange between two people.

Right?

But deep down, Cindy knew better. She'd already sacrificed too much for those tiny tablets: her dignity, her sanity, her savings... and the people who used to care about her. Was she really about to give her art, her soul's voice, in exchange for a high?

A deal was a deal, wasn't it?

Then why did it feel like a trap?

"M-maybe some other time," Cindy forced herself to say, her throat dry.

There was no way she was going to accept the tablets. Not here. Not now. Not in front of Judy.

Judy gave a casual smile and slipped the bag back into her purse as if it meant nothing. As if it hadn't just ignited a war in Cindy's chest.

I can't believe I just turned down the tablets, Cindy thought, her mind spiraling. *It's like I turned down a million dollars. What's wrong with me? I need one. Just one. Just to level out. Just to think straight. Just to escape. Could she possibly have...other things I could try too? That are stronger than Dan's?*

Her hands trembled.

"Sure, I can dig," Judy chirped, her grin wide and weightless, like she hadn't just tried to break someone.

Cindy nodded, barely able to hold herself together. Every part of her was screaming to change her answer, to ask what else Judy had to offer, to grab the bag and disappear, but somehow, she stayed put.

For now.

A few of Cindy's classmates began to trickle into the studio, making her envious of their laughter and cheerfulness.

"Well, class is about to start," Judy said with a breezy sigh. "And I've got an engagement to catch, doll. We'll talk again— I'm sure of it."

She winked, then strutted off, her perfume trailing behind, something expensive and smug that lingered longer than it should have.

Doll? Cindy blinked. *Did she just call me doll?* Was that a pet name or some dismissive nickname? Did Judy say that to everyone, or was it aimed at her specifically? What did it mean? Was it a code for something? *She's weird!* She had pet names for both Paul and Ryan, two guys she might have a thing for, but why Cindy? They weren't friends. Judy didn't like her. So why "doll"? Was she being sarcastic? Mocking her? Or worse...toying with her?

Cindy continued to work on her paintings and attended her last class of the day, printmaking. She was glad that her schedule was light that day, and she was free to spend the remainder as she wished.

Unfortunately, her mind kept drifting to something she didn't need.

Judy has acid tablets, Cindy thought, the idea looping through her mind like a stuck record. *I can't stand her, but if she has what I need, maybe we could work something out. Shit, I feel like I'm about to lose it. All this stress is making me lose my fucking mind. A good trip can make it all go away. Fuck, I need that acid. But what if they're weak, like Gordon's? Oh, that wouldn't work, not even close. I need to try one, just to see if it's decent. Damn, I should have taken a sample. What else does she have—ludes, bennies, Valium? Other good shit? I need to find out.*

Without wasting time, Cindy made a beeline to the other side of campus where all the sorority houses were, stopping in front of the one that Judy belonged to. She knocked urgently, hoping the evil tramp would answer.

Sure, it was possibly a trap, but at least she wasn't dumb enough to accept the offer back in the art building where Ryan was. At the sorority house, she could say she was there to do more sketches. After all, Judy had asked for several before, so why change things now? If it *was* a trap, she could always threaten to tell Ryan what was going on behind his back. Everyone had something to lose.

It cracked open a moment later, revealing a familiar face: Bonnie, one of the few people in Judy's circle who genuinely appreciated Cindy's art.

"Cindy, hi," Bonnie said warmly. "Can I help you?"

"Yeah," Cindy replied, trying to keep her tone casual. "Is Judy here? I needed to talk to her."

"Sorry, she left a few hours ago. I'm not sure when she'll be back," Bonnie said. "But I'll let her know you stopped by."

"Thanks," Cindy replied with a polite smile, then turned to head toward the bus stop.

As she walked away, her thoughts buzzed louder than the wind in her ears.

Shoot...maybe I should find Gordon and see if he has something else I could try instead of acid. But, what if I waste more money on him, and then Judy comes around? Hmm... if she mentions anything to Ryan, I could throw it back at her. How does she know what the drugs are if she doesn't take them herself? How'd she even get them? Then Ryan couldn't do anything to me without dragging her down too. An eye for an eye.

Her stomach twisted.

We'd all be equally guilty.

If Ryan does acid, Cindy thought angrily, *wouldn't that make him a hypocrite? Tripping big time while helping his girlfriend supply it to me? That's something else!*

Cindy tossed her head back and scoffed.

He had the nerve to say my time in the program would be over—over a suspicion. What a joke. He probably only said that because he works there. Playing Mr. Professional like he's better than the rest of us.

She smirked.

Shoot, we could've just chilled and done acid together. Who knows? It might've actually loosened him up.

The thought spiraled, and she laughed to herself, picturing it vividly:

"Honey, I'm home," followed by Judy greeting him with a kiss and an acid tab balanced on her tongue.

Ridiculous. But... not entirely impossible.

Cindy had reached the center of campus when she spotted Millie heading toward her.

"Hey, Cindy," Millie said with a sigh, tension tightening her voice.

"Hey," Cindy replied, barely slowing down.

"Wait." Millie's voice sharpened, stopping her in her tracks. "We need to talk."

Cindy glanced back, guarded. "About what?"

"It's Dan," Millie said. "He's finally lost it. He told everyone to meet him at this weird place. I thought we were going to try out something new, but it was an ambush. He started pacing around, demanding everyone prove they were loyal to him. Then, out of nowhere, he accused Ann and Eileen of stealing his wallet and said he was going to make an example of them."

She swallowed hard.

"Dan had Jackie and Ellen hold them down while Drew force-fed them sand. Then they stuck needles under their fingernails and threatened to beat them with a hammer. I was so scared. I thought if I ran or said anything, they'd hurt me too. All I could do was stay still, close my eyes, and hope I wouldn't be next."

Millie's voice cracked. "They were beat up pretty bad when we got back to campus. But what's even scarier is… I don't think he's done with them. He said if anyone reports what happened, they'd be next and won't be seen again. I'm done. I didn't know Dan could get that violent or that he could talk other people into helping him do something like that. I'm never going back there again."

Cindy stayed quiet.

Dang, no wonder Gail left... Wait...Did she leave on her own or...Oh crap... If she did, did he go after her? Shit...That could've been me. It almost was. My apartment...He needs to be locked up and the key thrown away, but how? If I say something and fail, what'll happen to me? Even if what Millie says is true, could she twist things and blame me because of what I told her? We both could end up in serious shit...I'd better keep quiet for now until I can figure out what to do next. It'd be easy to let this go since he's not targeting me anymore, but what if he flips and comes back to blame me? Shit!

Millie looked at her, her voice low and urgent. "After what I saw... I just hope he didn't do anything awful to you too."

Cindy blinked, unsure how to respond.

"I'm done taking tests for him," Millie said quickly. "I never wanted to in the first place. But I'm too scared to stop now. What if he comes after me for saying I want out? What if 'no' isn't an option? He's too unpredictable. Since you haven't been around, I thought maybe you got out. Maybe you figured out how to get away. I'm trying to do the same."

Cindy nodded faintly. "Just keep away from him, or maybe tell him the class is getting too hard and you don't want his grade to slip before the next test. But it might mean bombing one or two on purpose so he believes you. Then, he could get someone else to do it for him. He's got someone we don't know on his side."

She hesitated.

"Another option is dropping the class. That gives him a reason not to expect anything from you. I dunno. Something like that. Just...try to cut ties if you can."

I don't know if she is setting me up or not, but that's the best I can come up with, other than going to the dean. I don't know if she's being tested by Dan herself. Or if I'm being tested too. I could be putting myself in danger just by helping her.

"If none of that works," Cindy added aloud, "then maybe talk to the dean. But just... be prepared for anything..."

Millie hesitated, then dropped her voice even further. "I know. Someone like Dan doesn't deserve to pass. But... Thanks. I'll think about what you said."

She paused.

"Also, be careful with Judy."

Cindy looked up, startled.

"She's been watching you," Millie added. "That's all I'm going to say."

And with that, Millie turned and walked away, leaving Cindy in the middle of campus with a chill creeping down her spine and more confused than ever.

Chapter 15

Cindy returned home and drew herself a bath. She sank into the warm water, letting her muscles loosen, her breath slow.

She kept replaying her exchange with Judy. That offer dangled just long enough to tempt her. Cindy felt strangely proud of herself for not taking the bait. She hadn't fallen for it. She'd almost said yes at the sorority house... almost. But something in her gut had stopped her, relieved that she did.

There was something off about Judy, something Cindy couldn't name, a weirdness that only deepened the longer she thought about it.

"I've got enough problems," Cindy murmured to herself, sliding deeper into the water. *Judy's not one I need to add. I don't even like her. I got to deal with school, money problems, Dan problems, and other crap that keeps piling on.*

Cindy closed her eyes, determined to enjoy her soak. *Mmmm.* Her body felt light, and her thoughts began to drift somewhere quieter.

Minutes later, she stepped out of the tub and patted herself dry. After changing into a nightgown, she reviewed the notes she'd taken in Dr. Ritter's class, focused and determined to memorize the material until it became second nature. Then, she moved on to her Spanish notes, studying until she felt she'd absorbed enough for the night.

Just as she was about to turn in, the shrill ring of the phone cut through the silence. She picked up the phone, and relief washed over her when she heard Margo's voice.

"Hey, Margo," Cindy said, smiling despite herself. "How'd things go?"

"Fine," Margo replied casually. "Sorry to call this late, but I figured you'd be up. Okay, here's the skinny. We all met at Paul's and went to a nearby disco. I think it just opened. None of us had ever been before. It was fun. Everyone danced most of the night. We ate, talked, and hung out for a bit afterwards."

"Who's 'we'?" Cindy asked.

"Yes, 'we' included Judy," Margo stated, getting straight to the point. "The rest was me, Joel, Greyson, Paul, and a few people he knows from campus. Laura couldn't come. She's working on a paper."

"Did they bring me up?"

"Yeah, actually," Margo replied.

Cindy straightened, listening more carefully as her friend continued.

"Everyone was talking about the campus events, and Paul mentioned the art show. Then Judy said she was buying your diptych to hang in one of her family's hotels. She even said she wants to ask if you'd make more. It sounds like she's trying to support your art."

"She's so fake," Cindy muttered. "Why would she do that after weaseling in and taking Paul, when she's with Ryan? Were they making fun of it?"

"Not that I could tell."

"Come on; be honest. Are they a thing?"

"Maybe. They danced to a few songs. Maybe she dumped Ryan, but still wants your art. Who knows?"

"Anything else?"

"Nothing about you," Margo replied. "But Paul, Joel, and Greyson were talking about making it a weekly thing, rotating hangouts at each other's places. I don't know if I want people over that often, but those three are pretty set on sticking together. "

"Back to Judy," Cindy pressed. "Earlier, she called me 'doll.' Isn't that weird? She calls Ryan 'baby' and Paul 'sweetie', but me? 'Doll'? We can't stand each other. Why would she call me that?"

"Well," Margo began, her tone cautious but honest, "when it comes to Judy, she does have this habit of calling people pet names: 'sweetie,' 'honey,' 'baby,' that kind of thing. It can be annoying sometimes, but that's just Judy for you."

"I wish she'd go away and disappear. How can I work things out with Paul if she keeps sticking around?"

"Honestly, how can you work on things with him when it seems like he's already moved on? I mean, sorry to say this, but it kind of looks like he did. He invited her, not you. Maybe it's time to move on and focus on yourself instead of him and Judy."

Cindy tilted her head and stared down at the floor, saying nothing.

There was a pause on the line before Margo spoke again, her voice gentle but firm.

"Listen, Cin... I know you like the guy and all, but just take a step back and think about what I said. I know it hurts, but doesn't that say something?"

Cindy didn't respond, but her silence spoke volumes.

"I know it's hard," Margo continued, "but it's time to let him go. You thought the same thing was happening with Betsy, remember? Don't let it keep eating away at you. You've got other things going for you, *good* things. Focus on those instead."

"I am," Cindy said quietly, trying to reassure her friend, and maybe herself. Either way, she was done talking for the night. She didn't need to hear one more thing about moving on, like it was that easy for her, like it was for everyone else. She let out a tired sigh. "I'm getting sleepy. Thanks for the call. Let's talk more later, okay?"

"Okay, bye," Margo replied before the line clicked dead.

Cindy hung up the phone and went to bed. Yes, there were a few things to be grateful for. She was no longer an active target for Dan. School was going okay. Her place was clean. The art show was coming up. There were a few other good things on the horizon. Still, she wished she had some sense of where her future was headed. Would things finally begin to move in the right direction, even with the loss of Paul? Could she move on from him easier than she had with Betsy?

It was tempting to visit a seer or two, just to glimpse at what might be coming. What would they say? That he needed more space and would be back in two weeks? That he was the one who got away?

Ugh, Margo said to move on, she thought. *But why should Judy win? Does she even deserve to? What makes her so special that everything seems to go her way? What about me? I am a good person, or at least I try to be. I know I'm better than that tramp. So why is everything always so hard for me? What did I ever do to deserve this? What has she done to deserve everything she has? It's not fair! Why does life have to be like this? Why does mine have to be so hard?*

Frowning, Cindy closed her eyes and drifted off to sleep.

Saturday morning, Cindy got up early to take a short walk around the apartment complex. It felt good to get some fresh air and see children playing between the buildings. From the looks of it, one group was playing hide-and-seek, and another was deep in a game of freeze tag. Two girls were playing hopscotch on the sidewalk, their chalk-drawn squares were faint but still visible.

Cindy smiled, thinking how lucky they were: so innocent and untouched by the complexities of adulthood.

Enjoy that time, she thought. *As everyone used to tell me growing up, "Those are the best years of your life."*

She stared at the children a moment longer. Maybe, if she wished hard enough, she could turn back the clock and return to that kind of innocence, even if it meant repeating the same game over and over. The repetition wouldn't matter, not if every time she relived it, she would be happy and laughing louder than she ever would again.

Back in the apartment, Cindy went to the bedroom closet and pulled out her bike. A ride around the neighborhood sounded like the perfect way to kill time. She barely made it to the front door when she heard a knock.

Who could that be? Cindy wondered, leaning the bike against the living room wall and stepping toward the door.

Knock! Knock!

Cindy exhaled. The moment she opened it, a joyful shriek escaped her lips. Standing there was a familiar figure: her mother, with thinning gray hair pulled neatly back, wearing a soft blue dress that caught the breeze, and white shoes planted firmly on the pavement. Cindy's heart surged.

"Momma!" she cried, throwing her arms around the woman. Tears spilled freely as she clung to her. "I missed you, Momma!"

"I missed you too, my sweet angel," Mrs. Spearman murmured, hugging her daughter close and pressing a kiss to her cheek. "It's so good to see my baby again."

Cindy pulled back just enough to see her mother's face, then lit up with a grin.

"And you brought Jacob!" she said, hurrying to the backseat of the familiar green car.

She gently scooped the toddler into her arms, showering him with kisses and soft laughter.

Jacob, with his tousled blonde hair and curious brown eyes, so much like his mother's, wore a striped yellow-and-green shirt, blue shorts, white socks, and bright white shoes.

"Momma," he giggled, wrapping his tiny arms around her neck.

"Come in," Cindy said, welcoming them into the apartment.

Mrs. Spearman looked around, her eyes lighting up.

"Oh, it's even better than I remembered!" she exclaimed. "Darling, did you get new furniture? It's so beautiful! Has the article about the art show come out yet?"

"Thanks, Momma," Cindy replied, smiling. "Yeah, it's new and worth every penny. The article should be published in a few days."

She turned to Jacob, who was already walking toward the sofa.

"Jacob's coming along amazingly," Mrs. Spearman said, pride shining in her voice. "He knows some of his colors, letters, and numbers. I want to make sure he's more than ready by the time he starts school. I can't believe he'll be turning three this year! Time's flying by."

"And it's all thanks to you," Cindy said warmly. Her expression softened. "Have you heard back from the doctor's office yet?"

Mrs. Spearman sighed. "Yeah... There was a mix-up with the scheduling. I got a call reminding me about the surgery, but they had it set for the same day as the art show. I told them that it had to be a mistake, but..." She shook her head. "Unfortunately, they couldn't change it, at least not without pushing it back even further."

She paused, her voice tinged with disappointment. "I really wanted to be there for your show, baby. But since I can't, I figured Sunshine and I could spend some time with you before I head back to Tennessee."

Mrs. Spearman reached out, her hand resting lightly on Cindy's. "I hope it's okay if Sunshine stays with you a little earlier than we planned while I recover. I'm sorry for the sudden change; I didn't see it coming either."

Cindy gave a small nod, absorbing the news.

Mrs. Spearman's tone brightened. "Since we're here, though...how about we go out for breakfast? You pick the spot, somewhere you like."

"How about Tony's?" Cindy said thoughtfully. "They have a good breakfast buffet on the weekends. They have pancakes, crepes, eggs— the works."

"I love pancakes. Let's go there," Mrs. Spearman replied with excitement. "Oh, and I made extra copies of your important documents in case you need them: your birth certificate, a spare Social Security card, some pictures of me and Jacob, and copies of everything I mailed, in case anything happens."

She handed Cindy an envelope containing the documents.

"Thanks, Momma."

Later that morning, Cindy, Mrs. Spearman, and Jacob went to Tony's. The dining room walls were adorned with peaceful landscape paintings, giving the restaurant a cozy, welcoming feel. Jacob happily dug into a plate of pancakes, already cut into smaller pieces by his mother. Mrs. Spearman enjoyed her pancakes with a side of bacon and eggs, while Cindy chose French toast, served with fresh fruit and eggs. The morning felt calm and comforting, lifting Cindy's spirits more than she expected.

"Gertrude's daughter, Pamela, will be graduating from college in a few months," Mrs. Spearman said, taking a sip of coffee. "In Home Economics. I think Troy had a lot to do with it. They're getting married soon—in Scotland, of all places! Can you imagine? A wedding in another country. We're invited, but we'll have to cover our own expenses, so I'm not sure if it's affordable."

"I wish I could go," Cindy said, setting down her fork. "But with school, the cost, and everything going on...I just don't know."

"I think you should consider it," her mother replied, leaning forward a bit. "It's a once-in-a-lifetime opportunity. If you talk to your professors, they might be understanding. Things like this don't come around often."

"*Brmph,*" Jacob began, making engine sounds with his lips. "*Brmph, br—*"

"Oh my, not at the table, sweetheart," Mrs. Spearman said gently, placing a soft hand over his.

"I'll see what I can do," Cindy replied, looking at her mother. "They're easygoing most of the time, but strict when it comes to deadlines and expectations."

She took a sip of orange juice before continuing.

"They've already told me that after I get my bachelor's, it would be best to move straight into a master's program. Thing is, they don't usually accept students from their own undergrad program into the grad program. So, I'll need to start looking at other schools, probably sometime before my senior year."

"Is there a particular school you're interested in so far?"

"Well, I'm hoping to find one closer to home this time. I get homesick sometimes, and I think that would be better for everyone."

"Oh? Are things not going well at Camellia University?"

"Things are okay," Cindy admitted. "It's not quite what I expected, but maybe it'll lead to something better. Besides, it's a beautiful campus, and there are some important people there."

Mrs. Spearman raised an eyebrow. "How are things with this Ryan person? I still don't know how I feel about students calling teachers by their first name. That just doesn't sit right with me."

"I know, but he's the kind who'd be upset if we didn't," Cindy said with a small smile.

"Strange. Absolutely strange."

Cindy softly wiped away a smear of syrup from Jacob's cheek. She steadied a glass of milk in his small hands as he took a sip, though some spilled down the sides of his mouth. Quickly, she tilted the cup to catch the drips and reached for a napkin to wipe away the mess.

"Oh, have you looked into daycares around town for Jacob while you're at school?" Mrs. Spearman asked.

"Yes, Momma," Cindy replied. "I took care of that a while ago, but I'll need to drop by again soon since Jacob will be staying earlier than expected."

They finished their meals, and Mrs. Spearman drove them to the Happy Time Daycare Center. A member of the weekend staff greeted them but explained they'd need to return on Monday to speak with the director and that there might be an additional fee. Cindy agreed to come back, saying nothing about the morning painting class she would miss.

Mrs. Spearman and Jacob stayed at Cindy's apartment for the rest of the weekend. On Monday morning, after grabbing breakfast from a nearby fast-food place, Mrs. Spearman stayed a little longer to help Cindy speak with the daycare director about admitting Jacob that day.

Fortunately, the director was able to accommodate the early start, though it did come with extra fees.

Glancing at the clock, Cindy figured she still had plenty of time to make it to her second class, but when she and her mother tried to leave Jacob at the daycare, he burst into tears and threw a tantrum. The toddler clung to her leg, refusing to let go, and followed her with every step.

The daycare staff reassured her that he would be fine, but the guilt gnawed at Cindy. In the end, she decided to postpone leaving her son in their care until the next day. Then the teen had her mother drop them off near the art building before saying her goodbyes and returning home to Tennessee.

As Cindy and Jacob walked toward the art building, they unexpectedly ran into Paul coming from the opposite direction.

Jacob spread his arms like an airplane and began running in circles, nearly crashing into him. Cindy braced herself, expecting Paul to ignore them, but to her surprise, a smile spread across his face.

"Jacob, watch where you're going," Cindy called softly.

The boy paused, glanced back at his mother, then hurried over to her side.

"Hi," Paul said. "Who's the little guy?"

A flicker of adrenaline ran through Cindy. *He's talking to me again... and it's not something bad?*

"He's Jacob, but his grandmother calls him 'Sunshine,'" Cindy answered, her pulse quickening. "He's... he's going to be three in a few weeks."

Paul smiled and knelt to Jacob's level. "Nice to meet you, Jacob. My name is Paul. Since you're gonna be three soon, can you show me three fingers?"

Jacob squinted, then looked up at Cindy, who held up three fingers as a guide. He pointed with one finger, then looked back at Paul. With a gentle touch, Paul lifted two more of Jacob's fingers, counting aloud, "One, two, three."

"See, that's you," Paul said with a grin. "You're going to be three. Me? I'm this old." He held up both hands and quickly counted his fingers until he reached twenty. "I'll be twenty-one later, so I'll show the extra one then."

Jacob giggled.

"All right, now show me three."

Jacob held up two fingers. Gently, Paul lifted one more to make three.

"Great job," Paul beamed, then glanced at Cindy. "Jacob's pretty sharp. Is he your little brother?"

A faint wave of panic washed over Cindy. She hesitated.

Paul had made it clear that he'd never date someone with a kid. He'd already been angry with her before. Telling the truth now might be the one thing that made him shut her out completely. If anything could guarantee losing him for good...it was this.

"He's actually my neighbor's kid," Cindy lied. "He looks like he could be my little brother, doesn't he? I watch him every now and then."

"Why today? Was there some sort of emergency?"

"Yeah. His mom's in the hospital, and his dad has to work. They couldn't find anyone else. I'm just helping out. I figured if I were in their shoes, I'd want someone to do the same."

"I see... My grandfather was hospitalized when I was in high school. I know how hard that is."

Paul paused, then added warmly, "It's really admirable of you to step in like that."

"Thanks. Jacob's a good kid, and we have lots of fun together. Right now, we're working on his ABCs so he'll be ready when he starts school."

Paul's smile faltered for a moment.

"I was heading to my next class. Would you like to catch up later? I'll understand if you say no."

"S-sure, that would be great."

"Great. I'll give you a call soon. Later."

Wow! Wow! Wow! Paul wants to hang out again! Oh my gosh! Finally! I can't believe it. Things are really turning around!

Rejuvenated, Cindy covered her mouth with her hand to muffle a scream of excitement.

Chapter 16

Cindy decided to skip her printmaking class as well. The studio was filled with too many hazards: sharp tools, dangerous chemicals, and heavy equipment. She didn't want to risk Jacob getting into something the moment her attention slipped. It just wasn't worth it.

Instead, she explained the situation to her professor and promised to return next time. She also informed Ryan and apologized for her earlier absence.

With that handled, Cindy shifted her focus to more practical tasks. She took Jacob along to run last-minute errands: picking up groceries and a few toys, anything to help keep him occupied in the days ahead.

Wow, Cindy thought. *I can't believe things are actually going well today. It's like some switch flipped, and for the better. What a relief.*

After returning home that afternoon, Cindy sat on the living room floor, playing along with Jacob as he quietly stacked his wooden building blocks. Cindy built a small tower of her own nearby, enjoying the peace, until the phone rang.

Glancing over her shoulder now and then, she made her way into the kitchen to answer it.

"Hello?" she said, a thrum of nerves in her chest.

"Hey, Cindy, it's Margo," came the familiar voice. "Wanna go shopping this weekend? Marcie's is putting out their new inventory, and they've still got their usual sales going on. I already asked Laura and Clair. They're coming too."

"I'd love to, but I'm low on funds right now," Cindy replied. "Jacob's back in town, and I had to do a lot of last-minute shopping for him."

"Oh, I didn't know he was back! Could you maybe get someone to watch him and still come hang out?" Margo asked. "It's been a while since we've done any real shopping. You don't have to buy anything, but you might want to think about getting a new dress for the art show."

Margo's tone turned more serious.

"A lot of important people will be there, people who could make or break your career. So, I'd strongly suggest dressing to impress. If you change your mind, some of the dresses will be 50 to 60 percent off. This is probably your best chance."

"I'd like to, but... I don't know," Cindy said, hesitation creeping into her voice.

"Like I said, even if it's just to hang out," Margo replied, trying to stay upbeat. "C'mon, I miss shopping with you!"

Cindy sighed softly. "Okay, but Jacob'll have to come with us. Otherwise, I can't go."

There was a long, awkward pause at the other end of the line.

"So... no one can babysit him?" Margo finally asked.

"I'd drop him off at the daycare," Cindy said, "but they charge extra on weekends, and I really need to save every penny right now. I had to spend a ton when I stayed at the hotel, and it pretty much wiped me out. My momma gave me a little money, but that's for Jacob. I'm trying not to ask for more unless I have to. She's struggling herself, so.... "

Cindy paused, then added with a hopeful lift in her voice. "Oh, guess what. Paul changed his mind about me. I think he wants to start hanging out again.

Maybe things didn't work out with Judy after all. This could be my second chance. I'm not gonna ruin it this time."

"That's neat and all," Margo said slowly, "but... does he know about Jacob?"

"Sort of. We ran into him earlier, and weirdly, things went well. Only, I panicked and told him Jacob was my neighbor." Cindy sighed. "I know that wasn't right, but I just needed to say something in the moment. Once Jacob goes back home with Momma again, things'll be back on track."

"How are you going to explain it if Jacob slips up and calls you 'Mommy' or something?" Margo asked.

"I don't know. I wasn't thinking that far ahead," Cindy admitted. "I guess I could say he feels close to me, like a second mom. Or maybe we're playing some new game called 'Mommy.' Or I could say he misses his real mom and is talking about her."

"That makes no sense," Margo snapped. "Who would fall for something that ridiculous?"

"I could always teach Jacob to call me by my first name."

"What? That'll never work. He's already used to calling you 'Mommy,' and kids his age don't do that unless it's the truth. You're probably better off coming clean and taking your chances. I mean, if Paul talked to you after being mad before, chances are he'll get over this too."

"Yeah, but look at how bad it got the first time he was mad," Cindy told her. "If he finds out Jacob's my son, that's another strike against me. I *will* tell him... I just need time. Wanting to tell the truth doesn't make me a bad person... or a bad mother, right?"

From the living room floor, Jacob stood up, stretched his arms out like airplane wings, and made engine sounds. *"Brmph, brmph, brmph!"*

"Jacob, stop," Cindy snapped, her tone sharper than she intended. She sighed. "Sorry... I hate it when he does that."

"Calm down," Margo said calmly. "He's just a little boy. It'll be alright."

"I'm just confused," Cindy murmured. "Why wouldn't Paul want to date someone with a kid but still get along with one? He said it wouldn't be fair to him or his own kid, since he wasn't there for his. But... why does he have to think that way?"

"I don't know," Margo responded. "Only he can answer that."

"You don't think there's more to it than what he told me, do you?"

"I wish I knew the answer to that," Margo replied thoughtfully. "But doesn't that mean you're both hiding things from each other, in a way? If Paul *is* hiding something... what would it be?"

"I don't know," Cindy said quietly. "But it makes me want to be careful. I wish I knew what happened. What was so bad that his ex doesn't want him in their lives?"

"Yeah... It's all very bizarre," Margo sighed.

"Well, maybe one day we'll find out what really happened. He said he'd call soon, so maybe he'll hint at something."

"Maybe..."

"Well, I'm gonna go. I'll see you back on campus. Bye."

"Later!"

Cindy waited eagerly for Paul's phone call late into the night, but it never came.

The next day, Jacob had another meltdown at the daycare when Cindy tried to leave. This time, though, she had no choice. She slipped out the door, heart heavy, hoping he'd eventually adjust to being left with someone who wasn't her or Mrs. Spearman.

The day passed quietly, without any surprises. Cindy picked Jacob up from daycare, then brought him to the nearby park, where he ran and spun in the grass. Later, she fed him macaroni and cheese at home, wiped his sticky fingers, and settled him on the couch for a quick nap.

She had just begun to doze off beside him when the phone rang.

Groggy, she walked into the kitchen, picked up the phone, and answered, "Hello?"

A familiar voice on the other end made her heart jump.

"Hey, Cindy. It's me, Paul. How's it going?"

Her pulse quickened. She sat up a little straighter.

"Great," she replied, trying not to sound too eager. "Just resting a bit after prepping some things for the art show."

"Cool, I remember you mentioned that. Has the article come out yet? I've been keeping an eye out, but I haven't seen anything about you or the show so far."

"It should be in the next edition," Cindy said. "Mrs. Everett thought releasing it a week before the reception would help boost the turnout. Exciting, huh?"

"Yeah, I've been doing a lot of networking around campus," Paul responded. "The feedback's been solid.

A lot of people said they're planning to come. I think the reception's going to be a big success."

She could practically see him grinning through the phone, maybe even giving that confident wink he always did when he was pleased with himself.

"Really?" Cindy perked up. "Sounds like it might be packed. The Crimson Gallery isn't exactly huge, but if that many people show, it could be a big chance to get my work and my name out there."

"It's all part of business," Paul said smoothly. "Networking. There are actually a lot of people on campus who really value the arts. More than I expected, to be honest."

Cindy smiled, warmed by both his support and hearing his voice on the phone.

"So," she ventured, her tone softening, "would you want to come over sometime? I still feel bad about what happened last time. I'd really like to make it up to you."

There was a pause.

"I'd like to," he said, "but I can't. I've got some catching up to do. A few of my classes haven't exactly been smooth sailing."

"Oh," Cindy said, trying to keep the disappointment from creeping into her voice. "Well... maybe some other time then. I almost flunked my Spanish test, but it worked out. I can't afford to fail. My GPA has to stay up if I want to keep my scholarship."

"I dig it," Paul said. "I used to be at the top of my game in high school, but now that I'm in college, it's like everything nosedived, especially at the start of the semester. That's on me though, too much tripping and too much partying. I've come close to overdosing more than once, waking up in places I don't even remember getting to. I missed classes and walked into the wrong ones. It was a total mess."

He let out a soft, self-deprecating chuckle. "I wasn't always like this. But... I've got no one to blame but myself. Dumb, huh?"

"No," Cindy replied. "It happens. I bet there are plenty of students, maybe even professors, doing the same thing. Moderation, remember? Though not the kind we had last time. I think we took that a little too far... but it *was* fun while it lasted."

Paul chuckled lightly. "I got into so much trouble that week. We definitely need to rethink what 'moderation' really means."

Cindy hesitated, then asked carefully, "Since the fallout with Dan... have you gone back to get more acid or anything?"

"No," Paul said, then added without pause, "but I've been able to get a few things from Judy. Hers are just as good as Dan's, maybe better."

Judy... Cindy paused, her expression dimming. *So, she's still around? A supplier, too? That explains a few things...*

"We could hang out and drop some acid," Paul offered casually, "but only when you're not babysitting. I don't believe in tripping around kids."

"It'll be fine," Cindy said, brushing it off. "Jacob won't know the difference. We'll be okay."

"I'll never agree to that," Paul said firmly. "He needs to be home with his folks."

"Okay, okay, I get it. You don't have to sound like Ryan."

"Who?"

"Ryan," she sighed. "One of my professors. He's also my advisor and kind of oversees my scholarship. I think the department paired us because we both paint and draw, but he really needs to chill sometimes."

"How are his classes?"

"They're okay. A little boring. He grades hard; getting an A in his class is almost impossible. He says 'nobody's perfect' and hands out Bs at the top. That's mostly what I get. It's not fair, but I'm stuck with him."

"Is there someone else you could take the class with instead?" Paul asked.

"Yeah, but her class fills up way too fast," Cindy replied. "And honestly, the quality of work from her students isn't that great. I've seen some of it...It looks pretty bad for college-level."

"Sounds like Ryan's your best bet, then."

"Yeah, but if he's calling me his best student, shouldn't I be getting an A instead of a B?"

"Sure," Paul said. "But that's just my opinion. I'm not the one grading the assignments. Like they say, sometimes we don't always get what we deserve."

"Funny you should say that. Let me tell you something that happened last year. One of the professors in the English department was sleeping with some of his students, and I guess he was grading them based on how good they were in bed. One girl got an A and the other got a C. The one who got a C got upset and reported him; that's how everyone found out about what went on."

"That was a nightmare waiting to happen," Paul said. "And there's a lot more going on behind closed doors on campus that would probably shock you. But honestly? Nothing surprises me anymore, you dig? Just try not to get caught up in the worst of it... If it can be helped."

There was a pause, then: "Hey, Cin, I've gotta go. I'll be at the cafeteria for lunch on Monday. I'll meet you there during your break, like we used to, okay?"

"S-sure. Sounds great! I'll be there!"

"Cool. Later, Cin."

The call ended with a soft click. Cindy slowly set the phone down and returned to the couch, curling beside Jacob, the silence wrapping around her like a blanket, both comforting and heavy.

Saturday morning arrived swiftly. Cindy caught the early bus with Jacob, heading to the grocery store to restock food for the week. The trip demanded constant juggling of grocery bags in one arm while trying to keep a restless toddler in check. Jacob darted toward shelves and displays, wide-eyed with curiosity, and his little hands eager to touch everything in sight.

"Stay close, Jacob," she reminded him for the fifth time. "Don't go wandering off now."

After checking out, they shared a banana while waiting at the bus stop. The ride home was quiet, and once back at the apartment, Cindy unpacked the groceries and tucked them into the refrigerator. Then, closing the fridge door, she paused.

Her hands trembled. The craving slammed into her — acid, weed, ludes, bennies —anything to take the edge off.

Shoot, Paul... why couldn't we meet today instead? Damn, I need a trip. A wild one. And honestly? Some good sex wouldn't hurt either...

True to her word, Margo arrived on time to pick up Cindy and Jacob, along with Clair and Laura, for a shopping trip to Marcie's at the indoor mall. Marcie's was Margo's favorite spot for everything: dresses, perfumes, hats, jewelry, and even shoes. Most of it was far too expensive, except during sales. On a lucky day, prices might drop 30 percent. Today was rare. Items were marked 50 to 60 percent off.

The women and child strolled through the clothing section, browsing rows of plaid and solid flare pants, sharp blazers, ruffled lace blouses, and swingy skirts. Everything shimmered beneath the store lights: beautiful, stylish, and entirely out of Cindy's price range.

She preferred thrift stores, where second-hand donations sold for a fraction of retail. Most of her wardrobe came from places like that. Still, if her friends loved Marcie's, the least she could do was pretend to enjoy it too, even if she'd never bought a single item from the store.

Forcing a smile, Cindy grabbed an armful of blouses just like the others, blending in with the group as they moved deeper into the racks.

"I'm heading to the fitting room," Margo said, carrying several outfits draped over her arm. Clair followed behind with her own selections.

Cindy was about to try on a few items herself. Suddenly, Jacob darted off, laughing as he ran up and down the aisles between the clothing racks.

Oh my gosh, Cindy thought, letting out a breath of quiet frustration. *I wish he would stop misbehaving for just one gosh darn minute.*

Jacob extended his arms out like airplane wings, fingers splayed wide, zooming between displays as he made engine sounds. *"Brmph, brmph, brmph!"*

"Stop, Jacob," Cindy called, trying to adjust the clothes in her arms without dropping them. She marched toward him and grabbed his arm. "You can't run around in the store, Jacob. Do you understand?"

Jacob's smile crumpled. He began to cry, the joy gone from his face. Cindy, jaw tight, led him toward the fitting rooms, clothes still clutched awkwardly in one hand.

"Sit here and be still. I mean it." Cindy warned him, guiding the tearful child to the small bench inside the dressing room. She dropped the clothes next to him and began trying on the outfits one by one.

Outside, her friends' voices echoed through the fitting area, light laughter, playful chatter, and cheerful compliments.

It's not fair, she thought, her eyes narrowing as a wave of anger surged inside her. *No matter how hard I work, I still have to work twice as hard just to get a little piece of what they take for granted. I should be able to afford anything I want! I deserve it. And they know it, too. Sometimes I wonder if they bring me here just to remind me how broke I am...Well, maybe not Laura. But she never speaks up. She just goes along with everything...*

She changed into another outfit and turned toward the mirror. The fabric hugged her figure just right.

This would be perfect for a date with Paul, she thought. *I can just see that look in his eyes if he saw me in this. Maybe then he'd quit chasing those floozies.*

Behind her, Jacob had stopped crying. He sat curled on the bench, thumb in his mouth, his quiet sniffles the only sound in the room.

Cindy tried on a few more outfits before stepping out of the dressing room. She handed the rejected clothes back to the attendant, then reached for Jacob's small hand. His fingers curled around hers automatically, but the warmth between them felt faint and distant.

As they made their way back toward the clothing section, Cindy spotted her friends gathered near a display of blouses, chatting casually.

All around the store, other families browsed with ease, children giggling, parents smiling, the air light with patience and routine affection. Cindy watched them for a moment. They looked so natural, so connected, like they belonged together.

She glanced down at Jacob. His eyes were still puffy from crying, his expression unsure, searching hers for some invisible cue.

Why is this so hard for me? Cindy wondered. *Why can't I connect with him the way other mothers connect with their kids? What's wrong with me? Why does it always feel like I'm failing, no matter how much I try?*

"I like the green top better," Clair was saying to Margo, holding the blouse against her chest. "See? Doesn't it complement my hair color?"

"It does," Margo replied, thoughtfully, "but the orange brought out your figure more."

Laura glanced over at Cindy, her eyes soft. She didn't say anything, but her expression carried an unspoken question: *Are you okay? I hope so.*

"Did you find a dress for the art show yet?" Margo asked, turning to Cindy with a cheerful curiosity.

"There was one I really liked," Cindy admitted, managing a half-smile, "but it was too expensive."

"Get it anyway," Margo insisted. "Especially if it makes you feel confident. Nights like this are about making an impression. You've got that article coming out in the paper, and who knows? Maybe even TV coverage!"

"The dress she wore at her first show looked nice too," Laura added lightly, a quiet nudge toward practicality.

"That outfit's fine for a regular day," Margo said, "but not for a night like this. You've got to turn heads. Go get the dress. I want to see how it fits."

Cindy faltered only a moment before returning to the dressing room. She retrieved the dress from the attendant and came back, pressing it against her body for the others to see.

"That one's much better than her old outfit," Margo declared. "It pays to be beautiful, so why not look it on a special night?"

If only I had time to put it on layaway, Cindy thought, falling even more in love with the dress now that Margo had praised it. *Maybe I can buy it, keep the tags on, and return it later with the receipt... If Margo thinks it's great, other important people will too. I can always make the money back doing sketches at the student union. It worked before. Also, if I can sell a few more pieces, that'll help cover the rest.*

"Okay, I'll get it," she told the others at last. "It doesn't hurt to splurge for something this important. I mean, it could really help my career. It's not like I buy expensive things every day."

Margo and Clair responded with bright approval, their attention already drifting toward another section of the store.

Laura lingered, her voice low. "Cin... are you sure you can afford a dress from here? Other stores at the mall might have something just as nice for less."

I'm not buying a cheap dress in front of everyone, Cindy bristled silently. *I already look pathetic enough. I should still have a little money left... I think. I hope.*

She glanced at the price tag again. Buying the dress would take more than half of the money her mother had given to help cover expenses while Jacob visited. She could afford it, but barely. It would stretch things painfully thin.

"I can afford it, no sweat," Cindy said aloud, flashing a smile she didn't quite feel.

And with that, she decided.

The teen held tightly to the one dress while her friends continued browsing, piling on more outfits with carefree ease.

"Next weekend, let's all hang out at Greyson's," Margo said, leading the way toward the checkout counter. "He's throwing a small get-together, and Joel and I are definitely going."

"Where does he live?" Clair asked.

"Across the hall from Paul," Margo replied. "Directly across. Greyson's a veteran, and his dad's a Four-Star General in the Marine Corps. The family's also big in real estate."

"I haven't met him yet," Clair said. "Is he handsome?"

"If you like muscular men with tiny heads," Margo said with a smirk, "he's a catch."

The women burst into laughter as they made their way toward the registers.

Cindy suddenly stopped.

Just a few feet ahead stood Mrs. Everett, flanked by two well-dressed teenage girls. Reflexively, Cindy put on her best smile and gave a small wave as they approached.

"Hi, Mrs. Everett," Cindy said brightly.

"Cindy! Oh, hello!" Mrs. Everett exclaimed, her smile wide and polished. "Fancy running into one of the university's best and brightest! Cindy, this is my daughter, Annabelle, and her best friend, Brooke. And who is this handsome young man? Is he your little brother?"

Cindy's smile flickered. Her eyes darted to Jacob, who had somehow grabbed a white blouse from a nearby rack and was waving it proudly in the air.

Where did he get that from? Cindy's mind raced.

"Yes, he is," Cindy said with a quick laugh. "His name's Jacob, and I'm babysitting him today."

"Oh!" Mrs. Everett beamed, placing a hand delicately over her chest. "That reminds me so much of my little sister Jan and me. We'd go shopping with friends on the weekends, too — though Jan was a little older than Jacob."

She glanced down at the toddler with light amusement. "Where are you two off to now?"

"We were just leaving," Cindy replied, nodding toward the checkout line where her friends waited. "It was nice running into you. I'm really looking forward to reading the article and seeing everyone at the show."

"A follow-up article would be perfect," Mrs. Everett mused, her voice bright with inspiration.

"*Students and the Siblings Who Inspire Them.* I think you and Jacob would be perfect! I'll jot the idea down as soon as I'm able. It was so nice meeting little Jacob and seeing you again, Cindy."

Cindy grinned tightly, her heart pounding.

"You too," she replied.

She walked with Jacob to the counter, gripping the dress like a lifeline. Reaching into her purse, she pulled out the envelope of money her mother had set aside for emergencies. As far as Cindy was concerned, this counted as an investment in her future.

At the register, the salesclerk grinned and glanced at Jacob.

"Would you like to include that item as well, ma'am?" the clerk asked, nodding to the white blouse in Jacob's small hands.

"That?" Cindy blinked. "No, I planned on returning it." She reached for it gently. "Jacob, we have to give it back."

"No," Jacob said, clutching it tighter.

"Jacob," she said again, trying to keep her voice steady. "Give me the blouse."

"No!" he shouted, louder now.

A few heads turned. Cindy's face flushed. She tugged the blouse gently but firmly, and Jacob erupted.

His small body flailed, and tears streamed. His wails rose in piercing waves that echoed across the store like a siren. The clerk's polite smile froze, and someone in the line sighed audibly.

Cindy stared at the dress on the counter as Jacob melted down beside her, and for a moment, she wasn't sure what felt more fragile: her wallet, her reputation, or her resolve.

"Oh my gosh," Margo muttered, placing a hand to her temple and glancing away, clearly embarrassed.

"I'm so sorry," Cindy said quickly, her cheeks burning as her arms tightened protectively around Jacob.

"Cindy, maybe you should take your son back to the car," Clair suggested softly, but not softly enough.

Cindy felt the world stop.

Out of the corner of her eye, Cindy saw it, Mrs. Everett's eyes widening, her mouth parting in surprise.

Oh no.

Cindy froze. The lie: Jacob as her little brother, hung in the air like glass, now shattered.

Mrs. Everett cleared her throat briskly and turned to her daughter and her friend.

"Why don't we look at the outfits on the other side of the store?" Mrs. Everett said, her tone clipped but polite.

Cindy couldn't speak, and for a moment, she couldn't move. Silently, she paid for the dress, keeping her eyes down. She followed her friends back to the car, Jacob still crying in her arms, and her thoughts louder than his wails.

Chapter 17

Sunday arrived heavy with tension. Cindy's frustration simmered beneath the surface as she tried calling her mother all morning, but the phone only rang, unanswered, cold, and relentless.

Jacob's cries pierced the quiet again with another meltdown fueled by missing his grandmother. The wails echoed through the apartment, unbearable.

Unable to take it, Cindy retreated to the bedroom, crawled under the covers, and pressed a pillow over her ears, desperate for silence.

I can't take this anymore, she thought, the pressure mounting. *Why won't he stop crying? He never does this when Momma's around.* A bitter pang hit her chest. *I want to be with her too, but she keeps ignoring my calls! I'm about to lose my mind!*

Suddenly, the phone rang. *Finally. Surgery or no surgery, she needs to take him back to Tennessee.* Cindy scrambled out of bed and hurried to the phone, tears streaming down her cheeks.

"Thank God," she sobbed. "Momma, I need you to come and get Jacob. He won't stop crying, and I just... I can't do this anymore."

But the voice on the other end wasn't her mother's.

"Cindy?" Paul's voice came, calm but concerned. "This isn't your mother. It's Paul. Is everything okay?"

"I'm sorry," Cindy wept, her voice breaking. "No, it's not. Jacob won't stop crying, and I'm just so overwhelmed right now. I don't know what to do."

"Hold tight," Paul stated gently. "I'll come over and help as best I can."

Her heart pounding, Cindy waited. When Paul arrived, Cindy rushed outside and let herself be held for a moment before leading him inside. By then, Jacob's tear-streaked face no longer shed tears; only soft, mournful moans remained.

"Hey there, little guy," Paul said, kneeling beside the toddler. "Not having a good day, huh? Uncle Paulie's here." He wrapped Jacob in a gentle embrace, patting his back with calm reassurance.

"Granny," Jacob whispered, voice trembling with sorrow and exhaustion.

"Poor kid," Paul murmured, still holding him. Then, turning to Cindy, he added, "He'll be fine. Sounds like he's just missing his grandmother."

Paul refocused on Jacob, whispering, "There, there. I'm sure she'll come to see you soon."

Cindy sank into a nearby chair, pressing her fingertips hard against her temple. Her adrenaline surged.

He's going to find out now, I bet. I'm doomed. Everything always falls apart when someone shows up to ruin my life. Why does Jacob always have to ruin things for me? First, the store with Mrs. Everett, and now this, with Paul! Thanks a lot. Why, Momma? Why couldn't you keep him with you in Tennessee?

Jacob's moans slowly softened as Paul whispered soothing words. The sound faded, and the boy's eyelids grew heavy. Carefully, Paul carried him to the couch and settled down, letting Jacob lean against him.

"Thanks for coming," Cindy said quietly. "You didn't have to, but you did..."

"It's no problem," Paul replied, his voice kind. "I was taking a break and wanted to check in. I'm glad I did."

Jacob, now calm, wrapped his small arm around Paul and drifted off to sleep.

"My best friend from high school came from a big family," Paul shared, voice low but steady. "I was an only child and always wished I had a brother or sister. So, I filled that space with cousins and friends."

He glanced down at Jacob and beamed.

"Look at that," Paul whispered. "He's out cold... How are his folks doing? Are things getting any better for his mother?"

"They're fine, thanks," Cindy answered. "I wish I had a magic wand to calm him like you did. Maybe you should be the babysitter instead."

Paul chuckled softly. "Nah, don't be so hard on yourself. You're doing great. Remember, kids have their good days and bad days."

Cindy's eyes lit up.

"Thanks, Paul," she said softly. "So... I know we've talked about the show before, but you're coming, right?"

"Yeah. Don't you want me to come?"

"Y-yeah... I do. It's just—" her voice wavered, "I've been disappointed so many times before and... well, I'm just happy to have someone I can rely on. I mean, outside of my momma and Laura."

Paul nodded, his gaze steady but unreadable.

Cindy bit her bottom lip, watching him carefully. *If he's still coming around, that means he cares... right? He's forgiven me?*

Paul glanced around the room.

"So, this is home sweet home," he said. The words were casual, but not unkind.

Cindy winced.

"It's embarrassing, I know," she muttered. "But, it's mine. For now, anyway. It's not much, but I worked hard for it. For all of this. Before I make it big, hopefully."

"There's nothing to be embarrassed about," Paul said. "Especially when it comes to the rewards of hard work. I'm confident you'll make it big, however you want to. You're already halfway there."

His tone was kind, but there was a shift. Something quiet and final threaded through his words.

"Since things have calmed down, I'm gonna head out," he added. "I've got a lot to do back home."

He gently transferred Jacob into Cindy's arms. She held the child close, but her eyes followed Paul, aching for something more. After laying Jacob down on the couch, she turned back toward the door, watching him move toward it.

"Are we still meeting for lunch on Monday?" she asked, trying to steady her voice. It still came out more needy than she wanted.

"Sure," he said, turning slightly. "Same time."

Cindy stepped closer and reached for Paul's hand. Her hand closed around his as she asked, hesitant but hopeful, "Does this mean...?"

Paul turned to fully face her. He paused, breathing in slowly before letting out a long, quiet sigh.

"Just as friends," he said gently, but firmly. "I know what you're hoping for, Cindy. I get it. But there's no part of that in me left to give. I'm sorry."

Her eyes brimming with tears, Cindy choked back a sob. She wanted to ask why. Was it because of Dan? Judy? Her being poor? Her not being good enough?

Then the harder question surfaced: *What was the point of asking if he didn't see her as being more?* He didn't want it. Not with her.

Something lingered in Paul's eyes, pain, maybe even regret, but vanished before she could make sense of it. His arm lifted slightly, as if on instinct, wanting to reach for her, but he stopped himself. His gaze dropped. Eyes closed, jaw tightening, he swallowed hard.

Without another word, he turned and walked out the door, shutting it softly behind him.

Bye, Paul, Cindy thought. *I wish we could be more, but if you only want to be friends, I'll take it. I can still have my own feelings, can't I? I can still love you, even if it's only as a friend... Wait...I love my friend? I guess I do...I'll do my best to think of you that way. Just a friend. Thanks for helping me with Jacob, and for supporting me... in your own way.*

Monday arrived with the buzz of undergraduates in motion: framing their pieces, brushing final details, and carrying canvases into the Crimson Gallery. Cindy worked alongside them, assisting where needed, but her eyes kept drifting toward the front entrance of the art and business school.

Where's the paper? Every Monday, like clockwork, the campus newspaper appeared by midmorning, but today, the rack was empty.

She brushed the thought aside, though a tight knot remained in her stomach. Her tears from the weekend had dried, but the heaviness lingered. And yet, she still chose to meet Paul for lunch at the cafeteria, as planned.

Part of her wanted to throw Paul and everything they'd ever been away for good. However, another part still clung to him, unwilling to let go just yet. She told herself she would walk away eventually on her own terms, in her own time. For now, she stayed close, not just to say goodbye slowly, but, if she was being honest, in some quiet, almost imperceptible way, to keep an eye on him too.

"Seen any newspapers around campus?" Cindy asked as Paul walked beside her toward the cafeteria.

"No," he replied, clearing his throat. "Maybe there'll be some at the union. They usually have stacks."

The walk was quieter and heavier. Cindy kept her arms close to her sides, resisting the urge to reach for his hand.

"Thanks again for yesterday," Cindy said tenderly. "For a moment, I thought I was going to lose my mind. I guess I'm just... not great with kids."

"Then why babysit?" Paul asked, not unkindly, just curious.

Cindy shrugged, offering a half-smile. "Maybe to be like you one day."

Paul laughed. "Be careful what you wish for; it might come true. But seriously, you're doing a great job, so keep at it. Got any plans for the summer?"

"Other than trying to stay sane? Not really," she replied. "Maybe I'll take a few more classes, just to get them over with. What about you?"

"Yeah, I'll be turning twenty-one," he said with a smirk. "I'm thinking about having a small get-together with friends. I also want to do a little traveling, maybe hit the beach. I heard the night bike rides down there were amazing. Ever thought about doing something like that?"

"I might. It sounds like fun."

"It does. Tell you what, let's see if we can get a group together one night and give it a go. That way, it'll be safer."

"Neat. Count me in."

"I saw a few people carrying canvases to the other side of the art building. Need help with anything? I can pitch in, outside of class, I mean."

"No thanks," Cindy said, blushing. "Everyone's still setting up, but I already hung my pieces. Now I'm just helping where I can. There's been a lot of buzz, thanks to you."

"I can't take all the credit," Paul replied, flashing a grin. "Just networking with the right folks. I'm still the new guy on campus, trying to figure out who's who and where I fit. But your art? It speaks for itself. That's what's getting people talking."

They reached the entrance of the student union. Paul stepped ahead and pulled the door open for her. Cindy offered a quick smile, doing her best to hide how much the small gesture warmed her.

Paul squinted his eyes, touched his throat, and cleared it.

"Did you catch up on your assignments yet?" Cindy asked.

"Almost. I've still got work to do for English Comp. I've been trying to dig myself out of a hole. Thank goodness I woke up before it got any worse. It's a pain trying to bring my grades up."

"What do you have in them?"

Paul winced. "I don't want to say."

"Tell me."

He hesitated. "Two Fs... four Ds."

Cindy's mouth dropped open. *Wait —what?* His grades are *that* bad? *Is he... slow or something*?

"What?" she blurted. "How'd they get that bad? I mean, I party sometimes too, but mine never tanked like that."

"I know," Paul exhaled. "Things just got out of control. I didn't do the work. I knew I should've, but I chose to party, trip, or just zone out. My head wasn't in the right place. I'm trying now, though. Believe it or not, they were *all* Fs at one point."

"Oh my gosh," Cindy said, her eyes wide. "I had no idea. If I'd known, I would've tried to help."

"I appreciate it," he said quietly. "But I made the mess, so it's on me to fix it. I knew better; I just didn't care enough back then. Sometimes... I still don't. But another part of me wants to now. I still have time to turn things around before the semester ends."

Paul shook his head and let out a dry chuckle.

"What a way to start college, huh?" he groaned. "I've been trying to buckle down more. Greyson's been on my case about rehab. He checks in on me a lot since we're friends, neighbors, and go to the same school."

"All that matters are the final grades," Cindy said. "If you can pull a C, it'll look way better than a D or an F."

They moved through the cafeteria line, grabbed their trays of food, and sat down. For a moment, it almost felt like old times: laughing, swapping stories, and simply being together. However, Cindy couldn't help noticing what was missing: the flirting, the light touches, and the little sparks that used to dance between them.

Paul cleared his throat again.

"Sorry," he muttered. "My throat's been acting up lately. It usually does this right before I get sick. I'm gonna stop by the store after class and grab some medicine. Hopefully, it'll help."

"If you gargle with saltwater, it might soothe it," Cindy offered. "Or try garlic. Even tea could help a little."

"Thanks, I'll keep those in mind," Paul told her with a small nod.

They finished their meals and wandered the student union in search of the latest edition of the school paper. Yet, all they found were back issues or empty racks. When they asked around, no one had seen the new edition. Eventually, they gave up and headed off to their separate classes. There was no paper that day.

The next morning, the paper finally appeared. However, the feature wasn't what Cindy had hoped for. Instead of the article about her, the spotlight shone on the female lead in the school play.

Cindy gasped. She wanted to call Mrs. Everett to apologize and plead for the promised feature in the next edition.

Still, deep down, she already knew. It was too late. The damage was done.

Ryan and a few other students were still working with the Crimson Art Gallery coordinator, arranging artwork throughout the space. Others who had finished were either starting new pieces or were scattered throughout the building, chatting, lounging, and laughing.

"Hey, Cindy," one of the art students called. "Wanna help in the gallery?"

Cindy ignored her, and the next few students too. Instead of talking, she made her way to the pile of recycled canvases. She picked one up, then another, repurposing them without care. Inside, though, she was on fire.

I should take every last one of these and smash them. Every. Last. One. No one better say a word about that stupid article. I hate this place. No article about me? Really? The theater department gets a front-page spread, and no one even cares about them! Who's Gwen Stevens anyway? A nobody. Her name doesn't mean anything!

The teen sat hidden behind the canvases in a quiet corner, out of sight. Tears spilled, but she stayed silent. There was no way she was going to cry in front of anyone. She would not give them the satisfaction of asking why. If anyone wanted to know what happened, they'd have to figure it out themselves. Maybe they'd forget the article was ever supposed to happen at all.

Taking a deep breath, Cindy tossed her head back and fanned her face, hoping for a little extra air. Then, a familiar scent caught her attention.

Her gaze dropped to the ground as the sound of footsteps crept closer. She spotted a pair of pink shoes approaching, then stopping just beyond the canvas, like some creepy, unwanted visitor who *wanted* to be seen. Squinting, she reluctantly peeked around the other side of the canvas. Judy stood there, casually grinning at her. *When did she get here? Doesn't she have better things to do?*

"Knock, knock," Judy giggled. "I knew someone was hiding back there."

Without asking, Judy grabbed a nearby barstool and slid it beside Cindy's, settling in as if she too were hiding from the world.

"I heard you were looking for me, Cindy," Judy sighed, her tone dreamy, like some strange thirst had just been satisfied. "I take it you changed your mind about my little offer?"

Shoot, Cindy thought. *I forgot I told Bonnie that I was looking for her.*

"Or would a dollar amount make it easier to say yes?" Judy asked, her voice smooth, almost playful.

Why now? Cindy cringed. I wasn't even thinking about her or any dumb deal until she showed up. Having extra money would be nice, especially after spending so much on my new dress... but an acid tablet, mesc, or even a bennie sounds even better.

Judy tilted her head, studying her.

"You look upset," she said thoughtfully. "I hope it's not about the art show. Aww, cheer up. You'll do fine. It's probably just nerves; I'm sure of it. If anything goes wrong, mistakes can always be managed."

"It's not that," Cindy said with a sniffle. "In fact, it's nothing... So, yeah, I came up with a price for the diptych, but since it's in the show, I can't give it to you until the show ends. Just so we're on the same page."

Judy nodded slowly after agreeing to Cindy's price for the diptych.

"Of course. I can wait." Judy said. "I'll pay as soon as I receive it. It'll be worth it when it's mine... Do you have any family coming to the reception? It's such an important night for all the art students."

"I wish they could," Cindy replied. "But they all live back home in Tennessee. They won't be able to make it."

"Aww, I'm really sorry to hear that," Judy said, her head still tilted slightly too long. "My family's out of town too, in Montana. That's why I joined my sorority. They're like my second family now. We'll all be there to support my honey's friend however we can."

"Excuse me?" Cindy asked, her voice a little sharper now.

"My honey, silly," Judy giggled. "Paul. You two are still friends, right?"

"We are," Cindy shot back, her smile tight. "Seems like we have a lot in common as Paul's friends, huh? I'm looking forward to seeing him, and every one of his friends, at the show."

A sliver of tension passed between them—thin, sharp, and silent.

"I brought you a little something," Judy added, shifting her tone with practiced ease. "Just a tiny gift. A good luck charm, maybe. With success comes small rewards, after all… and it's good to support one another in every way possible." Her voice was light, but her gaze lingered just a second too long. "I'll see you at the show. Or maybe sooner. Who knows?"

With that, Judy slid off the barstool and walked away, her steps light.

Cindy exhaled slowly, relief pooling in her chest, until she noticed the barstool.

There, resting on the seat, was a small bag.

White tablets?

Chapter 18

Later that evening, the police were called to Cindy's apartment. The window was shattered, the furniture overturned, and Jacob was found crying uncontrollably on the floor.

Residents gathered outside, forced to witness the teen's arrest as she thrashed and screamed, her body jerking with erratic, wild movements. It was like watching someone possessed: detached, unraveling, and slipping into something far beyond reason, right before their eyes. It took several officers to restrain her.

Mr. Tanner, the Grigsbys, and others stood in stunned silence as Cindy was dragged out, still kicking and screaming. Her tearful son was taken away in a separate vehicle.

It wasn't until a few days later that Cindy fully came to her senses. She awoke in a jail cell, dazed, shocked, and unable to comprehend how she got there or where her son was. That's when an officer explained the situation. She had been arrested for child endangerment, drug possession, disturbing the peace, and several other charges. She would be held for another 24 hours and evaluated by a psychiatrist to determine her next steps.

Out of everything the officer listed, only one thing truly mattered: Jacob had been taken away.

"No! Jacob! Not my baby boy!" Cindy's voice cracked as she covered her mouth, her body folding in on itself as she collapsed onto the bench. She began to sob, rocking back and forth. "He'll be so scared without me or his grandmother. I need to see my baby boy.

Please! Oh God, no. I'm sorry! Please give me my baby back! Please!"

No response came to her pleas, as if she were damned, and unwittingly, so was her son.

It's all my fault. My fault! My fault! My fault!

Cindy stared ahead blankly for a while until time no longer mattered. Then she slipped to the floor, unworthy even of the hardened bench in a jail cell. She deserved far worse.

Curled on the ground, shamed and silent, she could do nothing but wait.

She missed her classes that day. Everyone on campus would notice, but no one would know why. She had no answer that wouldn't crush her beneath the full weight of shame.

Later that day, the psychiatrist arrived. Cindy sat hollow-eyed and shaking. Her only thoughts were of Jacob: if he was safe, where he was, who was caring for him, and whether he was afraid.

She answered the psychiatrist's questions numbly, fingers twisting the hem of her shirt.

Listening carefully to the teen's responses, the man nodded and scribbled onto a document attached to a clipboard.

"You don't seem dangerous," he said at last, almost to himself. "But you don't seem stable, either."

After a tense deliberation, Cindy was released the following day, the day after the art show, but had a date to appear in court within thirty days.

Numb, Cindy walked home in silence.

By the time she reached her apartment door, a notice flapped against the peeling paint. ***Eviction***. She had five days left to leave. The window had been boarded up again with a sheet of plywood.

She stared at the paper until the words blurred. Part of her wanted to keep walking, past the door, past the street, past everything, until it all stopped. Yet, the memory of her son held her like a tether, still ghosting the corners of her mind.

Cindy opened the door.

The apartment was in disarray, as if a hurricane had torn through it. Still, it was quiet. Not just silent, but absent.

Jacob was gone. His favorite blue blanket was gone, and so was his favorite plush toy. The emptiness hit harder than any scream.

She drifted to the center of the room and stood there, arms limp at her sides, staring at the spot where she'd last seen him. She imagined him there, playing and giggling, but he was gone. In five days, even that emptiness would be taken from her.

There was no money for storage, no money to move, and no one left to call.

Her mother was still away. God, how devastated she'd be if she found out how far everything had fallen.

Cindy's legs gave out, and she sank slowly to the floor, curling into the place where her son had once sat. Her knees were drawn tight, her hands clenched under her chin.

She lay still in the silence, wishing she could disappear too.

For days, Cindy didn't move. She stayed in the same spot on the floor, her body curled into itself like a discarded rag doll in a trash heap.

She didn't eat. She didn't sleep. She didn't answer the phone when it rang, or the knocks that came and went at the door. The world outside could keep spinning if it wanted. She wasn't part of it anymore.

The spot where Jacob had last sat felt sacred. As long as she stayed there, maybe he wasn't really gone. Maybe if she stayed long enough to disappear into it, she'd vanish with him.

The bathroom was too far. The fridge didn't matter. School, the art show, the eviction notice taped to the door, none of it pierced her numb cocoon.

Let them take everything, she thought. *There's nothing left to protect. Nothing left to fight for.*

"Cindy?" a voice called through the door, muffled but insistent. "Cindy, are you home? Cindy?"

"She's not there," said a second voice, more clipped, dismissive. "We should go. This place feels dangerous."

"I'm heading to the office," the first voice said with urgency.

A long silence followed. Then, a knock, sharper and impatient.

"Ms. Spearman?" a third voice spoke, professional but tired. "Ms. Spearman, are you home?"

"Oh, just open the door already," snapped the first voice impatiently. Cindy's ears registered the tone but processed it like static.

A key turned. The door creaked open. Footsteps entered, hesitant at first, then more determined.

"No, Cindy!" the voice cried. Someone rushed toward her and knelt beside her. She was weightless in their arms. A shadow of strength stirred in her, just enough to open her eyes.

It was Paul.

His face was pale with panic. "Cindy, can you hear me? Cindy, are you alright?"

The smell of the apartment hit him like a slap, but he didn't pull away.

"God, it reeks in here," Judy muttered. "Look at this place. How does anyone live like this?"

Mr. Tanner exhaled loudly and started toward the kitchen.

"Where are you going?" Paul barked. "Get help! Get an ambulance!"

"I'm calling the police," Mr. Tanner muttered over his shoulder. "Maybe this time, they'll lock her up for good. She's been nothing but a problem."

Paul turned back to Cindy, shielding her with his presence. She could barely hold her head up, but she saw the anguish in his eyes.

"Hey, hey," Paul called out. "The *ambulance*. Can't you see how far gone she is? She needs *medical* help. Not handcuffs!" His voice cracked with urgency as he gently tried to rouse her.

"Maybe," Judy said coolly, arms folded. "Or maybe the police are exactly what she needs. At least she can't hurt herself around them. This place alone should be more than enough for anyone to see that she's crazy."

"Cindy," Paul said again, leaning closer. "Cindy, answer me. Cindy."

Judy yawned, unbothered, then grimaced at the urine-soaked floor.

"I'll wait outside," she added with a wrinkle of her nose. "Someone should guide the officers. Make sure they find the right mess."

Paul carefully laid Cindy back onto the floor, then took the phone from Mr. Tanner's hand. "911? No, we don't need the police involved, just an ambulance. Right away!" His voice was steady but urgent.

Minutes later, paramedics arrived and transported Cindy to the nearby hospital. Paul stayed close, refusing to leave her side. Hours passed before Cindy was discharged, but instead of letting her return to her apartment, Paul brought her to his own place. He gently settled her on the couch, sliding a pillow beneath her head and covering her with a blanket.

"I'll be back soon," he said softly, kneeling beside her. "I don't know exactly what's happening, but I promise I'll do everything I can to fix this. Just hold on for me, okay?"

He stood, crossed the room, picked up the phone from the kitchen, and dialed quickly.

"Hi, this is Paul Boudreaux," Paul said, polite but firm. "I'm a friend of Cindy Spearman's, and I need to talk to someone about contacting her family. She just got out of the hospital and is staying with me."

He paused, clearing his throat and squinting slightly as he listened.

"What?" Paul exclaimed, his voice growing hoarse. "She has to be out of the apartment by *when*? There's no way we can clear everything out in just half a day. Is there any chance we could get a few extra days? She's going through a really difficult time right now."

He paused, listening. Then his brows furrowed.

"By *tonight*? That's impossible. How are we supposed to do that without even enough time to rent a moving truck?"

He pulled the receiver away for a second, exhaling in disbelief, then returned it to his ear. "Alright then, what if I take over the lease? I'll rent the place myself for the rest of the month."

He swallowed hard, suppressing a cough. "What? Oh, come on! What kind of business are you running? Fine. We'll get out what we can."

Swearing under his breath, Paul stepped into the hallway and crossed over to knock on the door across from his.

"Hey, Paul," Greyson greeted him, opening the door. "I was just about to head out."

"There's been a change of plans," Paul said quickly. "I know this is gonna sound weird, but I need help moving. There's not much time, and I can't explain everything right now."

"What? Moving? Right now? Where to and why all of a sudden?"

"Look, I'll fill you in on the way, I promise. But we have to leave. Now."

Greyson hesitated, glancing back into his apartment, then nodded. "Alright. Lead the way."

Back in Paul's apartment, Cindy heard the sound of the door click, their voices fading, and then nothing. For the next few hours, silence wrapped around her again.

Then, the front door creaked open, and soft footsteps crossed the room toward the couch. Cindy barely stirred. A faint floral perfume lingered in the air, familiar.

Fingers snapped twice in front of Cindy's face.
No response.

Judy didn't speak. She simply hummed a light, tuneless melody. Leisurely, she reached down and grabbed the edge of the blanket tucked beneath Cindy's chin and yanked it up over her entire face, as if she were dead.

With a rustle, Judy set her heavy handbag directly on Cindy's stomach, as if she were no more than furniture. The humming didn't stop. Judy's heels clicked lightly against the floor as she walked away.

Then silence was followed by the clicking of something being used with a low ring.

Judy's voice answered smoothly. "Hey, baby. It's me...Yeah, things are fine. In fact, they couldn't be better..."

There was a pause, then Judy continued to speak.

"Oh, the art reception? I still have *no* idea where Cindy is. It's like she just disappeared. I hope someone finds out what happened to her soon."

There was a second brief pause.

"I know, you've tried talking to her before...Yeah, but it seems like she doesn't care, does she? It was her big night, and she didn't bother to show up. Honestly, I don't think she respects you or herself. Maybe one day she will...You should think twice about giving her another chance."

More silence.

"Yeah," Judy continued, "I'll ask her boyfriend if he knows anything the next time I see him. Maybe *he* can clue us in. I just hope she's okay... poor thing."

She lowered her voice a bit more, then came a soft giggle.

"Yeah, I should be home soon. You know how it gets, planning events at the sorority house..."

A brief pause.

"Mmhmm... Love you too. I'll be home as soon as I can."

Click.

More clicks followed.

"Hey, Carol," Judy said. "It's me. Looks like we're done here. She's as good as gone. Tell Dan I got Millie to help with his little problem. Honestly, it was too easy."

She paused, then laughed softly.

"I get why he kept her around. Cindy's entertaining, in a sad, pathetic way. Watching her unravel was the best part. She's so gullible, so desperate, like she ever had a shot at making it big here? Please. As if we'd ever allow someone like her to represent our school."

Judy giggled.

"Dan was over her the second she stole his wallet. He figured if he was gonna cut her off, he might as well use her for sex first. Gross, right? Doesn't she like girls too? Total freak."

Judy sighed.

"What a weirdo. I'll be glad when she's finally gone. I don't see what Ryan sees in her. Sure, she can paint and draw, but she's a mess. She had to go."

Judy paused again.

"Millie? Yeah, she played her part, but seriously, do we really need someone like her in the sorority house? She did what we asked, but she's...average. We don't need her anymore. Let's just make something up and drop her. It won't take much effort. She'll fall for anything. What a dummy. Bless her heart."

Judy laughed out loud.

"Don't remind me of Ryan. He's so boring; such a lame duck. I'd rather hang out with Paul; he's more fun to be around. I can see why Cindy liked him. I think I do too, but he cares too much about people like her. Lame, huh? Maybe one day he'll wake up and realize girls like Cindy aren't worth rescuing. I might have to nudge him a little more until he sees things our way."

Knock! Knock! A sharp knock interrupted her.

"Judy," Paul's voice called from the other side of the door. "Judy, open up."

"I gotta go," Judy said hurriedly into the phone.

Click. She hung up. Her footsteps shuffled in a hurry across the floor. She yanked the blanket off Cindy's face and lifted her purse, setting it carefully on the coffee table. Then she fumbled with the lock.

"Coming," she called. "Give me a minute."

The door clicked open. Paul stepped inside, his eyes going straight to the couch where Cindy still lay.

"What happened to the spare key?" he asked, striding over. "How could it just go missing?"

Judy tucked a loose strand of hair behind her ear. "I don't know. Maybe someone stole it."

Paul sighed and winched slightly as he straightened up. "Well, give me my original key back. I'll get another one made."

He let out a sharp cough and rubbed his lower back. "Thanks for dropping by to check on Cindy. Normally, I wouldn't ask, but I needed someone to keep an eye on her."

"No problem," Judy said, handing him the key. "I'm here to help."

"She still seems out of it," Paul said with a frown, rubbing the back of his neck. "The doctors said it might be a while before the medicine wears off."

His voice was hoarse, and he grimaced mid-sentence.

"God, I nearly threw my back out, and Greyson's in no better shape. I've still got stuff crammed in the trunk. There was only so much we could fit in our cars. We couldn't find a single moving truck this late, so we just hauled what we could. We had to ask the folks next door if we could stash some furniture outside their place. It was a mess."

Judy offered a small smile. "She's lucky to have a friend like you around. You've earned your rest." She tilted her head slightly. "Care to go upstairs? I'll be up in a minute... to make you feel a whole lot better."

Paul coughed hard into his sleeve, his shoulders shaking.

"I can't," he muttered, his voice rough and cracked. He rubbed the back of his neck with a wince. "My throat feels like it's on fire. God, I'm so damn sick of this cough."

Judy flinched.

Paul clenched his jaw, clearing his throat again. He dropped down onto the edge of the couch and slammed his fists against the cushion in frustration.

"Why won't this thing go away?" he snapped. His fingers curled like claws before tightening into fists again. He punched the air in front of him. "I'm about to lose my damn mind!"

He rose to his feet and paced once before turning toward the stairs.

"Just go home, Judy," he said flatly. "I'm not in a good mood. Whatever I have, I don't want you to end up catching it."

"But, I—" Judy stammered. "What about her?"

She pointed to Cindy.

"Couldn't she catch something too?" Judy demanded. "Why should I leave while she stays behind?"

"Stop forcing me to talk," Paul growled, not turning around. "My throat's killing me. I'll just stay upstairs. Go home. I mean it."

He stormed up the stairs, coughing as he went, then disappeared behind a closed door.

Judy stared up after him, her expression slowly contorting with rage. Without warning, she snatched her purse from the coffee table, raised it high, and slammed it down on the couch, narrowly missing Cindy's face. Then she turned and stormed out of the penthouse, not bothering to close the door behind her.

The next morning, laughter and conversation echoed through the hallway as other residents made their way to the elevator. They passed by casually, until Greyson, across the hall, cracked open his door and peered inside.

"Paul?" he called out. "Hey, Paul. Are you alright in there?"

He stepped inside and saw Cindy asleep on the couch.

"Paul?" Greyson called out again, frowning. He headed into the kitchen, then up the stairs.
When he returned, his expression was tense, his brow

creased with concern. Grimacing, he rubbed his lower back as he stepped into the living room.

Moments later, Paul came down the stairs. His face was pale and drawn, as if he hadn't slept at all. He hadn't changed clothes since the day before. One hand clutched his throat.

"You should see a doctor, buddy," Greyson said, stepping toward him. "Could be that bug going around campus. And if it is, blondie might need to head out before she catches it too. Don't worry about the furniture. I'll round up a few guys to help. It's handled. Just go."

Paul didn't say a word. He walked into the kitchen, scooped salt into a glass, poured in hot water, and began gargling. When he finished, he spit into the sink. His eyes stayed low, his movements slow and mechanical.

"I don't know if you knew this," Greyson continued, "but the door was wide open when I came in. And the spare key's missing too…"

Paul reached for a pen and scrap of paper. He scribbled quickly: **Could you call Judy?**

"Judy?" Greyson blinked. "What for?"

Paul winced, then motioned toward Cindy on the couch.

"Don't tell me you expect *Judy* to take care of anybody," Greyson shot back. "What about Margo or Laura? Aren't they her friends? They'd pitch in way more than she ever would."

Paul wrote again: **Judy knows. They don't.**

Greyson scoffed. "Isn't she supposed to be planning another event for her dumb sorority today? I doubt she'll answer."

Paul struggled to swallow and wrote, **Could you watch her, then?**

Greyson stared at him. "Are you kidding me? You want me to babysit her?"

Paul shoved the notepad into Greyson's chest. ***Then, who can I trust not to blab? I need to see a doctor! Right now!***

"Fine," Greyson grumbled. "But make it quick."

Paul's eyes expressed his gratitude. He scribbled, **Thanks, buddy!**

He quickly walked out the door, leaving Greyson alone with Cindy.

"Great," Greyson muttered. "Just great. All this before breakfast..."

He sank into the loveseat and closed his eyes. He barely had time to breathe before a soft, broken sniffling from the couch forced his eyes open again.

Cindy had begun to stir, as if awakening from some deep spell.

"My little boy," she wept. "Where's my little boy?"

Greyson tilted his head, glancing in her direction.

"Jacob..." Cindy sobbed, her voice cracking. "I'm sorry. I'm so sorry..."

"Who on Earth is that?" Greyson asked, frowning as Cindy buried her face in her hands and let out a long, gut-wrenching wail. "Now wait a minute. What's going on here? I didn't sign up for any of this!"

He glanced toward the door, unsure whether to bail or call Paul back in, if he was even still around.

"Please," Cindy begged, crawling from the couch toward him. "Please help me get my little boy back."

Greyson jumped up and hurried away from the loveseat. "Wait a minute. I think *Judy* is exactly the person you need to help find Jacob or whatever his name is."

"My little boy," Cindy wailed. "I need my little boy."

Greyson rushed to the kitchen and grabbed the phone. He dialed quickly, shifting his weight nervously while keeping one eye on Cindy, now curled on the floor, sobbing. He prayed that she wouldn't come crawling after him again.

He slammed the receiver down and immediately dialed another number.

"Joel," he said hurriedly, "there's an emergency. I need help here. I can't say what it is, or Paul'll lose it. Is Margo there? Put her on."

A pause.

"Hey, Margo. I need you to come to Paul's place... No, he's fine. *I'm* not. I just— I can't say over the phone. I just need someone here. Now. Please. Make it fast."

Greyson hung up the phone and lingered in the kitchen until a knock came at the door several minutes later.

"It's open!" he called, hoping whoever was on the other side would hear him.

The door creaked open. Margo and Joel stepped inside. Margo rushed straight to Cindy, who was still curled into a ball on the floor, sobbing.

"Cindy!" Margo cried, kneeling beside her. "Cindy, what happened?"

She looked up, spotting Greyson in the kitchen.

"What did you do to her, you monster?"

"Monster? *Me?*" Greyson shouted, pointing at Cindy. "She's the monster! Have you seen her apartment lately? I'm the one who should be scared."

"My little boy!" Cindy wailed. "Give me my little boy back! Please!"

All eyes turned to Greyson.

"I don't have him!" he shot back. "Why is everyone looking at me?"

"Where's Paul?" Joel inquired.

"He went to the doctor and told me to watch her," Greyson responded. "Look, I don't know what's going on. She was asleep on the couch, and then she started acting crazy. Can you guys handle it from here? I need to go home. I'm hungry, and I don't want to be here."

"What do you expect us to do?" Joel asked.

"I don't know," Greyson replied with a shrug. "You two are smart. I'm sure you'll come up with something."

"They took my baby away," Cindy cried.

"Who?" Margo asked gently. "Who took Jacob away?"

"Is he some imaginary person she talks to from time to time?" Greyson asked, glancing at Joel.

"He's her son," Joel said quietly. "Obviously... something happened to the kid."

"Well, don't tell Paul I said anything," Greyson began, "but yesterday, we had to go back to her apartment and clear a bunch of stuff out. I guess she got evicted or something, but I never knew she had a son. I mean, nobody's ever mentioned it until today."

"Paul doesn't know," Margo said firmly. "And we're keeping it that way. She's been through enough already."

"What?" Greyson asked. "Why?"

"Don't ask," Joel said, clearing his throat. "Just go along with it."

Greyson shot his friend a look.

"Cindy, we'll get him back," Margo assured her friend. "But we need to know who took him."

"The police stole my baby," Cindy sobbed.

"Joel," Margo said quickly, turning to him, "can't your dad do something? He's a judge. Doesn't he know someone who can help Cindy?"

"Maybe, but you know how rotten he can get when it comes to favors," Joel grumbled.

"Ugh, my family and he can work something out," Margo groaned. "Just get him to help us fix this. It's not like they haven't worked together before."

"Fine, but it won't be pretty," Joel mumbled, stepping away to use the phone in the kitchen.

"See? Things are gonna be fine, Cindy," Margo told her friend. "Jacob's going to be back real soon."

"But she got kicked out of her home," Greyson reminded her. "How's she gonna get him back if she's homeless?"

"That's for us to worry about," Margo said. "Aren't you supposed to be back home eating something?"

"Yeah, but if I leave and Paul comes back, he won't trust me anymore," Greyson replied.

"You're not helping much from the kitchen, are you?"

"Well, I *did* call you over, didn't I?"

"Oh, go home already," Margo scoffed. "That's where you belong and where you wanna be. When's Paul coming back?"

"Beats me. That's why I'm sticking around," Greyson shot back.

"My baby boy's coming back?" Cindy asked, her voice softening.

"Yes, he's coming back," Margo said. "And you'll see him again soon to give him all your kisses and hugs, just like always."

"But where will they live?" Greyson asked. "I've been to her place twice, and both times it was a wreck. How is someone like her supposed to raise a kid? Maybe he's better off where he is."

"Will you *shut up* already?" Margo yelled. "Stop talking about her like she isn't right here!"

"Momma's gonna be mad at me," Cindy wept, rocking slightly. "Everyone's always mad at me..."

"I'm sorry," Margo said, softening her tone. "I wasn't trying to upset you. Nobody's mad at you." She shot a glare at Greyson. "Well, maybe *he* is. That's a different story..."

Joel reentered from the kitchen, brushing his hands on his jeans.

"He's gonna make a few calls," he said. "But I hate to say it...Greyson's not wrong. She needs something solid. Not just for Jacob, for herself, too."

Margo curled her lip, arms folding tight across her chest.

"Yeah," she admitted. "But I don't think she should be alone right now." She glanced at Cindy, whose eyes had gone glassy. "What if she cracks again?"

"Since she's here with Paul, he probably wouldn't mind her crashing with him a little longer," Joel said, running a hand through his hair. "But, man, he's been struggling a lot lately. He's holding on by a thread."

"Can't she stay with us?" Margo asked, her voice tight with concern.

"I want her to," Joel sighed, "but your sister's already staying over. It wouldn't work out."

He hesitated, then added, "I don't know about calling her mom either. Cindy might not want her to know... and with her mom still in the hospital, it might break her even more. Regardless, she's gonna need someone to look after her, at least until she gets her own place again, especially with her family being out of state."

Greyson motioned for Joel to follow him outside. With a heavy sigh, Joel dragged his hands down his face and stepped out after him. The door clicked shut behind them.

Inside, Cindy remained curled in Margo's arms, worn out and silent.

A few minutes later, both men returned.

"I'm gonna round up a few guys to help get the rest of her stuff into storage," Joel said, heading toward the door.

"Isn't Greyson going with you?" Margo asked sharply.

"He will, after Paul gets back," Joel replied, hesitating.

Margo rolled her eyes. "Ugh. Completely useless. As useless as they come."

Greyson shot her a cold look as he walked into the kitchen without a word. Joel fished his keys from his pocket and left the apartment, letting the door shut behind him.

Margo turned her attention back to Cindy and gently helped her to her feet.

"Come on, let's get you cleaned up," she said softly, guiding her upstairs to the bathroom. "Then I'll fix you something to eat. I bet you're starving."

Greyson winced in the kitchen just as the phone rang. He snatched up the receiver. "Hello?"

"It's Paul," came the hoarse reply. "How's Cindy?"

"She's fine," Greyson said sharply. "How'd it go at the doctor's?"

"I went to the campus clinic. Got some medicine," Paul replied. "I'm heading back now. Just hang in there."

Greyson's voice softened. "Alright, buddy. See you in a few."

He hung up and glanced toward the stairs. The faint sound of running water drifted down from above. With a sigh, Greyson eased himself back onto the loveseat and closed his eyes.

Fifteen minutes passed.

The door creaked open.

Paul stepped inside, a small paper pharmacy bag tucked under his arm. He moved with the weight of someone who hadn't rested in days. He scanned the living room. Cindy was gone, and Greyson was knocked out cold on the loveseat.

Paul's eyes flew open. He scanned the living room in a panic, darting from the couch to the staircase. Cindy was gone.

"What in the world?" he muttered, his voice barely audible. He lunged toward Greyson and grabbed his shoulder, shaking him hard.

"Where's Cindy?" Paul barked, his voice low and strained.

Greyson jolted awake, groggy and confused.

"She's upstairs," he mumbled drowsily.

Paul bolted for the stairs, taking them two at a time. A light flicked on in the hallway. He pushed open the bathroom door, and a scream cut through the air.

"You scared the life outta me!" Margo shrieked.

A moment of silence followed. Then, Paul reappeared, walking down the stairs. His eyes were now cold, sharp, and locked on Greyson.

"Why'd you call Margo?" he demanded in a low, biting voice.

Greyson rubbed his neck. "Cindy scared me, and I didn't know what else to do."

"She's a *woman*," Paul snapped hoarsely. "What, exactly, could she do that scared you so bad?"

Greyson opened his mouth, ready to explain the way Cindy had crawled after him, begging for her son, but stopped short. He decided to change the subject.

"What'd the doc say about your throat?" he asked.

Paul sighed and dropped onto the couch.

"He gave me a shot, a few pills, and said to come back in a few days." He winced. "It feels like I swallowed sandpaper."

"Joel's out trying to find a few guys to help move Cindy's stuff into storage," Greyson added. "We can head that way after I get something to eat. Will Cindy be staying here a while?"

"Might as well, now that everyone knows you can't keep your mouth shut," Paul muttered. "We'll get you something along the way. Let's go."

Chapter 19

Two hours had passed since Margo left. Paul had returned not long ago and was now upstairs resting. Cindy sat curled on the couch, quiet and unmoving. As much as she wanted to tell him everything, about the dream, about the voice, he looked so drained, more exhausted than she'd ever seen him. So, she remained downstairs.

She wasn't sure what to think. Was the voice even real? The one that whispered things about Dan and Millie? It sounded like Judy. That same smug tone, like she knew everything, but why would Cindy dream about Judy, of all people? The voice hadn't said anything kind. In fact, it had been cruel.

Cindy pressed her lips into a thin line. *Maybe I've finally lost it.*

What if she told someone? What if they decided she really did need to be locked away? She could already hear the judgment in that voice, Judy's voice. And the worst part was...a part of her was starting to believe it.

God. Her voice. Even I think I'm going crazy. Thank goodness Paul's upstairs.

She frowned and shifted on the sofa, poking at the takeout container in her lap. Paul had picked it up earlier, shrimp creole supreme from Ackerman's. It was delicious, like always, but something about eating it alone made it taste bland. She missed him and missed how things used to feel before everything went wrong.

I hope he gets well soon, she thought. *I wish I weren't such a burden to him...or to anyone else. I'm nineteen. Why do I feel like this? Needy and incompetent... Adults are supposed to be able to handle life, right? So, what happened to me?*

She took another bite, slowly and mechanically. Her gaze lifted toward the staircase, resting there for a while.

Get well, Paul, she thought. *And...thanks for helping me, even now.*

Cindy kept eating until the container was empty. For a moment, she thought about saving it. The habit of scarcity spoke louder than logic, but this wasn't her place, and Paul probably wouldn't want it.

With a quiet sigh, she carried the box into the kitchen and tossed it into the trash, hesitating just a second before letting go.

She went back to the living room and flicked on the television. A movie was already playing, something about a woman reclaiming her life and living freely. Cindy pulled the soft blanket around her shoulders and curled up on the couch. Gradually, her mind relaxed and swept into the storyline like it was a warm tide.

Then came the sound, a sharp click at the front door.

Cindy's body went stiff. Her eyes darted toward the entrance just as the door creaked open, slow and unhurried. Someone turned the knob from the outside.

Then, Judy stepped in.

Their eyes met. For a moment, neither moved. The surprise that passed between them felt cold and electric.

Judy's smile faltered but didn't fall. She shut the door softly behind her.

"Well, hello there," she said sweetly. "How are you, doll? Feeling better?"

Cindy didn't respond. She stayed under the blanket, motionless, and her heart climbed into her throat.

Judy's heels clicked softly as she crossed the floor and sat down right beside her.

"Aren't you going to say hi to me?" Judy asked, tilting her head with her lips curved into a forced pout. "Cat got your tongue? I *did* help take care of you, after all."

The scent of Judy's perfume hung in the air, thick, sweet, and sharp. It used to smell luxurious. Now, it turned Cindy's stomach.

Their eyes locked, and Judy moved to brush a strand of hair from Cindy's face, causing her to flinch. Judy's smile remained the same, but her eyes said everything: *I knew you'd be scared, coward.*

Quietly, Judy refocused her gaze upstairs, then stood. Light on her feet, she made her way to the stairs, each step deliberate and practiced.

Cindy's breath caught in her throat.

Warn him, her mind screamed. *Say something.*

Yet, her voice and body refused to move. By the time she gathered the courage to shift, Judy was already in the hallway. Then the bedroom door creaked open.

Cindy sat frozen beneath the blanket. A tremor passed through her.

Oh no, Paul...

Laughter echoed faintly down the stairwell, Judy's voice, followed by silence. Then another giggle.

Cindy's brow furrowed, her stomach twisting.

Maybe...maybe he's not as sick as I thought.

Tears welled up in her eyes.

"Oh, come on," Judy called playfully, her voice just loud enough to carry downstairs. "You can't be *that* sick. You're avoiding me, aren't you?"

A pause followed. Cindy leaned forward slightly, straining to hear Paul's response, but all she caught was a faint mumble that was low and muted.

Then Judy again: "What? I didn't steal your spare key! You *gave* it to me, remember?"

Another stretch of silence followed.

"Don't be so hostile, sweetie," Judy's voice was heard again. "I only wanted to show how much I care by dropping by. Haven't I been good to you? I watched that zombie downstairs, didn't I?"

More silence. Cindy's jaw clenched.

"What about *me* and how I feel?" Judy demanded. "Doesn't that matter too?"

Moments later, Judy reappeared. Her footsteps thundered down the stairs. Her hand covered her mouth, her shoulders tight and trembling. Her eyes, once gleaming with arrogance, now shimmered with unshed tears. Her lips quivered as she reached the bottom step and turned to face Cindy.

For a moment, her expression faltered as if she'd forgotten her script. Then, she turned and rushed out the door, one hand still shielding her face as though trying to catch the emotions spilling from it.

The door clicked shut behind her.

Cindy wrinkled her nose, her brows drawing tight in suspicion more than sympathy.

Paul appeared at the top of the stairs. He stood for a moment, saying nothing, his eyes unreadable. He turned and went back into the bedroom.

Slowly, Cindy refocused back to the television set, though the movie now seemed distant. Somehow, something stirred in her chest. She witnessed Judy fall apart. Strangely, it felt...refreshing. Was it wrong? To find satisfaction in someone else's breakdown? Maybe, but with Judy? Maybe not.

Later that evening, Paul emerged from the bedroom. He looked slightly better, less pale and steadier on his feet, but there was still a weariness behind his eyes that hadn't lifted. He approached the couch and sat down beside Cindy.

"Hey," he said, his voice still raspy. "Feeling better?"

"Yeah, you?" Cindy asked.

"A little. I'm not supposed to talk much, but we need to talk about something important."

He closed his eyes for a moment before reopening them. They were heavy with regret and didn't meet hers at first. They had a sadness that made Cindy brace herself.

"I'm sorry, Cin," Paul continued. "Tomorrow...we both need to go to the campus clinic. The doctors think I might have oral gonorrhea."

Cindy's breath hitched. Unblinking, she stared at him.

"I won't know for sure until the results come back," Paul added, "but you need to be tested too, just in case..."

Cindy went completely still.

"W-what?" she whispered, her eyes widening in disbelief. "I don't have it! I don't have any symptoms!"

"Some people don't," Paul told her, "but it doesn't mean you're in the clear. It's been going around campus. If there's a chance you may have it...you should get checked, so it can be treated."

Squeezing her eyes shut, Cindy lowered her head. *How could this be happening? It makes no sense!*

"We can go together," Paul offered. "You won't have to do it alone. Okay?"

Her posture stooped, Cindy reluctantly nodded.

"Okay," she murmured, but on the inside, she wasn't okay at all.

The next morning, Paul and Cindy went to the campus clinic, where Cindy was tested and told she would be given her results in the next few days. Regardless of the outcome, she was given an injection, a prescription, and a firm warning: no kissing or sexual activity until she was medically cleared. Afterwards, she was given a doctor's note to give to Ryan.

Cindy closed her eyes slowly and shook her head. *Ryan is going to kill me for missing the art show and being absent the last couple of days. I'm toast...Damn. What else could happen today?*

Paul walked with her back to the courtyard. There, he gave her a small comforting hug.

"I'll see you after class," he murmured, then disappeared down the walkway to go to his class.

Cindy watched him go, then slowly turned toward the art building. Her feet felt like they were sinking into the pavement with every step. She entered the art building, bracing herself for potential questions about her whereabouts and, worst of all, Ryan's wrath.

However, she immediately noticed that the door to the painting studio was open, and her classmates were inside, busy at work, but Ryan wasn't there. Squinting her eyes, Cindy thought about going straight to her work area to pretend she hadn't missed the first half of class, but she heard Ryan's heated voice coming from behind his closed office door aimed at someone.

Great, she thought. *He's already mad at someone, and I'm next.*

"Don't come crying to me at my job and expect any sympathy!" Ryan's voice bellowed behind the closed door.

Cindy froze.

"No, I will not lower my voice!" Ryan shouted. "What's the point in being embarrassed now? Let the whole campus know who and what you really are. Who is he, huh? I'd *love* to meet the guy, shake his hand, and say *thank you!*"

His voice thundered throughout the studio.

"Don't even think about finishing your classes. By the time I get home, you and everything you own better be gone!"

Cindy stood motionless. Her classmates stopped what they were doing, their eyes flicking nervously toward Ryan's office.

Then came Judy's voice, defiant but trembling.

"What did you expect, Ryan? We weren't even doing anything together anymore. You ignore me! I never get any attention! You're always here, at that other college, or off at some stupid, boring art museum!"

"Well, one of us has to work to earn money," Ryan bellowed back. "I don't have the luxury of calling Mommy and Daddy every time I'm in a pinch! I may not have been born with a silver spoon in my mouth like most people around here, but I earned this job.

Something someone like you wouldn't understand, much less appreciate."

There was a moment of silence.

"And to think..." Ryan growled, his voice lower now but no less bitter, "I was working my ass off trying to surprise you with a nice house when you graduated."

Another moment of silence followed that was thicker and heavier. Then, there was a final blow.

"Get out of my office. I have a class to teach."

Cindy and a few of her classmates grimaced right before the office door creaked open.

Judy staggered out, looking like she'd just emerged from a long, losing battle: drained, disarmed, and stripped of whatever pride she had left. Her makeup was smeared, and her mascara was trailing down her cheeks in long, shadowy streaks. Her hair hung limp and uneven across her shoulders. Gone was the sorority glam and sultry attitude, replaced by a simple gray blouse, worn jeans, and white tennis shoes. She didn't speak to anyone. She didn't even look around. Her head hung low, and her eyes were vacant. Quietly, she walked out of the art building.

Ryan's office door remained open. From where Cindy stood, she could see that his face was red, he was breathing hard, and he was the angriest she'd ever seen him. He scraped his fingers through his hair, then dragged a hand down his face, like he was trying to peel off a mask he no longer had the energy to wear.

The professor's eyes met Cindy's. His expression flickered, his rage giving way to weariness. He pressed his lips into a thin line and stepped forward but stopped at the threshold of his office. With a quick gesture, he motioned her over.

Cindy's knees nearly gave way, but she made her way toward him. *Oh, no, I'm next!*

"Cindy," he said, voice urgent but far gentler than the one he'd unleashed on Judy. "We'll talk later, alright? For now, let everyone in class know that class is canceled. I won't be back today."

Cindy did a double-take. *Ryan? Canceling class?*

Had the whole world gone mad, or was it finally snapping back into place after a long, twisted spell of chaos? Either way, she wasn't about to question it.

Let reality realign however it wanted; this version was far easier to live in. The spotlight had finally shifted, and for once, it wasn't burning her. Everyone's attention was fixed on Judy's public downfall, not Cindy's, and she had no complaints. In fact, all she could think was: *It's about damn time Judy got her just deserts.*

"Yes, sir," Cindy replied, with a quiet nod, then walked into the painting studio. She delivered the news that class was canceled, and Ryan had left.

Then something unexpected happened.

One by one, her classmates turned to her with genuine warmth.

"Hey Cindy," one said. "Your diptych was a hit. Everyone loved it!"

"We missed you!" said another, giving her a soft pat on the back. "It's good seeing you back! We were worried!"

"Lots of people were talking about the paintings and drawings that you did, Cindy," a third exclaimed. "One of the professors from the Humanities Department bought one of your drawings to put in his office."

"So, did my mom," a fourth added. "She's a big fan of the drawings and wanted to buy another one, but that one sold before she could buy it!"

Cindy stood there, stunned. *They...missed me? Do people care about me after all? They liked the art that much?*

A wave of disbelief washed over her, followed by something warmer and brighter.

Oh, my God, this is the best day I've ever had on campus. I could cry right now.

She waited until the last student filed out of the studio. The room fell into silence. Then, unable to hold it in, Cindy sprang into the air, her fists raised like a victorious boxer. A grin stretched across her face widely. For once, even if just for today, she was the clear victor.

Chapter 20

Later that day, as Cindy and Paul walked back from the cafeteria, they spotted Joel sitting alone in the courtyard. His elbows rested on his knees, and his head was slightly down, like he'd been waiting for them.

"Hey, pal," Paul greeted him. "Ready to head to class?"

Joel didn't move right away, and his eyes flicked toward Cindy.

"Yeah. I'll catch up in a minute," he said. "I need to talk to Cindy first, in private."

Paul raised an eyebrow but didn't press.

"Alright," he muttered, walking off toward the business building.

Cindy watched him walk away, and her gut tightened as Joel stood and exhaled deeply.

"Okay," he began, "here's the deal. Since your case involves drugs, the court's gonna require a few things. First, you'll need to go to rehab. Second, you'll have to pass a scheduled drug test. And third, you need a stable place to live. Something official, in your name."

He let that hang in the air, giving Cindy a second to absorb it.

"If you check all those boxes," he added, "there's a chance you could get Jacob back within a few weeks. But if you don't, if you miss even one, there's a strong possibility they'll terminate your custody rights or Jacob could stay in foster care long-term."

Cindy sighed deeply.

"I haven't done anything in the last couple of days," she said defensively. "I haven't heard a word about rehab. Since I'm staying with Paul, doesn't that count?"

Joel shook his head slowly. "Nope. Not in the eyes of protective services. You're not on his lease and don't pay bills there. You need to show the court that *you* can provide stability for Jacob. Everything, the lease, utilities, and proof of income must be in your name."

He paused, his gaze steady but not unkind.

"As far as the court's concerned," he continued, "you could vanish tomorrow, and it wouldn't affect Paul's stability at all."

"Oh," Cindy said quietly.

"Also," Joel added, "since your move was sudden, your caseworker probably sent paperwork to your old address. You'll need to check with your former landlord and see if anything's waiting for you. If you miss an intake date for rehab, that could count against you."

Cindy nodded slowly, still processing the information.

"Margo's stopping by later," Joel said. "She's going to help review a few housing options. Do this right, Cindy, and it'll go a lot smoother. Get clean, secure a place, and Jacob can come home."

"Thanks," she said, subdued. "I appreciate everything you're doing."

"No problem," Joel replied, then hesitated. "But there's one more option you need to think about. You're not going to like it, but it might give you the best chance of getting your son back sooner."

Cindy felt a quiver in her stomach.

"If you decide to get your mother or another trusted adult involved," Joel said carefully, "you could arrange for one of them to take temporary emergency custody while you complete the program. If you choose your mother, she will need to come to Alabama to file. Either way, going this route could help get Jacob out of foster care sooner. He'd be with family or someone you trust, not strangers, and not lost in the system."

"Oh, okay," Cindy said, her voice shaky and barely audible. "Let me think about it. It's...It's a lot to process now..."

Joel gave her a firm nod.

"Sure, in the meantime, let's get you back on track," he said, before heading into the business building.

Cindy stood frozen.

I'm toast no matter what. Momma's gonna kill me once she finds out. She might even hate me after this...What if she gets so mad that I'll never see my baby boy ever again?

Frowning, she slumped down on the bench.

If I don't do anything...if I stay quiet... Jacob's going to be alone, scared, and miserable, like he probably already is... Oh, God, Jacob, I'm sorry. I failed you. I failed as a mother. I wouldn't blame you if you and Momma never spoke to me again.

Cindy began crossing and uncrossing her arms.

I have nothing to offer. No home, no food, no plan...Maybe Jacob's better off with Momma, maybe for good.

She began to bite her lip, then her nails.

Momma, I'm sorry I couldn't be the mother Jacob needed. I'll try harder. I swear I will... Give me one more chance before you decide I'm not worth it. Please, don't throw me away.

Twisting a strand of her hair, Cindy forced herself to walk toward the art building and slipped into her printmaking class, where she couldn't focus. The weight of the choice, between keeping secrets to protect herself or telling the truth to protect Jacob, pressed down like a vice.

But none of this is Jacob's fault, she thought, swallowing hard. *He shouldn't be punished for my stupidity...*

Then another thought hit her.

What if Momma's been trying to call this entire time? It's not like I've been reachable since moving in with Paul for now. I need to call her, but...What if this call is the thing that makes her finally tell me that it's my problem to fix on my own? She wouldn't allow Jacob to suffer because she'd be mad at me, would she?

After her printmaking class had ended, Cindy still had time before Paul would arrive in the courtyard. She rushed to a nearby payphone and attempted to call her mother's number, but all the phone did was ring unanswered. She would have to try again later.

When Paul arrived, he agreed to drive her to the office of her old apartment complex, where the landlord let her retrieve mail from her former box. Inside was a thick envelope with official-looking paperwork. One document listed two approved rehab programs. She was required to attend at least one. Another confirmed that parenting classes were mandatory. A drug test was scheduled soon. A note at the bottom added a final blow: proof of stable housing was still required.

Cindy sighed deeply.

There's so much to do... but I'll get through this. I have to.

"Got everything?" Paul asked as she climbed back into the car.

"Yeah, thanks," Cindy said, slipping the envelope onto her lap. "I guess this means I've got to try harder at getting clean, huh?"

"Me too," Paul sighed. "We'll manage. We've both had a chance to see how things *shouldn't* be done. Now, it's time to turn things around."

"Right." She glanced at him. "You sound a little better."

"My throat still hurts," Paul said, "but not as bad as before. I still shouldn't talk much, but if it is oral gonorrhea, I'm glad it can be cured."

"I know. It's scary... just knowing we might have caught it."

There was silence between them, not heavy, but aware.

"Let's make another deal," Paul said finally. "If it turns out that either of us has it, I won't tell, if you won't."

Cindy gave him a small, tired smile. "Deal."

"Not trying to sound nosey, and you don't have to tell me anything, but are you okay?" Paul asked. "Joel had a talk with you earlier, and I'm here to help too, if you'll let me."

"Things are fine. It's nothing," Cindy said. "He and Margo are helping me find a new place to live. My mom is going to kill me, though. It was my first apartment, and I needed her to co-sign. Now I'm going to have to ask her again for a different place."

"Greyson's family knows real estate, but they focus on bigger stuff," Paul said. "Do you have enough for the security deposit or application fee, if there is one required?"

"Maybe, it depends on how much it is," Cindy told him. "I was told I sold a few pieces of art at the reception, but I can't touch the money until the show ends. I get more from my stipend tomorrow, but it's usually not much. I could always do more sketches in the union to earn a few dollars really quick if I have to."

"I'll help cover the security deposit and application fee," Paul offered.

"Thanks, but I should do it on my own. I'm the one who put myself in this situation. You've done so much already by giving me a place to rest my head for now."

"Well, we did promise to help each other out, so why not?"

"Thanks. That means a lot... So, Margo's dropping by later today to help me find a new apartment."

"Got it. Anywhere else you needed to go to before heading home?"

"Nope, thanks for asking, though."

Paul started the car, and they made their way back to Lakeland Square.

"Mind if I check the trunk real quick?" Cindy asked. "I need to grab a few art supplies."

"Sure," Paul said, parking the vehicle and popping open the trunk.

Everything was neatly arranged. Cindy pulled out a sketch pad and a handful of drawing pencils.

"Need anything else?" Paul asked.

"That's all for now, thanks," Cindy replied.

Paul closed the trunk and walked with her back to the penthouse. Once inside, they settled in and began cooking dinner together: spaghetti with meatballs, garlic bread, and a tossed salad.

Like old times, Paul's competitive spirit shone through in the kitchen. He made everything into a game: seeing who could roll the most meatballs in under a minute, guessing ingredients in the refrigerator, and spelling them out before tossing them into the salad. Even the bread became part of the challenge. They passed it back and forth like a relay before sliding it into the oven.

Their laughter filled the apartment. Every moment shimmered with adrenaline and joy, as if the most ordinary tasks had suddenly become something worth remembering.

Margo arrived shortly after to join them for the hearty meal. Over plates of spaghetti and bursts of laughter, they discussed apartment options. Margo and Cindy had narrowed it down to four promising leads and planned to tour them with Laura over the weekend.

There was a catch to three of Cindy's choices: higher rent than her old place, questionable neighborhoods, or, in one case, a previous rejection.

Later that evening, after Margo had said her goodbyes and Paul had gone upstairs to rest, Cindy lingered on the couch, alone.

It was time again to see if she could contact her mother. She went downstairs to a payphone and dialed her mother's number. The phone rang twice.

"Hello?" Mrs. Spearman's tired voice answered, low and edged with caution.

"It's me, Momma," Cindy stated, her voice low. She tilted her head back, closed her eyes, and slowly exhaled, the weight of the moment pressing against her chest.

"Sweet angel," Mrs. Spearman exclaimed, a flood of relief in her voice. "I'm so happy to hear your voice. I tried calling so many times, but no one—"

"I messed up, Momma," Cindy blurted out, her voice cracking as the tears spilled freely. "I'm so sorry. I ruined everything."

"What do you mean? I don't understand."

"Jacob's gone, and it's all my fault."

There was a sharp intake of breath on the other end of the line.

"What?" Mrs. Spearman asked. "Sunshine's gone? What do you mean he's gone? What happened to him? Tell me!"

Clutching the phone like a lifeline and with trembling words and long pauses, Cindy told her mother everything: how she'd relapsed, how Jacob had been taken away, how she had been jailed, and how she had lost her apartment. It was heavy. It was shameful. It was the kind of truth she never imagined saying out loud.

Her mother didn't hang up. She listened and agreed to meet with Cindy the next day to file for temporary emergency custody.

The following morning, Cindy attended her first few classes as she waited for her mother to arrive. By early afternoon, Mrs. Spearman showed up on campus and took Cindy with her to the courthouse. Together, they filed a petition requesting an emergency hearing with a judge. Once the paperwork was submitted, Mrs.

Spearman checked into a nearby hotel and dropped Cindy off on campus to finish her remaining classes.

Early the next morning, a call came from the court clerk. The hearing was scheduled for that afternoon, and Cindy and her mother were required to be present.

Later that day, after reviewing the documentation and hearing their case, the judge granted Mrs. Spearman temporary custody of Jacob. The transfer was scheduled for the following afternoon.

Once Jacob was returned to his grandmother, Mrs. Spearman had no choice but to take him back with her to Tennessee immediately. The reunion between mother and son was brief, bittersweet, and ended with yet another promise from Cindy to make things right before the next court date.

Over the weekend, Cindy, Margo, and Laura toured the five apartment options.

The first was Margo's top pick: spacious, with updated appliances and a pool, and only a few blocks from campus, but it was far beyond Cindy's budget.

The second had less space, no pool, and was slightly farther from campus. It was still too expensive.

The third was even smaller, without a pool, and far enough from campus that Cindy would need to rely on the bus again or pedal her bike. The neighborhood looked decent at first glance, but rumors painted a mixed picture when it came to safety.

The fourth option was in noticeably bad shape: an old building that looked half-abandoned, with cracked windows, a crooked *No Trespassing* sign, and trash littered across the pavement. A used condom lay near the stairs like a warning.

"Uh, uh," Margo protested, shaking her head hard. "No way. We're not even getting out the car for this one."

Without hesitating, she hit the gas and drove off.

"How about the third one?" Laura suggested from the back seat. "It's kinda like your old place, just a little farther out. Or maybe even the second one? It's closer to school, which is always a plus. And you *did* say you could earn extra from your sketches."

"Maybe, but what if things slow down?" Cindy replied, glancing out the window. "It's not that consistent. I can't ask my mom for more help either, outside of co-signing. She's already struggling... probably more now because of me."

"Well, which one's it gonna be?" Margo asked.

"The third's my best bet," Cindy replied. "I'll fill out the application and take it back with Paul on Monday."

"Not to sound like a downer," Laura added, "but what if they don't approve it? Like... if they find out about your old place?"

Cindy closed her eyes and sighed deeply. "Then it'd have to be the fourth. I don't really have a choice. It's all I can afford right now."

"That's ridiculous," Margo stated, shaking her head. "Can't the school give you more money? It's not like giving you a little extra is going to bankrupt them. I think you need to talk to Ryan about the amount because you shouldn't be struggling this much. They should be ashamed of themselves."

"I can try talking to him on Monday," Cindy sighed. "If he's there. He's been out the last couple of days, which is not like him at all."

"When are you supposed to start attending the rehab program?" Laura asked.

"In a few days," Cindy replied, rolling her eyes. "Tuesday and Thursday evenings, right after the parenting classes. I'm going to be even busier during exams, no less...Perfect."

Margo wrinkled her nose, her brows knitting together.

"I was just thinking," she said. "Are you still going to keep the dress you got from Marcie's? I mean, the entire point of getting it was to show off at the art show."

Cindy gasped. Her eyes widened as her mouth dropped open.

"Oh no," she muttered under her breath. "I forgot all about it! I—I don't even know where it is! We had to clear everything out... It could be in the storage unit where Joel put everything, or maybe in Paul's trunk. But he's not home, and neither is his car!"

"Let's try Joel's first," Margo said. "I know he's home."

She drove them straight to the Gardere Apartments. Once there, she jumped out and dashed inside while Cindy and Laura waited anxiously in the car. A few minutes later, Margo returned and drove them to a nearby storage facility.

Using the key Joel had given her, she unlocked the unit, but to their dismay, everything inside was stacked tightly: the bed frame was upright, the couch was tilted sideways, and the table was buried under chairs and taped-up boxes.

Cindy and Laura tried squeezing through but couldn't make it past the tangle of furniture and endless boxes.

"Joel," Margo muttered through gritted teeth. Her gaze flicked towards the sky, and she let out a long, frustrated groan.

Off to the side, a man in a storage facility uniform leaned against the fence, sipping from a can of soda as he watched them with lazy curiosity. Margo stared back at him, expecting him to do something. He didn't budge. She tilted her head. Still, nothing happened. With a scoff, she marched over.

"Can't you see we need help moving that furniture?" Margo snapped. "Are you going to lend a hand, or just stand there doing nothing?"

"A 'please' wouldn't kill you," the man said flatly.

Margo spun toward Cindy. "Well? Tell him, Cindy."

Cindy wanted to roll her eyes, but muttered through her teeth, "Please."

She said it like it physically pained her, and for a second, she seriously considered smacking Margo for dragging her into such an awkward situation.

The man eventually came over and helped them shift the heavier items while Margo rifled through the clutter. After a few tense minutes, they finally found the dress tucked deep inside one of the boxes. Cindy's heart gave a small leap, until she noticed a streak of dried blue acrylic paint smeared across the side of the fabric.

Shoot.

Quickly, Cindy folded the dress and set it aside, disappointment curling in her stomach. Her friends and the storage attendant began restacking the items back into the cramped unit.

Once finished, Cindy thanked the attendant and handed him a few bills for his help while Margo locked the unit tight. She passed the key to Cindy before driving them back to the clothing store.

Though the dress still had its tags, it was wrinkled and carried dried paint. Cindy held it in her arms, silently hoping that some gentle care would make it look presentable when the time came.

The women hurried into Marcie's just before closing. Cindy and Margo headed straight for the counter while Laura dashed off to the restroom. Behind the register, a young salesclerk sat hunched over a thick textbook, not bothering to look up.

She twirled a lock of hair around her finger and popped her gum loudly, her eyes glued to the page as if the customers in front of her didn't exist.

Margo tapped her fingers on the counter, then cleared her throat. Nothing.

Growing tired and increasingly impatient, Cindy narrowed her eyes. She wondered if the clerk was deaf, blind, or just didn't care.

"Ahem," Cindy said as loudly as she could.

The clerk jumped, sending her book sliding to the floor. A folded, stapled paper partially slipped out and landed near Cindy's feet. Before the clerk could react, Cindy lifted the dress and held it out, forcing her attention back to the task at hand.

"I'd like to return this dress," Cindy said.

The clerk's expression soured, as if she were being inconvenienced by their presence.

"We're closed," she told them, her voice dismissive.

"We still have ten minutes," Cindy replied to the woman, who hesitantly reached for the garment with the tips of her fingers, unfolding it like it was contaminated. Her nose wrinkled as she caught sight of the faint smear of blue paint.

Cindy placed the receipt firmly on the counter.

"We cannot accept this dress back," the clerk said, placing it directly on top of the receipt.

"I have the receipt, and it's still within the return period," Cindy argued, her heart heavy.

"The dress needs to be returned in the same condition it was in when it left the store," the clerk told her. "This one clearly has stains and smells."

"Excuse me?" Cindy shot back. "What do you mean it smells? I haven't even worn it since the day I bought it. How could it possibly smell? And what stains? Are you just trying to be nasty right now?"

The clerk lifted the dress again, flipping the fabric to reveal a faint swipe of blue paint and a dried chalky patch near the underarm, deodorant remnants Cindy hadn't noticed.

Margo leaned in and shook her head.

"What good is a receipt if the return policy isn't honored?" she asked. "Every dress here has been tried on by half the town. The deodorant stains could have come from anybody. How do you know it's hers?"

"She wouldn't have purchased the dress if it already had stains and a bad smell," the clerk said, her voice dripping with condescension.

"It could have been there, and she didn't see it until later," Margo countered. "And what smell? Why would it smell bad if it has deodorant on it? This sounds like an excuse not to give her the money back. Is this store that desperate?"

"No, but we aren't taking back soiled clothing either," the clerk argued back.

"Then *clean* it," Cindy snapped, losing her patience, "because I'm not leaving without my money back!"

"It doesn't even fit her," Margo added. "Why should she keep something that doesn't fit, even with a receipt? Where's your manager? You clearly need more training in customer service. What a rude employee!"

"*What*?" The clerk exclaimed, her mouth dropping open in disbelief.

"She said get the manager, stupid," Cindy shot back. "Or are you refusing service because you're scared of what we might say?"

The two women locked eyes, hostility sparking between them like a silent storm about to burst.

"I'll get the manager," the clerk said through clenched teeth, spinning on her heel.

"What a bimbo," Margo muttered under her breath to Cindy.

Moments later, the clerk returned, accompanied by an older woman who inspected the dress with a scrutinizing gaze.

The manager pointed to the underarm area. "There's deodorant buildup here, and this smear of blue acrylic paint...We can't take the dress back in this condition, sorry. It's written in the receipt—"

Margo quickly jumped in. "Are you saying that it's now the customer's job to inspect every dress with a magnifying glass before buying it? Just to protect ourselves from other people's deodorant stains? Does this store even clean the dresses between customers trying them on? Ridiculous!"

"What about the blue paint?" the young clerk demanded before being shushed by the manager.

"How are we supposed to know where it came from?" Cindy challenged. "Maybe this store needs to be cleaner!"

"I shop here every week and spend thousands of dollars," Margo pressed, "but after this, I'm taking my business elsewhere. I'm reporting this to corporate and will be telling everyone I know not to support this store. You don't even follow the basics of retail. If we have a receipt, then take the dress back!"

The clerk was about to argue again, but the manager raised a hand to silence her. Sighing, the manager reluctantly handed Cindy her money back and stormed off toward her office.

"Rude," Margo whined. "I'm done shopping here. Where's Clara? They need to make her the new manager, because everyone working today acts like it's their first day."

"Tell me about it," Cindy agreed, slipping the cash into her wallet. As she turned to leave, she accidentally kicked the clerk's textbook aside. The stapled paper underneath flipped open, revealing multiple-choice questions with several highlighted answers, and others marked with handwritten answers.

Squatting down, Cindy tilted her head, furrowing her brows as she examined the document. At the top, in bold letters, were the words: **Spanish II Midterm Exam**.

"Why do you have a copy of a midterm exam?" Cindy asked, her eyes narrowing.

The clerk hurriedly stepped away from the counter, reaching to grab the paper, but Cindy stomped her foot down on it, narrowly missing the woman's hand.

"None of your business," the clerk snapped, tugging at the exam beneath Cindy's shoe. That's when Cindy noticed the pink and white sorority pin on the clerk's blouse, marked with the same Greek letters as Judy's.

"You go to Camellia University?" Cindy inquired.

"Listen, you got your money back. Now leave before I call security," the clerk barked.

"I want to know where you got the exam from."

"You're crazy! Buzz off! I'm calling security!"

"Go ahead! That way, we'll have proof you stole a university exam, and maybe get you expelled. Now, where did it come from? Or will security have to ask all three of us questions? I'm sure the Dean of Students would love to hear everyone's story too."

"Security," Margo called out, her voice dripping with mockery.

"Shut up," the clerk begged, her tone suddenly pleading. "Okay, okay, I got it from my boyfriend."

"How'd *he* get it?" Margo pressed.

"He's a graduate student and sometimes makes copies of the tests and exams for the Foreign Language professors." The clerk's voice cracked as tears welled up. "Please don't tell anyone. We'll both get in trouble, and neither of us can afford to get kicked out of school. I won't be able to transfer anywhere else, and my student loans will ruin me."

"That's not our problem," Margo said flatly, folding her arms. "You knew what you were doing before you got caught."

"Yeah, tell your boyfriend hi for me," Cindy told the clerk. "I think I've met him before, through his work, when he tried to fail me on purpose. Consider this payback."

"Please, don't," the clerk begged. "He'll lose everything and blame me."

"It'll be okay," Margo assured her. "Once he gets over it, he can help hold your hand while you both cry about your loans. Boohoo. So sad."

"Yeah," Cindy agreed. "Where was all that compassion when he was trying to ruin me?"

"I'm sorry for him," the clerk offered weakly. "Please don't tell anyone about this. I'll do anything."

"I'm not falling for that," Cindy snapped. "I bet this is another one of Dan's little stunts, huh?"

"No, we don't even like him! He's only going along with whatever Dan wants because he's blackmailing him."

"How would we know if that's the truth or not?"

"I don't know!"

The manager stepped out of the office and reminded everyone that it was closing time.

Cindy stared at the clerk carefully. The woman was trembling, and her eyes were full of dread. She wasn't sure if it was all an act or not, but even though the clerk had been rude earlier, she didn't do nearly as much as others had.

Cindy picked up the exam, folded it, and tucked it into her purse.

"We're taking the exam," she stated, "for insurance. You keep quiet about it, and we'll forget you and your boyfriend ever existed. I'm sure he can make another copy since this one got 'misplaced.'"

"How do I know you won't go to the dean on us anyway?"

"I guess we'll have to trust each other and find out, huh?"

"And don't think of double-crossing her," Margo warned. "We know where you work and can pinpoint your boyfriend now. Who knows what we're capable of?"

The two women walked briskly away and headed to the restroom where Laura was washing her hands. After Cindy and Margo finished and washed their hands, they met Laura near the door to walk back to Margo's car.

"Why take the test?" Margo whispered to Cindy. "She could always claim you stole it since you're the one holding it now."

"She might try it," Cindy whispered back, "but that would only get her boyfriend in trouble too. How else would I have the test unless he's the one copying them? They're better off staying quiet. Either way, we've got leverage."

"Don't be stupid like her and walk around with that exam in your purse," Margo warned. "You'll blow the whole thing. Hide it at home somewhere safe until you figure out what to do with it."

"Got it," Cindy said.

Cindy wasn't exactly sure about what she was going to do with the exam, but one thing was for certain: Dan and Judy seemed to be pulling the strings behind the scenes. Manipulating even graduate students? That was confirmed. How high up the ladder did their network go? If she had been double-crossed, apparently, others probably had been too.

Her thoughts turned sharply to Judy.

"Tell Dan I got Millie to help with his little problem," Judy's voice was overheard bragging. *"Honestly, it was too easy."*

Cindy pinched her lips thin. *I've been through too much to let any of this go. It was all easy, huh? I guess it was easy to ruin my life, and everyone else's. Well, bitch, let's see how easy it's gonna be now that things are about to change, one way or the other.*

Chapter 21

On the way back to Paul's penthouse, Margo dropped Laura off at home, then pulled over to a payphone. Cindy stepped out, fed a few coins into the slot, and gripped the phone as she dialed her mother's number.

"Hi, Momma. It's me," Cindy said.

"Hi, Sweet Angel!" Mrs. Spearman replied, her voice light. "I was just thinking about you."

"I'm sorry, Momma," Cindy told her. "For everything I've put you and Jacob through. I'm trying. My friends and I have been looking for an apartment, and I've put in several applications. I'm about to start the rehab program and take parenting classes. I won't mess up again. I promise."

"I know you will," Mrs. Spearman said.

"How are you and Jacob doing?"

"We're doing fine. Sunshine's been quieter lately, but is slowly starting to come back around. He sure does miss you, though. I told him we'll see you again soon. As for me, the doctor says I'm healing like I should."

"I'm glad. Summer's just around the corner. Once I get a new place and things start to settle down, I hope to see both of you again. We could go to the beach and enjoy ourselves."

"That sounds wonderful. Sunshine loves playing in the sand. I wish I could have taken you more often when you were little. You loved building sandcastles and flying kites. I miss those times, but now we'll get to make new memories, even better ones, with Sunshine."

"Yes, Momma. We could all use that break and have something good to look forward to, especially after everything that's happened."

"Before I forget, any news on the article?" Mrs. Spearman asked.

Cindy hesitated before speaking.

"They decided not to run it," she admitted. "I was hoping they would, but they went with someone else from the theater department instead."

There was a pause at the end of the line.

"That's shameful," Mrs. Spearman sighed. "For them to make a promise like that and not honor their word. I have half a mind to call there and file a complaint."

"It's fine, really. I've moved past it," Cindy said, trying to sound unfazed. "I don't need some silly article to get recognition. Like my friend Paul told me, the art speaks for itself."

"But you deserved that recognition. We both know how much that article meant, not just to you, but to everyone. They had no right to pull the rug out like that."

"I know," Cindy said, keeping her tone light but firm. "But, from what other people said, the show was a success, and I managed to sell most of my art. So, it was a hit, even without the article."

"I'm glad," her mother stated. "That shows them what you're made of. I'm proud of you, baby. Never forget that."

"Thanks, Momma...I just don't know why I keep messing things up. I think something's wrong with me."

"No, Sweet Angel. There's nothing wrong with you. You're young and still navigating life. We all go through things, but we learn and grow from them."

Cindy wiped away a tear that slid down her cheek.

"I'm proud that you took accountability for your actions," Mrs. Spearman added. "We got Sunshine back, and you are getting the new apartment, getting clean, and getting life back in order. Keep doing that."

"But what if I fail?"

"But what if you succeeded too? Keep trying, baby. It'll work out. Just believe in yourself, that you can do it. I believe that you can, and you will."

"Thanks, Momma."

"All I want for you is to be happy. Nothing more. Always remember that I love you, Sweet Angel, alright?"

"Yes, Momma. I want you to be happy too. I love you too, and Jacob as well."

There was a short pause, but Cindy knew it was her mother smiling quietly on the other end of the line. They spoke for a few more minutes before Cindy hung up the phone and returned to Margo's car.

She was dropped off at Paul's place and entered the home.

Paul was sitting on the couch, as if waiting for her. Their eyes lit up at the sight of each other, but only briefly.

"Hey, Cin. Any luck with the search?" Paul asked.

"A possibility for one... and a miracle for two," Cindy admitted, sitting down beside him. She glanced at the notebook in his lap, filled with notes.

"Don't sweat it," Paul said. "Whichever one you decide on, the guys and I will help with the move. Only next time, let's try to plan it earlier than the day of."

"Don't remind me," Cindy groaned, covering her face with her hands and dragging them down. "Thanks for helping me then, and now. Believe me, I'm working on getting everything sorted and moving as fast as I can. I'm sure you'd like to have your place back to yourself."

"Well, it's also nice to have company," Paul beamed. "I was a latchkey kid growing up, and it got pretty lonely. I started playing sports just to be around other people after school, at least until I was old enough to start helping with the family business."

"I'd just stay a little longer after school," Cindy sighed. "If it had just been Momma and me, I think I would have been happier. I don't know if she would have been. There was a short time when it was just the two of us, but sometimes I wonder...if I had been the daughter my dad wanted, would their marriage have lasted longer?"

"Would you have been happier too?" asked Paul.

"I don't know," Cindy replied. "Have you ever regretted something so long, and been through so much, that you can't remember what real happiness feels like anymore?"

"Yeah," Paul admitted. "But, it is out there, in different ways. Not in anything Dan ever gave us."

"Yeah," Cindy softly echoed. "I thought if I could just numb myself, I wouldn't have to feel anything. Feeling sad all the time is draining, and I don't want to be sad anymore."

Paul's eyes softened. He pulled her into a hug, one that lingered just a moment longer than casual.

"Whatever happiness feels like to you," he said, "hold onto it. Even if it's just a memory you have to rewind a thousand times, but always be open to making more."

Cindy giggled.

"And more and more, I get it," she laughed. "So, how'd your morning go? You left early."

"I dropped by the clinic," Paul admitted, "They had the results from the first day. It was positive, but I'll be okay. I've been taking the meds, so I'm already on the right track."

"I don't think I have it in me to go back," Cindy confessed. "I'll just finish the treatment and try to put it all behind me."

"If you change your mind, I'll go with you."

"Thanks...How are classes going?"

"The pressure is definitely on," Paul chuckled nervously. "I'm still trying to make sense of some of these notes. I had to make copies of Greyson's notes for one class we take together. It's...a lot... that I was dumb enough to miss."

"Do you know if any exams are circulating around?" Cindy asked.

"I'm sure they are, but I'm not getting involved. I've got enough on my plate. If I pass a class, great. If not, I'll take it again next semester."

Cindy nodded, then hesitated.

"I have a quick question," she added.

"Go for it."

"When you hang out with Judy, has she ever given you any white tablets?"

"You mean acid tablets?"

"Not quite. They're bigger, but white. Do you know what they are?"

"I'm not sure. I don't know everything that's floating around campus. I could ask Judy."

"No, it's nothing. I was just curious."

"Why? You need some?"

"No, forget I said anything," Cindy said, forcing a laugh. She began to stretch. "I need to get serious about these art history notes."

"Get them out," Paul said. "We might be studying for different classes, but since we're both here, we might as well hit the books together."

"Cool, let's do it," Cindy smiled.

On Monday, it was time to return to Ryan's painting class, but before Cindy could step inside, the professor stopped her at the door and motioned her into his office for an unwanted detour.

Cindy nearly rolled her eyes. She resisted the urge to toss her head back or throw her hands in the air. *Another lecture. Just great. Here we go again.*

Ryan folded his arms across his chest and leaned back against his desk. His voice was steady, though a touch of disappointment showed through.

"I wanted to check in," he told her. "You were gone for a while and missed the reception. We haven't had a chance to talk about it."

"Well, a lot happened during that time," Cindy responded, keeping her tone polite but guarded. She wasn't about to explain that she'd been arrested, had her son taken away, was currently homeless, and was now staring down rehab, along with a dozen other problems she was barely keeping afloat. "It's very personal. I hope you understand..."

Ryan tilted his head.

"I had a chance to talk to Mrs. Everett about the missing article," he continued. "I'll be honest. I'm disappointed by her decision, and I'm sure you are too. She told me her reasoning, but I can't say I agree. Unfortunately, this is one of those harsh realities of life. Yet, where one door closes, another opens. I spoke with a few professors at the local state and community colleges, and we thought it might be a good idea to have our students showcase their work at one of the downtown galleries this summer. It would give you a chance to meet other art students in the area and build your network."

"Really?"

"Yeah, I think it would be a great way to expand beyond our campus," He glanced at his watch. "Well, it's almost time for class."

They were about to leave when Cindy stopped at the door.

"Can I be honest about something?" she asked. "I don't want to say too much, but I wouldn't bring it up if I didn't need to. I can't keep going like this. I've been struggling a lot this past year. I can't afford to stay in the program with so little money to live on. Something came up, and now I need to move, but finding a decent place with what I'm making feels impossible."

"Most students think our scholarships are more than generous," Ryan told her, squinting his eyes. "How much more do you need?"

"More than I have now," she said. "I just need something livable, especially if I'm not allowed to work anywhere else."

Ryan drew his head back, as if to say, *she can't be serious*. He turned to his file cabinet, rifled through a few folders, and pulled one with Cindy's name on it. It contained documents regarding her scholarship. He flipped to the page showing the amount she was supposed to receive.

"How is that not enough?" he asked. "We've had plenty of students over the years get far less without complaint."

Cindy leaned forward to read the document. Her stomach twisted.

"But, I'm not receiving that much," she said quietly. "It's way less."

Ryan squinted at her, clearly thrown off.

"If it's less than that, it wouldn't be correct at all," he said, shaking his head. "And you've been getting less for a whole year?"

Cindy nodded.

"After class," Ryan instructed her, "go to both the financial aid office and the bursar's office. Tell them there's an issue with your scholarship funds. I'll give you a copy of your scholarship paperwork to take with you."

"Thank you," Cindy replied, her voice unsteady with a jittery swell in her chest.

Straightening her posture, she followed Ryan into the studio where other students were beginning to file in. He instructed the class to bring their current projects to the front for the usual lineup.

Cindy made a beeline for her usual painting space, but froze.

She stared at her newest incomplete painting. Across the canvas, smeared in bright red paint, were large, jagged letters: **Bitch.**

Cindy's eyes went wide. The world seemed to spin. Her hand flew to her mouth, which had fallen open, but no sound came out. Desperately, she pushed the easel closer to the wall just as the first few students trickled in.

No, no, no. Not today. Not now.

"Alrighty then," Ryan called out to his students, snapping his fingers. "Line them up, everyone. Line them up."

No, not today!

Faintly, Cindy watched her peers carry their paintings forward, one by one, placing them in line near the front of the studio for the critique. The last student scooted her stool forward, and Ryan moved among the paintings, arranging them in the usual judgmental lineup.

It's over. Any hope left for me is gone. She thought about all the hours she poured into the piece. Now, it had been violated, and so was she.

"Any time, Cindy," Ryan said, standing at the front of the studio where the others gathered.

Oh my God, this isn't me. This isn't a reflection of everything I worked for. I didn't do this.

She thought about refusing to take the painting up there. But with Ryan, that was never an option. He didn't allow excuses, and she was trapped.

Shit. Shit, shit, shit.

Clenching her fingers briefly into claws, Cindy reluctantly carried the painting to the front of the room. They wanted a painting, and this was all she had. Her heart pounding, she set it down hard in front of the class. Gasps echoed across the room. A few students chuckled. Others stared, wide-eyed, whispering to their neighbor.

Ryan's glasses nearly slipped off his nose as he stared at the painting.

There. I hope everyone is happy now, Cindy thought bitterly as she hurled herself into a chair.

For the first time, there was a lingering hush in the studio. All eyes remained fixed on Cindy's vandalized painting, and Ryan did not move it from where it had been placed.

"I... I like it," Ronald said, breaking the silence and a class rule. All eyes bounced between him and Cindy, then back to Ryan, who rubbed his chin. "I mean... it speaks to me. The red paint shows anger and hostility, which contrasts with the calm, cool colors underneath. It expresses tension in a way..."

"I can see that," another student chimed in. "It could mean that, even behind anger and bitterness, there's a hidden person crying out for help. That's what I get from the blue figure underneath. I see hidden feelings..."

Ryan sighed. Then, to everyone's surprise, he picked up Cindy's vandalized painting and placed it in first place, right at the front of the class.

To Cindy's surprise, more compliments followed, with students adding layers of interpretation. They spoke of freedom of self-expression, the fragility of the psyche, being overly self-critical, projecting emotions onto others, vanity, and more.

The conversation became so impassioned that Ryan had to remind the class there were other paintings still to review. By the end, Cindy had received more praise and feedback than she ever expected. Several classmates even called it one of the most powerful critiques of the semester.

As the class returned their canvases to the easels, Cindy began gathering her things to leave. Ryan stepped into the doorway to speak with her.

"Stellar painting," he said. "While I don't typically condone vulgar language, especially when directed at women, your piece made me reflect on the inner and outer conflicts women face today... The harsh and often unfair expectations, the strain on mental health, the constant social scrutiny, and the reality of harassment. It holds many compelling layers. This is your strongest work yet. Congratulations."

With that, he stepped aside, offering a subtle smile that barely reached the corners of his mouth.

After class, Cindy went to the financial aid office, where it was determined that there had been a clerical error. They filled out paperwork for her to give to the bursar's office and sent her there. The bursar's office informed Cindy that she would receive the correct amount of money owed, including a lump sum of the missing funds from the previous year.

Enthused, Cindy felt a heaviness lifted off her shoulders that she hadn't realized she'd been carrying until that moment. With the extra money, she could finally afford either of her top two apartment choices.

When she met with Paul again to drop off the apartment applications later that day, she smiled as she filled out the forms. For the first time, living there wasn't just a distant dream, it was an actual possibility.

With the right approval, it could be the beginning of something new.

A week had passed, and Cindy had begun attending her rehab and parenting sessions, scheduled every Tuesday and Thursday for the next three months. After a brief medical evaluation, she was placed in a group therapy session with women much older than herself, making her the youngest in the room. The experience was awkward and humbling. She sat silently, listening to their stories, each one shaped by hardship, regret, and the quiet strength it took to speak aloud.

Cindy felt too ashamed to contribute. She wasn't ready to admit how far she had fallen, not at nineteen. She wasn't ready to admit that she had started using even earlier, at fifteen, when her life began to unravel after she kissed a former friend, a girl, and was ostracized for it. That memory lingered, vivid and unresolved. And now, somewhere deep inside, she wondered if she was repeating the same pattern with Paul, desiring him in ways she couldn't quite name, needing him to want her back, just to feel whole.

She began to feel more at ease when the women shared stories about losing their children and their homes. There was a quiet sense of camaraderie in the room of pain recognizing pain. Still, it felt too early for her to speak. What would she even say? That her father, Mr. Spearman, once called her a walking lunatic and blamed her for the end of his marriage? That she lost her virginity to a neighbor who practically abandoned her after "showing her what it felt like to be with a guy"? It all sounded pathetic in her head. Who would want to hear that?

She could already picture their faces, polite, maybe even kind, but silently judging. She didn't want to look stupid. Not again.

After Cindy's first session ended, she stepped out into the parking lot where Paul was waiting, leaning against the car with his arms crossed. He smiled faintly as she approached and opened the passenger door for her.

On the drive back to the penthouse, Paul grabbed the day's mail from the lobby and thumbed through it.

"Here you go," he said, handing her a thin white envelope as they took the elevator. "Looks like something from that apartment complex you applied to."

Cindy graciously took the envelope and waited until they were back inside Paul's place to open it. She sat down on the edge of the couch, carefully sliding her finger under the seal while Paul wandered into the kitchen for a soda.

Cindy tore it open, her breath held tight with hope. Yet, as her eyes scanned the paper, her stomach dropped.

No.

Her hands trembled slightly.

Oh God, no, she thought, blinking rapidly. *They must've found out something from Mr. Tanner... or maybe it was the old income records. But I need somewhere to go. I need a place so I can move forward. I need to prove I can be a good mother and prove to myself that I can build something better. How am I supposed to show I'm trying if nobody gives me a chance?*

"What'd they say?" Paul asked, sitting beside her, concern clouding his eyes.

"I got denied," Cindy said, her voice flat and hollow. She scrunched the letter into a ball and set it on the coffee table. Leaning back into the couch, she looked up toward the ceiling, then down at the floor.

"That's one place," Paul told her. "You applied to others."

"I won't get either of them," Cindy muttered, swallowing a sob and swiping at the corners of her eyes. "Not after what happened with Mr. Tanner. I might as well crawl to that dump that Margo hated. Maybe they'll take me. Maybe that'll be the only shoo-in I get."

"You can always stay here," Paul offered, "for as long as you want."

"I can't," Cindy whispered, shaking her head. "It has to be mine. Otherwise, I'm a failure."

"But you're not—"

"I'm sorry," she interrupted. "I'm just frustrated. I don't want to overstay my welcome."

"I get it. Just take a breath. Waiting is hard, but you need to be patient. There are still other options. We'll look again this weekend, alright? There's bound to be something out there."

"Thanks," Cindy murmured, her voice heavy with fatigue.

Paul reached out and gave her hand a soft squeeze.

A knock at the door broke the moment. Paul walked to the door and answered it. To Cindy's dismay, Judy strutted in, her voice already raised.

"Ugh, I hate Ryan," she fumed. "That bastard thought he was hurting me by kicking me out? Please.

I'm gonna have Daddy pull a few strings and get him fired. Let's see how he likes *that*. How about them apples?"

Judy came to a sudden halt, spotting Cindy on the couch. Her eyes flicked from Paul to Cindy, narrowing with distaste. She pressed a hand to her temple and squinted her eyes as if Cindy's mere presence triggered a headache.

"Some things never change," Judy uttered, slapping her hand against her thigh.

"Let's go out to the balcony," Paul told Judy, who followed him.

Cindy stayed frozen on the couch, but their voices carried through the barely cracked balcony door.

"What's the deal?" Judy hissed. "What's she still doing here? Are you two dating now?"

"That's our business," Paul shot back. "The real question is, why do you keep showing up wherever I go?"

"If you'd stop lying to me, maybe I wouldn't have to," Judy countered. "The only reason I didn't dump Ryan sooner is because *you* said you didn't want anything serious. Yet, every time I turn around, there you are, eating with Cindy in the cafeteria, walking around like some couple...and now she's moved in?"

"Someone's been busy playing spy," Paul said coldly.

"Well, then, maybe your girlfriend would like to know you gave me gonorrhea."

"You're not gonna pin the whole gonorrhea issue on me. I didn't even have gonorrhea until after I got to the school. For all I know, you gave it to me. It's not like you haven't been sleeping around either."

"Oh, please," Judy scoffed. "Look at who you're sleeping with. You've been sleeping with that walking infection, and I'm the one paying for it! Don't even try to compare what I've done to the garbage Cindy's pulling. That little gutter rat's been manipulating everyone around her just to climb her way up. I thought you, of all people, would be smarter than this."

"I think you should leave," Paul groaned. I don't have time for this jealousy crap."

"Why won't you open your eyes? We'd be *great* together. Don't you want me anymore, or was all of it fake?"

"Come on. We both knew what it was. Just sex, remember? No strings."

"Why does it *have* to be that way?" Judy demanded. "Is it because of her? Is Cindy better than me? Is *that* what this is about? She's disgusting; you saw how she was living!"

"Stop it," Paul snapped. "I'm not going to stand here and listen to you badmouth Cindy. None of this should be happening! You and I were *never* a couple! Yeah, we hung out, fooled around, whatever, but I never dated you and never led you on. So, why are you still showing up?"

"Oh, I get it now. I was used and tossed aside, right?"

"No, not by me, but a *lot* of people on campus could say that about *you*. So, why would I take someone like that seriously?"

"You're a jerk, you know that?"

"Fine, I'll be a jerk. I'll be anything you want, if it gets you to leave and never come back."

Fuming, Judy stormed back into the home, her eyes locking on Cindy like daggers. Her expression said it all: *This isn't over. Not by a long shot.*

Paul reentered the home, his eyes scanning the tension that still lingered in the room.

"For God's sake, Judy, go home," he told her, his voice firm.

Judy choked back a sob and stormed out of the penthouse.

At her wits' end, Cindy briefly considered leaving too, just to escape. However, she wasn't about to step outside with that stalker still hanging around. It was better to wait until the coast was clear.

"Cin," Paul said, lowering himself onto the couch beside her. "I'm so sorry about that."

"I'm going to call Laura," Cindy replied. "I'll see if I can stay at her place. Obviously, I'm not welcome here."

"What?" Paul's head shot up. "You can still stay. I wouldn't have let you in if you weren't welcome."

Cindy turned slightly toward him, her expression unreadable. "So...was she your girlfriend?"

"No," Paul said quickly. "She wanted to be, but I'd never date someone like her." He exhaled slowly and added, "Actually... I think I'm done. I'm taking a break from trying to see what else is out there."

Cindy's heart sank.

"I thought dating around would help," Paul admitted. "I figured if I kept moving forward, I'd stop looking back, but it's the same thing, over and over again."

He took a deep, pained breath.

"I still love my ex," he continued. "I'd give up everything: this apartment, my savings, everything, just to have her back. She's the one I really want, and the truth is...I'm not ready to let go. I don't know if I ever will be."

Paul cleared his throat.

"And you know what's worse?" he asked. "Not knowing if she still loves me as much as I love her."

"Then why break up?"

"We...we never did," said Paul, lowering his head. His eyes brimming with tears, he rose to his feet and quietly ascended the stairs. A moment later, he disappeared into the bedroom and shut the door softly behind him.

Cindy lingered on the sofa. She was tired.

I think I'm done too, she thought. *I think it's time to move on. Why should I keep waiting and hoping for something that isn't there? Paul's been honest, but I haven't been honest with myself. He's waiting for someone, and it's not me. I deserve love. Real love, with someone who's waiting for me.*

Chapter 22

Wednesday morning, Cindy sat alone in the courtyard. She didn't care if Judy, Dan, or anybody else was spying on her. She was done being sad, done hiding, and done overthinking. It was time to move on, without letting someone puppeteer her next move.

"Hey, Cindy."

Cindy turned to see Gordon approaching.

"I got more acid, if you're looking to buy some," he offered.

Cindy smirked, then scoffed.

Paul was right, she thought. *Nothing he or Dan offers will ever help. I'll just end up back in reality again, so I might as well face it now.*

"No, thanks," she sighed, breathing in the crisp air.

Gordon nodded and started to walk away.

Cindy looked up at the beautiful clock tower. Fifteen minutes until painting class. If she had more time, she'd start a new piece, one with more hope. Maybe of someone starting over. Maybe of someone finally living their truth.

She stood up and quickly called out.

"Wait," she said, hurrying after him.

Gordon stopped and turned.

"Do you have any white tablets?" Cindy asked.

"Lots," Gordon said. "What are you looking for?"

Cindy began describing the white tablets she had taken before, the ones left by her adversary.

"You want PCP?" Gordon said. "I got some, but be careful. That stuff can get ugly. People go into frenzies. One guy poked his own eyes out after taking one."

Judy gave me PCP? Cindy blinked, stunned. *She wanted me to lose it. I lost my apartment, my kid, and my freedom because of that night. Sure, I took it, but I didn't know what it was or what it would do. She tried to ruin me. Then Dan, Millie, Eileen, and Ann. They all must have had a field day at my expense.*

"No, I was just asking," Cindy said with a calm smile. "I'll see you around."

As she walked away, her thoughts boiled. *Judy had the nerve to start fights with both Ryan and Paul, and they didn't back down. So why should I? Why should she get a pass after everything she did to me?*

It was time to start leveling the playing field, her way.

Cindy turned sharply and made her way toward the administration building. At the dean's office, she approached the secretary.

"I need to speak with Dean Kelly. It's important," she said.

I might fail, she thought, settling into a nearby chair, *but I've got to try.*

She slowly exhaled.

Ok, Gail and the dean failed to get rid of Dan last time, but only because nobody else wanted to come forward. People were either too scared, indifferent, or just as bad as he was. Did he send Millie to scare me with that story? Was it true or bait?

Cindy shifted in her chair.

I don't know, she thought, *but it was a tactic to read me. Same with Eileen and Ann. They played nice, questioned me like friends, only to stab me in the back.*

Cindy began to bite her nails while staring down at the rug.

Then there was Dan. He was bold enough to show up in art history. That proves he'll do his own dirty work if pushed hard enough. One guy defended me, but it's too much to ask him to go against a whole network of people.

She eyed the exit but remained seated.

And Judy? She'd deny everything. Even though she was behind it, she'd tell the dean about the night I went off the rails, call me a PCP addict, and bring up the apartment, the arrest, and Jacob. Everything I lost. She could flip the truth into a weapon. Dan could too.

Cindy closed her eyes and took a calming breath.

What I need is proof. Something solid. Not just words pointing fingers...Maybe that moment in the store...perhaps it was a blessing in disguise. It's small, and it has its flaws, but it's something.

Minutes later, a student exited the office, and Cindy was called inside. She entered, closed the door behind herself, and took a seat across from the dean.

"What brings you in today, Ms. Spearman?" Dean Kelly asked, folding his hands on the desk.

The dean, a bald man with clear blue eyes, wore a dark navy business suit, a checkered light-blue-and-white tie, and polished shoes. His office was immaculate: plush executive furniture, a shelf of honor plaques, framed photos of him shaking hands with campus officials, and a large window that looked out over the well-manicured campus lawn.

"I'm sorry to disturb you, sir," Cindy said. "But do you remember when a student named Gail Roberts came to speak with you about Dan Jones?"

Dean Kelly nodded slightly. "I do recall that time. Go on."

"Back then, you asked several students if we knew anything," Cindy continued. "I had my reasons for not coming forward sooner. But I'm here now because I can't keep silent anymore. I need help, and I think you're the only one who can provide it."

She took a breath, steadying herself.

"These past few months have been miserable, not only because of Dan, but because of other students working with him. They've been selling drugs, stalking people, using blackmail, and helping others cheat. If I was questioned back then, then clearly I was close enough to know something. If I was that close before, I still know something now. I've seen and heard things."

Dean Kelly remained quiet, listening.

"There's a sorority girl named Judy Bowman," Cindy went on. "She's working with Dan. She's helped stalk people. She encouraged cheating. And...she's drugged students. She drugged me with PCP. I didn't know what it was at the time, but it ruined my life. I lost my home, my child, and my freedom over that."

Her voice trembled for a second, then steadied.

"I'll admit I took the tablet, but I didn't know what it was. What kind of person would willingly throw their life away like that unless they were being manipulated? And I was."

Dean Kelly leaned back, still listening intently.

"Before I say more," Cindy asked cautiously, "I need to know, can I get in trouble for coming forward with this? For what I'm about to say?"

The dean folded his hands again. "That depends on what you share, but I need something more than words. If you want my help, I'll need evidence, something with real weight behind it."

"If you can find a way to send someone to Dan's place on a Monday night, around 10 p.m., you'll see it for yourself," Cindy continued. "That's when the parties happen. He and a bunch of others do all kinds of illegal drugs."

She leaned in slightly.

"There's a pattern. Sometimes the parties are at his place, sometimes at nearby apartments. But it's always in the same area, always around the same time. He rotates between his unit and about four others. It's like clockwork. He doesn't just do it for the money. He gets a kick out of it, watching people spiral. Then he uses it against them later. He gets people hooked and blackmails them."

Dean Kelly sat forward in his seat, visibly more attentive now.

"And it's not just drugs," Cindy added. "He and students like Judy Bowman have been circulating copies of professors' exams. They help other students cheat. I've seen it with my own eyes."

The dean raised an eyebrow. "That's a serious accusation. Do you have any evidence to support these claims?"

"Yes, sir. If you check the attendance records, you'll see that Dan rarely attends class, especially this semester. Yet somehow, he keeps acing his exams. That's because he's not the one taking them."

Dean Kelly leaned in slightly, squinting his eyes.

Cindy explained further. "In Mrs. Garcia's class, for example, there's a student named Millie Fellows who's been taking his exams for him. Have Mrs. Garcia show you the handwriting. Compare Millie's handwriting to the test sheets that supposedly belong to Dan. Also, you might find matching samples on any attendance forms. If professors started making copies of their exams, counted them before and after distributing, or used multiple versions of the same tests with the questions in a different order, without telling the grad students, you'd be able to catch them in the act."

"That's Dan," Dean Kelly said with a nod. "What about Judy Bowman? Do you have any evidence against her?"

"Yes, sir," Cindy replied, her voice low. "But I don't want to get expelled for showing it to you."

"What is it?" the dean asked. "I still need something tangible to work with. Otherwise, these are just accusations."

After a brief hesitation, Cindy reached into her purse and removed the folded exam. She handed it to the dean, who began to scan it with his eyes.

"This is a Spanish II exam..." Dean Kelly uttered.

Cindy nodded. "It's one of the tests Judy and her sorority sisters have been circulating. I got it from one of them, and she told me directly that Judy was the one who gave it to her."

Dean Kelly's gaze sharpened. "And the name of this sorority sister?"

"I can't say," Cindy replied. "If she's exposed, they'll trace it back to me."

"That's understandable," the dean said slowly. "But how do I know you're not the one using this exam to cheat?"

"It's a Spanish II exam," Cindy explained. "I'm in Spanish I. That test wouldn't help me at all, except as proof of what I'm telling you."

Dean Kelly sighed, glancing between Cindy and the exam.

"I'll need you to file a formal written grievance outlining everything you've told me about the students involved," he said. "From there, I'll initiate an internal investigation. Your identity will remain confidential. Only administrators directly handling the case will be informed, but keep in mind, those students will still have their right to due process."

He handed Cindy a grievance form. She carefully documented everything she told him, including the exact addresses of the other locations where Dan hosted his parties. She also placed the bulk of the blame on Dan and Judy. It was a stretch claiming that Judy's sorority sister had directly accused her, but at this point, Cindy reasoned, Judy had to be taken down by any means necessary. If Judy could play dirty, then so could she. For all she knew, Judy had been behind it all along. Let the cards fall where they may.

She included Millie's involvement, and out of spite, listed Eileen and Ann's names as well. If they wanted to betray her and sleep with Paul, they'd have to face the consequences too.

Fighting the urge to smile or laugh with relief, Cindy handed the completed form back to Dean Kelly, who immediately began reviewing it.

"Thank you for bringing this to my attention," he said.

Cindy left the administration building with a surge of triumph welling inside her. She was tempted to jump into the air, shout for joy, and even throw in a heel click.

That'll show them for messing with me, she thought fiercely. *They should've left me alone. Maybe now, they'll know what it feels like to take what they've been dishing out on me and on other students. If they can work in a network, so can I. They think I'm powerless? I'll use power to fight power.*

"Hey, Carol," Judy's voice said back then. "It's me. Looks like we're done here. She's as good as gone. Tell Dan I got Millie to help with his little problem. Honestly, it was too easy."

Easy, huh? Cindy thought, her eyes going cold. *Looks like I'm finished here too, bitch. I'm done playing your stupid games. The dean's helping me now. Let's see how easy things are when he starts investigating and calls you into his office.*

Chapter 23

Over the weekend, Paul left the penthouse to work on a paper at the library. Cindy stayed behind and brought in the mail. Among the usual envelopes, one stood out, another letter from one of the apartments she'd applied to.

Her heart sank as she opened it. Another rejection.

Still, she refused to give up. With a determined sigh, she picked up the phone and called Laura.

An hour later, the two pulled up outside the building. It was the same rundown place Margo had refused to enter.

I don't like this place either, Cindy thought, *but if this is what it takes to make a way for myself, so be it. No one else is giving me a chance.*

Grimacing at the surroundings, Laura hesitated at the door. "Cin, are you sure about this?"

"It's not like I have a lot of options," Cindy told her. "I need a roof over my head, and I can't stay at Paul's forever."

Inside, the owner met them with a flat expression.

"It's just a room," she said bluntly, "with a month-to-month lease. No co-signer is needed, as long as you've got the cash. You could move in today."

"I have it," Cindy said, "but could I see the room first?"

The owner led them up the stairs and down a dim hallway. As they walked, the sound of harsh coughing and throat-clearing echoed through the narrow corridor, exposing how paper-thin the walls were. A tall, skeletal man with sunken eyes and a sickly pallor shuffled past them, like some ghostly figure from a fever dream.

Startled, Laura gasped and instinctively pressed herself against the wall to avoid him.

Cindy saw him too, heard the rattle in his chest, but forced herself to act like it didn't bother her. She walked on, pretending everything was fine, even as unease settled over her like dust.

The owner unlocked the door to the room. Inside, there was only a single bed with a worn, bare mattress. A window without blinds or curtains let in pale afternoon light.

Laura's face tightened, concern evident as her hand rose to her lips. The wallpaper peeled away in strips, and the floor groaned beneath their steps. A single bare light bulb hung from the ceiling, its flickering glow offering little comfort.

"Cin, are you sure about living here?" Laura whispered, her voice thick with desperation. "You could stay with me. This place isn't safe. Honestly, I don't think I could leave you here. I'd never forgive myself."

"Everything's fine," Cindy said firmly. "It just needs the right touch. With some care, it'll look as good as new."

Suddenly, a hurried noise echoed down the hallway, causing both women to flinch.

Laura shook her head quickly, raising her voice as if she no longer cared about offending the owner. "I'm not letting you stay here. I just can't."

"Well, where am I supposed to go?" Cindy whispered back.

"Anywhere but here," Laura replied. "This place? It's not suitable for a child, or for you! Cindy, I'll pay for a better apartment, one that's safe and secure. I'll even sign for it myself."

Cindy took a deep breath. "No, I can't rely on people to do everything for me, like I'm some little kid."

"Cin," Laura pleaded, "if you stay here, you'd never regain custody of Jacob. This place isn't safe."

"Ugh, what exactly does everyone expect me to do?" Cindy snapped, frustration rising in her voice. "It's damned if I do, damned if I don't!"

Suddenly, a loud bang echoed from the side wall, sharp and irritated, cutting through their conversation. Laura flinched, clutching her chest and shutting her eyes for a moment.

A rat darted across the floor, prompting both women to scream and stumble back in surprise. The banging grew louder, pounding against the wall once more. Without a second thought, they turned and ran, leaving the owner behind, flying down the stairs, and bursting out of the building. They dove into Laura's car and sped off down the street.

"Now will you listen to me?" Laura cried out in the car, her adrenaline racing through her veins.

"Okay, I'm sorry," Cindy cried out in an equal amount of intensity. "I'll find somewhere else!"

For the remainder of the afternoon, they went to different complexes to apply to more apartments.

Hours later, Paul was upstairs at the apartment, while Cindy sat alone downstairs with the television on. She blinked hard at the screen, not watching, just stewing.

Don't any of these damn apartments need money? I'm not that bad of a tenant to be getting rejected this many times. Ok, I messed up, but even people like me need a place to live. Maybe I should move back to Tennessee. It feels like this state's trying to push me out. Don't worry, Alabama. I want to leave too, but can't I at least finish the art program first?

The phone began to ring.

Cindy glanced towards the stairs, unsure if Paul was still asleep. After a moment, she rose from the couch and walked into the kitchen. The phone kept ringing. She picked it up and pressed it to her ear, just as voices came through the other end.

"What was that?" Judy's voice snapped, sharp and suspicious.

"I don't know, wasn't it on your end?" Paul responded.

"No," Judy said. "Weird..."

Cindy froze. Her thumb hovered near the receiver. She was about to hang up, but paused.

Why should I? I've played nice long enough. Maybe it's time I listened. Let Judy spill something herself. Let her hand me the dirt.

"You've got to help me," Judy said. "Someone went to the dean on me, and I don't know who it could be. They're accusing me of stealing and distributing exams. Who would be crazy enough to do that?"

"Well," Paul sighed, "that's gonna be tough to figure out. You've rubbed too many people the wrong way; it could be anybody. Maybe if you were nicer to people, this wouldn't be a problem, would it?"

"But, I didn't cheat," Judy insisted, "Why would I distribute a Spanish II exam? I'm not even taking Spanish II!"

"Well, maybe it's someone who is," Paul yawned.

"You think it's Ryan trying to frame me?" Judy asked. "I wouldn't put it past him. He probably typed up a fake test and wrote all the answers to get back at me."

"For a Spanish test?" Paul said skeptically.

"Yeah, so it could look like someone else's test, or maybe he got hold of one of their old exams and used that for revenge."

Paul paused. "Well, you did say you were gonna try to get him fired."

"He deserves to be fired," Judy told him, "but I shouldn't go down with him, especially for something I didn't do! He's got me in trouble with my sorority and the school! I could be suspended or expelled, and that's not okay!"

"I'm sure your father can work his magic," Paul said flatly. "He's trying to get Ryan fired, isn't he? Why can't he try to save you? I don't know why you're calling me. What do you expect me to do?"

"I don't know, maybe listen like someone who gives a damn. I thought you'd want to help."

"I don't know about that. I'm busy over here spreading gonorrhea, remember."

"I'm sorry, okay. Can't you get over that? This is more important! My future is on the line! If I get expelled, I'll have to explain it to my parents, and if I do, they'll probably cut me off financially! They've already said that if I got in trouble again, they would."

"So, you've been in trouble before?"

"Stop making it sound like this is all my fault! It's not! Someone is framing me. I know I've done a few things in the past, but I don't deserve this! Isn't your uncle friends with the dean? Can't you get him to talk to the dean and pull a few strings? I'll owe you."

"I'm not exactly on the dean's good side either. Involving me won't help your case."

"So, you're not going to try? I don't have time for this. If you're just gonna sit there, be lazy and do nothing, I can hang up the phone right now."

"I'll try as far as listening. That's about it."

The phone clicked on the other end. Then clicked again.

Cindy carefully hung up the phone. She opened the refrigerator, grabbed a soda, and took a slow, satisfying sip. Nodding to herself, she thought, *The day started rough, but it sure got easier just now.*

Let her suffer, Cindy thought. She deserves everything that's coming her way. She didn't care if Judy got suspended or expelled. Either one or both would be fine, as long as it brought down her network. Maybe they'd all turn on each other to save themselves. They seemed like the type who would.

Well, Cindy mused, *I guess I had a bigger network than I realized.*

Paul, Ryan, and the dean were in her corner now. They might not know it, but that didn't matter. What mattered was that she knew.

Chapter 24

Monday came around, and the union cafeteria buzzed with its usual lunchtime crowd. Alone, Cindy grabbed a soda and a bag of chips from the vending machine. She was about to leave when three sorority sisters from Judy's circle stepped in front of her, blocking her path.

Cindy recognized them: Nedra, Jennie, and Maxine. She'd sketched each of them before.

"Got a minute, Cindy?" Nedra asked, folding her arms tightly across her chest. Her tone was sharp. "We heard you stole Judy's new boyfriend and turned him against her. We want to know what the deal is."

"What new boyfriend?" Cindy replied, voice steady but tight. "Who'd be crazy enough to date her?"

"Paul liked her, until he started hanging out with you," Maxine accused her. "And now you're living with him? How low can you get? I feel bad for ever supporting you after what you did to Judy."

"I didn't do anything to her!" Cindy shot back. "Paul's not even dating Judy. Did any of you bother asking him if they were together? Judy's lying. She's crazy!"

"You calling our sister crazy—crazy?" Jennie countered, then gave Cindy a shove.

Cindy stumbled, then pushed her right back.

Maxine didn't wait. She shoved Cindy hard into the wall.

Without thinking, Cindy lunged and tackled her to the floor.

"Hey! Fight!" someone shouted.

Heads turned. Chairs scraped. A student at a nearby table gasped, clutching their tray.

"What's going on?"

"Move over!" someone shouted. "You're blocking my view!"

A crowd gathered fast, voices rising in excitement and disbelief.

Nedra grabbed Cindy by the arm and yanked her off Maxine, but not before Cindy rushed to clutch a fistful of Maxine's long brown hair, dragging her back down to the floor.

"I'm betting on the blonde!" an overly eager student laughed from the sidelines.

"I dunno, man," his friend countered, eyes wide. "That brunette's got serious fight in her."

Jennie lunged in to grab Cindy from Maxine, but Cindy twisted, swung around, and landed a clean punch right in Jennie's gut.

Jennie doubled over with a loud gasp, staggering backward as the crowd erupted in shocked cheers and laughter.

"Out of the way!" one of the union staff shouted, forcing his way through the swelling crowd. "I said, move!"

Nedra shoved Cindy off Maxine, giving her sorority sister time to scramble upright. But Cindy recovered just as fast. She grabbed Maxine by the arm and hurled her hard into the side of a table.

Maxine let out a sharp cry and collapsed to the floor. Nedra attempted to shove Cindy again, but Cindy managed to backhand her rival.

The crowd howled.

Cindy charged again, seized a fistful of Maxine's hair, and began dragging her back like a rag doll.

"Break it up!" the staff member shouted, grabbing Cindy around the waist and trying to yank her away.

Maxine shrieked, still tangled in Cindy's grip, just as another staffer grabbed her from the other side.

The two women screamed in unison as they were dragged in opposite directions, Cindy still clutching Maxine's hair like a lifeline.

"Her hair!" someone from the crowd cried. "She's still holding her hair!"

"Some of it's already on the floor!" another student cackled, hopping up and down and pointing at the strands of brown hair scattered across the tiles.

Somehow, Maxine managed to bite Cindy's arm. Cindy yelped, instinctively recoiling, finally releasing her grip.

The fight came to a ragged halt as the girls panted, tangled and disheveled, glaring through smeared mascara and tousled hair.

"All four of you girls, come with us," the staff member barked, gesturing sharply as other employees dispersed the jeering crowd.

Students cleared a path as Cindy and the three sorority sisters were marched down the hall like delinquent royalty. Whispered comments and sideways glances followed them all the way to the Dean of Students' office.

There, each girl was separated and called in one by one.

When it was Cindy's turn, she sat across from the dean, nursing the bite on her arm and trying to steady her voice.

"All this fighting... over a boy?" the dean asked dryly after she finished explaining. He folded his hands on the desk. "You're now saying Judy sent her sorority sisters to attack you because she's jealous over Paul Boudreaux?"

"Yes, sir," Cindy said, her voice rising with urgency. "She's crazy. She thinks he's her boyfriend, and he's not. She thinks I stole him from her, but that's a lie! He and I aren't even together! She's trying to turn other people against me!"

The dean sighed deeply, rubbing his temple as if her words were giving him a headache. He leaned back in his chair, looking at her like he wasn't sure if he should believe her or call someone.

"Let me remind all of you that this is an institute of higher learning, not some junior high school where immaturity is to be expected," the dean said, fixing her with a disappointed glare. "Ms. Spearman, I understand you've been helpful before, but fighting like middle school children is unacceptable, especially from a scholarship recipient."

Cindy's knuckles ached from the fight, but the dean's words hurt more.

"We have a Student Code of Conduct to uphold...Are you aware that this fight could put you at risk of having your scholarship revoked, being put on probation, suspension, or even expulsion?"

"They assaulted me first," Cindy shot back. "I was minding my business until they came after me! I only defended myself. What was I supposed to do, let them beat me up? I told you before; it's Judy's doing."

"I will speak to them further," the dean said curtly. "Since this is your first offense and you've been helpful before, I'm going to let you go with a warning. But don't assume you're off the hook. If there's another incident, I will move forward with additional measures that won't be as forgiving. Am I clear?"

"Yes, sir," Cindy muttered, leaving the office. The three sorority sisters lingered near the stairs, staring her down as she had no choice but to approach and descend the stairs.

"Thanks a lot, Cindy," Nedra snapped, folding her arms. "Now we could all get expelled...from the sorority or even the university. This is what happens when they start letting just anybody from the streets into our school."

"Good, now we'll all be on the streets together," Cindy shot back, "Welcome to the other side, skank."

Jennie huffed. "My father's an attorney. If I get kicked out of school or the sorority, he'll sue your ass, Cindy. Then hopefully we'll never see your ugly face on our campus again."

Cindy smirked. "What's he gonna get from me? A cardboard box and a drawing pad? I'm from the streets, remember, dummy?"

"She's finished on this campus," Maxine said under her breath, flicking her hair with a sneer. "She doesn't come from anything to worry about."

"Whaa whaaa whaaaa," Cindy mocked in a baby voice, "I can't do anything without my mommy, daddy, and their money. Get them to change your diapers while they're at it."

She made a loud fart sound with her lips, then turned, descended the stairs, and walked away. Moments later, she reached the courtyard that separated the art building from the business building.

Cindy swore under her breath, realizing she'd forgotten to get a note from the dean to give to Ryan.

You know what, she thought. *Fuck it. I don't give a shit anymore.*

She entered the art building, but stopped when she noticed the door to the painting studio was open, and once again, loud voices echoed from behind Ryan's closed office door.

Jesus, Cindy thought, rolling her eyes as she recognized the voice. *I'm so sick of that evil bitch.*

"If it wasn't you, you've got to help me then," Judy's voice pleaded from inside the room. "I'll lose everything I've worked hard for if the dean decides to expel me. He's already doing that to Dan, and if there's any part of you left that cares about me, you'll go to the dean and talk to him. You're a professor. He'll listen to you."

Ryan's response came flat and unimpressed. "Don't come crawling back to me asking for any favors. Get the guy you've been cheating on me with to go to the dean."

"I'm sorry I cheated, okay," Judy continued, her tone shifting to something softer, more desperate. "Isn't forgiveness a part of loving someone? I was lonely and didn't realize what I had until you were gone. I miss you, but if I get kicked out of school, I won't be able to stay. We won't be able to start over. I'm sorry. We can work things out, but it's up to you to decide."

There was a pause.

Then Ryan answered, cool and sharp: "You'll only end up lonely again, and part of loving someone is knowing when it's time to let them go."

"I bet it was Cindy," Judy hissed. "Who else could it be? She's always been jealous of me, even when I tried to be her friend and supported her dumb little art shows. She stalks me, spreads lies about me, and is turning everyone against me. Now I'm losing everything...even you."

"I don't buy that for a second," Ryan replied, arms likely crossed in disbelief. "How does she have all this time to plot against you when she's always in the studio working? If anything, *you're* the one obsessed with her."

Judy's voice rose. "I am not! She's got you wrapped around her finger, doesn't she?"

"Could've fooled me," Ryan shot back. "You're always hanging around the studio, staring at her like a ghost while she's trying to work. Maybe focus on graduating instead of harassing her."

Judy's tone turned cold. "So now you're on her side? You think I'm crazy too, huh?"

Ryan let out a dry scoff. "She didn't have to. I've seen enough to figure that out on my own."

"I'm *not* crazy!" Judy's voice shrieked loud enough to carry down the hall, drawing glances from several studio doorways.

Ryan's reply was cool and sharp. "Yelling isn't exactly the way to win people over, is it?"

"You don't love me anymore," she accused him, her voice quivering. "You love Cindy. That's why you gave her the scholarship. I bet she seduced you and got you to turn against me to see that I have nothing left. Now, there's nobody left to care about me."

A sudden crash followed, something falling or being shoved aside. The office door burst open a second later, and Judy stormed out like a cyclone, her eyes locking onto Cindy with a hatred that burned like fire.

Judy didn't say a word, but the look said everything: *You're next.* She shoved the front door open and stormed out of the building.

Cindy swallowed hard, her eyes locking with Ryan's. He said nothing, just narrowed his gaze and began quietly gathering the books and artwork Judy had knocked from his desk.

Still trembling, Cindy walked to the painting studio where Ronald and several others were working. She tried to focus, collecting her paints to continue her piece, when a student burst through the door.

"Hey!" he shouted, breathless. "Someone's trashing the Crimson Gallery!"

"What?" Ronald gasped.

The studio emptied as students rushed downstairs. At the gallery entrance, a crowd had formed. Inside, Judy was in a frenzy, ripping paintings from the walls, including Cindy's, and destroying anything she could grab. Ceramic pieces shattered as she hurled them to the floor. Drawings crumpled under her feet.

Gasps and murmurs spread through the onlookers.

Ryan and the other art professors rushed downstairs, pushing through the crowd, trying to clear students from the gallery entrance.

Inside, Judy stood amidst the wreckage, clutching another ceramic piece. Her movements paused. Something in her had either snapped or possessed her. Slowly, she turned her head toward the doorway and locked eyes with Cindy.

Her expression twisted into a sneer.

With a furious scream, she hurled a ceramic piece across the room. It missed Cindy's head by inches, shattering against the doorframe.

Students screamed. Some ducked. Others froze. Judy ripped Cindy's painting off the wall and flung it across the room. She grabbed another student's painting, threw it on the floor, and kicked it.

Ryan shoved past the last few bodies and stepped into the doorway beside Cindy, just as Judy charged. More students screamed, now trying to push their way back from the gallery entrance.

"Get back!" Ryan shouted.

He stepped in front of Cindy just as Judy lunged, her nails digging deep into his forearm. Blood welled instantly as he wrapped his arms around Judy, struggling to hold her back.

"Judy, stop!" one of the professors yelled.

Yet, Judy didn't stop.

She thrashed and screamed, fighting to break free from Ryan's grip, clawing toward Cindy. Several students were knocked over as the crowd surged in panic, retreating up the stairs.

Two campus police officers pushed their way through the thick crowd of onlookers and scattering students.

They moved to detain Judy, but it only made matters worse. Now, she was scratching, kicking, and biting the officers. One officer cried out as she sank her teeth into his leg, even as he tried to pin her down. The other struggled to get the cuffs on. Three more officers rushed to the scene.

Cindy tore the sleeve from her blouse and wrapped it tightly around Ryan's arm, trying to stop the bleeding.

"Everyone clear out!" several professors shouted, ushering students up the stairs and away from the gallery.

Paramedics rushed in, immediately tending to Ryan.

Cindy wanted to stay, to do more, to be there for Ryan, but firm hands guided her and the others away. She climbed the stairs, her blouse and skirt stained with streaks of blood.

"Are you okay?" one of the officers asked, glancing at the dark red stains on Cindy's blouse.

"Yes, sir," she replied, her voice even but distant. "It's... not my blood."

She moved up the stairs in a daze, blinking against the light as more students crowded outside the art building. The evening air felt sharper now, laced with confusion and adrenaline. Faces blurred past her until three familiar ones cut through the noise.

"Cindy! Are you okay?" Paul rushed forward, his expression drawn, eyes locking onto the blood smeared across her skirt. "What happened?"

"She's bleeding blood," Greyson shouted, already waving toward a paramedic. "Hey! She needs help!"

"I'm okay," Cindy said quickly. "It's someone else's blood..."

"What?" Paul and Joel said in unison, stepping closer, unsettled.

Before she could explain further, the paramedics emerged from the stairwell with Ryan. His arm was bandaged and his face pale. They loaded him swiftly into the back of the ambulance. The doors slammed with a finality that made Cindy flinch.

Siren lights washed over her skin. She didn't realize she was shivering until Paul gently reached out and touched her shoulder.

The crowd gasped at the sight that followed. Two officers emerged at the top of the stairs, half-carrying Judy, her body tightly bound in a heavy wraparound blanket. Her hair was wild and tangled, her face contorted in something between rage and madness. She kicked and writhed, shrieking animalistically through gritted teeth, as though the blanket alone held back something feral.

"Is that Judy?" someone in the crowd asked in disbelief.

"What's wrong with her?" another student whispered.

"She's completely lost it," a third muttered.

All eyes followed as the officers dragged her down the walkway. But then Judy's head twisted toward the crowd and her gaze locked onto Cindy and Paul. She stilled.

A moment of silence hung in the air.

Then, from deep within her throat, came a rasping, high-pitched laugh: sharp, manic, and victorious. Her eyes blazed with a knowing glint, like someone who had pulled off something terrible... and knew no one would understand until it was far too late.

Even as the officers dragged her off, that laughter clung to the air, echoing in the ears of everyone present and leaving a cold, uneasy chill in its wake.

Chapter 25

Later that evening, back at Paul's penthouse, the television hummed in the background. Every station seemed to echo the same headline: the violent incident at Camellia University, where a professor was hospitalized and a student, Judy Bowman, was placed under psychiatric evaluation.

Cindy sat beside Paul on the couch, freshly showered and dressed in an old shirt and pants.

Paul had asked her three times if she was alright. Four, if she counted the moment he'd woken her from a short nap just to ask again.

"I'm fine," she repeated.

He nodded, but the look in his eyes told her he didn't believe it.

On the screen, footage replayed the chaos outside the art building. Students scattering. Police. Blood. Judy's twisted laughter echoing as she was taken away, restrained in a heavy wrap. Cindy winced and looked away.

She wasn't sure if the story would stay confined to local news. Deep down, she doubted it. Judy had always wanted control...desperately and obsessively.

In a bitter twist, Judy had made headlines. Her name, her face, and her madness were broadcast across every living room in the city. Maybe the country.

"She got what she wanted," Cindy muttered. "Just not how she planned it."

Paul glanced at her but said nothing.

Onscreen, a red-faced university spokesperson tried to salvage the school's image.

"Camellia University does not condone such isolated incidents on our campus," he said stiffly, eyes darting nervously between cameras. His suit looked a size too large, and he gave the impression of a man cornered into making a statement he hadn't rehearsed, nor believed. "We are currently undertaking a thorough review of our policies and procedures to reinforce the safety and security of our campus community. Our commitment to providing a secure and supportive environment for learning, teaching, and research remains unwavering."

Cindy's gaze lingered on the screen a moment longer before she turned it off. Silence filled the room like fog.

"She's gone now," Paul said, trying to offer reassurance.

But Cindy wasn't sure.

Judy was gone for now, but for how long remained the question. Still, it was a relief to finally have some breathing room without Judy lurking in the shadows, unchecked. Now, it was time to focus on what really mattered: securing the apartment and working hard to do whatever it took to regain custody of her son.

Later, Paul returned with the day's mail and came through the door grinning. He handed Cindy an envelope. Cindy tore it open. She scanned the document, then again, and again, in disbelief. She'd been approved. It was not for just any apartment, but one in a clean, quiet neighborhood not far from campus.

Cindy shrieked with joy, waving the document in the air.

"I got it," she cried, her voice bright and breathless. "I got the apartment! The one I thought I'd never get! I got it!"

"Really?" Paul beamed. "Wow! Sounds like we need to head down to Ackerman's to celebrate, with some shrimp and meatloaf!"

Cindy's eyes brimmed with tears of joy. This was her big step forward. She finally had something real: a space of her own, a place to call home. It gave her hope and something to hold on to as she kept going to rehab and worked to get custody back.

Days later, more news surfaced about Camellia University. News outlets buzzed with updates on the growing campus scandal: more arrests, more names, and deeper ties to illegal drugs, academic dishonesty, and blackmail.

A prominent attorney representing the Bowman family called for damages and Judy Bowman's reinstatement, accusing the university of negligence in protecting students from individuals such as Dan Jones, who preyed on the vulnerable. He also urged the administration to adopt stricter drug-free campus policies.

"Had the university done a better job protecting students from individuals such as Dan Jones," the attorney stated, "my client never would have unknowingly ingested PCP, a dangerous drug known to cause the very effects witnessed in recent days. We are moving forward to ensure that the university makes meaningful changes and upholds its commitment to a drug-free campus that is safe for all students. My client does not see herself as a victim, but as a fighter who is willing to come forward and share her story to promote student safety and protect others from campus predators at universities nationwide."

Cindy scoffed at the article, tossing the paper aside.

If the world could still call someone like Judy a fighter, she thought, *then it sure as hell could make room for one more.*

Author's Note

This book is a spin-off from the *Love Fumbles* series, told through Cindy's voice and on her own terms. You do not need to read the original series to follow her journey, though some characters and events may overlap with Paul's story. Thank you for reading. I hope Cindy's story says something that stays with you.

www.ingramcontent.com/pod-product-compliance
Lightning Source LLC
Chambersburg PA
CBHW071342300726
48976CB00006B/1746